# BLIND JUSTICE

NATHAN BURROWS

# 1

_____

I jumped as the thick metal door slammed shut. It wasn't just the sound, but the physical force of it closing that affected me. The pressure changes inside the small cell were palpable. I could feel it in my ears, like that feeling you get on an aeroplane, and my heart thudded in my chest a couple of times before returning to normal. If only the rest of me could calm down, things would be a lot easier.

I looked around the cell, taking in the four white walls that would be my home for the next fifteen years. They seemed so close, almost suffocating. The cell was maybe six feet by ten. There was a small window high on one wall with a glow coming through it I knew was from the street-lights outside. I'd considered trying to see out, but even if I climbed up to the window, I wouldn't be able to see anything through the opaque reinforced glass. The only other light in the room was a bright fluorescent shaft of light from the observation window set into the green metal door. Even though it was my first night, I knew in about ten minutes that light would disappear as the prison guards turned off the main lights to the wing.

Other than the bunk-bed I was sitting on and the bare toilet in the corner, the only furniture was a small table with a chair and a cabinet bolted to the wall near the window. I lay back on the bottom bunk, wriggling to fit myself into the bed. They weren't made for people my size. That much was for certain. I'd been told that my cellmate, who was in the hospital wing for a few days, had already claimed the top bunk. I couldn't see any point in making a scene about it. Not on my first day, anyway.

The events of the last few weeks ran through my mind as I examined the bottom of the mattress above me. Being arrested, being remanded, and being tried. Being found guilty.

Maths had never been my strong point, but I tried to do the sums in my head. I wanted to know how many times the cell door would slam before I would be eligible for parole. There were three hundred and sixty-five days in a year, so I needed to multiply that by fifteen. When I realised it was over five thousand, I gave up trying to work it out. Fifteen years was a long time, but it was the minimum term for my crime.


Murder.

I remember meeting Jennifer for the first time like it was yesterday. God knows I've relived it in my mind hundreds of times over the last couple of months. I'd gone to the pub to meet Tommy, my business partner, for a drink and a chat. Calling him my business partner isn't quite true. He was more my partner in crime. Tommy and I had been what the police would call 'petty thieves' since we both left school at fifteen without a single GCSE between us. Our careers, such as they were, had begun ten years ago back in the winter of two thousand and seven. Aged fifteen, we had both clambered over a fence into a builder's storage yard and relieved the owner of some tools that were lying around. Later that evening, as we sat in the park drinking the cheap cider we had bought with the proceeds of our endeavours, I realised that we had earned twenty-five quid between us for what was around fifteen minutes work.

Our futures started to look a lot different from that point on until here I was in the pub with Tommy, years later. I looked at him now over the top of my pint of lager.

He was wearing what he usually did — a threadbare hoodie — even though he was way too old for them. I'd told him many times that blokes in their mid-twenties didn't wear hoodies, but he wasn't having it. As I looked at him, he scratched his head through untidy black hair, somehow making it even scruffier.

It was a cold, miserable night in November. I had just bought us both another pint of lager and was sitting with Tommy facing the door of the pub. We were expecting the third member of our little crew, David, to arrive at any moment. As Tommy talked about a business he had cased earlier on in the day with less than effective security, I took a sip of my pint and half listened to him. We had a few rules we were all happy with — no residential properties, no violence, and only low-risk jobs. Tommy had been in prison twice. They were both short stretches, but still long enough to put him off going back. It didn't stop him getting prison tattoos, as the dark green spider web on his hand showed. David, the third musketeer, was late as usual.

"Maybe David's been nicked?" Tommy said with a smirk as I checked my watch for the second time in as many minutes.

"It wouldn't surprise me," I replied. David wasn't the sharpest tool in the box at the best of times when it came to burglary. His day job was working as a courier, but his real skill was with anything electronic. This made him handy to have around, but he wasn't good at the more physical elements of the job. He was also the least likely of the three of us to keep to our unofficial rules and often supplemented his income with what he called 'other opportunities'.

The pub we were sitting in was a typical drinkers' pub on the eastern edge of Norwich. It was called The Heartsease after some flower and run by an ex-boxer and part-time criminal, Big Joe. He wasn't called Big Joe because he was fat. He was known as Big Joe because he was a hard-looking bastard. His main talent, other than the fact he was as nasty as he looked, was his discretion. How the place even stayed open was beyond me as there never seemed to be more than four or five people in it at any one time. Tonight was no different even though it was a Saturday night. Apart from Tommy and I, there were only three other people drinking. I looked around the pub, taking in the yellowed walls which hadn't seen fresh paint since before the smoking ban had come in years ago, and at the mismatched, battered tables and chairs. It was a depressing place.

I looked up as the door to the pub swung open, expecting to see David's greasy-haired head pop through it. It wasn't David though, but a bloke I didn't recognise. He looked around the pub as if looking for someone or checking to see who else was there. Behind him was a woman who looked even more out of place than he did. They were both dressed as if they were going for a night out somewhere else, somewhere far posher than The Heartsease, which they might have been. I had no idea. The man was about five feet nine with a runner's build and smart, freshly ironed shirt and trousers. The pub we were in wasn't the sort of place where you wore smart trousers, so that marked him out straight away. He strutted his way to the bar and the woman with him followed. My first impression was that the woman, how can I put this without sounding crude, was stunning. She was shorter than him by one or two inches and was wearing a canary yellow short summer dress under a thin coat which reached to just above her knees. The woman wasn't dressed for the weather. From what I could see, her legs were slim, toned and tanned despite the time of year.

I've always had a thing for legs, and hers ticked all the boxes.

As she followed him across the pub rubbing her hands up and down her arms, she glanced around, and our eyes met for a few seconds. She had the deepest, most striking green eyes I'd seen in a woman for a long time. To be fair though, I didn't spend that much time around women. She looked away almost immediately, and I wasn't sure if she'd noticed me at all.

"Gareth?" I heard Tommy say. "Gareth?" I looked at him and caught the smile on his face.

"What?" I said, annoyed with him for breaking my concentration.

"You're staring, mate," he said, laughing. "With your mouth open."

"Piss off, Tommy," I replied. "I was not." He picked up his pint glass from the table and took a sip of lager.

"You bloody well were."

"Whatever," I replied. The door to the pub swung open again, and I looked across to see David walk in. I looked at my watch and frowned. "About bloody time." He ambled his way across to our table, dressed in a T-shirt advertising a heavy metal band I'd never heard of. The crotch of his trousers hung somewhere halfway down his thighs, revealing the upper band of his grubby boxer shorts. They made him look every inch the loser he was. He ignored the woman in the yellow dress, and she didn't look at him either. Neither of those things surprised me. I liked David. He was a mate, but he wasn't a ladies' man by any stretch of the imagination.

The three of us sat deep in conversation for the next twenty minutes, Tommy describing the off-licence he'd been having a look at over the last few days. There were CCTV cameras inside and out that Tommy swore were fake, and he and David were talking about the best way of finding out if they were real. As David prattled on about camera feeds and power supplies, my attention drifted back to the smartly dressed couple. They'd moved away from the bar and were sitting at a table on the other side of the pub. Their conversation didn't look quite as companionable as ours, though. The woman was leaning back in the chair, her arms folded and her legs crossed. My earlier assessment had been correct. She had very nice legs indeed. Her drinking partner was doing most of the talking, punctuating whatever he was talking about with a pointed finger on the surface of the table between them. Occasionally, she would take a breath as if she was about to say something, only for his finger to thud the table and silence her. I'd always enjoyed watching people — I even daydreamed about going back to school and studying psychology — but I didn't need to be an expert of any kind to tell that they were in the middle of the mother of all arguments.

That might explain why they'd come here. Maybe it was neutral territory for their discussion? Maybe one of them lived around here, although looking at the way they both dressed, I doubted that. I watched them, wondering what the bloke could be saying that needed such dramatic punctuation. She glanced back in my direction, holding my gaze for a few seconds longer than before. I raised my eyebrows a few millimetres, unsure if she'd be able to see the gesture from across the pub. Her green eyes were something else. That was obvious even from this distance.

David drained the last of his pint and scraped his chair backwards.

"Right then, I'm off. Got stuff to do." He got to his feet and swept his fingers through his hair. I hoped that he wouldn't put his hand out for us to shake. "I'll have a look

at those cameras tomorrow, Tommy, and come up with a
plan of some sort."

"That'd be good. Cheers. See what you think," Tommy
replied before finishing his own drink and clunking the
empty glass back onto the table. "I'd better bugger off as
well." I looked down at my glass. I was about half a pint
behind them.

"Alright then, gents. I'm going outside for a smoke, so
I'll see you both tomorrow," I said, raising a hand to them
both. "Same time, same place?" They both nodded in
unison before heading for the door, and I smiled as I saw
Tommy's unsteady gait. I'd suspected earlier that he'd been
in the pub for a while before I arrived, and it looked like I
was right.

I stood outside in the dismal excuse of a beer garden.
In reality, it was a small concrete walled yard with a well
decorated table and bench set. Well decorated with graffiti,
at least. I lit my cigarette and read the clumsy writing,
wondering if Jane actually did perform the sexual act the
graffiti suggested she did for twenty quid a time. Even if
she did, I wouldn't touch her with a barge pole. As I
enjoyed my cigarette, thinking not for the first time I
should give up, I could hear raised voices coming through
the cold night air from the other side of the wall. First a
man's, and then a woman's. Being a nosey chap, I stepped
up onto the bench to look over the wall and see what was
going on.

The couple from the pub must have left at around the
same time as Tommy and David. They were now
standing on a street corner about twenty yards from the
pub entrance. I couldn't hear what they were talking
about — shouting would be more accurate — but I was
close enough to read their body language and see the
clouds of their breath in the cold night air. He was

waving his arms, pacing. She was standing still, her arms folded across her chest. It was obvious the woman was scared.

I crushed my half-smoked cigarette into the broken flower pot that served as an ashtray and walked back through the pub, nodding to Big Joe as I left through the front door. As I approached the arguing couple, I slowed down. All I wanted to do was to make sure that the woman was okay.

Ever since I was a kid, I'd always hated bullies. One advantage of being quite a big lad was that I didn't get bullied. At least, not for long. The first proper fight I ever had was with a boy called Marcus who fancied himself as the top boy in the playground and preferred other children's money to his own. To his credit, he was a quick learner, although the bloodied nose and black eye I gave him almost got me expelled.

Remembering Marcus and the satisfaction I'd got from putting him on his back, I stopped about ten feet away from the woman in the yellow dress and her companion. With my hand clasped in front of me in the classic bouncer's pose, I cleared my throat.

"Everything okay?"

The woman looked at me, her green eyes striking even in the glow of the streetlights. The look of fear on her face being replaced by relief still haunts me to this day, and it told me everything I needed to know in an instant. I took a step closer to the couple, rolling my shoulders as I did so. Her companion glanced up at me. I was a fair bit taller than him and had at least a two-stone weight advantage. None of it fat. I'm big, but I'm not a bloater. Lucky genes, I guess. It's not from the gym.

"Nah, we're good, mate. Thanks." He reached his hand out and grabbed the woman's arm just above the elbow before trying to drag her away from me. I took another step closer as she resisted.

"Let go, Robert," she said, trying to pull away from him. Robert? What a poncy name. The least he could do would be to shorten it to Rob. I took another step closer and was now well within arm's reach of Robert. Close enough to see the grooves in his hair from too much gel. "Please, you're hurting me." The woman looked up at me, her eyes wide. This was the nearest I'd been to her, but I didn't want to take my eyes off Robert to see what she looked like up-close.

"Robert," I said. "I think you need to let go of the lady." My voice was low and full of menace.

"Piss off, fella," he replied, tugging again at her arm. I could see white patches on her skin around his fingers. "This has got fuck all to do with you, so just leave it, would you?" He looked at me with a dark expression on his face. He was either brave, stupid, or both. Being brave and stupid was usually a road to nowhere in my experience. I relaxed my arms, letting them hang at my side, and flexed my fingers before bunching them into loose fists. A recognisable signal to most people that things were about to get serious.

"Robert, let go. Now," I said, almost whispering. Another signal. "I'm not going to ask you again."

In response, Robert took a step backwards. The woman let out a squeal of pain, raising her free hand to prise his grip off her arm. That was the decision made right there for me. I stepped towards him, snapping my right arm up as if I was going to smack him under the chin with a deft uppercut, but I didn't ball my fist. Instead, I shot my hand out and grabbed him by the neck, forcing his head back. I dug my thumb and middle finger deep into the soft tissue between his jaw and ear and pushed him back, away from the woman. As I'd predicted, he let go of her as he tried to get me to loosen my grip on his neck. I took a step forward, moving him away from her, and tightened my fingers. I'd had the same move done to me once, so knew how bloody painful it was. All you can do is try to release the pressure under your ears. It's a sensitive spot which was why I'd chosen it. He had both his hands on my right arm, leaving my left one free. All I wanted was for him to let go of the woman, which he'd already done, and to send him a message.

"Are you listening, Robert?" I asked, easing up on his neck so he could speak.

"Yes," he replied through clenched teeth. His face was already red from the pressure on his throat.

"I'm going to let go of you in a minute, and you're going to walk off nice and quietly," I said in a soft voice. "Because if you don't, you're going to get hurt." I squeezed his neck to illustrate the point. "Really hurt. You got that?" He nodded in response, so I lived up to my word and let go of him, taking a half step backwards in case I needed to use my hands. Robert took a deep breath and stood there, looking at me with a mixture of fear and anger on his face. He rubbed at his neck where red finger-shaped welts were forming. I pointed over his shoulder.

"Go on Robert," I said. "Off you fuck."

He stared at me, and for a moment I thought he was going to claw back some of his pride with a swing. Instead, his gaze flicked over my shoulder. I could tell he was thinking of something to say to the woman behind me. Probably something impolite from the look on his face, so I took half a step towards him. He backpedalled and then saw sense, turning to walk away. I watched him for a couple of seconds, until I was sure he'd not retreated for a run-up back at me, and then turned to the woman. She was watching Robert walk away, rubbing her arm where she had similar welts to the ones on his neck. What goes around comes around.

"Are you okay?" I asked. She paused and looked at me before replying.

"I am, yes. He's such an arsehole."

"Boyfriend?"

"Ex-boyfriend," she said. "As of this evening. He just isn't adjusting to it very well." At last, I could look at her face. Even though it was bathed in the orange glow of the street lights, she was beautiful. A small button nose with a sprinkling of freckles, framed by high cheekbones. She smiled a quick nervous smile that gave me a glimpse of slightly crooked front teeth before they disappeared. "I'm sorry you had to get mixed up in all that."

"No problem at all. Look, there's a taxi office just down the road. Why don't I walk you to it in case your mate Robert is still hanging around?" She looked at me and smiled again, holding it for longer this time. It was only one front tooth out of kilter, and for me, that was the prettiest thing about her. I held out my hand, conscious of the fact that a few seconds ago it had been choking the life out of her ex-boyfriend. "My name's Gareth." She took my hand and shook it; her fingers cool and delicate in mine. I suddenly felt stupid, shaking this woman's hand so formally.

"I'm Jennifer," she replied. "Nice to meet you, Gareth."

## 3

To be honest, I never thought I'd see Jennifer again after I'd walked her to the taxi office. We'd chatted on the way, but it was only a few hundred yards away from the pub. It wasn't because I didn't want to see her again, but it's just not how the conversation went. It was small talk, nothing more. When we reached the taxi office, all I knew about her, apart from her name, was that she worked in Human Resources somewhere. She had been going out with Robert for about a year, and he was an absolute arsehole. I didn't get the chance to tell her anything about me other than the fact I worked as a bouncer on the doors of pubs and clubs in Norwich, and she didn't ask. I couldn't exactly tell her I was also a part-time burglar.

When we got to the taxi office, I asked the bloke behind the counter for a cab. We waited in silence for a few minutes before one turned up and I did the gentlemanly thing by opening the rear door for her. As she put her seatbelt on, I opened the passenger door to talk to the driver.

"Hi, mate, you alright?" I said as I dropped a twenty-pound note on the passenger seat, careful to keep the money out of Jennifer's sight. Wherever she lived in Norwich, twenty quid would be more than enough to get her home and leave a healthy tip. "Can you do me a favour?" I reached for the driver's ID card dangling from the rear-view mirror. "Jim, is it?" I looked at his surname, but it had too many consonants for me to even try to pronounce. "Could you drop this young lady wherever she needs to get to, and then just hang around for a minute to make sure she gets inside okay?" The driver looked at Jennifer in the rear-view mirror and then back at me. "Her tosser of an ex-boyfriend is about somewhere, and we've already had words. I think he got the message but just in case, yeah?"

"Sure, boss," he replied in an Eastern European accent, or maybe somewhere else. Not a local boy. "I look after her, no problem." I stood on the kerb for a few seconds after the taxi had left, watching its red lights disappear down the road. What an interesting end to the evening it had turned out to be.

About a week later, maybe longer, I was back in The Heartsease to meet up again with Tommy and David. The job we'd been talking about earlier in the week was coming along well, and we were planning on doing it at some point over the next few nights. Tommy and David were already huddled in the corner with full pints when I got there, so I didn't bother going over to see if they wanted a drink. Big Joe regarded me with rheumy eyes. He didn't bother asking me what I wanted and was already pouring a lager.

"Alright, Joe?" I asked him.

"Yep, all good," he replied. "I've got a message for you behind the bar. I'll grab it in a sec."

"What sort of message?"

"From that bird who was in here the other night." Joe

looked at me with a smirk. "I hear you worked her boyfriend over." He returned his attention to the pint.

"Where did you hear that?" I asked, annoyed. I didn't like things like that being public. It wasn't as if it was bad for my reputation. I didn't want a reputation at all. The smirk disappeared from Joe's face.

"I just heard, mate. Keep your knickers on." He put the pint on the sticky counter between us and turned to get an envelope. "Here you go." He handed it to me and I saw 'Gareth' written in child-like handwriting on the front. I waited until Joe had disappeared to do whatever it was he did around the back of the bar and then ripped it open. There was a single piece of paper inside with a phone number and the words "Can you call me?" written in the same childish scrawl. I stuck it in my pocket, figuring Robert had come back and she wanted a big ugly friend to stand between him and her again.

Later that evening, after Tommy and David had gone, I nipped back outside to the beer garden for a smoke before heading back to my flat. I dug into my pocket to find a lighter and pulled out the note I'd shoved in there earlier. With five and a half pints in my stomach, I decided to give Jennifer a ring to see what was going on and what she wanted. Where's the harm in that, I asked myself. If she was a damsel in distress, maybe I could be her knight in shining armour? I was giggling at the thought of me trying to ride a horse as I punched the numbers into my phone. Why doesn't someone make phones with big buttons for people like me with larger fingers? At the third try, I got the numbers in the right order and pressed the 'Call' button.

"Hello?" Jennifer answered the phone before the second ring, catching me off guard. I'd got the phone wedged between my shoulder and my ear so I could light my cigarette, and I almost dropped it trying to sort myself out.

"Oh, hi. Jennifer?" I said. "It's Gareth." There was silence on the other end of the line. "From the other night?"

"Hey, Gareth," Jennifer said, her voice slow and deeper than I remembered. Maybe she'd been drinking too. "Thanks for calling." There was another silence, this one bordering on uncomfortable.

"So… you left me a note?" I asked, my cigarette now under control. I sat on the bench, realising too late it was wet with either rain or urine. "Is Robert still being an arse?"

"He is, yes, but that's not why I called. I'm not after a bodyguard, don't worry." Her laugh echoed down the phone. "I thought maybe I should say thanks or something, you know, for coming to my rescue and everything." She paused, and I heard her take a breath. "I mean, it would have been fine, but I appreciate you stepping in."

Even though I was pissed, I was sure it wouldn't have been fine. It might have been okay that evening, but I knew Robert's sort. At some point in the future, it would go downhill. It would start with a slap in the heat of the moment, followed by profuse apologies, flowers, and promises it would never happen again. Great sex. Then the next time it would be a fist, not a slap. Maybe somewhere it wouldn't bruise, or maybe it would be a punch in the face? That pretty face, with a button nose and ever so slightly out of line front tooth.

"Are you still there?" Jennifer's voice on the phone made me jump.

"Oh, I'm sorry, I was miles away," I replied, trying to concentrate on something other than how much I liked her crooked tooth. Another silence. I had to break it, fill the void. "I was just thinking about, er, thinking about…" Shit. What should I say?

"What were you thinking about, Gareth?" Hearing her say my name sent a shiver down my spine. This was getting weird. I shouldn't have called her after one beer, let alone five. In fact, I shouldn't have called her at all. The only thing I was achieving was making a fool out of myself.

"Sorry, I've had a few pints," I said. "I'm not pissed. Well, just a bit. Maybe ever so slightly pissed." Her laugh brought a smile to my face.

"Can you keep a secret?" she said, her voice so faint I struggled to hear it.

"That's one thing I can definitely do," I replied, trying to put some confidence in my voice.

"So am I," she said. It was my turn to laugh at her. "I'm sitting in my flat with an empty bottle of wine listening to Celine Dion."

The image this brought to my mind made me laugh out loud. I'd gone to see *Bridget Jones Diary* at the cinema with a date. The only thing in the film I thought was funny was the blonde actress singing "All by Myself" into an empty bottle of wine. That was the most memorable part of the whole miserable, but short-lived, relationship. There was no second date.

"No, no, no," I said. "You're listening to the wrong song."

"Okay, so what would you recommend then?" Jennifer's voice had shifted, become much more conversational. I racked my brain for a moment before coming up with what my beer-soaked brain thought was the perfect answer.

"Gloria Gaynor," I said. "Definitely, Gloria Gaynor."

"Help me out here," she replied. "Bit before my time, I think." I thought for a second about singing down the phone the first few lines of the song I had in mind, but I wasn't that pissed.

"I will survive," I said. "First I was afraid, I was petrified," I continued, managing not to sing. She laughed.

"Oh God, yes," she said. "I know it. It's not on my iPod though." I kept quiet. It was on mine.

We spent the next fifteen or twenty minutes going back and forth, relaxing into an easy conversation about music, films, and what we both enjoyed doing in our spare time. All nice and safe, nothing controversial. Nothing about her idiot ex-boyfriend. Big Joe stuck his head out of the rear door of the pub at one point, no doubt to see where I'd gone or to make sure I wasn't trying to break into the back. He disappeared, reappearing a few minutes later with a fresh pint which he put on the table in front of me. If he wasn't such an ugly bugger, I could have kissed him.

I'd discovered Jennifer's favourite death scene in a movie was Dennis Hopper being killed by Harvey Keitel in *True Romance*. In return, I'd shared the fact I'd cried when King Kong died. In fairness, I was only seven. But I'd still cried like a baby. We'd both blubbered at *Watership Down*, so it was honours even. The conversation had slowed down, not because we'd run out of things to say, but I think because we realised we had so much more to talk about. Not how I'd imagined the conversation playing out at all. Jennifer said something else, but I didn't catch what it was she said.

"Sorry, I missed that," I said. "What did you say?" There was a pause before she replied.

"I said, are you free tomorrow night?"

"Er, yeah I think so."

"Do you fancy going out for a drink?" Jennifer said. "I owe you at least one to thank you properly."

So the next night, we went for a drink. It wasn't at The

Heartsease though. That was the last place I wanted to take her. We went to a smart wine bar in Norwich which had not long opened. Even though it was only a drink, so she could say thank you, I still made an effort and was what I thought passed for a perfect gentleman. It must have worked as the weekend saw us at the cinema. Then a meal the week after, then a few more drinks the weekend after. If I didn't know better, I'd say she liked me. I knew deep down that wasn't the case though, just based on the fact women like Jennifer never went for men like me. She was just too — I'm not sure how to describe it — too bloody nice. I hate the word nice, but it's the best one I can think of to describe her.

I was sure all Jennifer wanted was some company. Someone safe who she could just chill out with who would keep her arsehole ex-boyfriend away. As far as she was concerned, I worked security on doors so would fit that bill nicely. But, the more I saw of her the more I liked her. It wasn't just because she was attractive, there was something more about her. One Friday night, a few weeks after the incident with Robert, we'd gone for a few drinks in a pub down by the river in Thorpe St Andrew. When I'd phoned up for a taxi to take Jennifer home before dropping me off at mine, there'd been a two-hour wait. Even though it was just before Christmas, it was a balmy evening with clear skies. A very pleasant night for a stroll, so we decided to walk back. We were about halfway back to her flat when I decided we could take a shortcut.

"We can cut up through here if you want?" I'd said, pointing at a path leading through some woods. It was a steep path, but I knew at the top was a recreation ground we could walk across to her flat. It would cut maybe twenty minutes off the walk.

"What?" Jennifer had said with her hand on her chest.

"You want me to go into the woods with you?" Her sly smile told me she was joking.

"I promise you'll be safe with me, young lady," I replied. "My intentions are entirely honourable."

"Are they?" Jennifer said before frowning, but the smile stayed on her face as she did so. "Damn. Okay then. If you insist."

Jennifer looped her hand through my arm, and we made our way through the woods. When we got to the end of the path, the sky opened out in front of us.

"Wow, look at the stars," Jennifer whispered, breathless from the steep climb. I looked up to see a black sky, dotted with white sparkling pinpricks of light. I'd never been one for stargazing, but I had to admit the sight was impressive.

"Let's sit down, get our breath," I pointed at a bench.

"Oh, you're not just a pretty face, are you." Jennifer laughed as she unhooked her arm from mine and made her way to the bench, sitting on it with an exaggerated sigh. I sat next to her and looked up at the sky. We sat in silence for a few seconds. "So," Jennifer said. "Are you into the astronomy side of things then?"

"Oh, yeah," I lied through my teeth, pointing up at the sky. "See, look there. There's Capricorn." I waved my finger around. "And that's Sagittarius just there." I looked at her as she stared upwards at the sky. The glare from the streetlights on the other side of the recreation ground shone on her face. In that moment, looking at her staring at the sky, I realised I liked her. Really, really liked her.

I looked back up at the stars and was about to put my hands behind my head when Jennifer punched me in the arm.

"Ow," I said, rubbing the spot where she'd hit me. "What was that for?"

"For talking rubbish," Jennifer said, moving herself a

couple of inches toward me so our hips were just touching. "I'm getting cold," she continued. "Shall we give it five minutes and then head away?" I could feel the warmth of her leg against mine and couldn't work out if she wanted me to put my arm around her. The truth is, I've never been great with women. I glanced across at Jennifer, who was staring back up at the sky, and a mad jumble of thoughts ran through my head. What did she think of me? Was I just safe company? Or was there maybe, just maybe, something more? The thought of her being on the rebound from Robert was front and centre of my thoughts. I knew I only had a few minutes before we'd be walking again, and the moment would disappear. I felt like a teenager about to ask a girl out on a date but decided, what the hell.

"Jennifer, can I ask you something?" I said, after a deep breath to calm my nerves.

"Sure you can," she replied, still staring up at the night. I paused, taking another deep breath and trying to keep my voice steady.

"What would you do if I kissed you?"

Jennifer turned her head and looked at me. She opened her mouth just a touch, as if she was about to say something, then she closed it again. Her expression was inscrutable, and I couldn't tell if I'd made a huge mistake.

"Oh," she said a few seconds later. "Well, I guess one of two things." I waited, desperate to hear what she would say. "I'd either slap you round the face hard and run off, or…" Jennifer paused.

"Or what?" I said a few seconds later.

"Or I'd kiss you back." There was another pause as we looked at each other. I couldn't read her expression at all.

"Which would it be then?" I said. She didn't reply but just carried on looking at me. I realised I would have to find out for myself. I leaned forward, angled my head, and brushed my lips across hers, only just making contact with them before I sat back and screwed up my eyes.

"What are you doing?" Jennifer said, and I could hear the smile in her voice.

"Waiting for a slap," I replied. She laughed, and I felt her cool hand on the side of my face. She slid it round to the back of my neck.

"You big daft lump," Jennifer said as she pulled me toward her.

We sat on the bench in the dark, like teenagers do, and kissed. Like teenagers do.

And it was very fine indeed.

**4**

The first time I spent the night with Jennifer, which I will always think about as when our relationship began, things didn't turn out the way I thought they would. We'd been out quite a few times since the night we'd puckered up on the bench. Other than a couple of chaste kisses at her door, it hadn't progressed beyond that. I wanted it to, God knows I wanted it to, but I needed to be sure she wanted more than a kiss. Each time I walked her back, I was desperate for her to invite me in but too nervous to suggest it myself. One evening before we met for a drink, I'd even blitzed my flat, giving the hoover a rare outing and changed the sheets. I'd had every intention of inviting her back to mine for a coffee, but I'd bottled it and settled for a kiss at her door and a wave goodnight as it closed.

It was three weeks to the day since our first kiss when that all changed. We'd been out for the evening to grab a quick bite to eat in a pub by the river called The Town House. It was a nice enough pub, nothing too flashy, just one of those chain pubs with the same menu whichever one in the country you went into. It was a very relaxed evening, but there was a massive part of me that still thought I was a convenient drinking partner, as opposed to a boyfriend. Jennifer was only just out of a relationship that was bordering on abusive. The last thing I wanted to do was to push her into another relationship even if I knew it wouldn't be one with any abuse in the slightest. An added complication was that I was fairly sure she wouldn't be interested in a relationship with a part-time thief.

I remember sitting there listening to Jennifer tell me a story about her work. I can't for the life of me remember what the story was about, but I remember thinking how beautiful she was. She was wearing a long brown jacket over a simple white t-shirt. Her blonde hair was in a loose ponytail, and she had a yellow daffodil in the lapel of her jacket. Black, skin-tight jeans, brown shoes that matched her jacket. Simple enough in terms of fashion, but she looked stunning. She continued her story as she shrugged herself out of her jacket, and as Jennifer turned to drape the jacket on the back of her chair, the t-shirt tightened against her chest for a few seconds. I tried not to stare but failed miserably

"You are so rumbled," she said as she turned back to face me, and I felt the heat rise to my cheeks. I mumbled an apology as she took a sip from her glass of wine before putting it down on the table and staring at me, a faint smile playing across her face. We sat in what was for me an uncomfortable silence for a few seconds before I tried to move the conversation away from my embarrassment.

"So, is the daffodil just for decoration, or does it mean something?"

Jennifer's smile disappeared in an instant, and her entire expression changed. I had no idea what I'd done, but I'd certainly managed to change the subject. She took a deep breath, blowing it out through her cheeks as she glanced back at the flower in her jacket.

"It's for Marie Curie," she said. I was none the wiser, and it must have shown. "The cancer charity. A kind of appeal thing they run every year." She reached out and ran her fingers up and down the stem of the wine glass, but there was nothing seductive about the way she did it. "My mum died of cancer. It was a while ago now, but it still hurts. You know?" The truth was I didn't know. My mother had died so long ago that she was a distant memory, existing only in the photographs I looked at once in a blue moon.

"I'm sorry," I said. "I didn't know." Jennifer reached out her hand and took mine, rubbing her thumb across the back of my hand.

"You don't have to be sorry, Gareth," she said, the smile returning to her face. "But I love the fact you are."

We spent the next hour in quiet conversation. Jennifer told me a little about her mother's death, and the way it had affected her father, but soon steered the conversation away from the subject and on to something lighter — her brother. She'd mentioned him on one of earlier evenings out — I wasn't sure whether they were dates or not — but I hadn't realised that they were twins. She was the baby of the family by just under two minutes, and her brother Jacob never let her forget it. We spent a few minutes talking about him. As I was an only child, the whole concept of a sibling was an alien one to me, and the idea of a twin sibling was even stranger. No, they weren't identical, and no, they didn't finish each other's sentences. One thing Jennifer told me was how protective Jacob was of her, and I wondered how much he knew about her ex-boyfriend Robert.

Jennifer finished her wine and declined a refill, saying she had to be up early for work.

"Do you want to walk back, or grab a taxi?" I asked. She looked at her watch, frowning.

"A taxi, I think. I hadn't realised it was so late." I pulled my phone out of my pocket to check the time and call a cab. It was only ten o'clock in the evening. Not late by my standards, but then I didn't have to get up early. The taxi turned up within minutes, surprising both of us, and in no time at all, we were pulling up outside her flat. Jennifer leaned across and kissed me on the cheek before she got out of the cab.

"I'll call you," she said.

As the cab pulled away, I sat back in the seat and sighed. Home alone again then. I caught the cab driver looking at me with one eyebrow raised in the rearview mirror, and I gave him a stare to let him know I didn't want to talk about it.

"Where to, mate?" he said, shifting his gaze back to the road.

"The Heartsease please," I replied.

Three pints later, and I was outside in the beer garden of The Heartsease, smoking a cigarette. I'd missed Tommy and David by about thirty minutes, and Big Joe wasn't in a conversational mood. I'd just finished my pint and was about to head home when my phone rang. It was Jennifer.

"Hey," I said. "You okay?"

"Yeah, I'm good," she replied. I waited for her to say something else. She'd called me, but all I could hear was the line hissing. The beer swilling round in my stomach wasn't helping, and I fought the urge to belch.

"Let me ask you something," Jennifer said. "And I want an honest answer, okay?"

"Sure, scout's honour," I replied, lighting a fresh

cigarette and waiting for her to continue. She laughed, and the sound brought a smile to my face.

"If you were here now," she said. "As in, here with me." A pause, but not an uncomfortable one. I imagined that scenario and wondered if she was doing the same. "What song would you play for me from your iPod?" I wasn't expecting that. I scrolled through my music in my head and it was my turn to pause. This was going to one of those throw it out there moments.

"You sure you want me to answer that question, Jennifer?" I said, wondering what her response might be. There was a silence on the other end of the line.

"Yes, but I want an honest answer. Not something by Frank Zappa." How did she know Frank Zappa when she didn't know Gloria Gaynor? "And if it's anything by Dire Straits, I'm hanging up." I closed my eyes, trying to picture her in my head. I took a deep breath and decided that if I was in for a penny, I might as well be in for a pound.

"It would have to be "Fix You", by Cold Play," I said and waited for a reply.

All I could hear down the line was silence, and I thought for a moment that Jennifer had hung up. Not everyone likes Cold Play. Then I heard the opening bars of the song come through the phone. I sat in silence, listening to the song through Jennifer's phone. As the final segment of the song faded away, I heard Jennifer say something but missed what it was.

"Sorry Jennifer, I missed that?"

"I said, where are you?" she replied.

"I'm at The Heartsease." There was another silence. Each one was more electric than the last.

"Do they sell wine?" Jennifer asked. I didn't have a clue.

"It's a pub, so I think they must," I replied. "It's probably piss water though." I was expecting her to laugh, but she didn't. I heard her take a deep breath, start to say something. Another deep breath.

"Can you do me a favour?" she asked, her voice a notch higher than it had been.

"Sure, of course I can," I replied. I waited for her to reply. It was her silence to break but as the seconds passed, I wondered if she was still there.

"Can you bring a bottle with you on your way over?"

I'd bought two bottles of overpriced wine from Big Joe — the only options he had available were red or white, so I got one of each. The walk to her flat didn't sober me up anywhere near the amount I'd hoped it would. I wasn't sure what to expect when I rang her doorbell, but I remember thinking things like this didn't happen to people like me while I waited. When she opened the door, Jennifer was still wearing her clothes from earlier, minus the jacket and shoes.

"Hey, hello again," she said with a smile that lit up her entire face. She'd removed what little makeup she'd been wearing, and let her hair down, but other than that she was just the same. "Come on in." Jennifer walked back into the flat, and I followed her through the narrow hallway into the lounge. Her flat was tiny. The white hallway was maybe ten feet long, extending to a lounge at the end of it, and I counted three other doors. Bathroom, bedroom, and kitchen, I assumed.

"I wasn't sure if you wanted red or white," I said as I walked behind her. "So I got one of each. I don't really drink wine." Jennifer looked over her shoulder at me and grinned.

"Perfect," she said. "I'm easy either way, and I haven't got any beer, so you'll have to help me drink it."

Jennifer's lounge was in proportion both to the rest of

the flat and to her — small. It had a sofa, a television, and not much else. The only thing different from my lounge was that Jennifer's didn't have empty beer cans and Chinese takeaway containers littering the floor.

"Have a seat, make yourself at home." Jennifer waved at the sofa. It wasn't as if there was anywhere else to sit, so I plonked myself on the end away from the cushions. I figured from the way they were crinkled that was where she sat. "I'll grab some glasses. Are they screw tops?" She nodded at the bottles I was still clutching.

"Yep, think so," I replied. She disappeared back into the hall. I heard a door open, and a few seconds later, some glasses rattling. I looked around the lounge while I waited for her to come back. There was a music channel turned down low playing on the television, and a small bookcase against one wall. A photo on top of the bookcase showed Jennifer and an older man hugging on a beach. A few of the books on the shelves were about astrology, with some romance novels dotted about. At the far end of the shelf was a copy of *Fifty Shades of Grey* with a very creased spine. Interesting.

Jennifer came back into the room holding two large wine glasses and put them on the small coffee table. I opened the bottle of white wine and poured us both a glass while she sat down at the opposite end of the sofa. The main reason I didn't often have wine was because it usually hit me like a sledgehammer, but I couldn't sit there and watch her drink it on her own.

"Here you go," I handed her a glass. "Chin Chin." We clinked our glasses together and Jennifer took a large sip from hers before sitting back on the sofa, crossing her legs as she did so. "So, let me guess," I said, pulling my face into an expression I hoped looked as if I was thinking hard. "You're a Capricorn, right?"

"Oh my God," she laughed. "I didn't know you were into astrology?" I wasn't, but I've always had a great line of bullshit.

I remember us talking for ages about nothing in particular. It hadn't taken Jennifer long to realise that I knew bugger all about astrology. I ended up confessing that I couldn't understand how a bunch of rocks floating about in space knew more about my day than I did, which she claimed was because I was a Pisces.

The white wine didn't last long, and the bottle of red turned out not to be a screw top. While Jennifer hunted in the kitchen for a corkscrew, I used her bathroom. As I peed, I looked around the small room. There was only a shower, a sink, and a toilet. Her bathroom was spotless and smelt pleasant, which was a distinct contrast to mine. The towels were neatly folded on a rail, not tossed on the floor, and the bottom of the shower was clean as a whistle whereas mine had a yellow ring effect around the plughole. I resisted the urge to peep in her bathroom cabinet and washed my hands after checking the toilet bowl for any sign of a poor aiming technique. At the last minute, I remembered to put the seat and lid back down.

When I got back into the lounge, Jennifer was sitting on the sofa, holding a large glass of red wine. Another glass, just as full, was on the coffee table. I picked it up and took a large mouthful. It was rancid. I didn't like wine at the best of times, but even a philistine like me knew this was bad. But over the course of the next half an hour or so, we managed to work our way through most of the bottle. By the time Jennifer filled up my glass with the dregs from the bottom of the bottle, I was feeling woozy. So, instead of drinking it, I lay back on the sofa and listened to her talking. So I could concentrate on the sound of her voice, I let my eyelids close just for a couple of seconds.

"Hey, sleepy head." I opened my eyes. Jennifer was kneeling in front of me holding a mug in her hand. I was stretched out on her sofa, with a blanket over me. No shoes but clothing otherwise intact. I groaned. I must have passed out last night, knowing me not long after we had started to drink the bottle of red. Anything stronger than lager just killed me. "I brought you a cup of tea," Jennifer said. She put the mug down by the side of the sofa and stood up. "I need to head off to work soon," she said. "In about twenty minutes."

"I'm so sorry," I said. "I wasn't rude, was I?" Jennifer laughed, and I grinned up at her despite a bastard of a headache behind my eyes. I must look like shit, unlike Jennifer who looked like she'd had a great night's sleep. I sat up on the sofa, running my hand across the back of my neck as the pain in my head shifted to a tight band across the back of my neck.

"Not at all," Jennifer said, still laughing. "I was in the middle of telling what I thought was a hilarious story about my brother when I looked over to see you'd passed out. Not quite snoring, but not far off." She laughed again, much more of a morning person than I was. I looked at my watch. Almost seven o'clock in the morning. I rarely got up much before ten, so being awake at this time of day was an unusual experience.

By the time Jennifer had finished in the shower, I had drunk the tea. She walked back into the lounge, still wearing her dressing gown and with wet hair cascading over her shoulders. She looked beautiful and I couldn't help but wonder if she was wearing anything underneath the dressing gown even though I'd just woken up and was hungover as hell.

"I'd better be going," I said. "I'll get out of your way, but thanks for the tea. It was perfect."

"No problem at all," Jennifer said. "And thanks for your company last night, it was just what I needed." Truth be told, I couldn't remember a great deal about last night beyond the red wine being opened. I remembered nothing about a funny story involving her brother, and I didn't remember her putting a blanket over me or removing my shoes. I hoped my feet weren't too offensive.

"Where do you want me to put this?" I asked, waving the empty mug at Jennifer.

"Oh, just leave it there. I'll wash it out later," she said. I walked to the front door of Jennifer's flat and opened it. The bright sunlight outside hurt my eyes, but the fresh air was just what I needed.

Across the road from her flat was a bright red BMW with a familiar face up behind the wheel. I turned back around, to see Jennifer holding the door open and peeping round it. This would not look good for matey boy sitting over the road. Jennifer seeing me out of her flat first thing in the morning when she was fresh from the shower.

"Why is Robert sitting outside your flat at seven o'clock in the morning?" I asked her. She groaned.

"Oh God, he's not, is he?" I stepped aside so that she could see him. If Robert hadn't seen her in her dressing gown, he could now. Oh well, some you win some you lose.

"Do you want me to have a word with him?" I asked her, looking back at the BMW. It looked brand new, but I don't really know much about cars. Tommy would know the make, model, and how to nick it, but he wasn't here.

"No, don't worry," she said. "He's been there twice this week and not said anything or done anything."

"Are you sure?" I asked.

"Honestly," she said. "It's fine."

"Okay, but if you change your mind, just let me know." I descended the steps outside her flat and walked toward the end of the road. When I turned to look to see if Jennifer was still standing at the door, it was shut. I was kind of hoping that she would be standing at the door, waving at me or something like that. As I reached the end of the road, I heard a car pull up alongside me. I turned to look, and sure enough, it was Robert. The look he gave me was one of absolute fury. I didn't want to make things more difficult for Jennifer, but I couldn't help winking at him and giving him a knowing grin. He wasn't to know I'd spent the night passed out on her sofa, so let him imagine away what might have happened. The BMW's tyres screeched as he sped up hard away from me, and I noticed his personalised number plate. It spelt 'RO3 ERT'. Robert.

What a cock.

## 5

I'd been going out with Jennifer for two months when she decided that it was time for me to meet her family. I couldn't remember the last time I'd met a girlfriend's family. It must have been while I was still at school. I guess that was because I wasn't the type of bloke that girls wanted to introduce to their families, or perhaps it was because I didn't have that many girlfriends.

Meeting the family seemed like things were getting serious between Jennifer and me, which in fairness they were. It had taken another couple of weeks after the night I'd passed out on her sofa for me to stay over again. Even now, after everything that's happened, I can't think about that second night in her flat without smiling. It was amazing. Jennifer was amazing. Was I amazing? I like to think so, but doesn't every man? I'd felt a massive sense of relief, emotional and physical, as I lay in her arms afterwards. We were both breathless, naked. Jennifer had used her thumb to mop a bead of sweat from my forehead.

"Well that was rather nice," she'd said with a sly smile that I'll remember until the day I die. "Can we do it again?" So a bit later on, we did. That night, I didn't have a drop to drink until we were both exhausted.

There was still a nagging doubt in my mind she wasn't interested in me as a person, but that I was useful to have around. I wasn't complaining though, and I tried to convince myself that it didn't matter if she didn't like me in that way. I was having fun, and I thought she was having fun. So where was the harm in that? The other problem was that she had no idea about my part-time job, and the more time I spent with her, the more uncomfortable I got about my secondary income. I'd even considered, but not mentioned it to a soul, giving it all up and going straight.

But, despite those issues that nagged inside my head, like me she did, and I have to say we made a good couple in the early days. Tommy didn't help when I told him that Jennifer and I were seeing each other. He'd said I was punching so far above my weight I needed a ladder. Despite him, the first few months of that summer was one of the happiest times of my life. I'd been so nervous as we drove to her Dad's house I'd almost bottled it and asked her to drop me off at the nearest pub. We drove towards Thorpe End, a village on the outskirts of Norwich where even the smallest houses had names, not numbers, and I would have stuck out like a sore thumb at any of the pubs we passed. I was wearing my only suit, which was much tighter around the neck and the waist since the last time I'd worn it. I'd bought it a few years ago when I was thinner, and even with the top button of both the shirt and the trousers undone, it was still too small. When Jennifer slowed down to turn into her Dad's driveway, I realised that the house couldn't be seen from the road but was hidden behind large, mature trees. The tyres rolled over the smooth weed-free gravel as we pulled into the drive, and she parked her Mini behind a brand-new Audi TT.

"My brother's car," Jennifer explained when she saw me admiring the Audi. "He got it with last year's bonus." I didn't know what it was he did, but to buy a TT with the bonus he got for doing it meant he must be doing well. I looked at Jennifer's Dad's house, which loomed above us as we walked toward it, our footsteps crunching on the gravel. The house was enormous, red brick, white windows on two stories with a steep roof. It loomed over us as we approached, not menacing but not friendly either. Either side of the front door the house jutted out like it had stately home style wings, and the grandiose effect was finished by a large garden. No nosey neighbours on this street. I wanted to ask Jennifer why she lived in a little flat on the edge of a council estate in Norwich when the rest of her family seemed to be minted, but I thought better of it.

The man who opened the door as we approached was the same guy I'd seen in photographs in Jennifer's flat. He was in his early sixties by my guess, and still in good shape. Six-foot two or three, about the same height as me, and he had broad shoulders. The man didn't have an ounce of fat I could see. Smart brown trousers, an open-necked blue shirt under a multicoloured jumper with a large diamond pattern. He wouldn't have looked out of place on a golf course, and I wouldn't have been surprised if he'd owned a golf course.

"You must be Gareth?" he asked, an inscrutable look on his face.

"I am, sir," I replied, following Tommy's advice about meeting the parents, or in this case parent. *Be respectful*, Tommy had said. *Always call them sir and ma'am, rhymes with jam*. I extended my hand outwards. "Pleased to meet you." He looked at my hand, frowning before his face split into a wide smile. He grabbed my hand and almost crushed it.

"Ha! I'm Andy, Jen's Dad, obviously. So you're the boy

who's had such an effect on my baby girl?" he said, shaking my hand up and down. I tried to grip his hand back, but he'd got my fingers like a vice.

"Dad, please," Jennifer said, her face reddening as she pushed past him and walked into the house. He laughed in response, a loud booming laugh that endeared him to me straight away.

"She's only my youngest by a few minutes, but she's still my baby girl," he said, looking at me. The wide smile on his face faded, and he looked at me with an earnest face. "I am pleased to meet you though, Gareth. She's not shut up about you for the last couple of weeks, and you look a hell of a lot better than most of the tossers she's been out with over the years."

I was suddenly uncomfortable. Although I'd been with Jennifer for a few months, we'd not discussed previous partners. I knew about Robert but knew nothing about anyone else. At least my revelations wouldn't take long — I'd been with exactly two and a half women in my life before meeting Jennifer. The half was an experience in Amsterdam that I'd rather forget, with a Thai lady who'd looked mighty fine in the window but turned out to be not quite as advertised.

"Come in," Andy said, still gripping my hand. "Please, come through. Welcome." He let go, and I resisted the urge to massage my fingers as he walked into the house. I followed him through the front door into a hall that was bigger than my entire flat. His downstairs toilet was probably bigger than my entire flat. Family photos covered one wall, and there were a few of a much younger Andy playing cricket and holding up trophies. As we walked through the hall, a bunch of framed medals on the wall caught my attention. They were mounted one above the other, large bronze discs surrounded a thick

walnut frame. Leaning towards them as I passed I saw
that they were medals for finishing the London
Marathon. The most recent one was only last year. Andy
went up in my estimation. Although I used to run a bit
when I was younger, I could barely run for a bus these
days, let alone finish a marathon, and he had to have
forty years on me.

We walked into a light, airy kitchen with an industrial
size cooker in the centre taking pride of place, and the
most fantastic smell of cooking meat in the air. Leaning up
against the cooker was a man who I knew was Jennifer's
brother, Jacob. I knew it was him as I was expecting him to
be there, but what I wasn't expecting was how much he
looked like Jennifer. She'd laughed when I'd asked her if
they were identical twins. Apparently that wasn't possible,
but they still looked pretty damned similar to me.

"Gareth, is it?" he said, walking toward me, hand
extended. Jennifer's family were big into handshakes.

"Yes, and you must be Jacob?" I replied, shaking his
hand. A normal handshake this time. "Jennifer's told me
all about you," I said. He sighed before replying.

"Oh, really? What's she said then? Just so you know,
I've got more dirt on her than she's got on me." He flashed
a smile at Jennifer, who was leaning up against the kitchen
counter with a glass of wine in her hand. She grinned in
response and raised her glass in our direction.

"Don't worry Jacob," I said. "It's all good."

"I should hope so," he replied, smiling again at
Jennifer. It was strange talking to him, knowing he was her
twin brother. He spent a fair bit of time in the gym, that
was obvious from his oversized arms, broad shoulders, and
tapered waist. But he shared some of her mannerisms, like
the way he stood and the way he smiled. Jacob glanced at
Andy and lowered his voice. "Jennifer told me how you

two met. That was good of you to help her out." I shrugged my shoulders.

"It was nothing. Her ex just needed some gentle persuasion, that was all," I replied.

"Is he still hanging around then, your ex?" Jacob turned to Jennifer. "You said he was the other night." I looked across at Jennifer. She'd not mentioned that.

"Robert's fine," Jennifer waved her hand at Jacob. "He's got the message, don't worry." I could tell from the look on Jacob's face he was worried and wondered if perhaps I needed to have another word with Robert. As I thought about the best way to do this, Andy walked up and handed me an ice-cold can of lager and a glass that felt like it was fresh from the fridge.

"There you go, Gareth," he said. "Get that down you. After you've had a couple of beers, we'll all seem normal." He laughed at his own joke, and the rest of us gave polite chuckles. "Right then," he rubbed his hands together. "Let's get this show on the road then, shall we?" I caught Jennifer rolling her eyes at her brother. In fairness to her, she had warned me about this. Dinner was a family affair in Andy's house, and that included the preparation.

For the next hour, I peeled potatoes, diced swede, and took the top of my finger off trying to cut an X into the bottom of a Brussels sprout. Jennifer and Jacob both gave up after about half an hour, Jacob offering to nip out to get more tin foil. Jennifer went with him, saying he'd need a hand. She avoided my eyes as she walked past me, but I could see her trying to keep a straight face. She pinched my backside as she brushed against me on her way out, and it was my turn to try to keep a straight face. Thinking back, they must have planned it in advance to give me some time alone with Andy.

"I meant what I said earlier, Gareth," Andy said, his

eyes meeting mine for a second before returning to whatever he was chopping up. "Jen seems thrilled being with
you. I've not seen her this happy for a long time." He
paused, knife mid-chop, and looked back at me. There was
a sadness behind his eyes. "Not since before her Mum
died, I'd say."

We took a break from the lunch preparation, and Andy
decided that we needed what he called a "cheeky drink".
For him, this was a very large whisky. I declined one,
deciding to stick to beer to be on the safe side. Andy slid
the patio doors open and stepped through them. I followed
him, realising for the first time just how big the garden was.
You could put a goal at either end of it and not be far off a
football pitch.

"It's getting warmer, isn't it?" he said as we walked
onto the patio. "I've heard we're in for a scorcher this
summer." Andy sat in a chair facing the long lawn and
took a deep breath. I joined him and we both regarded the
garden in companionable silence, bathed in the weak
sunshine.

"They're very close, the two of them," Andy said. "Jen
and Jacob, I mean."

"Less than two minutes, I'd heard," I replied, proud of
myself for coming up with that one on the fly. Andy
laughed.

"Superb, Gareth," he replied. "I can see why she likes
you. Seriously though, they are. Well, they're twins but
even so. He'd do anything for her, but half the time she
refuses any offers to make her life easier. Wants to make
her own way, she says. I'm comfortable enough, and
Jacob's doing all right for himself. We've both tried to help
her out here and there, but she won't have it." I wondered
if Andy knew how Jennifer and I had met when she most

needed some help. It wasn't my place to tell him if he didn't know.

"I take it that Jen's told you about Jacob, has she?" he said a few moments later.

"Er," I replied. "I'm not sure what you mean."

"That he's a left-handed batsman?" he said. I thought for a second before replying.

"No, sorry. I'm not with you." I had no idea where he was going.

"Sits on the top deck of the bus. You know? Plays for the other team," Andy said. I looked at him, none the wiser. "That he's gay?"

"Oh, yes. I see what you mean. No, she didn't tell me he was gay." Left-handed batsman? I had never heard that phrase before. We sat for a moment and I took a large sip of my beer to cover the silence.

"I'm quite keen on grandchildren, you see. I think I might have to call you 'Obi-Wan' if that's okay?" Andy paused before continuing. "You're my only hope." I snorted, inhaling beer and coughing. It wasn't helped by the fact that I was trying to laugh at the same time. He roared with laughter, slapping me on the back, just as the patio doors opened and Jennifer and Jacob looked out.

"So this is getting lunch ready, is it boys?" Jennifer stood with her hands on her hips. She had a stern expression on her face, but she couldn't stop the corners of her mouth twitching. Jacob was just behind her, holding a roll of tin foil in the air as proof they'd accomplished something.

By the time Jennifer and I were driving back home that night, I was in a fantastic place. We'd eaten until we couldn't eat anymore. Andy and I had got drunker throughout the day while Jennifer had switched to diet coke after her earlier glass of wine. I'd tried to persuade her we could get a cab back, come back and get the car tomorrow, but she wasn't having it. Andy had even suggested that we both stay over, in separate bedrooms but that wasn't on the cards either. The whole day had just been so comfortable, and I'd experienced something that I'd not experienced for years, if at all. At the risk of sounding dramatic, I felt as if I belonged.

We were lying in her bed, both exhausted but wide awake. Jennifer turned and propped herself up on her elbow.

"Thank you for today, Gareth," she said.

"What? Thank you for bleeding to death doing the sprouts and laughing at your Dad's awful jokes?"

"No, you know what I mean. I know you weren't happy about the whole meet the family thing, but they liked you." She looked at me in the semi-darkness. "I knew they would." I wasn't quite sure what to say to that, so I chose the easy option and said nothing.


Jennifer snuggled against me and slid her arm across my chest. "So, thank you," she murmured, closing her eyes.

# 6

The night I finally decided to go straight is another evening I've relived in my mind time and time again. It was April, but freezing cold outside. The early warm snap hadn't turned into the expected scorcher just yet. I was huddled in the corner of The Heartsease with Tommy and David. The proceeds from the off-licence job had long since disappeared. Most of the stock was now behind the bar, sold to Big Joe so he could sell it on with a hefty markup.

Tommy was telling us about a grand idea he'd had to rip off a fish and chip shop, of all things. He was waiting for the bus one morning when he noticed a delivery driver pull up to one near his house. The delivery driver had dropped off several large sacks of potatoes in exchange for what was, as far as Tommy could see, a not insignificant amount of money.

Tommy had since worked out that there was a potato delivery every week, and that the fish and chip shop near his house was just one in a large round that the delivery driver made. Every transaction was in cash, and Tommy estimated that by the end of his round the delivery driver would have had at least a few thousand pounds. All in cash. His plan was to relieve the delivery driver of that cash at the end of his round. David was sitting on the fence, no doubt waiting to see which way the decision went between the two of us.

I wasn't convinced in the slightest. It was one thing doing over a business like an off-licence or office at night, with no one around. Even stuff like that I was becoming uncomfortable with as I knew every time we did a job there was a risk involved. If that risk was realised, and we were nicked, then all three of us would go to prison. It wasn't something I'd been bothered with before I had met Jennifer, as it was an occupational hazard for people like us, but it was weighing on my mind now that things seemed to be getting more serious between us.

"He won't care," Tommy said. "He's only the delivery driver." Tommy had been following the delivery driver, as discreetly as he could, for the last couple of weeks and had identified an ideal spot to pull the van over just outside the city centre. "It's not as if he's going to put up a fight or anything, is it?"

"So how are we going to get the van to stop then, Tommy?" David asked. I'd been wondering the same thing myself.

"Well, I guess there are a couple of options," Tommy replied. "We could, I don't know, stage a car accident or something. Get him to follow us, slam the brakes on at a roundabout so he goes into the back of the car. Then pull into the lay-by to sort out the insurance details and relieve him of the cash."

"But that still doesn't answer the question of how we get the cash from him, Tommy, does it?" I said. Tommy's plan so far was rubbish.

"We'll just threaten him a bit," Tommy replied. That's what I'd thought he would say. "I mean, come on, you and me? We're both big guys. He's not. He's a streak of piss, smaller than David, and got to be in his fifties at least."

"I don't like it, Tommy," I said, crossing my arms and leaning back in the chair. "We've never done that before. It's always just been buildings, never people."

"I'm not convinced either," David said. "I mean, what if he has a heart attack or something?" Nine times out of ten, David would follow my line of reasoning, and tonight he was true to form.

"Oh for God's sake, the pair of you are just not listening," Tommy replied. "We're talking thousands here. This could set all three of us up for months."

"So how do you propose that we threaten him then, Tommy?" I asked, leaning forward and tapping my finger on the table just hard enough to make the beer glasses wobble. "Just stand there looking bigger than he is until he hands over the money?"

"Well, we could take a bat or something?" Tommy replied. "Wave it about until he gets the message?"

"Wave it about?" I asked, louder than I'd intended. I lowered my voice to a whisper. "Wave it about? Really? Tommy, I've known you for a long time, but you've lost the plot on this one."

"Why?" Tommy replied, whining. "This is a big job. You've got to take a bit of risk for a lot of reward." I looked across at David and saw his eyes flick between me and Tommy.

"Mate," I said, putting both hands flat on the table in front of me and staring at Tommy. "You're talking armed robbery. Do you know what you get for that?"

"That's not armed robbery," Tommy said. "Not with a baseball bat it's not."

"I think it is, Tommy," David said, looking across at me for approval. "Isn't it, Gareth?"

"Yeah, as far as I know, it is. A baseball bat is a weapon unless you're on your way to play baseball somewhere," I said. "I think it would be difficult to persuade the Old Bill that we were on our way for a game of baseball in the park when we happened to have an accident with a van driven by a man with a lot of money in his pocket. Which we then decided to take for ourselves," I said. Tommy sat back in his chair and sighed, deflated.

"I didn't realise I was having a beer with a couple of lawyers," he said.

"Tommy," I said. "Don't be daft, mate. You know what the maximum sentence for armed robbery is, don't you?"

"No, sorry Your Honour. I don't," he said. "Perhaps my learned friend could enlighten me?" David smiled at his response, but my reply soon wiped the smile off his face.

"It's life, Tommy."

I didn't tell Tommy or David how I knew that the maximum prison sentence for armed robbery was life. Nor did I tell them how I knew even with a baseball bat, it would still be armed robbery. Over the last couple of days, weeks really, I'd spent hours on the Internet looking at various legal websites to find out how long you could get put away for. Going to prison had always been at the back of my mind, an occupational hazard. But while I didn't think that a couple of months inside for theft would be too hard to deal with, one thing that I drew the line at was life in prison. Ironic really, considering where I am now.

The main problem I had was Jennifer had no idea how I earned my money. As far as she was concerned, my sole source of income was from working the door on clubs and pubs around Norwich. To be honest, the thought of spending a couple of months inside and losing Jennifer when she found out the truth about what I did for a living was getting to me. I pushed my chair back and got my feet.

"I'm going for a smoke," I said. "Back in a minute."

Standing outside in the cold, I remembered looking over the wall of the beer garden and seeing Jennifer and Robert arguing. That had been the start, and I realised as I smoked my cigarette that in a sense it was also the beginning of the end. I stubbed out my cigarette in the broken flowerpot on the table and stood for a second, thinking. Tommy's plans were becoming increasingly risky. The problem with that was that David was easily influenced and if I wasn't careful, it would be a situation where it was two against one. I knew my bollocks were big enough to resist that sort of pressure, but even so, the time had come. I considered having another cigarette, but decided against it and walked back inside the pub.

"Tommy, David," I said, looking at the three full pints on the table in front of me as I did so. Tommy must have got a round in while I was outside having a smoke. It was his shout after all. "I've got something to tell you both." I picked up my pint and took a large sip of the cold lager to buy some time. Tommy leaned back in his chair and folded his arms across his broad chest. From the look on his face, he knew exactly what I was going to say. David, by contrast, was more interested in scratching what looked like a nasty spot on his neck. "I'm quitting, boys," I said, trying to say it in a voice that meant it was obvious I meant business.

"What, smoking?" Tommy replied. "You've been saying that for years."

"No, not that. I'm going to go straight. I've had enough." There it was, out in the open.

They both looked at me for a few seconds as if they

were wondering what to say next. I was pretty much in the
same boat. Until the words had left my mouth, I wasn't
one hundred per cent sure I was convinced that was the
right course of action for me to take. I regarded David,
who was deep in thought. He looked across at Tommy and
grinned. He had obviously thought of something funny
to say.

"See, Tommy," he said, giggling like a child. "I always
said he was gay." Tommy didn't laugh but looked at me
with stern eyes.

"You can't go straight, Gareth," he said. "You wouldn't
last five minutes in the real world. What would you do for
money? You're thick as mince at the best of times, and the
only things you're any good at are robbing and looking
ugly on the door of a club." I knew he was angry with
what I had just said, but there was no need to be rude.

"Piss off, Tommy," I replied. "You're the one suggesting
we pull off an armed robbery. Just because I don't think
that's a fantastic idea doesn't make me thick as mince." It
was Tommy's turn to bristle. "What you're suggesting is
way out there. It's one thing risking a couple of months
inside for burglary but quite another risking a life
sentence."

"When did you decide this then, mate?" Tommy said.
"What, you went outside for a cigarette and while you were
smoking it decided that you would go straight. It's not like
you mentioned it before, is it?"

"I've been thinking about it for a while," I replied. "It's
getting more difficult with Jennifer."

"What, she doesn't know you're on the rob?" David
asked. He looked across at Tommy as he asked the
question.

"I think she knows I don't just work on the door of
clubs for a living."

"Seriously? She doesn't know anything?" David said.

"No, and I don't want her to find out either," I said. Tommy was still looking at me with an impassive expression, his arms still folded. He was leaning back in his chair. I mirrored him, leaning back in my chair and crossing my arms. Ignoring David, I held Tommy's stare.

Truth be told, I wasn't sure what I wanted Tommy to say. Was I looking for him to agree with me? Did I want validation of my decision? Or did I want him to accept it? Tommy looked at me for what felt like ages before speaking.

"I've seen that look on your face before," he said.

"Really?" I replied.

"Yes," he said. "Laura Hutchinson."

Now that was a name I'd not heard for many years. Laura was my first ever girlfriend, and at the time I was going out with her I was convinced that she was the one, the one I would spend the rest of my life with. In fairness, I was only fifteen at the time so that was quite an unlikely outcome for the relationship. I'd gone out with her for maybe four months before she unceremoniously dumped me for a lad who looked as if he was at least eighteen, if not older. This meant he could buy booze. That was how seriously she took our relationship. When she finished with me, it was if the bottom had dropped out of my world, and I was heartbroken in only the way that a fifteen-year-old boy whose first ever girlfriend has just ditched him can be. People say girls grow up quicker than boys. Well in Laura's case, that was definitely true.

I looked at Tommy, wondering why he had brought Laura up in the conversation when I realised what he meant. He still had his arms crossed and was still leaning back in his chair, but the ghost of a smile was playing on his face.

"Yeah?" he said. "You know what I mean?" I knew exactly what he meant, and while bringing her up in this conversation made him a bastard, it also confirmed he was the man who knew me better than anyone else. I guess that's what friends are for. David looked at Tommy, then back at me, then back at Tommy. He hadn't got a clue what we were talking about, which is probably just as well because I didn't feel like explaining it to him.

We sat in silence for a few minutes, sipping our drinks. I was waiting for Tommy to say something. The only thing is I was too proud to ask him if he thought I was making the right decision. He might have been my best friend, but we're still both blokes. Maybe if David hadn't been there, it would have been different, but I didn't think it would be. We all reached the end of our drinks at more or less the same time as people used to drinking with each other often do. David got to his feet and saying nothing, picked up the empty glasses from the table before walking across to the bar to get them refilled.

"Tommy?" I said. "What do you think?"

"What would I know?" he said, the faint smile returning to his face. "But you are as thick as mince. We both are." I laughed before replying.

"Yeah, you're probably right," I said. It was his turn to laugh.

"Gareth," he said. "You've got it bad, I can tell. And you know what?" He glanced over his shoulder to make sure that David was still at the bar. "If I'm honest, I'm jealous." I wasn't sure what to say to that, so said nothing. Tommy paused before continuing. "She's a lovely girl, and you look good together. In all fairness, I've been waiting for you to say something like that for a couple of weeks." We both sat in silence while we waited for David come back from the bar.

David managed to carry all three pint glasses back from the bar, his hands clasped in a triangle around them. He put them on the table, only spilling a bit. Tommy and I both reached forward at the same time to grab our pint glasses. Once David had sat down and picked up his pint, Tommy raised his in the air.

"Gentlemen, I propose a toast," he said. David and I raised glasses in response.

"What are we toasting?" David asked. I looked at Tommy and his eyes met mine. I knew what his toast would be, and I loved him for it.

"To Jennifer and Gareth, and their crime-free life. May it last for a long time." David smiled and glanced at me and Tommy. I wondered for a moment if he'd had the presence of mind to leave us alone for a moment, but looking at him I decided that he probably hadn't.

"I'll drink to that," I said, looking at Tommy with a slight nod of my head as I did so to thank him. The three of us clinked our glasses together, said "Cheers" in unison, and took large swigs of the lukewarm lager. Almost as one, we put them back on the table. Tommy grinned, and I knew from the look on his face, he was going to say something he thought was funny.

"Of course, it'll never last," he said, with a sly wink. "In less than a year mate, you'll be single again."

The saddest thing is that Tommy was right.

## 7

I stood in my kitchen, the phone pressed to my ear, and looked out at the sad patch of yellow grass that passed for a garden while I waited for Tommy to pick up. Even though it was only spring, the grass was still dead from the previous summer.

"What is it Gareth?" Tommy's irritated voice finally came on the line. "It's bloody well crack of sparrows, mate." I looked at my watch. It was almost half past nine, hardly first thing in the morning. But I guessed it was early enough for Tommy. In all the years I'd known him, he'd never been a morning person.

"I need some help, Tommy," I said. "Jennifer's Dad needs a hand shifting firewood. It sounds like there's a fair bit of it. Can you help?"

"Oh, for God's sake, really? What's in it for me?" he grumbled.

"My gratitude for one, and Jennifer's. You'd be helping me out big time, mate. I'll see you right, don't worry." As always, the promise of some money got Tommy's attention. He paused for a couple of seconds, weighing up whether or not it was worth his while. Even when he was silent, I knew what he was thinking about.

"Okay," he sighed. "Give me a while, though. Need to clean up in here. Had some company last night if you know what I mean?" I laughed in response. I think the last woman who'd been in Tommy's flat was his mum, and she'd only gone round there to give him an earful about forgetting a birthday or something like that.

"Yeah, I'm sure, Tommy. I'll pick you up in an hour?" I said. His only response was a grunt before he hung up.

An hour later, almost to the second, I was sitting outside Tommy's flat, leaning on the horn of the car. He appeared and from the look of him, it had been a wild night. I still doubted he'd had any company, but he seemed happy enough even if he looked like shit.

"Morning, mate," I said as he threw himself into the passenger seat. I could smell the faint odour of stale alcohol on his breath as he spoke. It was just as well I was driving.

"Yeah, well it was until you bloody phoned up," he retorted. "You don't want to know what I was in the middle of when you called." He was right. I had no interest in what he'd been doing when I phoned, especially as he'd almost certainly been alone. I handed him a cardboard cup of coffee. "Oh you're a star, you are. I knew there was something I liked about you," he said as he took the cup from me.

"Three sugars, mate," I said. "Just how you like it." He smiled as he took a sip from the cup.

"Perfect," he replied. "Nice one."

We pulled up outside Andy's house and got out of the car. I locked the car, and we walked into the driveway where there was a huge pile of wood strewn on the gravel drive. Andy's car was hemmed in behind the logs. It was a lot of wood, all cut into small pieces which I presumed were fireplace size. Tommy stood back a few feet taking in the house and front garden as I rang the doorbell.

"Nice place," he muttered just as Andy opened the door.

"Gareth, thank you so much for coming over," Andy said, the relief obvious in his voice. "You must be Tommy?" He looked over my shoulder at Tommy, who stepped forward with his hand extended. "Gareth said he would ask you to help."

"Yep, that's me, Mr Elliott," Tommy said as they shook hands.

"Please, it's Andy. And thank you so much for coming." Andy pointed at the log pile. "I wasn't expecting so many logs. I shifted a few barrow loads last night, but then my bloody back gave out." He rubbed his lower back for effect. "Not as young as I used to be."

"I know that feeling, Mr Elliott," Tommy laughed, as did Andy as he turned around and walked into the house. He didn't look like a man with a bad back to me, but then again why would a guy in his sixties shift a load of logs if there were other people who would do it for him?

"Come on in, we'll have a quick cup of tea before you two get cracking," Andy called over his shoulder. I looked at Tommy, who grimaced. We walked through the hallway, following Andy into the kitchen. I watched as Tommy looked around, his practised eyes taking in the interior of the house. I knew exactly what he was doing, and the anger rose in my chest.

Andy made us all a cup of tea in the kitchen before opening the back door and walking through it. There was me thinking we'd all have a nice cup of tea and a chat but no, it was straight down to work.

"I've only got one wheelbarrow, I'm afraid," he said.

I'd followed him through the back door before turning to see Tommy examining the lock on the door. He was wriggling the jamb, testing how secure the door was. I knew he would just claim professional curiosity, but I'd not brought him around here so he could case the place.

"Tommy," I said, louder than intended. He jumped and then followed me onto the patio. I shot him a warning glance, and he pulled a face in return. Like butter wouldn't melt.

There was a solitary wheelbarrow with a half flat tyre in the middle of the lawn, and a tiny pile of logs stacked up against the wall of the shed. It was more of an outbuilding than a shed and even had double glazing. Even my flat didn't have double glazing.

"What do you think, mate?" I asked Tommy. "One of us on the barrow, one stacking the logs? Then we can swap over."

"Sounds good, Gareth," Tommy replied. "You start on the barrow, though. I need to use the toilet. Just pile them there, and we can stack them against the shed slow time," he pointed at a spot on the lawn. "I'll catch up in a second." He turned to speak to Andy. "Can I use your facilities, Andy?"

"Of course you can, Tommy," Andy replied. "Follow me."

As the two of them walked back into the house, I saw Andy slap Tommy on the back as if they were old friends. I wheeled the barrow round to the front of the house and filled it with logs. I moved a couple of loads to the back of the house, not helped by the flat tyre.

"He's a nice chap, Andy, isn't he?" Tommy said when he reappeared, his voice bright. "Nice place, too."

"Tommy, you even so much as think about coming

back here I'll cut your balls off," I said, emptying another barrow load onto the pile.

"Woah, relax fella," Tommy said, his palms out in a placatory gesture. "I wouldn't dare. He's your family, isn't he?"

"As good as," I grumbled. "I mean it though, don't even think about it."

"Oh come on, Gareth," Tommy retorted as he picked up a couple of logs and stacked them on the pile leaning up against the shed. "How long have you known me? You really think I'm going to do over my own?" I knew he was serious, but I'd seen how he'd been looking at the place. I was sure he didn't need the toilet either but just wanted to have another look to see what was inside the house.

We soon settled into a routine of moving and stacking the logs. Each of us would do five trips on the barrow while the other one stacked them before we swapped over. It was almost therapeutic, doing the stacking. Like a giant jigsaw puzzle. Working out what was the best way to stack them so they all slotted in together was quite satisfying. After an hour, we'd shifted about half of the pile in the driveway and took a break. I poked my head back into the kitchen and called Andy's name. There was no reply, so I figured he must have gone out. One less cup of tea to make then. Tommy and I stood in the kitchen while we waited for the kettle to boil.

"How long would it take you then, mate?" Tommy asked, waving his hand round the kitchen.

"How long would what take?" I replied.

"To get in," he said. I raised an eyebrow in response.

"I've gone straight, Tommy. Remember?"

"Hypothetically, I mean. If you were still on the rob and wanted to get in here, how long would it take you?" He looked at me with his eyebrows raised.

"Hypothetically?" I said, knowing that Tommy was throwing down a gauntlet to me regardless of whether I'd gone straight or not.

"Yeah," he replied. "How long?" I shrugged in response before replying.

"Two minutes," I said. "Tops."

"That long?" he said. "I reckon a minute. Loads of different ways in, and some nice stuff in here, too. There's a Bose sound system hooked up to the telly in the front room. I could shift that for a couple of hundred easy, and probably another couple of hundred for the telly as well. I can see the look on Big Joe's face if I turned up with that for The Heartsease." I gave Tommy another dark look, as mean as I could get without looking constipated.

"Come on, Gareth," he said. "Don't give me the look. You know I wouldn't even think about it. I'm just saying, that's all." Tommy regarded me, his expression one I'd known for years. One I couldn't help but love, but also one I wouldn't trust an inch. "You should tell him," he said.

I laughed. "Yeah, sure. Andy? In my professional opinion as an ex-burglar, your house is wide open to pikeys like me. I can see how that would go."

"You don't have to tell him that, Gareth," he said, grinning.

I made tea for us both and threw a tea bag into another cup for Andy when he got back. I was thinking about what Tommy had just said as I was stirring the cups when something struck me.

"When did you go into the lounge?" I asked. "You went to the toilet, but that's off the hallway. You can't see the telly from the hallway."

"Er, I saw it through the glass door," Tommy replied.

"I think I need to go your opticians, mate," I said. "I

can't see a thing through frosted glass." Realising his mistake, Tommy laughed. Despite myself, I soon joined in.

We took our cups outside and got back on the case with the wheelbarrow. It took about another hour, but eventually, Tommy put the last of the logs onto the now impressive stack against the shed. We were both sweating in the sunshine even though it was still cold.

"Job done, fella," Tommy clapped me on the shoulder. "Time for a pint, is it?" I looked at my watch. It was almost one, and we'd not eaten yet.

"We could get a bite to eat and then have a cheeky pint I suppose," I said, walking back toward the house. As I stepped into the kitchen, I saw Andy sitting at the kitchen table reading a newspaper.

"All done?" Andy said, looking over the top of his glasses at me. He got to his feet and looked through the kitchen window at the logs piled up against the shed. "Wow, fantastic job. Thank you so much. At least I'll be able to get the car out now."

"No problem, Andy," I replied. The number of brownie points that this would get me with Jennifer made it well worthwhile. "I'm just nipping to the toilet, then we'll be on our way." I walked through the hallway to the toilet, glancing at the frosted glass door to the lounge as I did so. I smiled to myself as I used the toilet before returning to the kitchen to find Andy and Tommy deep in conversation. They stopped talking as I walked back in, and I stood looking at the pair of them for a few seconds.

"So, er, Gareth," Andy said eventually. "Tommy tells me you're concerned about my security?" I looked at Tommy, who was wearing his butter wouldn't melt expression again. I frowned at him before replying. Had he mentioned something to Andy about our area of expertise?

"Well, kind of," I said. "There are a few areas you could look at."

"You think?" Andy replied. "Fancy a flutter?" I wasn't sure where Andy was going with this. "Tommy here reckons that you could get in here in under a minute." That was a lie. I'd said two. Andy reached into his pocket and pulled out his wallet before throwing a couple of twenties and a tenner onto the kitchen table. "If you get in here in under a minute, you can keep it. Just don't break anything."

"That's really not my thing, Andy," I said. "I don't do that sort of security."

"Oh, come on," he replied. "I'm sure that you've got some, let's call them hidden talents. From the past, perhaps?" I looked at Jennifer's father, wondering how much he thought he knew about me. Was I that transparent? Jennifer didn't seem to have any idea, but did Andy? I glanced again at Tommy, but he was still expressionless.

Even though a silent alarm bell was ringing in my head, I'd always been a sucker for a challenge so I stepped outside the kitchen door and watched Andy through the glass as he locked the door, pushing a bolt across it. He mimed starting a stopwatch on his wrist. It wasn't the money. I knew I wouldn't keep it, but Andy had thrown down a glove and I'd never refused a challenge like that from anyone yet.

I dug into my pocket and pulled out my keys. Selecting a standard Chubb key, I stepped up to the outside of the kitchen door and worked the end of the key into the cracked putty surrounding one of the panes of glass. The putty fell out almost instantly, just as I knew it would, and I worked the key around the glass until the whole pane fell outward into my other hand. I put the glass down on the path and leaned my arm in through the gap it left, releasing the bolt and opening the door. As I stepped through it, Andy looked at his watch, eyebrows raised in surprise.

"Under thirty seconds," he said in a quiet voice. Tommy was standing behind him, his eyes on the fifty quid on the kitchen table. No doubt he was considering how to persuade me why we should go halves on it.

"And where, Gareth Dawson, did you learn how to do that?" Jennifer's voice, as cold as ice, rang across the kitchen. I'd not seen her come in, but she was standing by the door to the hallway, arms crossed tight across her chest. There was a look of absolute thunder on her face, and the twin red spots on her cheeks told me she was very, very pissed off.

Shit.

## 8

"I knew it, I bloody well knew it," Jennifer said, leaning up against the sideboard in the kitchen of her flat. "Every bloody time," she sighed. "Just when I think I've met a decent bloke, he turns out to be an arsehole." I stood in front of her, not sure what to do with my hands. We'd argued before, but nothing like this. The way it was going it could well be the last argument we ever had.

"Jennifer, please?" I said, trying not to sound too desperate. "It's not how you think."

"Oh, really?" She laughed, but there was no humour in it. "I nip round my dad's house to see how you and your mate were getting on, and I find you giving my dad a lesson on breaking and entering."

That's exactly what she had just found. After she'd seen my little demonstration of how insecure Andy's house was, Jennifer had left without saying another word. Tommy and I had gone to the hardware shop to get some window putty so we could fix the pane of glass I'd taken out. On the way to the shop, I'd made the mistake of asking Tommy for his advice. I should have known by then that Tommy's advice was, while well-meaning, almost always rubbish.

"All she saw, mate," Tommy said, "was you taking out a pane of glass so you could open the door. It's not like she caught you red-handed leaving his house wearing a striped top and carrying a large bag marked 'swag', is it?"

"Thanks, Tommy," I'd said. "That's really helpful. What the hell am I going to say to her? You saw the look on her face."

"Fair one," Tommy had replied. "She didn't look thrilled, did she?" That was the understatement of the century.

"Shit, Tommy. What the hell am I going to do?"

"Not much you can do, mate," he replied, unhelpfully. "You're nicked, I reckon. Just a case of waiting to see what the sentence will be. You might get off lightly, no sex for a couple of weeks or something like that. Or you could be out on your ear."

"Thanks a bundle," I said. "You're wasted as a crook mate, you should train to be a bloody marriage counsellor." Tommy laughed in response. It wasn't supposed to be a joke.

"Well, you're not married," he paused for a second before continuing. "But I don't think I'd need training, anyway." I looked across at him, his smug face irritating me, before I returned my eyes to the road in front of us, drumming my fingers on the steering wheel.

I dropped Tommy back at Andy's house, warning him to play nicely and just fix the window, before carrying on to face the music back at Jennifer's flat. When I knocked on the door, not wanting to use my key, she opened it and just walked back into the flat. I followed her through to the kitchen.

"Jennifer," I pleaded. "Listen just for a minute." I

watched as she folded her arms across her chest and pushed her lips together until they could barely be seen. This would be a tough sell.

"Go on, I'm all ears," she said, arching her eyebrows as if no matter what I said she wasn't going to believe it. Which was probably true.

"I admit that, when I was younger, I did some stuff I'm not proud of now," I said. "But that's not me now."

She glared at me, her eyes piercing. "It explains a hell of a lot," she said. "How you suddenly have spare cash floating about every once in a while, for example."

"I've told you, Jennifer," I said. "I'll have a flutter on the horses, and sometimes they come in." As Jennifer looked at me, I realised that she knew I was lying through my teeth.

"So your horse is on at five to two against, and you put ten pounds down each way. It comes in second. How much do you win?" She looked at me, her eyebrows arched again. I hadn't got a clue what the answer was. What I knew about horses could fit on the back of a postage stamp and still leave room for what I knew about betting.

"Er, well," I replied, trying to buy some time so I could come up with a convincing answer. "So, it's five to two against?"

"Don't even bother, Gareth," Jennifer barked at me. "It's a stupid bet. You wouldn't win anything. I've never seen you go anywhere near a bookie, or study the form in the newspaper, or any of the things that people who like horses do. That money is coming from your little sideline, mugging old ladies or whatever you do to get it."

"Jennifer, I promise you, I have never mugged anyone in my life," I said, in a desperate attempt to defend myself.

"You've lied to me, Gareth Dawson. You let me believe that you're a decent bloke, but you conveniently forgot to mention that you're not." She shouted the last two words of the sentence, and her words cut through me. I looked at her, and saw a tear appear in the corner of her eye. Jennifer brushed away before it could fall down her cheek, but for some reason the sight of that tear ripped me apart. "So what are these things you did when you were younger?" she asked. "Please, enlighten me." There was no way around it. This would be difficult.

"Come on, let's sit down and I'll tell you everything," I said. Perhaps if I could get her to sit down things would calm down a little. Jennifer wasn't having any of it, though.

"I don't want to sit down, Gareth. I just want you to tell me the truth," she replied, her voice half an octave higher. I took a deep breath.

"When I was younger, I admit that I used to very occasionally break into places and steal stuff." There, it was out in the open. Well, some of it was out in the open. I looked at Jennifer, knowing full well that she had me on the ropes. The look on her face was not one I ever wanted to see again. "But," I said. She laughed — a sharp laugh with no humour at all — so I carried on talking. "But I never, ever hurt anybody. I never broke into anyone's house. I never took anyone's personal possessions. It was only ever businesses, and it was only when I was desperate and didn't know what else to do." That last part was a lie, but the rest of it was true. Jennifer's stare bored into me, as the two red spots on her cheeks reappeared and grew.

"When was the last time you broke into one of these businesses?" she asked, using her index fingers to put air quotes around the word 'businesses': "Exactly how much younger were you?"

I looked at her, not wanting to reply. If I lied, she'd almost certainly know I was lying, but if I told the truth, I didn't know what would happen. I could say nothing, but that would be about as bad as telling the truth.

"Gareth," she said in a quiet voice. "I asked you a question." I took another deep breath as I decided to front this one out and tell the truth.

"About three months ago." It wouldn't take her long to do the maths and realise that this was after we'd got together. A second after I'd said three months, her mouth opened and then shut again. I was right, it hadn't taken her long at all to do the sums. "But I've quit, Jennifer. That's not me, not now. I've quit all that."

"After we'd met," she said. This wasn't a question. I looked at the floor. I wasn't just on the ropes here. I was in the corner getting the crap beaten out of me, and it was all my fault. My mind was racing as I tried to figure out the best way to tell her that was the past, that I'd gone straight, but I never got the chance. Jennifer spoke in a very small voice, and as I looked up, I could see that she had her hand outstretched with the palm up.


"Give it to me,' she said. "My door key. Give it to me and get the hell out of my flat."

## 9

The weeks after Jennifer threw me out of her flat were an absolute nightmare. I'd tried calling and texting her, but she ignored everything. I was sure that the relationship was over before it had begun. The only thing I knew for certain was that I missed her so much that it hurt. I wanted to go round to her flat, lean on the doorbell until she had no choice but to answer the door, and then just tell her how sorry I was, and that I loved her. To make her understand. The only thing that stopped me, apart from my stubbornness, was the thought of coming across as an absolute arsehole when I'd been caught bang to rights lying through my teeth.

But I loved her, despite my shame. I didn't realise how much until she'd thrown me out. The only thing I was holding on to was she'd not told me the relationship was over, although I'd had no contact from her at all. I was clinging to the faintest of hopes she was just making me suffer to prove a point. At the same time, I didn't want to be like Robert and act like a petulant ex-boyfriend who wouldn't take no for an answer. I didn't have a clue what to do.

I was in Sainsbury's exactly one month after I'd been thrown out on my ear as Tommy would have put it when I bumped into Jennifer's brother. The basket I was carrying had essential provisions in it. A microwave lasagne, eight cans of strong Belgian lager, and a Pot Noodle. Chicken and Mushroom, my favourite.

"Jacob, how you doing? I said.

"Hey, Gareth," he replied, beaming. "How are you, mate? Not seen you for a while." Had Jennifer not told him what had happened?

"Yeah, I've not been around much, to be honest," I said. His smile faded before he hiked it back up again and glanced down at my basket. I moved it behind my legs so he couldn't see how sad the contents were.

"Jen mentioned that you'd had words," he said with a brief frown. "About you being a naughty boy." I managed a wan smile.

"You could say that," I said. We stood in awkward silence for a few seconds before he shuffled his feet, keen to get away from his sister's ex-boyfriend no doubt. Sod it, I thought.

"Do you fancy a pint?" I asked. "When you're done shopping?" Jacob tilted his head to one side, the same way that Jennifer used to when she was trying to decide something.

"I don't drink, Gareth," he replied a few seconds later. Oh well, I thought. Worth a try. "But I'll have a coffee and watch you have a pint?" I could have hugged him, but that would have been emotional. We arranged to meet in a pub just around the corner, and I had a spring in my step as I headed towards the till to pay for my evening's entertainment.

I sat in the pub waiting for Jacob for what seemed like ages, nursing a lager. After about twenty minutes, I figured that he wasn't going to show. I'd been stood up before, but I'd never been stood up by an ex-girlfriend's gay brother. You live, you learn, I guess. I'd just decided to stop nursing my pint and neck it when he walked in.

"Sorry, Gareth," he said, breathless. "I met a friend in the car park and couldn't get rid of him."

"Hey, no problem," I said, getting to my feet. "Any particular coffee?"

"Do they do a flat white?" he asked. I had no idea what a flat white was, but fortunately for me, the barman knew and knocked one up for Jacob. I returned to our table and sat down. Jacob and I exchanged small talk for a few moments before I broached the subject I wanted to talk to him about.

"How's Jennifer?" I asked, trying to be nonchalant. He looked at me for a few seconds before replying.

"I don't want to get involved, Gareth," he said. I didn't understand why he was here if that was the case.

"You don't have to get involved, Jacob," I said, trying not to sound annoyed. "All I want to know is how she is. That's all, mate." He leaned in towards me, putting his forearms on the table. I instinctively leaned backwards before realising it. Jacob was quite an intimidating bloke, and I don't intimidate that often.

"Listen, mate," he said, echoing my words. "Jen's my little sister, and I would happily kill for her, but you've taken the piss out of her and I don't like that one bit. You get me?" I realised that the only involvement he was interested in was protecting his little sister. I couldn't fault him for that.

My hands went up in a placatory gesture.

"Woah, woah. Hang on Jacob." I said. "I think we're

going down the wrong road here. How am I taking the piss out of her?" He stared at me, his forehead creased, but I carried on. "Yes, I was on the rob, but I stopped because of her. I never wanted her to find out. I did one job while we were together, and that was right in the first few weeks. Before I knew things were getting serious. Or at least, I thought they were getting serious."

"Have you told her that?" he asked.

"She never gave me a chance," I replied. "She threw me out of her flat and hasn't answered the phone or replied to texts. Nothing. What else can I do?" Jacob's frown eased.

"What, you're asking me for relationship advice? You sure about that?" he said, the beginnings of a wry smile appearing on his face.

"No, Jacob. I'm asking you because you're her bloody brother."

"Jesus Christ," Jacob said, sighing and leaning back in his chair. "You're both as bad as each other."

"What do you mean?"

"Jen's as stubborn as they come," he said. "The last thing she's going to do is come grovelling back to you, especially when you're the one in the wrong." I wasn't sure what he meant. The last thing I would expect her to do is to come grovelling back. "And it sounds like you're exactly the same."

"How come?" I said. "I'm not with you Jacob. Help me out."

He looked at me before replying. "So you've tried calling, and you've texted her?"

"Yeah, lots of times."

"And she's not responded at all?"

"Not once."

"Have you been round there? Maybe, I don't know, with some flowers and a lot of humility?"

"No," I replied. "I don't want to be, well, like Robert."

"That idiot. You know he's still hanging around like a bad smell?" he said. I couldn't help but bristle at this news. Not for the first time, I considered tracking Robert down and having a word, or perhaps just giving him a smack. "Gareth, you're nothing like that loser," Jacob continued. "And Jen likes you. She's been cut-up the last few weeks, and I mean really cut-up." I could feel my heart beat slightly faster. "But a few calls and texts aren't going to work. You're going to have to be the bigger man here, tell her what an absolute idiot you've been and just park your sorry backside on her doorstep."

"Really?" I asked, not quite believing him.

"Yes really, Gareth," he said with a sigh. "At least then she might stop bloody going on about you. Like I said though, I'm not getting involved. You're big enough and ugly enough to sort your own problems out." He drained his coffee and placed the cup back on the table. "But I know she really likes lilies. Lots of lilies." He turned to walk out of the pub before looking back over his shoulder. "See you soon, yeah?" I could have kissed him, but I figured that probably wouldn't be what he wanted me to do.

Half an hour later I was standing on her doorstep, a carrier bag with instant food and beer in one hand and a huge bunch of white lilies in the other, waiting for her to answer the door. It opened halfway, and she peeped out. God, she was beautiful. I stood there like a hopeful school-boy, suddenly wishing I'd ditched the carrier bag.

"What?" she said with a fierce frown.

"I, er, well," I replied, wishing that I'd at least thought about what I was going to say, "I brought you some flowers." I held up the lilies, wishing I'd bought a larger bunch even though the ones I was holding up had cleaned me out. Jennifer looked at the flowers, and I thought her face softened ever so slightly. Silently thanking Jacob, I continued. "Please, Jennifer, hear me out. I've been an arse. I just didn't realise how much of an arse I was until I met you. All of that," I paused, unsure what to say, "all of that nonsense is in the past. I promise you."

"So what made you change your mind?" she said after a long and painful pause. "About your career aspirations?" One thing Jennifer did very well was cutting sarcasm.

"Meeting you," I replied. I didn't have to think about that answer. "It was meeting you." She crossed her arms over her chest, and looked at me. I looked at her, and for me at least, time stood still.

"Well, you took your bloody time," she said after what seemed like hours. "I suppose you want to come in and grovel?" My heart thumped.

"Can I?" I said. She opened the door fully and stood in front of me, a small smile on her face that was getting bigger all the time. I dropped the carrier bag and held my arms out for her to step into them, which she did. As we hugged on her doorstep, I could hear one of the cans of lager fizzing where it had burst as I'd dropped the bag.


That was collateral damage I'd take any day of the week.

## 10

Five months after we'd got back together, almost to the day, Jennifer and I got married. I wouldn't say we rushed into it, but in the aftermath of the few weeks we'd spent apart, I think we both realised that we were onto a good thing. Something we'd almost lost by both being as pig-headed as each other.

We were sitting in a pub one night, having a few drinks after going to the cinema. I can't remember what we went to see, only that it was a romantic comedy I'd not been that bothered about. The two main characters had got together, split up, then got back together and ended up getting married so they could live happily ever after. It would have been a shit romantic comedy if the last bit hadn't happened, I suppose. Jennifer was going on about the lead male character in the film, and about what a romantic bloke he was. She wasn't having a go at me for not being romantic; she was just talking about the film.

"They were a bit like us, I guess," Jennifer said, looking at me over the top of her glass of wine. I took a sip of my beer before replying.

"I suppose so," I said. "Next thing you know, we'll be getting married."

Jennifer's jaw dropped an inch, and she stared at me open-mouthed.

"Gareth Dawson," she said in a high-pitched voice. "Did you just propose to me?"

"No, I did not," I replied, laughing. "I definitely did not."

"I think you did."

"I don't think I did," I laughed again. "You'd know if I did because I'd be naked in the road outside your flat, singing a song with a red rose clutched in my butt cheeks, before taking a knee and asking you properly." Jennifer started laughing.

"So what song would you be singing, then?" she asked. I had to think for a few minutes before replying.

"It would have to be something by Snow Patrol." Jennifer wrinkled her nose at my reply. She wasn't a massive fan of Snow Patrol, but it was something I was working on.

"What song then? Is it one I know?"

"Probably not," I replied, pulling my phone from my pocket and flicking through my music. I found the song I was after and played it, putting the phone down on the pub table so that Jennifer could hear it. We both sat in silence, listening to the song for a moment. Jennifer leaned across the table and flipped the phone around so it was facing her. She prodded the screen to turn it on and read the title of the song. "Just Say Yes".

"You soppy old thing," Jennifer smiled at me. "I was expecting something completely different." She reached across the table and took my hand. "Of course I'll say yes, but you will have to ask my Dad before the big day." And that was that.

A few weeks later, I was round at Andy's house, supposedly to ask him for Jennifer's hand in marriage. Jennifer and I had talked about the whole marriage thing, and the more we talked about it the more the idea grew on me. If nothing else, it would put to bed the feeling I still couldn't shake that Jennifer wasn't that serious about me. Looking back, I think she realised that at the time and knew if we got married, those feelings would go away. The problem was we'd only been going out together for about six months, so the whole thing was definitely in whirlwind romance territory, but it all felt right to me.

The last time I'd been round to Andy's house was a few weeks after Jennifer and I got back together. She'd insisted that I come clean to Andy about my background. It wasn't something I'd wanted to do, far from it, but she would not let me get away with it. She'd already told him all the sordid details but wanted me to tell him myself. Andy had sat on the other side of his kitchen table, listening as I'd stumbled my way through a full and frank confession. Andy had sat there for a few minutes, looking at me until I started to wriggle on the chair.

"Gareth, look me in the eyes for a second," he'd said. I did as he asked. "Do you promise that you'll keep her happy?" I nodded my head, keeping my eyes fixed on his.

"Absolutely, Andy," I said, trying to sound as sincere as I felt. "That's all I want."

"Because if you get banged up for burglary, she won't be happy at all."

"I know," I'd replied, looking away and at my feet.

"Gareth, I've been in business for many years," Andy had said. "And I've done all right at it. But I've left a fair few casualties behind me, mark my words. We're not that different, you and I. We see something, we want it, we take it." I wasn't convinced about the analogy, but Andy was giving me a way out of the whole sorry mess. "But you need to work out how to do that on the right side of the law, and I might be able to help you." He stood, as did I, to mark the end of the conversation. As we shook hands, he asked me to promise him something else, something which with hindsight I failed miserably to do. "Just keep her happy, son," he'd said. "Keep her happy and keep her safe. That's all I ask of you."

So there I was, sitting again in Andy's kitchen a few weeks later, sipping a cup of tea and yawning as I did so. I'd been working pretty much every evening as a bouncer on one club door or another for weeks, trying to make up the money now that my alternative income source had stopped. It was going well, and I was getting a lot of repeat bookings.

"Jen mentioned that you might pop round, Gareth," Andy said as he put a plate of biscuits on the table and sat opposite me. "I've been wanting to talk to you for a while." I'd not been expecting him to say that and was stuck for something to say. It didn't seem like the right time to launch into the whole 'do you mind if I marry your daughter' speech I'd got prepared in my head. "I have to say, I'm delighted that you've sorted things out with Jen, though. I've never seen her happier than she has been the last few weeks." Andy laughed before continuing. "But my God, the look on her face when you popped that window out. That was an absolute picture, that was." I was glad he found it funny as I certainly didn't.

"So what was it you wanted to talk about, Andy?" I asked, keen for him to get whatever he wanted to say out of the way so I could say my bit and be done with it.

"I've got a proposal for you," he said. "A business proposal."

For the next twenty minutes, Andy outlined his grand

idea. It built on the theme of me proving to him how vulnerable his house was. He'd been playing golf with some friends a few weeks after it had happened, when me and Jennifer were not talking, and had told them about my impromptu demonstration. To cut a long story short, two of his friends had asked Andy if he would send me round to their houses to have a look at them. They'd also offered to pay me for the privilege.

"So, there's a market there for someone with your, er, your background, to set yourself up as a security consultant," Andy explained. I laughed, remembering that was the phrase I'd used to describe myself when Jennifer and I had first met. It was just back then the context was a bit different. Andy outlined his proposal, which was for me to set up a company and advertise my particular skill set. As an ex-burglar who had gone straight, seen the light and was now committed to preventing crime.

"I'm not convinced, Andy," I said. "That just sounds like an invitation for the Old Bill to come and nick me, help with their stats." Andy grinned at me.

"Nope, not at all," he replied. "I've got a good friend who works in the legal side of things. I've run it past him, and he thinks it's doable. All you need is some creative marketing and you'll be good to go."

We chatted through his proposal for a while, and the more he told me the more I thought it was a sound idea. He'd even printed out a proper business plan for me. At least, I assumed it was a proper business plan. I'd never seen one before. I looked through the document, trying to understand it. There was one bit I did understand, which was a table marked 'Startup Costs'. It listed a bunch of items, company registration fees, advertising, that sort of thing. There were even three months office rental at a place just outside the city in a business park close to where

I lived. The one line that caught my attention the most was the total at the bottom of the table. Just under five grand. I put the paper back on the table.

"That's me out then, Andy," I said, pointing at the bottom of the page. "I've not got five grand, and the rate I'm going it would take me years to put that together." I felt stupid, coming round here to ask him if I could marry his daughter, and then having to admit that not only was I skint, but I was also likely to remain so for quite some time.

"That's where you're wrong, Gareth," Andy said, his face serious. "I want in."

I shook my head from side to side, remembering Jennifer's absolute refusal to accept any help from her family.

"Sorry Andy, I can't take your money," I said. "Jennifer would—"

"Gareth, leave Jennifer to me," Andy interrupted. "Besides, I'm not giving you the money. It's a loan, repayable with interest, in exchange for a small share in the company. Well, smallish share." I still wasn't convinced. I had an image in my mind's eye of Jennifer with her arms crossed, red spots in her cheeks, asking me to tell her again how much her father had given me. "This isn't charity, Gareth. It's a business arrangement. You've got a marketable skill, believe it or not, and people will pay you for it. Look at these projections." He pushed another sheet of paper toward me, which I studied for a moment. I was no maths whizz, although I had scraped a GCSE in the subject, but they looked good to me. "Those are conservative estimates," Andy explained. "I think with the right marketing support, and I know just the man for that, the actuals could be twice that."

Twenty minutes later, we'd shaken hands and become business partners. I'd signed a bunch of paperwork that

Andy had prepared. He must have been sure I'd come round at some point. My only concern was what Jennifer would think, but he'd promised to speak to her and explain it all. Once the paperwork was signed, we shook hands to seal the deal.

"So," Andy said, relaxing back in his chair. "That's the business part out of the way. What was it you wanted to speak to me about?"

"Oh, yeah," I replied, racking my brains for the speech I'd prepared. When it didn't come to mind straight away, I decided to just front it out. "I was wondering if, um, I was wondering if you would mind if me and Jennifer got married?"

Andy looked at me, open-mouthed.

"Fuck off," he said. Not the answer I was expecting or hoping for. A simple "no" would have been enough if he wasn't keen on the idea. "Are you serious?"

"Er, well, I was until just now," I replied. He just carried on staring at me, his jaw slack. Then he did something I wasn't expecting. Andy slapped his hands on his thighs, leaned back in his chair, and roared with laughter. I sat there, not knowing what to do. Once he'd calmed down, he struggled to his feet and wandered off out of the kitchen into the lounge. I could still hear him chuckling as he walked off. A few seconds later, he returned with two tumblers and a bottle of what looked like a very nice whisky indeed, even though it wasn't even eleven o'clock in the morning.

"From ex-burglar to company director, to future son in law, all in the space of about thirty minutes. That's good going, Gareth. I think we should have a drink to celebrate."

One month later, to the tune of "Take Me Home" by Jess Glynne, Andy walked Jennifer down the aisle of the local registry office and handed her over to me. It was a small do, just as we'd wanted it to be. The only guests were Jacob and his partner on Jennifer's side, and Tommy and David on mine. David doubled up as the official photographer, using a very nice-looking Nikon camera he'd stolen just for the event. The photos were fantastic, and he even did some video clips for us. The whole day was perfect. I looked at Jennifer as we said our vows. The words that come back to me most were "Till death do us part". I had hoped that it would be years and years until that happened, but I was wrong.

The way it turned out, it wasn't long at all.

**11**

It was eight weeks after Jennifer and I got married when everything changed. Technically, it was seven weeks and four days, but that's close enough to eight weeks for me.

That particular Saturday started off like any other. I'd been working in the morning. Well, if you can call sitting at the kitchen table and using the laptop work. Jennifer and I had moved into a rented two bedroom flat close to where we both lived before we got married. It wasn't fantastic, but it was ours. At some point in the future, when we'd got a bit more money together, we were going to buy a place of our own. Until then, we were renting which irritated me as all we were doing was paying someone else's mortgage. Jennifer was a lot more pragmatic about it, and as she was the one who was better with money, I left it up to her. I suspected that Andy had offered to lend her the money for a deposit on a place of our own, and that Jennifer had said no, but it was never discussed.

Andy's idea for starting up a business, and his cash, was going well. I wondered if the whole thing was Jennifer's idea to get me on the straight and narrow, but I kept my suspicions to myself. What surprised me more than anything was when I told Tommy and David about the business plan, they were both keen as mustard to get on board. Maybe I wasn't the only one who thought going straight was a good idea? Two weeks after Andy had offered the cash, we were up and running, although I was still working most nights on the doors of pubs and clubs in Norwich.

The temporary office on the business park was in an ideal location, and we were getting plenty of work. Word was getting around, although I was ninety nine per cent sure that a lot of the clients in the first few months were friends of Andy's. I wasn't complaining, don't get me wrong. They all paid well, and they told their friends about our services, which meant the bulk of the new customers were recommendations. I'd arranged two assessments for later in the week and written up reports from the visits we'd done in the last few days. So far, so good. The only other exciting thing I'd done that Saturday was go to Sainsbury's and buy food for supper. There was a lasagne recipe on a website that looked amazing in the picture, so thought I'd try it. The chances of it turning out anything like the one in the picture were remote, but I was sure it wouldn't be far off. I was just in the middle of slicing peppers when Jennifer came home from work.

"Hi Jennifer," I'd said as she walked into the kitchen, throwing her handbag on the table, missing my laptop by inches. It was a business expense and therefore tax exempt, or so Andy told me. The kitchen table wasn't the best place to keep a computer, but even so, I still winced.

"What a crap day," she frowned. "Bloody clients messing me about all bloody day." The cut and thrust of the Human Resources world was right there for me to see.

Jennifer walked over to the fridge and grabbed a half full bottle of white wine. I stopped trying to slice the pepper and watched as she unscrewed the top and looked at the bottle with a curious expression. For a moment, I thought she was going to swig straight from it, but she got a glass out of the cupboard and filled it to the brim before taking a large gulp. "Oh my God, that's better," she said as she put the bottle back in the fridge. No drink for me then, even though there were four cans of lager in there. "How about you? You been busy?"

"Yeah, kept myself busy. Finished those reports for the new customers, anyway." I returned to my chopping. "You hungry?" She looked at me as if she'd only just realised that I was preparing something.

"I'm out tonight," she said. "It's Lucy's birthday, so we're going to the Old Buck by the river for some food. They've got a new menu out." The Old Buck was a pub that had reopened as a restaurant a few months ago, and would be dishing up better food than I would be. I tried not to show my irritation, but I was sure that Jennifer hadn't mentioned going out. "I told you a few weeks ago," she continued.

"Did you?" I said. "I don't remember." Even though I'd tried to keep my voice even and not sound pissed off, Jennifer saw straight through me.

"Oh God, don't you start," she said, turning and walking out of the kitchen.

I listened to Jennifer moving about in the bedroom as I scraped the sorry looking lumps of pepper into a bowl. Opening the fridge to keep the peppers for another day, I looked inside to make sure there was beer and something to throw in the microwave later. Good result on both counts, so I grabbed a beer and cracked the can open before walking into the lounge and turning the television on. I sat there for maybe half an hour watching rubbish on the television before Jennifer came in, but I wasn't just watching television. I was stewing over the fact I'd been looking forward to spending the evening with my wife, eating what could have been an amazing lasagne, and just chilling together. She'd definitely not told me she was going out; I had a good memory for things like that.

"What do you think?" she asked me, turning on her heels. Jennifer was wearing a simple black dress that showed off her slim curves. She'd tied up her long blonde hair in a loose ponytail which highlighted her cheekbones, and she had just the slightest touch of makeup on. She looked amazing, almost to the point where for a second or two I thought maybe I should be concerned about her going out looking so good without me. But I wasn't that kind of bloke.

"Yeah, you look okay," I replied like a spoilt child. She'd spent ages getting ready and that was all I could manage.

"Thanks," she said. The next sound I heard was the front door closing as she left the flat.

I sat drinking beer and watching re-runs of *Top Gear* on the television, stewing in my stupidity. After a crap day at work, so what if Jennifer wanted to go out with her friends? She shouldn't need my permission. I was, I concluded, being a muppet. I reached across to the coffee table for my phone and tapped out a text message.

*Sorry for being an idiot, Jennifer. You look amazing — good enough to eat. Have a great night, can't wait until you come home. I love u loads... xxxxx* It was always five kisses at the end of our text messages. It was our thing, the thing that let us both know everything was cool. I watched television for the rest of the evening, checking my phone every few minutes to see if Jennifer had replied, but there was nothing. I ate half a microwave meal before throwing the rest in the bin and wondered what she was having for dinner. Whatever it was, it would be a damn sight better than the rubbish I'd just had. A few more episodes of *Top Gear* later, I looked at my watch. It was almost ten o'clock, an hour away from closing time, but being a Friday night they'd be going on to a club, anyway. There was still no reply from Jennifer, so I decided to go to bed once I'd finished my last can of lager. Jennifer would wake me up when she got in, especially if she'd had a few too many glasses of wine. I could make it up to her then.

In the end, it was me who had a bit too much to drink. I woke with a start on the sofa, disorientated. I wasn't sure what had woken me up, but rain was lashing against the window pane. I looked at my watch — just gone eleven. I gathered up my empty cans from the lounge carpet and carried them into the kitchen. Might as well go to bed. As I walked through to our bedroom, a low rumble of thunder sounded. That must have been what woke me up.

The next thing I knew it was half past three in the morning, or at least that's what my bedside clock told me it was. Something had woken me up, but it wasn't Jennifer stumbling around the room trying to get into bed. I padded my hand across the bed, expecting to find Jennifer already curled up under the duvet. There was nothing there except a cold bed. As I lay there, cursing about the fact I was awake and wondering where the hell she was, there was a knock at the front door. I muttered to myself as I looked around the dark room for my boxer shorts. She must have forgotten her keys or was just too pissed to get them in the door. I was struggling to get my legs into my boxers when there was another knock, way more insistent. That wasn't Jennifer. It wasn't her knock, but one which was much louder, much harder. I stumbled to my feet, walked to the front door and looked through the spy hole. What sort of security consultant would I be if I didn't at least do that? Though the spy hole, I could see the distorted outlines of two figures standing on the doorstep. Dark figures, black or navy-blue uniforms. Old Bill, without a doubt. Bollocks.

I tried to clear my head as quickly as I could. It must be the off-licence job. I'd done nothing since, but that was ages ago. Maybe Tommy or David had been nicked and turned me over. I doubted it. Tommy was solid as a rock, and David wasn't far behind him for all his faults. Whatever the Old Bill wanted, there was nothing I could do about it, so I opened the door. Standing on the doorstep were two coppers, looking less distorted than when I'd seen them through the spy hole. The younger of the two was standing a couple of steps behind his colleague, obviously the junior boy. He looked almost scared to be there, which might explain why he was standing behind his boss.

"Mr Dawson?" the older policeman said. I paused, realising for the first time they both had their hats tucked under their arms, before nodding my head. A terrible feeling started growing in my guts. I hadn't had much to do with the Old Bill in the past, which was more from luck than judgement, but one thing I did know was they rarely took their hats off. The policeman swallowed. "Can we come in, sir?"

We sat in an awkward triangle in the lounge. I'd grabbed my dressing gown from the bedroom and fastened it around me as the policemen stood in the lounge. As I walked back in, I caught the younger one looking at a photo of me and Jennifer on the bookcase and then looking at his colleague before nodding ever so slightly. My stomach started to churn.

"Mr Dawson, I'm PC Turner. You're married to

Jennifer. Is that correct?" the policeman said. I felt sick, the churning increasing.

"Yes," I replied in a whisper. "Yes," I repeated in a louder voice. "Has something happened?"

"There's been an accident, Mr Dawson. Your wife was involved in a traffic accident earlier this evening and has been seriously injured."

"No, that can't be right," I said, relieved. There must have been a mistake. "She wasn't driving. She's only gone out for a meal with her friends. It's Lucy's birthday, and there's a new menu at the Old Buck so they'd all gone there." I was speaking far too fast, but needed to explain to them it couldn't be her.

"Mr Dawson, a young woman who we believe to be your wife was knocked down earlier this evening by a car," PC Turner said. I looked at him. His eyes were a light green, not far off Jennifer's colour but nowhere near as intense. The other difference was that PC Turner's eyes looked very sad. "I'm sorry to have to tell you, but we're sure it's her. We need to take you to the hospital." I jumped to my feet and ran into the bathroom, getting to the toilet seconds before my stomach erupted and I filled the bowl with the remains of eight cans of lager and a half-eaten microwave meal.

A few minutes later, I was sitting in the back of their marked police car as the younger policeman steered it through the narrow streets of the estate. I don't think I'd ever got dressed so quickly in my life. I stared through the window at the houses flashing by. There wasn't a soul around, which wasn't surprising considering the time of night and the awful weather. The police car was approaching the main ring road around the outskirts of Norwich when PC Turner's phone rang. He answered the call with a curt "Yes?", and listened to the voice on the other end. I couldn't hear what was being said. A few seconds later he ended the call and looked across at his colleague. Without a word, PC Turner reached forwards and flicked a switch on the dashboard, turning on the flashing blue lights on top of the car. I felt myself being pushed back into the seat as it sped up.

If there'd been anything left in my stomach, it would have been on the floor of the police car.

## 12

The police car pulled up outside the Accident and Emergency department at the Norfolk and Norwich Hospital, coming to a sharp stop near the door. It didn't quite screech to a halt, but it wasn't far off it. Before PC Turner had even undone his seatbelt, I was out of the car. The automatic glass doors crawled open as I ran up to them, so I ignored the sign taped to them asking people not to force them open and did just that. I ran into the waiting area and stopped, looking around to get my bearings. It was years since I'd been here. I tried to stay away from hospitals as much as I could as in my experience bad things happened in them.

I made my way through the waiting area to the reception desk, ignoring the curious looks of a drunk bloke with a filthy bandage wrapped around his hand. He said something as I walked past him, but I didn't hear what he said or bother replying. The receptionist looked up at me when I got to the desk. She was maybe in her mid-thirties, no real distinguishing features as far as I could see, but then again, I wasn't looking for any. She smiled, showing off a set of perfect white teeth that contrasted against her light olive skin as she did so.

"Can I help——" she started speaking, but I cut her off and her smile faltered.

"My wife," I said. "My wife's in here, she's been in an accident." I knew I was babbling, but I didn't care. "Please, you've got to tell me where she is."

"What's her name, sir?" the receptionist said. I was about to reply when I heard a male voice behind me.

"It's the young lady in resus, Jessica." It was PC Turner. The receptionist looked at me again, her hands poised above the keyboard. Her smile disappeared, and her mouth formed a small 'oh' shape. "I'll take him through to the relatives' room. Could you get somebody to come and speak to him?" PC Turner continued. The woman nodded and hurried through a door in the back of the reception area. I turned to the policeman, feeling helpless. He put one hand on my shoulder. "If you come with me, Gareth, I'm sure one of the doctors or nurses will be free to speak to you soon." I nodded, speechless.

The relatives' room was a windowless cubicle off the staff corridor. There were some nondescript prints on the wall, IKEA furniture, and a half-used box of tissues on the coffee table. I sat down but jumped to my feet a few seconds later, far too wired to just sit there. I couldn't believe what was happening. Should I phone Andy? Let him know Jennifer was hurt? Or should I wait and see what happened next? Questions bounced around inside my head, too many of them for me to answer.

"You want me to see if I can rustle you up a cup of tea, Gareth?" PC Turner asked.

"Yes, please," I croaked.

After what seemed like hours, PC Turner came back into the relatives' room with a mug of tea in his hand. He was followed by the other policeman, and a young man dressed in what looked like green pyjamas. PC Turner handed me the mug of tea, gesturing to the sofa as he did so.

"Have a seat, Gareth," he said, sitting on the other sofa. "This is the doctor." I sat down and looked at the man in the pyjamas. Embroidered across his breast pocket were the words *Norfolk and Norwich Hospital Accident and Emergency Department*, and he had a lanyard around his neck with some identification cards attached. He was thin, tired looking, and didn't seem old enough to be a doctor.

"Mr Dawson? My name is Dr Raout and I am one of the emergency department doctors working tonight," the man in the green pyjamas said in a quiet voice. He looked Indian but spoke with a much more cultured British accent than I did. "I'll take you through to see your wife in a moment." I took a deep breath as my heart thudded so hard I could hear the blood rushing in my ears. If they were taking me through to see her, then she must be okay. Thank God for that. "But I have to warn you," Dr Raout continued. "She has been very seriously injured and we need to take her to the operating theatre for emergency surgery in the next few minutes. There is a chance she may not survive the operation." I swallowed, suddenly nauseous again. I had never felt as out of control of a situation as I felt then.

Doctor Raout's mouth was still opening and closing, but the only thing I could hear were the words "might not survive" echoing in my head. I looked at PC Turner, imploring him to help me. He looked back at me with a blank face. I shook my head to try to clear it and concentrate on whatever the doctor was saying. It didn't work.

There must have been a mistake, I told myself. This couldn't be happening to Jennifer, to me. To us. It must all be a horrible mistake.

The door opened, and I saw a young woman with a shock of blonde hair peer into the room. She was wearing the same pyjamas as Doctor Raout, but I had no idea who she was. Nurse? Doctor? Not a clue, nor did I care.

"Dr Raout?" the woman said. "We need to go soon." She looked at me and smiled, but it was a sad smile that didn't reach her eyes. "Do you want to come with me?" she asked. Even though I didn't know who she was, she obviously knew who I was and why I was there. I got to my feet, knocking over the cup of tea which spread a wet brown stain across the carpet. I looked down at it and then at the tissues on the coffee table.

"Don't worry about that, Gareth," PC Turner said. "I'll sort it out."

"It's Gareth, is it?" the woman asked. "I'm Bridget, the senior nurse on duty tonight." I noticed a faint Irish accent. "Did Dr Raout tell you about your wife's injuries?" I sat back down and looked across at the doctor before replying.

"He did, kind of," I said, "but Jennifer will be okay, won't she?" The nurse shot the doctor a withering look.

"Your wife has suffered some quite serious head injuries, and she needs to have an operation to try to fix some of the damage," Bridget said. I felt the colour drain from my face, glad I was sitting down. Hearing this woman say the same thing as the doctor had made it a bit more real. Head injuries? What did she mean by that? "Now she's been put under an anaesthetic, so she's not in any pain, but you might be quite shocked when you see her. She's connected to lots of tubes and different pieces of equipment. They're all there to help and to keep her comfortable, so just try to ignore them if you can."

The nurse turned and opened the door. I stumbled to my feet without a word and followed her out into the corridor. When we reached a set of double doors, she paused and turned to me. She smiled again, the same sad smile as before, and reached out her hand.

"Are you ready?" I felt her cool fingers on my forearm. I nodded in reply, unable to speak. She pushed the door open and walked into the resuscitation room. I followed her, looking around. It was just like something off the television. In one corner of the room was a hospital trolley with more people in green pyjamas gathered around it. Bridget walked towards them, announcing my arrival. The pyjamas all looked at me as I approached, stepping away as I reached the side of the trolley.

The figure who lay on the trolley looked nothing like Jennifer, and as I stood there I couldn't help but hope again that there had been a mistake. That this was some other poor woman who'd been knocked over who had head injuries. Thick bandages came down to just above her eyes, covering her eyebrows. Her eyes were taped shut over ugly bruises below each one, and a green tube came out of her mouth. It wasn't until I looked at the woman's nose and saw the familiar freckles that I realised it was Jennifer. My Jennifer. Any hopes I had about it all being a case of mistaken identity disappeared in an instant, and in that moment of realisation, my life changed forever.

As I watched, a machine to the side of the trolley hissed and Jennifer's chest rose before falling back again. There was a horrible smell in the air, a mixture of lots of different things. The only one which I could identify was the metallic, coppery smell of blood. I looked down at Jennifer's body, covered in an inflatable sheet. Ugly looking tubes snaked underneath the sheet, connected to a variety of bottles hanging on a metal stand attached to the side of the trolley. The machine hissed again, breathing life into Jennifer. Did that mean she couldn't breathe for herself? Was she so badly hurt she couldn't even breathe?

"Gareth?" I heard Bridget whisper beside me. "We really need to go to the operating theatre now." I felt my throat tighten and tears in my eyes. I'd not cried for the best part of twenty years, and I'd never cried in front of strangers, even as a child. Not once. The nurse was asking me to say goodbye to Jennifer, and I didn't know if I would ever see her again.

"Can I kiss her?" I asked, barely able to speak. "Please?"

"Of course you can," Bridget said. I leaned forward, my hands gripping the safety bars on the side of the trolley. As I kissed Jennifer on the cheek, one of my tears dropped onto her face. I wiped it away with the back of my hand. Her skin was freezing, like ice. I felt Bridget's hand on my forearm again and I stepped back from the trolley. The medical team folded back around the trolley, and I saw Dr Raout pick up a phone.

"We're on our way," he said to whoever it was on the other end of the line. "Two minutes." I glanced around the room. There was a chart of some sort on a table, lots of different coloured lines all over it. I had no idea what they were, but I could see all the lines were pointing downwards. I watched as the team manoeuvred the trolley with Jennifer on it and all the equipment she was plugged into, through another set of double doors at the end of the room.

Back in the relatives' room, PC Turner had made me a fresh mug of tea and done a decent job of cleaning up the previous one. We exchanged small talk for a while, and he explained that he was waiting for the Detective Inspector who was in charge to get to the hospital. After a few minutes, we fell silent. I wondered how Jennifer was getting on, but they would have only just started the operation. I didn't even know what the operation was for. She had head injuries, but what that actually meant I didn't know.

I was standing outside the hospital entrance smoking a cigarette I'd cadged off the drunk man with the bandaged hand when a police car pulled up. The same young policeman from earlier was driving, and when he saw me he nodded in my direction, saying something to the man sitting next to him.

"Mr Dawson? Gareth?" the passenger asked as he got out of the car.

"Yep, that's me," I replied. He walked toward me, hand extended.

"I'm Detective Inspector Griffiths. The senior officer in charge this evening." He had a firm handshake, confident but brusque. "Please, call me Malcolm." Under any other circumstances, I would have grinned at his name, but not tonight. He wore a suit, with a shirt and tie I recognised from Next. I'd almost bought exactly the same set for my wedding, but decided against it at the last minute.

We walked back into the hospital, and Malcolm led the way back to the relatives' room. I followed him, wondering how often he had to do this sort of thing. He was quite a big man, not quite as tall as me but well built. The same physique as Tommy had, but the policeman was in much better shape. Malcolm opened the door to the room, and PC Turner stood up as he walked in.

"Sir, good to see you." From the look on his face, he meant it.

"John, thanks for holding the fort up here," Malcolm replied. "You couldn't do me a massive favour, could you?"

"Tea?" PC Turner asked. "No problem. I've found out where the nurses hide the decent tea bags." He hurried off, looking almost pleased to have something to do.

Malcolm sat down and I sat opposite, getting a good look at him for the first time. He had quite a craggy face, acne scarred from the look of his cheeks. I was sure none of the other kids took the piss out of him when he was younger, though. He looked like a serious bloke.

"So, what happened?" I asked, unable to hold back. Malcolm opened a small notebook and read for a moment.

"This is what we know so far," he said, looking at me with tired eyes. "Your wife," he glanced back down at his notebook. "Jennifer," he nodded. "Jennifer left The Old Buck just after closing time. Her friend, er Lucy, wanted to go to a nightclub, but Jennifer was keen to get home and was walking to a taxi rank. No one saw what actually happened, but she was crossing the road and was hit by a car travelling down the Yarmouth Road, sustaining what the doctors have described as 'life-threatening' injuries."

I looked at him intently, waiting for him to continue, but he said nothing for a minute or two. Finally, he continued.

"We've got a forensic team down there now, examining the scene, but the weather was horrendous at the time of the accident. There's not a great deal for them to go on in terms of evidence. It was pouring with rain when the accident happened." I remembered the thunder from earlier. I also remembered waking up. Had that been the time of the accident? Malcolm continued in a low voice. "We have arrested the driver of the car, though." I should bloody well hope so, I thought. Some maniac mows down my wife, that's the least they should do. Hopefully, he'll get a good old-fashioned kicking in the cells by the coppers, but I doubted it. Malcolm said something else that I didn't quite catch.

"Sorry, what was that?" I asked.

"The driver was over the limit," Malcolm replied. "He's been arrested for drink driving." My fists tightened at this, knuckles whitening. I hoped he'd be put away for a long time. A very long time. Either in a hospital or a prison. Or even better, both. Malcolm looked at me closely, as if he was trying to decide whether to tell me something. "There's more, though," he said, deciding that he should.

"What?" I asked, clenching and unclenching my fists to try to ease the tension in my hands.

"According to Jennifer's friend, the driver of the car knows your wife."

"What?" I repeated. "How does he know her? Who was the driver?" Malcolm looked down at his notes one more time and then his gaze met mine.

"His name's Robert Wainwright."

My heart thudded in my chest, and I could feel my back teeth clench together as I absorbed this news. Robert. Robert fucking Wainwright. I could picture him hunched behind the wheel of his BMW, waiting for Jennifer to leave the pub. How had he known that she was in there? Jennifer had mentioned a couple of times that he was still hanging around, but I'd not done anything about it because she hadn't wanted me to. She figured that he'd get the message and drop it, but obviously, he hadn't.

"What did you say you'd arrested him for?" I asked Malcolm. "Drink driving?" Malcolm sat back on the sofa, looking spent.

"That's what we've got him for at the moment, yes. He claims she ran out in front of him without looking and that there was nothing he could do. Before he realised she was there, he'd hit her." I could tell from the look on Malcolm's face he was thinking what I was. That story was bollocks. Malcolm looked at his notes again. "An unfortunate coincidence. That was the phrase he used when I interviewed him." My teeth really started to hurt. "I've been a copper for too long to believe in coincidences," Malcolm said. He paused for a second before continuing. "We'll have him, don't worry about that."

"If you don't, I will. I swear to God I will," I replied almost in a whisper.

"Please, Gareth. Whatever happens, leave it to us," he said, but with no real conviction in his voice. I figured he was just saying that because he was Old Bill and I glanced down at his wedding ring. What would he do if it was his wife in the operating theatre, I wondered? I stood up, shaking my head, trying to clear it.

"I'm going for a smoke," I said. The drunk bloke in the waiting room had disappeared, so I ended up going to a corner shop and buying a packet. It was going to be a long night. As I stood outside the hospital smoking, I tried calling both Andy and Jacob, but neither of them answered.

When I came back inside, PC Turner had returned with two mugs of tea and was sitting on the sofa like a spare part before Malcolm dismissed him. We sat in silence, sipping our tea, waiting. About two hours and numerous smoking breaks later, there was a tentative knock at the door. Malcolm got to his feet and opened it, stepping back to let Dr Raout and Bridget into the room. Their faces were inscrutable, and I couldn't read them at all. We sat, Malcolm shuffling to let Dr Raout sit next to him while Bridget sat next to me.

"Gareth," Bridget said. I looked at her and a hammer hit me in the chest. I knew exactly what she was about to say. My heart thumped and bile rose in my throat as she continued.

"I'm afraid we've got some really bad news for you."


With that simple phrase, my world tilted on its axis until it was upside down.

## 13

Andy, Jacob, and I sat on the hard, uncomfortable chairs at the back of the courtroom. I don't know why they called it a public gallery as it was nothing like a gallery. It was just a row of seats with a small wooden barrier in front of it, set against the back wall of the courtroom. If I'd known the next time I would sit in the courtroom I'd be on trial myself, I would have been less bothered about the uncomfortable seats. Opposite the three of us on the other side of the room was the judge's bench which was currently empty. We'd spent the last three days in this room, listening to the various legal arguments, only some of which I understood. The one thing I understood, beyond any reasonable doubt to use the legal term I'd heard, was that the man sitting on the left-hand side of the courtroom as we looked at it had killed my wife, Jennifer. Murdered her as far as I was concerned. The law didn't see it that way, though.

It was three months since Jennifer had died. Three long months when I'd wished that every day was my last. There'd been a post-mortem, which I wasn't happy about, but it wasn't my choice. The minute Jennifer had died she'd become the property of the coroner, wife or no wife. I'd had no say in the matter. The only part of the trial I'd not sat in this courtroom for was when the coroner had given evidence about her injuries and the post-mortem. Andy had sat in for it, while I paced outside the courtroom and smoked, Jacob watching me. When Andy came out to get us both and tell us that the coroner woman had finished, he'd aged ten years in less than an hour. He told Jacob and I that when Jennifer had been hit, her head had hit the windscreen so hard that they had both shattered. I guessed that he was trying to tell us both she didn't suffer, but it didn't work. Not when he had tears streaming down his face.

Jennifer's funeral had been held a fortnight after the accident. It was a small affair, not because she wasn't popular but mostly because we'd put people off coming. The three of us had decided that it should be a family affair, which limited attendance to hardly anyone. A few of her closest friends had come, such as Lucy, but that was it. Just the way we all wanted it. Only the people who loved Jennifer, really loved her, put her to rest.

The last three months had been the worst time of my life by far. There was no doubt at all about that. The pain inside me was palpable. I could feel it every day like a malignant cancer in my chest when I woke up. The worst mornings were when I'd been dreaming about Jennifer. For a few tantalising seconds after I woke up, she was still alive and I reached across the bed for her more often than not. Then reality kicked in, and I would remember she was dead, bringing my entire world crashing back down as I lost her all over again. Happiness to despair in the blink of a tearful eye. They were the worst mornings. The only thing I could do to stop the dreams and numb the pain was to drink before I went to bed. It wasn't working, though. I'd thought coming to the trial would help, provide closure but all it was doing was fuelling the anger.

Robert was being tried with dangerous driving. Not murder. That was all that the law allowed, so the British legal system said. Malcolm had been through it with us many times in the last few months. For a copper, he was a top bloke, but he came across as being just as frustrated as we were. The stakes were different for him, though. He'd given evidence in the trial, and at one point I thought he was going to leap across the witness bench and give the defence lawyer a well-deserved slap. As I thought about this, I looked across at Robert's lawyer, a weedy looking man in his early thirties with glasses that sat halfway down his nose. He probably thought they gave him an air of gravitas, but they didn't. They made him look like an idiot which, fortunately for Robert at least, he wasn't. The lawyer was deep in conversation with Robert as I looked at them. I wondered what they were discussing and then started to wonder how many times I could punch Robert if I leapt across the barriers myself. He was flanked by a couple of burly court security guards, so it would probably only be one slap if that. It was nowhere near enough. Robert glanced at me briefly before looking away again immediately. He'd spent the last few days doing that.

"What the hell's the judge doing back there?" Jacob said, unfolding his arms and rubbing his hands on his thighs. Andy stirred and looked at him. We'd been sitting here for the best part of an hour, waiting for the judge to come back out from his chambers. He'd disappeared into them a while ago after Robert's lawyer had finished his final statement.

"Reading the paper, having a whisky? Maybe he's

leaning out of his window having a cigarette?" Andy's attempt at humour fell on deaf ears.

"Do you think I've got time for another one?" I asked them.

"Jesus, Gareth," Jacob said, frowning. "You smoke like a sodding chimney." I looked at him, trying not to get annoyed. Both he and Andy were suffering as much as I was. It was just that they seemed to be dealing with it a hell of a lot better than me. I was getting worse with every day that passed. I'd even been to my general practitioner at Andy's insistence and the doctor had referred me to a grief counsellor. The doctor had gone on about the stages of grief, and about how anger was normal. Apparently, I was supposed to move on to bargaining with God or some shit like that at some point soon. I'd got as far as making the appointment with the counsellor and then spent the afternoon in the pub.

We sat there for a few more minutes in silence, and I was just about to give in to my nicotine cravings when there was a knock on the door behind the judge's chair. The door opened, and a man dressed in black robes stepped into the courtroom and cleared his throat. He had an easy job as far as I could see. All I'd seen him do through the entire trial was what he was about to do. I was already halfway to my feet by the time he spoke.

"All rise," the man barked as the judge walked through the door and took up his throne. I looked at him as the courtroom settled back down. He was maybe in his mid-sixties, with a kind face. I could see him as a favourite grandfather, the sort of man who was loved by almost everyone. Except for the criminals he put away, I supposed. As I watched, he shuffled his papers in front of him and looked around the room, waiting for everyone to look at him which we all did. Right at the start of the trial, he'd explained that although this was a magistrate's court, he'd been brought in as a county court judge owing to what he called "unusual circumstances" in the case.

The door beside us opened, and Malcolm walked in and sat down next to Andy, nodding at the three of us as he did so. Just behind him, two serious looking men in suits also walked in. They sat down a couple of seats down from Malcolm, and I guessed that they weren't with him. The two men looked like Old Bill to me, though. Short hair, both well built. But then as they sat down, I overheard them talking and realised they weren't speaking English. I had no idea who they were, but they weren't coppers.

"Mr Wainwright," the judge said, directing his gaze towards Robert who sat up straighter in his seat for a second before slumping back down. His lawyer nudged him and waved his hand upwards, motioning to Robert to stand up. My wife's killer got to his feet and clasped his hands behind his back. I concentrated on the back of his head, imagining putting an arm around his neck and strangling the life out of him. The judge spoke, his voice echoing around the courtroom. "Mr Wainwright, you have appeared before this court to answer to the charge of drink driving, for which you have pled guilty as charged." The judge paused, looking down at his notes. "However," he continued, "even after all the discussions in this courtroom, the pre-trial hearings, it is still beyond me why this is the only charge for which you have been brought to bear." He had a way with words, and I had to concentrate to follow him. "It is often said the law is an ass, and in this case it most certainly is."

He directed his gaze towards the defence lawyer, and the stare he gave him was a long way from a favourite grandfather. "Mr Daniels, you have done a fine job defending the accused. You have applied the law in a way that has served your client well. However, speaking as one lawyer to another, you should be thoroughly ashamed of yourself." The defence lawyer became interested in his notes, looking down at his lap. The judge looked up, and I realised that he was looking at us.

"This case involves the death of a young woman in the prime of her life." Jennifer. My wife, Jennifer. She wasn't just a young woman, her name was Jennifer. As if he'd read my mind, the Judge continued. "Jennifer Dawson was cruelly cut down by your actions, Mr Wainwright. But she is not the only victim here. Her family," he nodded in our general direction. "Her family are also victims of your actions and their pain must endure." He was looking directly at me. "I suspect that for some it will endure for a very long time." I could feel my throat tighten as he spoke these words.

The judge turned his attention to Malcolm. "I feel the police must share some culpability in this case. Their inability to prove any form of intent, discover any useable forensic evidence, or provide the Crown Prosecution Service with anything that could bring a higher charge is, quite frankly, disappointing." I glanced across at Malcolm who was looking very uncomfortable. I felt for him. We'd become friends of sorts over the last few months, about as close as a copper and a former burglar can be friends. I knew how frustrated he was. He'd confided in me once, on the understanding it was only between him and me, that he thought Robert should be on trial for murder. But, and this was an enormous but, the Old Bill couldn't prove anything. No one had witnessed the accident, the rain had destroyed any hope they had of forensic evidence, and Robert hanging around a couple of times didn't prove that he meant her harm.

The entire defence had been based on what the prick

of a defence lawyer had called "a hugely unfortunate series of coincidences". Robert had, apparently, just happened to be driving down that particular road at the exact same time that Jennifer had run across the road in front of him. In the middle of a heavy shower. He hadn't had time to do anything, the lawyer had said. Not even time to try to stop. Robert had hit Jennifer, my Jennifer, hard enough for her head to smash the windscreen of his BMW and when he had managed to stop, she'd been thrown straight onto the unforgiving surface of the road. That was the narrative that Andy had sat through when the coroner's assistant had described Jennifer's injuries. A terrible accident, the lawyer had said, but the only thing that his client was guilty of was driving while under the influence of alcohol. Not causing death by dangerous driving. Not murder. No proof. It was only a terrible accident, according to the law.

The judge put his notes down on the desk in front of him. He stared at Robert.

"Mr Wainwright, my intention is to sentence you with the maximum sentence available to me as a judge. I hereby sentence you to a driving ban of twenty-eight months. You will also complete one hundred and eighty hours of unpaid work during a twelve-month community order." There was absolute silence in the courtroom. "You are also to pay eighty-five pounds court costs and an eighty-five pound victim surcharge." My jaw dropped. Eighty-five pounds. Eighty-five fucking pounds. That's what Jennifer's life was worth. I stared at Robert as he turned to look me in the eyes for the first time in the entire trial. Then he made a huge mistake. He smirked.

I was on my feet in an instant, shouting. I managed to get one leg over the barrier in front of me before Jacob grabbed one of my arms and Andy got the other. Malcolm got himself between me and the barrier, pushing me backwards, speaking words I couldn't hear. All my attention was focused on Robert's smirking face. I shook one arm free and pointed at him, screaming words that would come back to haunt the next time I was in this courtroom. Between them, Andy, Jacob and Malcolm manoeuvred me back toward the door of the courtroom. As they pushed me through the door, I saw the Judge looking at me, his hands flat on the desk. He'd not said a word, not banged his gavel and shouted "Order" like I'd seen on the television. He was just looking at me.

"Please," I looked him in the eyes as I shouted just before I was unceremoniously shoved through the door.


"Please, this is wrong."

**14**

---

Once Robert's trial had finished, and he'd been led into one of the back rooms to sort out his sentence, such as it was, Andy, Jacob and myself went to the pub next door to the courtroom. I guessed that no one who worked in the court went anywhere near the pub, as it would be full of people visiting the court. Just like we were. I ordered a round of drinks for all of us, and sunk the first pint in about twenty seconds before going back to the bar for a refill.

"Gareth, slow down, mate," Jacob said as I sat down. I stared at him as I drained half the pint glass.

"Why?" I replied, not even trying to hide the rage in my voice.

"It won't help," he replied. I knew he was right but really didn't care. I sat there, waiting for the gas in my stomach to disperse so I could drink some more when Andy joined in.

"Jacob's right, Gareth," he whispered, sipping at his lager. "It's not going to do anything, change anything. The only thing it'll do is make you even angrier than you already are." I took a couple of deep breaths, trying to control myself. I didn't want to lose it in front of these two, the only connection I had left to Jennifer. The next thing I knew there were tears streaming down my face and I was blubbing like a baby. Jacob just looked at his pint glass while Andy put a hand on my shoulder for a moment. Without a word, I got up and walked out of the back door of the pub, ignoring the look that the barman was giving me. I figured I wasn't the first person to break down in his pub given its location, and wouldn't be the last either.

I sat on the bench outside in the smoking area and lit up a cigarette. As the nicotine kicked in, I felt myself calm down. That was bloody embarrassing. Not that long ago I could walk into a pub and look around, seeing people glance my way and then avoid my gaze as if I wasn't someone to be messed with. Now I just walked in and started crying. I heard the door to the pub open behind me and, hoping it was Andy, turned to see Jacob walking across to join me.

"You okay, mate?" he asked, a look of genuine concern on his face. I could feel the tears well up again.

"No, I don't think I am," I replied a few seconds later. "This whole thing, it's bollocks. He's got away with it, Jacob." I looked at Jacob for confirmation. "Hasn't he?" Jacob didn't reply straight away.

"I think he has, yes," he said, the sadness obvious in his voice. "Times like this, I wish I smoked." He looked at the packet of cigarettes I'd thrown onto the table.

"Help yourself if you want one," I nodded my head in the direction of the packet. He smiled wryly.

"No, I'm good thanks."

"Do you know what really gets to me, Jacob?" I said a moment later.

"What?"

"We'd had a bit of a barney that night, me and Jennifer. I'd forgotten she was going out, and she got the arse on with me about it."

"Yeah," Jacob said. "She was good at that sometimes."

"So I sent her a text after she'd left, just to say I was sorry, she looked great, that sort of thing." Jacob didn't reply, but just looked at me. "And then after she'd died, the Old Bill gave me back her phone in a plastic bag. It was all smashed up, covered in stuff." It was blood, but I didn't tell Jacob that. Someone had tried to clean it up, unsuccessfully. "I could see she had one unread text message. The one I'd sent her to say sorry. I never even got to say sorry."

I leaned forward and put my head in my hands. As the sobs racked my body, Jacob shuffled his way up the bench and put an arm around my shoulder, squeezing me tight. God knows what anyone would have thought if they'd seen us, but at that moment in time, I couldn't have cared less.

We both sat like that in silence for a few minutes, each lost in our own thoughts. I started to get a grip, helped by just having him sitting with me. He'd not said a word, just sat there with his arm around me while I cried, and I loved him for it.

"I was talking to Dad last night, Gareth," Jacob said eventually, moving away so he could look at me. "About everything." He looked at me. "About you."

"What about me?" I replied, not liking where I thought he was going.

"Well," he continued, crossing his arms loosely over his chest. "We both wanted you to know, that no matter what, you're still family. You've got us, and we've got you." I was on the verge of welling up again, so I kept quiet and waited for him to continue. Jacob just sat there, silent. I reached forward to pick up the cigarettes and shove the packet back into my pocket.

"You sure you don't want one, mate?" I asked, trying to smile as I did so. To my relief, he smiled back.

"Nah, thanks. Bit late for me to be starting, really." Another silence, this one a lot more comfortable, sat between us before I decided to ask him something I'd been wondering about for ages.

"Can I ask you something, Jacob?" I said, tentatively.

"Of course you can mate, you know that," he replied with an earnest look. I paused, not sure quite how to continue.

"Well, I've been thinking. You and Jennifer being twins and all. The night it happened." I paused, lost for words. How could I ask this?

"Did I feel anything?" he replied. "Did I know something had happened to her? Is that what you're wondering?" I nodded in reply. "No," he said, almost under his breath. "I went to bed, and when I woke up the next morning, she was dead."

I considered telling him about waking up on the sofa, unsure why I'd woken up, at what I now thought was the exact moment Jennifer had been hit. Was it a crack of thunder from the storm, or was it more than that? But I thought better of it. He was her twin brother and might wonder why he felt nothing. Knowing someone else might have wouldn't help him, would it? I finished my pint and added another cigarette butt to the overflowing plant pot on the table before standing up at the same time as Jacob. We stood there for a couple of seconds before he stepped toward me and wrapped his arms around me, pulling me into a bear hug. It felt like the most natural thing in the world, and I squeezed him back as the tears reappeared in my eyes and streamed down my face.

It was probably ten minutes later when I felt together enough to walk back into the pub. Andy saw us walking in and stood up, collecting his empty glass from the table and walking towards the bar. I diverted to the toilet to get some tissues to blow my nose and make sure I didn't look like too much of a mess. I needn't have bothered. Confirming I looked awful wasn't going to help. As I looked at my red-rimmed eyes in the mirror, I felt some of the sadness fade away, to be replaced by what was going to become a very familiar friend. Cold, hard, anger.

We only stayed for one more pint in the pub before leaving. Andy called a taxi, and he and Jacob dropped me off at my flat on the way past. I still couldn't get used to the idea it used to be Jennifer's and mine, and now it was just mine. Standing on the pavement, I watched the taxi as it drove off. As soon as it was out of sight, I turned and walked in the opposite direction to the off-licence at the end of the road. A few minutes later, I was unlocking the door to my flat with a bottle of cheap whisky in my hand. I knew it wouldn't solve anything, but I couldn't help myself. I walked into the flat, wrinkling my nose at the musty odour inside. Maybe I should open a window or something?

I made my way into the lounge and took up my usual position in the middle of the sofa, ignoring the half-empty containers of Chinese food that littered the floor. As I prodded at the remote control to turn the television on, I nestled the bottle of whisky between my thighs and opened it. No point creating any more washing up, I thought as I took a long slug from the bottle. The television came to life, and I started up the DVD that had been in the player since Jennifer's funeral. As I watched David's home movie of our wedding day start up, yet again, I took another much longer drink.

I don't know, was it one hour, two hours, or six hours when I came to on the sofa. I blinked my eyes rapidly, trying desperately to recall the dream. Jennifer was in it, we'd been at the beach or the park, or somewhere. I was running after her, and she was laughing as she skipped away from me. Her laughter pealed in my head as she stayed just out of my reach, my arms reaching toward her but always staying just out of range. My chest ached as I realised I'd been dreaming, and then she died all over again. I sat on the edge of the sofa, my mouth suddenly full of saliva. I slipped off the sofa and onto to my knees, knocking the almost empty bottle of whisky over. As the last remnants spilt on the carpet, I leaned forward, and a vile jet of half-digested whisky and bile splattered over the rug in front of me. Eyes watering, I looked up at the television to see the DVD player stuck on the last frame of the movie. Jennifer's face looked down at me, the smile on it reminding me of the happiest day of our lives.

Then I threw up again on her favourite carpet.

---

## 15

Thinking back, I don't remember the exact moment I decided that I wanted to go after Robert. It wasn't as if I woke up in my flat one morning, looked in the mirror, and thought "Right, that's it. I'm going to kill the fucker". It was much more gradual than that. It had started with idle daydreams about how I could track him down, hurt him really badly. These daydreams had got more frequent, almost to the point of being intrusive thoughts. They also got increasingly complex as I planned various ways to hurt him. To teach him a lesson he'd never forget. To punish him for what he'd done to Jennifer, to me, to all of us.

Over time, the thought of just hurting him became not enough. No matter how badly I hurt him, he'd still be walking around. Jennifer wasn't, so why should he be? The drinking wasn't helping either, and back then, I was getting through a massive amount. Every night. I knew why I was drinking. It was a futile attempt to block everything out, to make the pain go away. To somehow make Jennifer come back. Except that I knew that wasn't going to happen, so I drank even more.

There wasn't an epiphany where I decided to pull myself together and quit the booze. I didn't go to Alcoholics Anonymous. I didn't go back cap in hand to see my doctor, there was no mutiny amongst my few friends to make me see sense, and the closest I came to rock bottom was the night I'd thrown up on Jennifer's carpet. My business had suffered, and I noticed little things like clients taking subtle steps back from me when I met with them first thing in the morning. I'd even tried to reorganise my meetings for the afternoon to give myself time to sober up from the night before. Tommy's face was full of concern when I turned up for work still half-cut from the night before, but he never said a word. I think he thought I'd punch him in the face if he had said something. The only person who came close to getting through to me was Andy.

I'd gone round to his house one evening, not for any particular reason, but just for a catch up. We tried to get together at least every couple of weeks. I knew Jacob was struggling with his workload in the city and didn't get back to visit his dad as often as he wanted to, so I kind of assumed the role of a surrogate son. Andy and I had sat there for the evening and demolished the best part of a couple of bottles of wine each. He'd got up and stumbled, laughing as he almost fell over. I got to my feet to help him and he commented on how I'd got a much better tolerance for booze than he had. He was right, of course. The wine had barely touched the sides, much less get me as pissed as I wanted to be. The saddest thing was that I started thinking about how much whisky I'd got back at my flat, and whether I'd need to pick up some more on the way home. I'd helped him up the stairs to make sure he didn't go arse over tit trying to get up them. At the top of the stairs, he stopped and looked at me with watery, red tinged eyes.

"Wine hath drowned more men than the sea, Gareth. Don't forget that," he said, his voice slurring as he spoke.

I waited for him to say something else, but he never did. He turned away and shuffled into his bedroom, leaving me to see myself out. When I got back to my flat that night, I looked up the quote he'd said on the internet. It was by some old vicar hundreds of years ago, but as I thought about them, the words made sense. That night was the first night for months when I left the whisky where it was and just went to bed.

A couple of days later, I found myself sitting in the doctor's surgery mentally rehearsing what I was going to say to him when I got called through. When my name was eventually called, only an hour and a half after the scheduled appointment time, I was still not sure quite how to say what I wanted to ask him. I walked into his room and took the seat that was offered before clenching my fists a couple of times.

"So, Gareth," he said, looking at me with kind eyes. "What brings you here today?"

I'd known Dr Riley for years, but he never seemed to age at all. He had to be in his early sixties, a shock of white hair that made him look like that Einstein chap. I'd always wanted to ask him to stick his tongue out, like in the poster, but could never bring myself to do it. He was dressed in a crumpled white shirt, cuffs rolled up to just below his elbows, and a pair of creased brown chinos. To be honest, he looked more like a mad scientist than a general practitioner, but the rows of fancy looking certificates on his wall were testament to his pedigree as a doctor. I looked at him before glancing away.

"I need some help, Doc," I said. He was always "Doc", never "Doctor", but I couldn't remember why that was. I paused, wondering what to say.

"With what, Gareth?" he asked after I said nothing else. "I can see in your notes you saw one of my colleagues a while ago. Is this to do with Jennifer? Or more specifically, how you're coping without her?" I took a deep breath before replying.

"Yes, I mean no. It's not to do with that." His eyebrows went up slightly. Busted. "Well, I guess it is, at least indirectly." Doc Riley said nothing but just looked at me with his eyebrows fixed, questioning me without a word. "It's the drink. I'm drinking a bit too much."

He looked at me for a second or two before turning away to rummage through some papers to the side of his desk. Once he'd found what he was looking for, he turned back to face me. For the next few minutes, he asked me a bunch of questions about boozing. Had I had any blackouts? Was alcohol the first thing I thought about when I woke up? Did I feel like I couldn't function without alcohol? The answer to most of the questions was "yes", which I knew wasn't good. We then went through the amount I was drinking, night by night, and morning by morning. The only question that I couldn't answer was whether any loved ones were concerned about my drinking. I didn't think I had any loved ones. Not anymore.

Doc Riley used a calculator to add the results up and then sat back in his chair. It creaked as he leaned backwards, looking at the paper through reading glasses that it had taken him a while to find. "Hmm," he said. "Interesting." I didn't reply, but just waited for him to continue.

"What do you think?" I asked when I couldn't stand the silence anymore. He looked at me, angling his head so that he could see over the top of the glasses.

"I've been a general practitioner for almost forty years, and I don't think I've ever seen anyone still alive who can drink what you're drinking." He had a faint smile on his face. "In fact, in my professional opinion, you should be dead already." Although the wry smile remained on his face, his creased forehead told me that there was a seriousness behind his words.

"That bad?" I said in a resigned voice.

"Can I be honest?" he asked. I nodded in reply. He put the paper on his desk in front of him. "This amount of drinking, it's not sustainable. I dread to think what state your liver must be in, but I have a professional admiration for its ability to process such vast amounts of alcohol." His frown smoothed out, and his smile broadened. "Can I have it when you die? Medical science could benefit from it, I suspect." I smiled back at him, not feeling like it but figuring that it was the best thing to do. He leaned forward, his face back to being serious. "I have one more question for you, Gareth. If I may?"

"Of course," I replied.

"I asked you just now if you had ever thought about harming yourself, and you denied it most vehemently." I wasn't sure what "vehemently" meant, but I had a rough idea.

"No, I would never do that," I whispered, unsure where he was going.

"Well Gareth, I hate to break it to you, but that's exactly what you're doing to yourself. Committing suicide, sip by sip, bottle by bottle."

I left the surgery about twenty minutes later, having gone way over the allocated ten minutes that was all the NHS allowed for each patient. The sign on the wall was telling the other patients still in the surgery that the waiting time was now two hours but try as I might, I couldn't summon up any sympathy for them. I had a bunch of paperwork in my hand that Doc Riley had printed off for me, and another appointment for a week's time. The other thing I had was something that I'd not had since the night Jennifer died. The tiniest shred of hope that things might turn around. The first thing I did when I got back to my flat was open the cheap whisky I'd bought the day before but had been too pissed to drink, and tip it down the toilet. It was ironic, as that's where it would have ended up anyway, but this way it hadn't been in my stomach for a while before making it to the toilet bowl. I looked at the wine in the fridge for a few seconds, thinking about emptying that as well. I decided against it, remembering Doc Riley's words about taking it one day at a time.

The next morning, I felt so much clearer despite a bottle and a half of wine the night before. One of Dr Riley's suggestions was to replace the drinking with something else, something more productive. Perhaps something I'd used to enjoy, but hadn't done for a while. I'd texted Tommy the night before to tell him that I was going to take the day off, so with the whole day in front of me I dug my old trainers out from the back of the cupboard that they'd lived in for God knows how long, and put them on. My original plan had been to go for a run, but I ended up just going for a walk as I didn't fancy being seen out running in daylight. One step at a time after all. That's what Doc Riley had told me.

I stuck to beer and the occasional bottle of wine, then gradually eased up on both as well over the course of a couple of weeks until I wasn't drinking much at all. I also managed to get out and go running a few times, which to my surprise was a big help. Doc Riley had been right. My biggest victory was knocking the cigarettes on the head, replacing them with large amounts of nicotine gum. Over the course of a few weeks, I went from a wheezing sweaty overweight jogger to a slightly fitter version, one who didn't have to stop and lean up against things every few minutes.

I still only went out at night though, to hide under the cover of darkness.

What I discovered was that the deep-seated anger still burning inside me wasn't affected in the slightest by not drinking, or more specifically, not drinking as much as I had been. It was always there, like a malignant companion. Being sober just helped to crystallise it to the point where my idle daydreams started to get more detailed. My need for alcohol had been replaced by something much darker, much more sinister.

The tipping point, for want of a better word, was when I was out running one night and I saw a familiar looking red BMW with personalised plates driving towards me. It was Robert, still behind the wheel although he was still banned. He'd kept the same car that he'd killed Jennifer with and was now driving around in it. I watched, incredulous, as Robert drove past me, music thumping from the stereo in his car. He was tapping his fingers on the steering wheel in time to the music and didn't even notice me as he drove past. Not a care in the world. If I had to pinpoint the moment that I'd decided to act on my anger, it would be that precise moment. Why should he not have a care in the world? Jennifer was dead, at his hands, and I was a broken man. That wasn't fair.

Finding out where he lived was easier than I thought it would be in the end. I saw him again a few nights later, but he was on foot this time. I just followed him home to a small block of flats on the Yarmouth Road where he let himself into the main door. I saw lights come on in a ground floor flat a few seconds later. I had been sure that he lived down on Riverside somewhere, in one of the posh new developments near the football stadium, and the more I thought about it, the surer I was. Jennifer told me once about Robert losing the plot over someone using his allocated parking space underneath the flats, and it turned out that it was some bloke who'd gone to a football match at Carrow Road. Robert must have moved since then, although why he would move from a nice flat on Riverside to a shabby looking block on the outskirts of the city was beyond me.

Once I'd got his address, I hung around outside the block a couple of times to get an idea of his routine. I was quite used to blending into the background. It was a skill that had served me well in my previous career. Over the course of a couple of weeks, I established a vague idea of where he went, and when. I watched him go to a pub called The Griffin one Thursday evening, which was probably the closest pub to his flat and would, therefore, be his local boozer. It was a squat white building just off one of the main roads back into Norwich from pretty much anywhere to the east of the city. Anyone driving from Great Yarmouth back to Norwich would have to drive right past it, but it wasn't the most popular of pubs by a long stretch. I'd been in there a few years ago, I couldn't remember why, but I remember that it was a bit crap for a pub.

When I watched Robert leave The Griffin that Thursday night, he'd obviously drunk a fair amount judging by the way he was walking. He was still leaving well before closing time, which I was quite happy about as I'd spent the previous hour waiting for him to leave. I watched from my vantage point across the road as he disappeared down an alleyway at the side of the pub, coming back a moment later zipping up his fly. He couldn't even be bothered to go to the toilet before he left the pub. I followed him at a distance as he made his way home. I'd already decided that if I saw him driving again, I'd call the police and grass him up, which was something I'd never done in my life, but other than that one evening I saw him he never seemed to use the car. The idea of him being arrested and jailed for driving while disqualified was a pale punishment, anyway. Him being on foot made it a lot easier to follow him though, so I wasn't complaining.

A couple of days later, I changed my routine and went for a run fairly early on a Sunday morning, joining all the other overweight occasional runners in the area. I made sure that I went past The Griffin pub as well as from the pub to where he lived. There was a sign outside the pub advertising "Quiz and Chips" on a Thursday evening. I stopped by the entrance to the alleyway, trying to look like a jogger having a breather, and looked to make sure that there was no one around. Seeing nobody, I walked down the alley to see what was down there. The main thing that I was looking for was security cameras, but as I'd figured, there weren't any. Tommy had done over this pub a few years ago. I couldn't remember why I'd not been on the job, but he'd said it was an easy entrance for almost bugger all reward. The pub obviously hadn't bothered beefing up their security since Tommy's visit. The alleyway led to a small enclosed yard full of empty beer barrels behind the pub. There was a trapdoor that led down to the cellar with a big thick padlock on it, but other than that there was nothing security wise. It was also not overlooked by anything or anyone.

I left the alleyway and jogged slowly towards Robert's block of flats. It was maybe a ten-minute run, so only a mile. I kept looking out for cameras, net curtains with nosey old people hiding behind them, anything that might make it a dangerous route for someone who wanted to avoid being detected. There were a couple of shops on the way. I made a mental note to ask David to have a look at them. He was much better at spotting things like cameras than I was although I couldn't see anything obvious.

As I reached the outside of the block of flats that Robert lived in, I had the beginnings of a plan in the back of my mind.

## 16

The day it all came together started off pretty much like any other day. I woke up, I went to work, and I did what I would do any other day of the week. It was cold for November, getting colder every day, but when I looked out of the window before I left for work I didn't think it would snow. I left the flat and then had to nip back inside to get a pair of gloves and a woollen beanie hat I'd forgotten. It was chillier than I'd thought.

It was a Thursday, which as well as being quiz night at the Griffin was also a day to catch up on office related stuff. Tommy and David had done a few home visits that needed writing up, and I'd undertaken an assessment of a marketing startup in the middle of Norwich. Why a startup wanted to spend hundreds of pounds on security was beyond me. There was nothing at all in the place that was worth nicking, but I left that part out of my final report.

The three of us had a quick lunch in the office before going our separate ways. I had to go back to a previous client for a follow-up visit, Tommy was going to see a

potential new client, and David had an assessment to do
for another friend of Andy's. Although we were well
enough established now to make it with no help from him,
pretty much every week a new client called who was "a
friend of Andy's". Given that all of his friends seemed to
be well off, we weren't complaining. There'd been several
visits I'd done with Tommy where I'd known we'd be able
to make an absolute packet from the place if we turned it
over. There was a painting on the wall of one of Andy's
friend's houses that Tommy swore was an original painting
by some eighteenth-century painter he knew. I'd been scep-
tical at first, figuring that Tommy knew as much about
eighteenth-century painters as I did, which was next to
nothing, but he'd kept going on about it and even shown
me a photo of the painting taken on his phone. The next
day, Tommy had brought a flyer from an auction house
he'd printed out off the internet. He'd waved it at me.

"There you go, Gareth," he'd said. "Bloody told you
so." I looked at the flyer and the small thumbnail picture
on it. Tommy was right, and the guide price for the
painting was £25,000 to £30,000. For a painting of a
boat.

Later on that evening, we'd met up in The Heartsease
for a few beers. I wasn't completely teetotal then, but not
far off it. I was on a three pint a night limit which worked
well seeing as there were three of us. One round each, nice
and tidy. By the time I got to the pub, the other two were
already there.

"Evening gents," I said as I walked up to them and sat
down on a rickety chair which creaked as I eased myself
onto it.

"How do?" Tommy replied, while David just nodded at
me. "You have a good afternoon?"

"Yeah, I did," I said. "Another happy client. Plus, we

got a good commission off the security stuff they bought. How about you?"

"Another big old house with an old couple knocking round it. Very nice area, just near Eaton. Like a bloody oven inside, though. God knows what their heating bill must be like." Eaton was one of the posher areas on the outskirts of Norwich which had aspirations to be a separate village but was in reality still a suburb. The usual demographic that lived there was rich and elderly. The fact it was close to the hospital no doubt helped with that, and I knew in the past the area had been a happy hunting ground for Tommy. "They wanted to have a think about it, but I reckon they're in for a few grand of security at least. We'll get an assessment out of it, if nothing else."

I nodded at Tommy, pleased that he was getting the hang of bringing new clients in. He had just the right mixture of cheek and guile, and older people loved him. I looked at David, who seemed lost in his thoughts.

"How about you, David?" I asked him. "How did you get on?" He regarded me through his greasy fringe, almost looking offended at the question. One thing was certain about David, he would never be front of house.

"Yeah, standard visit really. Easy money. Not much in the way of improvements to suggest in the house itself." He glanced sideways across at Tommy. "At least not that I could see." David was very much the junior member of the team in that respect. His skill set was far more technical. "So then I did the assessment of his home network." I knew this was the main reason for the visit, and that the security assessment of the house was more for show than anything else. David took a sip of his beer, flicking his fringe as he put the glass back on the table.

"Well, how was it?" Tommy said, his impatience obvious. David paused before replying.

"Man, he had the largest collection of porn I've ever seen in my life," David laughed, a rare sight and as I saw his yellowed teeth, I was reminded why this was. For a while, I'd been considering stumping up for him to go to a cosmetic dentist as a kind of staff benefit, but I'd not had that conversation with him yet. "He was talking about how tech-savvy he was, and that his network was pretty much impenetrable while I was stealing his wi-fi and scrolling through his files." Tommy and I both laughed at the thought of it.

I'd not seen David this talkative for a long time but had heard a rumour — from Big Joe, who else — that there was a lass working in the supermarket down the road who David was sweet on. About bloody time, I thought, before making a mental note to phone up a dentist and get a rough quote for the lad.

"Gareth?" I heard Tommy call my name. "You still with us, mate?"

"Yep, sorry, got distracted," I replied.

"I said, is tonight the night?" he said in a stage whisper, although we were the only people in the pub apart from a couple sitting on the opposite side of the bar well out of earshot. David leaned in before speaking.

"The CCTV out the front's all set up," he said, nodding like a wise old man. We'd persuaded Big Joe to let us install a camera over the front door to the pub. I'd paid for it, mind. It would provide proof for anyone who might need it that they were at the pub. At least, it would provide them with video showing they'd arrived, and left. This was why, when I'd arrived at the pub, I'd made sure the camera got a good look at my face as I walked in through the front door.

"Yeah, I reckon so," I replied. I looked at my watch.

"I'll head away in about an hour. He normally leaves The Griffin at about ten, straight after the quiz."

"You all set then?" Tommy asked.

"Yes mate, good to go," I replied.

"And you're sure you don't want me to come with you?" I looked at Tommy as he asked me this. Part of me would have loved him to come along, even if it was just to stop me bottling it at the last minute, but this was something I needed to do myself.

"I'm good, cheers. Just make sure you stay in here so we can all leave together in case I need an alibi." I glanced at David who nodded in reply. "Right then gents," I got to my feet and looked at their glasses. "Same again?"

About thirty minutes later I left The Heartsease by the back door and stopped for a smoke in the beer garden. As I finished my cigarette, I ran my hand up and down the battered baseball bat in my jacket pocket. It was a child's baseball bat, about half the size of a proper one, but it was made of wood and solid as anything. I pushed the picnic table over to the fence and used it to get over the fence. There were no cameras behind the pub or on the other side of the fence where a strategically placed wheelie bin provided an easy way to get down into the alley. I pushed my gloved hands into my pockets, shivering against the cold as my breath appeared in front of me in white clouds. It was definitely getting colder. The Griffin pub was only about a ten-minute walk if I'd taken the most direct route, but if I'd gone that way I would have been picked up by about three cameras. At least, that's what David had told me, so I took the route he'd recommended as being the safest.

By the time I got to the car park opposite The Griffin, I was breathing hard. When I was about halfway there, I'd realised that it would take me longer than I'd thought, so

I'd had to get a shift on. I stood in the shadows of the community centre over the road from the pub where I hoped Robert would be. I was sure I couldn't be seen where I was hiding, but I pulled my beanie hat down to just above my eyebrows just in case anyone spotted me. I wasn't sure if Robert had already left or not and started to get anxious in case he'd left early. I looked at my watch, figuring I'd give it fifteen minutes, twenty at the outside, before heading back to the warmth of The Heartsease. In the end, I'd timed it right.

Only five minutes after I'd arrived, a familiar figure opened the door and stepped out into the night. Robert shivered, blowing into his hands before turning left and walking through the car park of the pub. Bollocks. I was hoping that he'd go into the alley down the side of the pub, but not tonight. There wasn't a Plan B, but now that I was here I might as well see what I could come up with. I gave him a few seconds head start before setting off after him.

I kept about a hundred yards behind him as he made his way down the road, running through various scenarios in my mind. One challenge would be getting close enough without him realising. A much bigger challenge was the amount of traffic on the road. I guessed that the fact it was so cold meant that more people were using their cars than usual, but the odds of being spotted if I tried anything in the open were high. I had two options. There was a patch of scrubland two hundred yards in front of him that was right next to the road. I knew that in the middle of the scrubland was a large patch of clear ground. Maybe I could drag him in there and away from the main road. As an alternative, there was a railway bridge further along where the footpath and road separated for maybe twenty yards. Beyond the bridge were a few shops and businesses with cameras, so whatever I did would have to be this side of the bridge.

Robert seemed oblivious to his surroundings as he almost lost his footing on the icy pavement. He didn't look behind him once, so I closed the gap between us to about fifty yards. I ran my hand over the baseball bat in my pocket, making sure I could pull it free without it snagging on the material of my coat and looked around to make sure that there wasn't anyone else around. To my dismay, I saw two men walking in the same direction as Robert and I, but on the opposite side of the road. They were both hurrying, dressed for winter in hats, thick jackets, and gloves. They were faster than I was, and I resigned myself to tonight not being the night as they walked past me. I swore under my breath as they overtook me, and I slowed my pace down as I considered the best way to get to The Heartsease. By the time I'd worked the route out in my head, the men on the other side of the road were only a few yards short of Robert, who was just walking past the patch of wasteland before the railway bridge. Although I was on my own, I was still lost for words when the two men broke into a run and crossed the road, each of them grabbing one of Robert's arms and dragging him through the bushes into the scrubland.

I swore again to myself as I broke into a run, reaching the edge of the wasteland a few seconds later. I stopped, trying to work out the best thing to do. I crept into the bushes just far enough to see what was going on. I was dressed in black anyway, and as long as I was careful I should be able to get near the clearing in the middle. In the end, I couldn't get as close as I wanted to. The frozen ground was noisier than I'd expected, so I settled for a spot on the edge of the clearing where I could just see the three figures through the gap between the bushes. Robert was standing between the two men, his arms either side of him with palms extended. I was too far away to hear anything other than muffled voices, not helped by the traffic on the main road only a few feet away. Robert looked as if he was trying to placate the men. The two men both had their backs to me, but I could see in the glow of the street lights that Robert was scared, his eyes wide. White clouds puffed from his mouth as he spoke quickly.

Robert was focused on the larger of the two men, who was also the one doing all the talking. I looked around, trying to see if there was a way I could get closer to them so I could hear what they were talking about when the smaller of the two men drew his fist back and hit Robert hard in the stomach. It was a nasty blow. Hard enough to make me wince even though it wasn't me that had been hit, and one that Robert hadn't seen coming. He went down on the icy ground with a sharp exhalation of air I could hear from my vantage point. The smaller man took a step backwards and pulled his foot back as if he was going to kick Robert in the head, but his companion put a hand out to stop him. The little guy shrugged his shoulders at his colleague and turned away. For the first time, I got a decent look at his face, or at least what little I could see of it under his hat. The only thing I could really make out was a solid jaw and small eyes. Not enough to recognise him if I saw him again.

The larger of the two men crouched down and said something to Robert before getting back to his feet. He turned to his colleague and nodded. The second man's foot drew back again, and he put the boot hard into Robert's ribcage three, maybe four times before taking a step back and looking around the clearing. I shrank back into the bushes as quietly as I could, thinking for a second he was looking directly at me. I held my breath until he looked away, not wanting to give him any sign I was here. From what I could see, he could be the other guy's big brother, but then again they were dressed almost identically. I watched as they both stepped back through the bushes towards the main road. Robert was now kneeling on all fours, and from the clouds coming from his mouth, he was breathing deeply. Probably trying not to be sick. I realised that I could finish it here and now. Just step out and give him the good news with the baseball bat, but somehow it didn't seem fair when he was down already. I wanted him standing in front of me, eye to eye, so I could look at him and he at me. I also had no idea where the two men had gone. After a minute or so, Robert got to his feet, rubbing his stomach and chest as he did so. He stumbled back toward the main road, pushing against the bushes to get back to the pavement. I watched him go, figuring that there'd be another time for us to finish our business, before I lit a cigarette and headed back to the pub.

It took me longer to get back to The Heartsease than I thought it would, and as I approached the alleyway at the back of the pub I realised that it was almost closing time. I climbed onto the wheelie bin, over the fence and down onto the picnic table before walking back into the pub through the back door. The only people in the pub were Big Joe, Tommy, and David. All three of them looked at me as I walked in, questioning looks on their faces. I nodded at Big Joe who was standing behind the bar holding an empty pint glass in the air. He started filling it up as I sat down next to Tommy and David.

"Job done?" Tommy asked, looking hard at me.

"Nope, nothing doing," I said. "He got a kicking all right, but not from me." I relayed the events of the evening to them both, stopping when Big Joe came across with a pint for me and starting again for his benefit.

"And you've got no idea who those blokes were?" Big Joe asked when I'd finished the story. "You'd never seen them before?"

"No, mate," I replied, taking a large sip of my beer. "Not sure I'd recognise them again, either. One big, one smaller but still a fair size. Didn't get hair colour, both dressed in black."

"What's this Robert joker's last name?" Joe asked. "I can ask about, see if anyone knows anything?" I shook my head. The last thing I wanted Robert to find out was that the landlord of my local was asking questions about him.

"Honestly Joe, it's fine," I said. "I'll catch up with him eventually, don't you worry."

It was proper cold by the time I left the pub and walked back to my flat. Ice was forming on the car windscreens, and I realised that I'd not put the heating on before I'd left earlier in the evening. When I got to the flat and opened the door, the temperature inside was almost as cold as it was outside. I got into bed as quickly as I could and lay there shivering.


It wasn't as if there was a warm person in the bed next to me. Not anymore.

## 17

It was almost a month before I caught up with Robert again. It was another Thursday, another quiz night. He'd missed the last couple of weeks' entertainment. I knew because I'd been watching from my usual spot over the road. I'd changed my routine, mostly to avoid messing Tommy and David about. Running past the pub the weekend after Robert had been sucker punched, I looked at the sign to find out what time the quiz started. For the next couple of weeks, I'd been in the community centre car park about half an hour before it began and had left a few minutes after the start time. I guessed that he was lying low as he never showed up on any of the nights I was watching.

That Thursday though, I'd struck lucky. About ten minutes before eight, a taxi had pulled up outside The Griffin. It had a large yellow canary on the side of it, and a sign that told the world it was a Canary Car. I suppose the bloke who ran the firm must have been a Norwich City fan. Robert got out of the car after giving the driver some cash and walked into the pub. I pulled a

phone out of my pocket and texted Tommy and David
to let them know it was on for tonight. It was a throw-
away phone, bought for a tenner off the market and
fitted with a sim that came with a couple of quid credit.
All bought for cash. My usual phone was back at the
Heartsease, in Big Joe's hands. I'd written out some text
messages for him to send from it at various intervals
throughout the evening so that if anyone looked, my
proper phone was there all along and I was using it in
that location. I'd been a bit hesitant giving him the pin
number for my phone, but needs must. I knew Tommy
and David would make their way to The Heartsease
once they'd got my text message, and they'd swear blind
I'd been there all night if anyone asked. My face was
already on the CCTV arriving at the pub and then, later
on, we would all be on the camera leaving together after
a hard night on the pop. A few seconds later, the throw-
away phone buzzed and I read the message from Tommy
confirming he and David were on their way to The
Heartsease.

I looked across at the pub and could see Robert
through one of the windows. He was sitting at a table with
two other men who I'd never seen before, although I'd seen
one of them walk in a few minutes before Robert had
arrived. I'd never seen Robert leave with anyone else,
either. He always seemed to leave just after the quiz
finished, on his own. I spent the next couple of hours
smoking far too much, watching Robert through the
window. It wasn't as cold that night as it had been when I'd
waited for him before, but I'd brought a small hip flask
filled with cheap whisky. My unofficial three pint a night
rule was only a guideline anyway, and a bit of Dutch
courage wouldn't hurt. I unscrewed the flask and took a
small sip before tucking it back into the pocket of the

hoodie I was wearing. Just enough to warm my stomach. I wanted to leave some for afterwards.

While I waited, a fog rolled in from the Norfolk Broads, which were only a few hundred feet behind The Griffin. It seemed fitting somehow, how the light changed and became much more diffuse. More threatening. I thought through my plan as I watched the swirling mist. I had a solid alibi in place, backed up with CCTV that proved I was where I said I was. The running clothes I was wearing were all disposable, bought from Snetterton Market with cash. It wasn't kit I would go running in, but I'd chosen it so that I could blend in by at least looking the part. The natural distrust of the stall holders at the market meant that nothing was recorded anywhere, either on paper or on film. My feet were freezing in a pair of cheap trainers, but all my clothes would be going into a yellow plastic bag at the end of the evening, along with the baseball bat. The only thing I would keep was my hat. I'd worn it on almost every job I'd ever done, and as I'd never been caught, this made it lucky. The plastic bag with the clothes in would be going to a friend of Big Joe who worked as a hospital porter at the Norfolk and Norwich hospital. One of his jobs was loading bags of clinical waste into the industrial incinerator, and for fifty quid a pop he'd throw in an extra bag of whatever you wanted him to as long as it wouldn't explode. Fifty quid was a lot for one bag, but the incinerator was big enough to cremate all sorts of nasty stuff from the hospital so was pretty much bulletproof in terms of destroying any evidence. Money well spent in my opinion.

I could see Robert laughing with his friends inside the pub, and I used this to psych myself up. I don't think I'd laughed properly since I'd buried Jennifer. Not like he was laughing now, that was for sure. Standing around in the cold for over an hour and a half didn't help. I looked at my

watch every few minutes until twenty to ten. Almost time
for Robert to leave, based on the time previous quizzes had
taken. I knew whatever happened, this was ending tonight.
I took another sip of the whisky, a large one this time, and
waited for the door of the pub to open.

A couple of minutes later, the door opened, and
Robert himself stepped out into the cold night air. Despite
the fog, I could see him clearly. He took a few steps forward
and stopped, looking down at his phone and jabbing his
thumb at the screen. Robert held the phone up to his ear
and spoke for a moment before disconnecting. I guessed he
was phoning for a taxi. Good idea, especially after what
had happened to him the last time he'd walked home. You
never knew what sort of people would be hanging around
this time of night, I thought as I patted the inside pocket of
my jacket to check that the baseball bat was where it
should be. I'd sliced a hole in the bottom of the pocket
liner to fit the bat into it, and a couple of times it had
slipped through the hole completely, but it was right where
I wanted it to be. Robert turned and walked towards the
alley at the back of the pub. It was on.

I crossed the road, looking left and right to see if there
was anyone around as I did so. The only person I could see
was a man in a strange looking hat walking a dog. He was
at least a hundred yards away and didn't look as if he was
hurrying. I wasn't going to hang around anyway, not with a
Canary Car on the way. I knew their offices were about ten
minutes away up in Thorpe St Andrew, but the car could
be closer. I pulled the baseball bat halfway out of my
pocket as I walked towards the alleyway, and slowed down
to deaden the noise of my footsteps as I walked into the
dark corridor. When I inched my way to the courtyard at
the back of the pub, I could see Robert with his back to
me, using the yard as a toilet. I stopped a few feet behind

him to wait for him to finish his business. His shoulder jerked as he finished and zipped up his trousers. I waited until he turned around.

"Hello Robert," I said as he turned to face me. "Remember me?"

I'll never forget his expression that night, not for as long as I live. It was almost comical. At first, he hadn't got a clue who I was, no doubt helped by a few beers. Then, as the penny dropped, his face changed completely. He didn't look scared like he had when he'd been talking to the two men in the clearing, just before he'd taken one to the gut. He didn't look scared at all. He looked absolutely terrified, which was exactly how I wanted him to look. I tightened my grip on the baseball bat hidden behind my back.

"I said, do you remember me?" I muttered through gritted teeth. This was it.

"What the fu—"

I never gave him the chance to finish the sentence. I whipped my right hand round from behind my back, putting as much weight as I could behind it. Just before it hit his head, I flicked my wrist to increase the velocity of the bat. It crunched into the side of his face with what was, with hindsight, the most satisfying sound I've ever heard in my life. It was like a carton of eggs being dropped to the ground from a great height. A solid thump, mixed with the sound of what I thought was cracking bone. A warm spray of blood splashed across my face as he wheeled round, unconscious before he'd even hit the deck. His phone span from his hand and skittered across the alleyway. I'd not even noticed him holding it and wondered for a second how he'd taken a leak with his phone in his hand.

Robert crumpled, making no sound at all apart from his body hitting the ground. I looked down at him, at the thin trickle of blood that was coming out of his nose. Had

I hit his nose? I'd been aiming for the side of his head, but maybe I had caught it. Not that it mattered in the slightest now. I held the bat with both hands in front of me like a sword. It was a solid enough little weapon, but the handle was a bit too small for me to get a really good grip on it so I adjusted my fingers until they were comfortable. As I prepared to smack him again, I looked across at the phone on the ground. The screen was still lit, and I could see a crack in the middle of it. I didn't know if that crack was a result of it hitting the ground, or if it had been there for a while. With a glance back at Robert, who wasn't going anywhere, I took a step toward the phone and had a closer look at the broken screen. The only thing I could see was a picture on the screen of Robert and Jennifer. I squinted, trying to make out the picture. In it, Robert was standing behind Jennifer, with his arms wrapped around her. They were both smiling at the camera. I couldn't tell when it had been taken, where they were or who had taken it, but the sight of Robert with his arms around my dead wife enraged me. It didn't matter that the picture was old and taken long before Jennifer and I had ever got together.

The fact he had it on his home screen was enough.

## 18

I looked at Robert lying on the floor of the alleyway as my throat tightened. What had I done? It wasn't as if I heard Jennifer's voice from beyond the grave, reprimanding me, but I might as well have. The satisfaction of smacking him with the bat had gone within seconds and was replaced by a growing sense of unease. This wasn't me. This wasn't the man that Jennifer knew, or would have wanted me to be. I threw the bat onto the floor where it bounced, narrowly missing Robert's phone. I wasn't bothered about fingerprints on the bat as I had gloves on, and everything I was wearing would be incinerated by this time tomorrow, anyway. There wasn't much time as the taxi could turn up any minute, so I hurried back to the end of the alleyway, stopping short of the entrance to make sure it hadn't turned up. That wouldn't be good, being spotted leaving the alleyway by a Canary Car.

There was no sign of a taxi, so I ducked out of the alley and crossed the road, pulling my hood up as I did so. I looked both ways and saw the dog walker I'd noticed earlier about fifty yards closer than he had been when I walked into the alley behind the pub. Silhouetted in the light of a streetlamp, he was watching his dog take a shit on the pavement. For a second, he looked like the priest on the posters for that film about an exorcist that came out years ago, except I couldn't remember the priest on the posters having a dog, or it shitting while he watched it. The mist meant that I couldn't get a good look at him, which was a good thing because if I couldn't see him then he wouldn't be able to see me, either. I hurried across the road, away from the dog walker, and cut down a narrow alleyway between two houses. I'd been through the alleyway several times over the last few weeks as I'd planned out my route back. When you're dressed as a runner, you can go anywhere with no one taking a blind bit of notice.

I reached the end of the alley and broke into a slow jog, wanting to put distance between the scene and me but without drawing too much attention to myself. A few months ago, I wouldn't have been able to run for a bus without wheezing, but my stamina had got a lot better since I'd cut right back on the booze and smokes. I knew the route I would take like the back of my hand, and I figured that I'd be back in The Heartsease with a pint before anyone came close to finding Robert. As I picked up my pace, I wondered if he'd even be found before the morning. I didn't care. It wasn't cold enough for him to die of exposure, and I'd shoved him onto his side so he didn't swallow his tongue. He'd wake up in a while with a banging headache, and crawl back under the stone he came out from. The message had been delivered, that was the main thing.

A few minutes later, I reached one of my favourite places in the whole of Norwich. It was here, on this bench, that I'd kissed Jennifer for the first time. If the graffiti was to be believed, a kiss was one of the milder things that had happened on this bench. I took a few deep breaths, pulling the hip flask from the inside pocket of my running jacket and loosening the lid before taking a large slug from it. As the cheap whisky burned my throat, I started laughing. This turned into a cough, and the next thing I knew I was trying to laugh and cough at the same time. Any unease I had felt earlier was gone. I was bulletproof, and Robert had got what he deserved. The justice that the court had failed to deliver had been delivered. I looked up at the sky, at the faint stars in the blackness, and for the first time since Jennifer had died, I felt a sense of peace. I raised the hip flask again and drained it.

Knowing the minute I walked into the Heartsease I would have to relive the moment with the others, I sat on the bench for a few moments just to get my head together. A few minutes later, I got to my feet and wandered across the park and through the back streets of Thorpe St. Andrew, heading for the alleyway that led to the back of The Heartsease. When I got there, the wheelie bin was in the same place, and getting over the fence was simple.

I was looking forward to seeing my mates, recounting the events of the evening. As I walked into the pub with a grin that almost split my face, the only people inside were the people I wanted to see — Big Joe, Tommy, David. They all looked at me expectantly, and I put both thumbs up in the air like a complete tool. I couldn't help it. I was too buzzed.

"You look like a man who needs a pint," Big Joe's voice came from behind the bar like a foghorn. Hearing this, both Tommy and David turned round to look at Joe. "All right, pints all round then," Big Joe said, a smile on his face. I sat down between Tommy and David, grinning like a child at Christmas.

"Well?" Tommy said. I paused for a few seconds before replying.

"Boom," I said before laughing at the pair of them. "Job done." David reached across and patted me on the shoulder, which was very unusual for him. Apart from the odd handshake, I didn't think we'd ever actually touched each other.

A few moments later, Big Joe came across to our table carrying a tray with four pints on it. He put one in front of the three of us and, to my surprise, sat down with the fourth in his hand. In all the years I'd known Big Joe, I'd never seen him drink. Tommy and I had even had an argument about it one night. I was sure that Big Joe liked a drink — he was a landlord after all, and had the face and build of a man who liked a pint — but Tommy was sure he was teetotal. Neither of us had got the bottle to just ask Big Joe, but I guess in the end I won that argument.

"So, how did it go then?" Big Joe asked, sliding my phone over the table toward me. "You sort him out?"

"I did," I replied, taking a large sip from my pint. "He went down like a sack of spuds when I smacked him."

"Good lad," Big Joe said. "Nice one." Tommy and David both nodded in agreement. "You'd better get changed, fella. Your stuff's out the back, in the cellar. Just go on through, but if you nick anything, I'll cut your bollocks off." I got to my feet and walked through the bar, listening to the sound of the three of them laughing. The last thing I heard as I opened the cellar door was Big Joe saying "finally, the boy done good".

I shivered in the cold of the cellar as I got changed. My original clothes — the ones I'd been wearing earlier for the CCTV camera — were freezing. As I shrugged myself into them and stuffed the running kit into a large yellow bag that Big Joe had got from his mate at the hospital, I thought about Robert lying on the ground of the courtyard behind the pub. Although I'd bottled it not long after hitting him, at least I felt as if justice had been done to a degree. Not the justice I had wanted, or that Robert deserved, but justice of sorts.

Despite the cold, I felt a broad smile creep onto my face as I walked back out of the cellar to join the others.

## 19

The next morning, I was woken up by the doorbell. Whoever it was then hammered four or five times on the door before ringing the doorbell again. I looked at my watch on the bedside table. It was just after six in the morning, and still dark outside. I sat on the edge of the bed and shook my head, trying to clear the alcohol fog. Last night had turned into a lock-in, and I'd had far more than my allocated three pints for an evening.

From the renewed hammering on the front door, I guessed that it must be the police which was unexpected, to be honest. For all his faults, I'd not got Robert down as a grass. Getting to my feet, I pulled the curtains apart and looked out into the back garden like I did every morning. I couldn't see anything at first, but then noticed a sudden movement behind the fence at the bottom of the garden. The doorbell rang again as I saw a man's face pop up over the fence before disappearing when he saw me looking straight at him. If it hadn't been so serious, it would have been comical.

I made my way to the front door, grabbing my

dressing gown from the hook on the back of the door. I tightened the belt around my stomach as I opened the door. Sure enough, it was the police. Malcolm had been the one doing the hammering, and behind him were two uniformed policemen. It wasn't the two who'd been around the night Jennifer had been run over. The two in uniform still had their hats on, and their serious faces told me they'd not popped round for a cup of tea and a chat.

"Morning Gareth," Malcolm said, pushing the door open and walking past me into the hall.

"Detective Inspector Griffiths," I replied. "Please, come on in."

"Get yourself dressed, Gareth," he said. "Sergeant Merrick, go with him please." As he said this, the older of the two policemen stepped forwards.

I walked back into the bedroom, followed by the policeman. He stood by the door watching me, as I threw on a pair of jeans and a t-shirt. I picked up my shoes and walked past him and into the lounge where Malcolm was standing, looking at a picture of me and Jennifer on the wall. He turned to face me, pointing at a chair.

"Sit down, Gareth," he said, no trace of warmth in his voice. I did as instructed and sat in the armchair. Malcolm sat opposite me while the other two policemen just stood by the door. I wondered for a second if this was nothing to do with Robert, but maybe something from back when I was on the nick. The thing was they wouldn't send round a Detective Inspector and two sidekicks to pick up a petty thief, and I doubted they would hide another copper in the back garden.

"What's this about, Malcolm?" I asked, trying to keep my voice steady. "Is this about Jennifer?" He stared at me, lips set in a tight line.

"Where were you last night?" he asked after a few seconds' pause.

"I was in The Heartsease, having a few beers with some friends."

"Between what times?"

"All evening. I got there about seven, and left a bit after closing time before coming home," I replied. I knew they wouldn't be able to prove that I was anywhere else, and I'd got enough evidence to prove that as far as they were concerned, I'd been there all night.

"Really?" Malcolm said, his disbelief obvious.

"Yes, Malcolm, really," I let a note of irritation creep into my voice, preparing to go on the offensive. "Why? What's this about? It's first thing in the morning, and you've turned up mob-handed for a chat?" Malcolm looked at the two uniformed policemen as if he was about to say that three of them weren't a mob. I carried on. "Don't forget the muppet out the back," I said. Malcolm frowned, obviously annoyed that his colleague minding the back of the property had let himself be seen.

"So you were in The Heartsease? All night?" he said.

"Yep, that's what I said," I replied.

"You can prove that, can you?" He looked at me, deadpan.

"I thought that was your job?" I said, allowing a half smile to form. "Yes, I can. If I have to." I wiped the smile off my face. "Are you going to tell me what this is about?"

"It's about Robert," he paused. "Robert Wainwright." I frowned at the mention of his name. Malcolm just stared at me, almost daring me to react.

"What about him?" I asked.

"He was attacked last night," Malcolm said.

"And you thought it might have been me?"

"I wouldn't be a very good copper if I didn't at least consider the possibility, would I Gareth?"

"Well sorry to disappoint you, Malcolm. But it wasn't me." I folded my arms in front of me before uncrossing them and leaning forward. "Look, I get it," I continued. "You have to go through the motions and I must be close to the top of your list in terms of suspects. So, what do you need from me? What can I do to help you?"

Malcolm tried to hide the brief look of relief on his face, but I still caught it. He got to his feet.

"Just give me a minute, would you?" Malcolm walked out of the lounge and into the hall, followed by the older of the two policemen. The other one stayed standing in the lounge, staring at a spot on the wall until he realised I was looking at him. He returned my gaze, lifting his eyebrows a couple of millimetres as he stared at me. I could hear Malcolm and the other copper talking in hushed tones in the hall, but their voices were too low for me to hear what they were talking about. After a minute or two, Malcolm came back into the lounge. He looked at the young policeman.

"I've sent Sergeant Merrick back to the nick," Malcolm said to him before turning to look at me. "And he's taking Kermit the frog from the alleyway with him." A sly smile appeared on his face. "Was he really that easy to see?" he asked me.

"Well, he stuck his head above the fence and then disappeared when he saw me looking back at him," I replied, grinning. Malcolm's smile broadened. This was looking up.

"Constable Barnes, could you do us a favour please?" Malcolm said. I knew what was coming and looked at the young policeman with a grin still stuck on my face.

"Can I have two sugars in mine please, mate?" I said.

"The kitchen's just through there." I nodded at the door, ignoring the look of annoyance on the young policeman's face. He looked at Malcolm.

"And in mine as well please, Constable Barnes," Malcolm said. The policeman left the lounge with a muttered "Yes, sir" in Malcolm's direction as he did so. I called after him.

"There are chocolate hob-nobs in there somewhere, mate. Bring them through, would you?"

A few minutes later, Constable Barnes had delivered two cups of tea and been sent back to the kitchen by Malcolm to make himself one. I sipped my tea as Malcolm sat back in his chair, wriggling to free a notebook from his pocket. He scribbled a few notes at the top of a blank page with a small pencil that looked as if it was from a golf course or bookies' shop. I guessed that even Detective Inspectors nicked things every once in a while.

"So, you were in The Heartsease, all night?" he asked.

"Yes, that's correct. From around seven until just after closing time. Well, quite a long time after closing, in fact."

"Who with?"

"Tommy Hayworth and David French." Malcolm frowned at the mention of their names. I figured that he must have crossed paths with Tommy or David in the past.

"I know Mr Hayworth, but I've not heard of the other chap," he said. "David French. Is he local?"

"Yep, he lives somewhere in Dussindale I think. I don't know his address though, sorry." I was kind of lying. I knew where David's flat was, but had got no idea of the street name or his flat number.

"Don't worry, I'm sure I can find him," Malcolm muttered. I was sure he could as well and noticed that he didn't ask for Tommy's address. "Was there anyone else in the pub?" I hesitated, suddenly realising that there was one small hole in my plan. I knew there was no one else in The Heartsease when I'd arrived at the start of the evening, and when I'd left with the others, but I had no idea whether there'd been any other customers. There must have been a few though. It was a Thursday night.

"Er, yeah, one or two." I managed to say. "No-one I knew, though. Big Joe was behind the bar, he'll be able to tell you who else was in, I would imagine." I closed my mouth, reminding myself that I was on thin ice here, so the less said the better.

Malcolm remained silent as he wrote this information down in tiny handwriting.

"What were you wearing?"

"Hoodie, tracksuit trousers, usual stuff," I replied.

"Shoes?"

"Trainers. These ones." I lifted my foot in the air to show him the trainers I was wearing. The ones I'd been wearing last night were almost identical, and with any luck had already been incinerated along with the rest of my clothes. Malcolm looked at them briefly before returning to his notebook.

"How about your phone? Did you have it with you last night?" Malcolm asked.

"Of course," I replied.

"Do you mind if I look at it?"

"Sure, I'll get it for you." I got to my feet and walked into the bedroom where my phone was sitting on the bedside cabinet. After a couple of deep breaths, I returned to the lounge pretty sure that this would turn out okay. I'd been a bit worried at one point earlier on, but the fact I was being interviewed here as opposed to down at the station had to be in my favour. I walked back into the lounge and handed the phone to Malcolm. He looked at it before stabbing a finger at the home button. "The PIN's

0109," I said. The first of September. Our wedding anniversary, but Malcolm didn't need to know that. He turned the phone over in his hands.

"Do you mind if we look at the phone down at the station?" I paused before replying. I'd not been expecting that. "It won't take long."

"It's my work phone, though," I replied. "I'm kind of stuck without it." Although I didn't want them taking my phone away and analysing it, I thought back to when I'd got the thing and remembered that it was after I'd gone straight. There wouldn't be anything incriminating on it, anyway.

"I'll have it back as soon as I can, Gareth. I promise," Malcolm said. "There are a couple of simple tests we can do on it to back up your movements, that's all." I knew there were, which is exactly why I'd left it in the pub with Big Joe for the evening. I also knew handing it over without putting up a bit of a fight would look odd.

"Well, can I get it back as soon as they're done then?" I asked Malcolm.

"Sure, I'll bring it back myself. How about that?" I nodded in reply. "Constable Barnes, could you do a receipt for the phone please?"

I signed the paperwork for the phone, including ticking a box to say I was content for the police to look at the data on the phone, and watched as Constable Barnes put it into an evidence bag.

"I'll try to get it back to you by lunchtime if I can. At least you'll have it back for the weekend." Malcolm said. This reassured me as if they didn't have it for too long then they wouldn't be able to do much to it. Or could they copy everything onto a computer somewhere? I didn't know and wished I'd looked into this more beforehand. David would know, but it was too late now, anyway. I answered a few more questions for Malcolm. What route I'd taken back from the pub to my flat, that sort of thing. About ten minutes later, he wound up the interview.

"Gareth, thanks for cooperating on this." He glanced down at his notebook. "I'll speak to Mr Hayworth and Mr French, and get your phone back to you." Malcolm got to his feet and headed for the door to the lounge, putting my phone into his pocket. Constable Barnes followed him out of the lounge and the two men stood at the front door. Malcolm turned and extended his hand. I shook it out of habit and tried to read his face. It was back to being impassive. "I'll be in touch."

"How is the little shit, anyway?" I asked, realising that I'd not asked or been told about Robert's condition. Malcolm stared at me, blinking once or twice before he replied.

What he said next made my heart race. I didn't have to fake the surprise on my face as it was real. Malcolm didn't say anything else, but just turned and walked down the steps to the pavement. I closed the front door behind them and took a huge breath in before blowing it out of my cheeks. That explained why the Old Bill had turned up so quickly. I walked back into the lounge, feeling faint as my heart pounded at God knows what speed. Sitting down, I took another deep breath. I swallowed, wondering for a second if I was going to throw up.

Robert Wainwright was dead.

## 20

Malcolm came back to the flat just after lunch with a policewoman and another male copper. At first, I assumed that they were returning my phone, letting me know they'd checked out my alibi and that I was off the hook. But that wasn't why they were there at all.

There was a piece of paper in Malcolm's hand when I opened the door. He waved it at me, explaining that it was a warrant to search my flat. A Section 8 warrant, apparently. He then turned and introduced the policewoman who was standing next to him. What she said would be burned into my memory forever.

"Gareth Dawson, I'm arresting you on suspicion of the murder of Robert Wainwright. You do not have to say anything, but it may harm your defence if you do not mention when questioned something which you later rely on in court. Anything you do say may be given in evidence. Do you understand?" She stumbled a few times over the order of the words, and I wondered if she'd ever arrested someone before.

"You're joking?" I looked from the policewoman to

Malcolm and back again. "You are joking, aren't you?" The next thing she said surprised me.

"Are you okay? Can I get you a glass of water or anything?" This couldn't be happening. She'd just arrested me on suspicion of murder, and now she was offering me a glass of bloody water?

"I don't believe this," I said, realising that my hands were shaking.

"We can talk down at the station, Gareth," Malcolm said. I held my hands out in front of me to see how badly they were trembling. Malcolm misunderstood the gesture. "I'm not going to cuff you, Gareth." As he walked me to the police car that was waiting outside my flat, he leaned over and whispered in my ear. "Don't say a word until you get a solicitor. Understand?" I nodded in response and looked at my next door neighbour who'd chosen that exact moment to put his recycling bin out. Nosy bastard.

As I was driven from my flat to the police station, I looked out of the window at the lush green trees and wondered how long it would be before I saw things like that again. We drove over a bridge that spanned the Norfolk Broads, and past a park called Whitlingham Broad where Jennifer and I had spent many happy hours. I racked my brains for what could have gone wrong. I was sure I'd covered everything. The only thing I could think of was that someone had blabbed. I was sure it wouldn't have been Tommy — he was my oldest friend — and it wouldn't be Big Joe. He had a reputation to protect, and being known as a grass would mean that the bulk of his customers would go nowhere near The Heartsease again. The only one left was David, but I couldn't see him rolling over either. Why would he?

When we arrived at the police station, I'd been "processed". Fingerprinted, swabbed, photographed, the whole works. I'd said nothing during the whole thing, doing exactly what Malcolm had advised. The only words I'd spoken were my name, address, date of birth, and the words "I'd like a lawyer, please". I couldn't see any point winding up the Old Bill. I was deep enough in the shit as it was. I'd been expecting to be put in a cell while I was waiting for the duty solicitor, but Malcolm had shown me into an interview room instead. It was still a locked room, but it had to be more comfortable than a cell. I wouldn't know for sure as I'd never been in one before.

The only furniture in the interview room were four chairs and a small table, with a complicated looking recording machine on top of it. The walls were covered with pale blue carpet tiles, and there was an air conditioning unit on the wall behind me. It whirred occasionally but did nothing about the stench of sweat in the room. There were at least two cameras in the small room that I could see. Was there someone on the other end of them watching me? I had no idea.

After what felt like hours, the door opened and Malcolm walked in. He was followed by the same policewoman from earlier. It was showtime. Malcolm put a grey laptop on the table and sat in one of the chairs opposite me. He left the door open and a young man walked in a few seconds later. He looked as if he was in his late twenties, very thin, and dressed in an off the peg suit. His blonde quiffed hair might have been fashionable in the eighties, but not since. He extended his hand and as I shook it, he introduced himself.

"I'm Toby Cooper, the duty solicitor. You must be Gareth Dawson?" He spoke with a Norfolk accent, but not a broad one. His handshake was firm and reassuring, and I reappraised my initial negative assessment of him. He smiled, showing a brief glimpse of white teeth, and the skin crinkled around his pale blue eyes. He looked like a man who smiled a lot, but I didn't know if this was a good sign or a bad one.

Malcolm shuffled in his chair and prodded at some buttons on the recording machine until a small green light came on.

"This interview is being recorded and may be given in evidence if your case is brought to trial. We are in interview room one at Wymondham Police Station, Norfolk. The date is the 24th November, and the time by my watch is 15.25." He was staring straight at me while he spoke, not reading from a card, and I guessed he'd done this a fair few times before. "I am Detective Inspector Malcolm Griffiths. The other police officer present is Sergeant Gemma Fitzsimmons. Also present is Mr Gareth Dawson, who has been charged on suspicion of murder. Gareth, please state your full name and date of birth." I did as he requested, my mouth dry. I thought about asking for a glass of water but decided against it. "Also present is Toby Cooper, duty solicitor," Malcolm continued before asking me if I agreed that there were no other persons present. I looked at the cameras before nodding in reply. "For the tape please, Gareth," Malcolm said. A bit pointless when there was a video camera pointed at me, but rules were rules.

"I agree, there's no one else in the room," I replied, my voice quiet. Malcolm rattled something off about free and independent legal advice, but I tuned him out and turned to look at the solicitor. He was sitting listening to Malcolm, an A4 size notepad at the ready. I glanced at the notepad. The page was empty, apart from my name and the date and time of the interview written across the top in neat, blockish handwriting.

"So, Mr Dawson. I interviewed you this morning at your flat, voluntarily," Malcolm said. No more first names then. "You informed me that last night you spent the evening at The Heartsease pub in the company of Mr Tommy Hayworth and Mr David French. Is that correct?" I nodded before remembering the tape.

"Yes, that's correct," I replied, glancing at the solicitor who gave me an encouraging smile.

"And you state you were there for the whole evening?"

"Yes, I was."

"For the tape, we have obtained initial telephone statements from both Mr Hayworth and Mr French corroborating this statement. We have also recovered CCTV footage from The Heartsease pub which shows the suspect entering and leaving the establishment at the times he states." Malcolm's language had changed, becoming much more formal, but from what he was saying it was so far so good. They wouldn't have arrested me without something, though. There had to be a reveal on the way. The only thing I knew so far was that I'd been wrong to doubt David. He'd come through.

Malcolm continued. "We've also analysed the suspect's phone, which shows that the phone was in The Heartsease pub for the stated period with several texts being sent during that time." Good old Big Joe had done what I'd asked him, too. Malcolm looked at me, inscrutable as always. "Do you maintain that this was the course of events last night, Mr Dawson?"

"Yes, I do," I replied, trying to put some authority into my voice for the tape. "I spent the evening with my friends, in the pub, having a few beers and talking nonsense." Malcolm's stare bored into me, making me uncomfortable. He knew something, he had something else, I was sure.

"Were you anywhere near The Griffin pub on the Yarmouth Road last night, Mr Dawson?" he asked.

"No," I replied. "I was not."

"Did you attack Mr Robert Wainwright last night, with a baseball bat, in an alleyway to the side of the pub?"

"No, I did not," I said, my voice wavering despite my attempts to keep it strong.

He reached down to pick up his laptop and placed it on the table. He also pulled out a bunch of photographs from his briefcase which he lined up face down on the table between us. Malcolm opened the laptop and stabbed at a button to turn it on. We all sat in silence while the computer whirred into life, Malcolm's face was bathed in the blue light of the screen. After a few seconds, he flipped the laptop around so that the screen was pointing at me.

"For the tape, I am showing the suspect the footage recovered from the occupants of a house in Yarmouth Road. The property is almost directly opposite The Griffin pub." He leaned forward and pressed a button on the laptop. I watched as a grainy video started playing. The camera was focused on a car parked by the side of the road, and in the background, the outline of The Griffin could be seen. A figure appeared from the door of the pub. It was Robert. I watched, knowing what was coming as he raised his phone to his ear before disappearing down the alleyway to the side of the pub. I knew what the next thing the camera would show and, sure enough, I could be seen crossing the road a few seconds later. Although the camera was showing my back, I looked left and right as I crossed the road and my face could be seen in profile both times. As I got to the other side of the road, the video showed my right hand pulling the baseball bat halfway out of my pocket.

In the bottom corner of the screen there was some white flashing text, showing a date of 1st January and 00:00hrs. I guessed that the date and time hadn't been set up properly on the camera, but I couldn't see how that would make any difference at all. I was still fucked. We sat in silence for a few seconds before I reappeared on the screen, this time walking directly toward the camera. My face could be seen without any problem at all this time, and Malcolm paused the video just before I disappeared from the shot. He turned over the photographs on the table to reveal screenshots from the video. There were three of them, one of my face from the right, one from the left, and one showing me looking directly at the camera. The camera which I hadn't seen despite scouring the area repeatedly. The photographs looked as though they'd been tidied up in Photoshop to remove some of the grain from the video, but there was no doubt they were of me.

"Officers have since visited Mr French, Mr Hayworth, and Mr Walcott to gain formal statements," Malcolm said, looking directly at me. Who on earth was Mr Walcott? Malcolm must have seen my confusion. "Mr Joseph Walcott, the landlord of The Heartsease," he continued. In all the time I'd been drinking there, I'd never known that was Big Joe's name. I must have passed under the sign above the front door with his name on it a thousand times without reading it. Malcolm carried on. "All three gentlemen have retracted their earlier telephone statements, claiming they were operating under extreme pressure from you. Additionally, Mr Walcott has admitted to sending text messages from your phone on your instructions." So, all three of them had rolled over. The only way that this could have happened is if the police had threatened them with perverting the course of justice or something like that. In a murder case as well. I think that would get me thinking if I was them. Me threatening Big Joe was a bit of a laugh though, and Malcolm must have known that.

He leaned forward and straightened up the three

photographs, lining them up. Looking at me, he pressed his lips together before speaking.

"I think we'll give you a few minutes with Mr Cooper." He looked at his watch. "I am pausing this interview at 15:35 hours." That had been the longest ten minutes of my life. Without another word, Malcolm got to his feet and left, followed by the policewoman. As the door closed behind them, Toby stood and shuffled round to the other side of the table so he was facing me. The look on his face was one of disappointment, almost as if he was looking at a child who's just been caught eating the posh biscuits. Not looking at a man who'd killed someone.

"Well?" he asked. "Where do we go from here?"

"I'm fucked, aren't I?" I sighed. "Absolutely fucked. They've got me on camera walking toward him with a baseball bat, and I've got no alibi for the evening. Plus he was the man who killed my wife, so there's motive in spades."

"Er, I think it's safe to say you're not in a fantastic position at the moment," Toby said. "Now you know this conversation is protected, don't you? The video cameras are now off, they can't hear us, and anything you say is confidential." I nodded to show that I understood, glancing toward the cameras. The red flashing light had gone off. "I take it you hit Mr Wainwright, then?" Toby asked.

What could I say to that? They had me on CCTV, and I had no alibi anymore. I felt numb.

"Yeah, I hit him. I knew he'd be there, and I made sure I was there as well." Toby scribbled in his notepad, glancing up at me a couple of times. "I'm surprised that the others rolled over so easily, though. I thought I was watertight with them."

"There were probably police with them up to the point

that you were arrested. Just to be sure they couldn't warn you," Toby said. "And in terms of them rolling over, they were probably threatened with being arrested themselves. The maximum sentence for perverting the course of justice is life. It's rarely given out, but that's a big stick for the police to have." I sat back in the chair, thinking about what Toby had just said. What would I have done if I'd been in their situation? If it was Tommy asking me for an alibi? I thought for a few seconds before realising that I would do exactly what they'd done. Friendship could only go so far.

Toby and I chatted for maybe about ten minutes before he summarised my situation.

"So, I think it's fairly sure you're about to be charged with murder." Hearing him say that in such a normal tone of voice made my blood run cold. "They've got a motive. They've got evidence which places you at the scene, and they've got evidence to suggest that you planned it throughout to try to get away with it." Toby looked at me, his face neutral. "That's a no-brainer for the Crown Prosecution Service."

"But I didn't mean to kill him," I said, knowing I was close to tears. "I only wanted to hurt him, to pay him back." Toby looked at me, his brow creased as he thought about what I'd said.

"Well, we're getting ahead of ourselves here but there may be legal options we can talk about further on down the line. Manslaughter might be your best option, but we'll get to that later," he replied. "Now DI Griffiths has got twenty-four hours to charge you, but knowing him he's probably already got the go ahead from the CPS to charge you now. There's nothing you can do, but I would advise saying nothing when you are charged."

"So, what happens next?" I asked through the lump in my throat.

"You'll be charged and remanded in custody until the case comes to trial. If they charge you with murder, then you won't get bail. I'd say you'd be looking at a trial in about three months." I could feel tears pricking at my eyes, but I didn't want to start blubbing like a baby in front of Toby.

It was maybe another ten minutes before Malcolm came back into the room, followed again by his sidekick, Gemma. Toby moved back to my side of the table, and I watched as Malcolm started the recording machine up again and went through the motions for the tape. I glanced up at the camera in the corner of the room and could see the red light flashing again. Then I listened as Malcolm charged me with the murder of Robert Wainwright, reading from a sheet of paper. He got to the end and looked at me.

"Do you have anything to say, Gareth?" I shook my head from side to side. "For the tape, please?"

"No," I whispered. "I don't have anything to say."

## 21

I t took three months to get to trial, just as predicted. Three months spent on remand at Norwich Prison. Toby had tried very hard to get me bail, but with the seriousness of the charges hanging over my head, that was never going to happen no matter how much money Andy promised to stump up. Looking back at it now, although being on remand was different from being in a proper prison, I was still locked up. There were more privileges, I had more rights for what that was worth, and I had more visitors. The only problem was that most of the visits were about either me being on trial for murder and how shit my situation was, or preparing for the inevitable long prison sentence after the trial. It was almost as if everyone was preparing me for a long time away, which they were.

As the trial itself approached, I was looking forward to it in a sense. At least it would end the limbo I was in. I would know one way or the other what my future held. The first two and a half weeks in the courtroom went past me in a complete blur. It was almost as if I was watching a film, but one with me as the lead character. I knew just beyond the doors to the courtroom was the heart of the old city. Riverside walks, mediaeval ruins, the world's supply of churches and a cathedral that even I had to admit was impressive were a few hundred yards away. They might as well have been on the other side of the world for all the good they did me. There was also a fantastic pub just near the courtroom. The Wig and Pen I think it was called. I'd been in there once when I went to court with Tommy to watch him get fined for theft. I can't for the life of me remember what he'd nicked that time though, it was all so long ago.

I was sitting in the courtroom dressed in a tailored suit that Andy had bought me for the occasion. Either side of me were prison officers, and we waited in silence for my future to be decided by twelve of my peers. The jury was being guided by Judge Watling, the same man who had let Robert Wainwright go with no more than a slap on the wrist. Throughout the trial, the judge had seemed disinterested, almost as if he knew this was an open and shut case and all everyone was doing was going through the motions. At the back of my mind were his closing statements at Robert's trial when he slammed the legal system that forced him to let Robert go. He still let Robert go, so his statements were meaningless anyway.

The prosecuting lawyer was maybe halfway through her closing statement which had started first thing that morning. I'd spent the previous couple of hours listening to her destroy me and my reputation, not that I had much of a reputation left by then anyway. Miss Revell her name was, with an emphasis on the second syllable but absolutely not the first, was an absolute witch. She had to be in her late thirties, maybe early forties. It was difficult to get a sense of her size given the flowing black robes she was wearing, but my best guess from the look of her hands and face is that she was stick thin underneath them. She had half-moon glasses on her face and she peered over the top of them so often that I wondered what was the point of her wearing them in the first place. Some small tufts of hair poking out from under her wig told me she had blonde hair. No wedding ring. Married to the law perhaps? I looked at her now, scribbling in her notebook as we waited for the jury to come back in after a short coffee break.

The only thing left once she had finished damning me was a verdict from the jury, so I had no idea what she was writing about. On more than one occasion, I'd wished that she was on my side. First thing this morning, once the judge had called the court to order, Miss Revell had got to her feet and torn me apart.

"Ladies and gentlemen of the jury, we are now approaching the end of my summary, and I will be shortly handing over to my learned colleague in the defence corner." Her voice was an octave or two lower than it should have been, looking at her. This, along with the crow's feet around her eyes and wrinkled mouth, hinted at a fondness for cigarettes. "They will attempt to persuade you that the defendant didn't mean to kill Mr Wainwright. Earlier in the week, we discussed the legal definition of murder and the difference between murder and voluntary manslaughter to which the defendant has pled guilty." I had indeed pled guilty to manslaughter because I had no choice. "But as we discussed, the defendant has admitted planning the attack on Mr Wainwright. He has admitted an elaborate attempt to establish an alibi which failed almost immediately." She paused and took a breath before continuing. "He has admitted lying in wait for the victim, approaching him when he was defenceless, and striking him with a weapon he had bought specifically for the purpose. Striking him time and time again until Robert Wainwright was dead." It was all true, apart from the very last part. She didn't need to be as good as she was, it was almost all true.

"The defence will no doubt focus on the most unfortunate circumstances leading up to the defendant's decision to do Mr Wainwright harm." The judge leaned forward slightly as the prosecutor said this, listening to her with a frown. "But these circumstances do not mitigate against the charge of murder. There was no loss of control, no sudden and immediate decision. This was a considered desire for cold revenge, nothing less." I tuned her out, aware that she was not only crucifying me but also taking apart the defence's case before they'd even said a word apart from their opening statement. Toby leaned across and whispered in my ear.

"Just relax, Gareth. You're not helping yourself here. No matter what she's saying, don't react at all. That includes the look on your face." I wasn't even aware that I had a look on my face, but I attempted to relax.

Toby had been an absolute star throughout the whole of this mess. The lawyer who was doing the talking on my behalf was a partner from Toby's firm, an older chap closer to the judge's age than mine. Apparently, Toby was too junior to be the lead, which was something I'd argued against. But I'd lost that argument, overruled by Toby's boss. I'd not been that impressed with the partner from the opening arguments. He was as dry and boring as he looked, quoting various legal references at the jury until their eyes glazed over. In contrast, the prosecutor was much more animated, and more of a storyteller.

"So, ladies and gentlemen, those are the primary reasons why you must find the defendant guilty of murder." Miss Revell turned the heat up at the end of her summing up. "You have no choice according to the law of the land, as I'm sure you're now aware. No matter how compassionate you may be feeling toward the loss of his wife, the law is unequivocal. He has, while of sound mind, unlawfully killed another human being in a premeditated and planned attack. The only option available to you is to find him guilty as charged." She paused, and even though she had her back to me I knew she was looking each juror in the eye before delivering her final blow. "Of murder."

I looked over at my defence lawyer as the prosecutor finished her closing statement. He sat with his robes pooled around him, polishing his glasses. To be fair to him, he didn't have a lot to go on, but he'd spent the previous week trying to prove that I was a broken man. Ruined by the death of my wife, he painted me as a desperate individual, hanging on to my sanity by a slim thread. The thrust of his defence was that the sight of Robert enjoying himself on a night out had provoked me to the point of taking action. The routine was pretty much the same for every witness he called. He would question them, try to make his point, and then sit down again while the prosecutor tore to shreds whatever argument he'd been trying to make.

At one point, he was trying to prove how distraught I'd been when Robert was sentenced for his crime. He'd called the previous court usher as a witness and was pointing out I was so upset at the verdict, I'd had to be restrained by Andy and Jacob. When my lawyer had finished, he sat down and the prosecutor got up to ask the usher some more questions.

"Did the defendant say anything when he was being restrained?" she asked in a quiet voice. The usher nodded before speaking.

"Yes, he did," he replied. I hung my head, not wanting to look at the jury. I knew what was coming. "Your

Honour, do you wish me to paraphrase?" I looked up to see the usher looking at the judge, and the judge looking at me with a dour face.

"No, there's no need," the judge said, looking down as the usher continued.

"The defendant shouted 'I'm going to fucking kill you myself, you bastard'. I apologise for swearing, Your Honour."

I had sat with my head down, not daring to look up at any of the jurors. I imagined them all sitting there, staring at me. Maybe a few of them were shaking their heads in disgust? I raised my head just so that I could see my defence lawyer. He had got to his feet and was standing with his hands on the table, stooped over it and looking down. His mouth opened and closed like a fish before he finally looked up at the judge.

"Does the defence have any more questions for this witness?" Judge Watling asked. The defence lawyer, the man with my life in his hands, looked up at the judge. Even though I couldn't see his face I could hear the defeat in his voice as he replied.

"No more questions, Your Honour."

"All rise."

In response to the court usher's shrill call to action, I rose to my feet along with everyone else in the courtroom. The two prison officers on either side of me were both smaller than me, and I stooped slightly as I'd been told to do by Toby and his team so I was closer in height to them. Something about being less threatening to the jury.

The door at the back of the courtroom opened and Judge Watling stepped through it, looking around his little empire as he did so. I watched as he settled into his seat, shuffling papers in front of him as he always did. He then looked across at me and nodded. Just as he had done every day we'd been in the courtroom. The first time he'd done it, it'd thrown me. Why had he done that? I asked Toby during a break what it was about, and he'd said it was the judge's way of recognising the situation I was in. Thinking back to Robert's trial, I tried to remember if he'd nodded at Robert. I didn't think he had done, so maybe the judge's nod was only for those really in the shit.

"Please bring in the jury," the judge said to the court usher, who hurried away to the back of the courtroom.

It was now lunchtime on Friday, three weeks after the trial had started. The jury had retired to consider the verdict yesterday afternoon, and the judge's summing up was bleak, to say the least. He didn't exactly tell the jury to find me guilty of murder, but he might as well have done. There was a real sense of deja vu when he was speaking. I was reminded of the end of Robert's trial when the judge's hands were tied by the law. The judge had focused in on the length of time between Robert killing Jennifer, and me killing him, suggesting that it made it difficult to prove that I'd just snapped. There was a lot of talk about intent, with the judge saying that if the jury believed that even if I only intended to cause grievous bodily harm to Robert, then they should return a guilty verdict for the murder charge. I'd followed Robert into an alleyway with a baseball bat. It was obvious to me that this would be seen as intent to cause grievous bodily harm. They only had to find me guilty or not guilty of murder, anyway. I'd already pled guilty to voluntary manslaughter, so if it was not guilty then I'd be sentenced for that charge anyway. No matter what they found, I knew I was going to prison.

I looked at the other side of the courtroom where the jury had filed back in and returned to their seats. Seven men, five women. I'd been watching them enough throughout the trial to work out that while there were some who were sympathetic, most of them weren't. I didn't fancy my chances with them no matter how good my lawyer was. The foreman was a hard-looking bloke who'd listened intently from day one. He was the only one who I'd never seen looking bored, tired, or disinterested. He sat there, ramrod straight, taking in every word. I thought he was maybe military from his short haircut and the way he held himself. If he wasn't on the jury I'd maybe have him down as a copper, but Toby had told me they weren't allowed to serve on juries.

The judge was in his usual position and looking over the top of his glasses at the jury foreman.

"Have you reached a verdict upon which you are all agreed?' the judge asked. "Please answer yes or no." The foreman nodded in response.

"Yes, we have, Your Honour."

"What is your verdict? Please answer only Guilty or Not Guilty." The foreman looked at me before speaking. I sat there, waiting, and I had never heard a more deafening silence in my entire life. It could only have been seconds, but it felt like a lifetime before he replied.


"Guilty."

**22**

---

Three months after I was sentenced, Paul Dewar came to see me for the first time. I was sitting in the recreation room watching television. I'd been transferred here, Her Majesty's Prison Whitemoor in Cambridgeshire, the same day I'd been sentenced. The prison was Category A, reserved for the worst of the worst. It had been dark by the time the van got here that evening, so I had no idea what the outside of the prison looked like and didn't really care. I wasn't going to be looking at it from the outside anytime soon.

The warder had only just reinstated television privileges after a fight between two prisoners over which channel to watch. One of them had wanted to watch *Britain's Got Talent*, the other one wanted to watch *The Voice*. I'd missed the fight itself as when it happened I was just sitting in my cell, not having the slightest bit of interest in either program. By all accounts the fight turned nasty pretty quickly. Blood was spilt. The warder's rules were clear. Any public disorder offences resulted in punishment for the whole wing. Most of the time this had the desired effect in that it was the wing population that policed itself, but the two prisoners who'd been scrapping were two of the biggest lads on the wing. No-one had fancied getting stuck in the middle of them.

There was a second-rate soap opera playing on the television. I was only watching it for something to do, not because I was that fussed about it, when I was interrupted by one of the prison officers.

"You've got a visitor, Mr Dawson," he said. I looked up, surprised. It was Mr McLoughlin. I didn't know what his first name was, but he was one of the more approachable guards. He was older than most of the guards, maybe mid to late forties, but he had a kinder face than most of them did, and I quite liked the bloke.

"Are you sure? I'm not expecting anyone today." I didn't really get that many visitors, not helped by the fact Whitemoor was an hour and a half from Norwich on a good day. It was only Andy or Jacob, and occasionally Tommy and David, but I always knew they were coming as they had to book the visits in advance. Big Joe had even been once, but never been back. According to Tommy, he still felt bad about having to roll over to the Old Bill with the phone messages. I'd tried to get a message to Big Joe via Tommy to say I was fine about it, that I would have done the same thing in his position, but he hadn't been back yet.

"Your visitor's a lawyer, so we let him in even though he's not booked in," Mr McLoughlin replied. "Not from your firm, though. His name's not on the list." He handed me a business card. I took it from him, turning it over in my fingers to read it. The card was very smooth, made from some sort of posh cardboard with a dimpled surface. The text on it read 'Paul Dewar' on one line, with 'Phoenix Trust' underneath. Both lines were written in a copper-plate handwriting font, but as I examined it I could see that it wasn't from a printer but proper handwriting. That was it. Just a name and a firm. No phone number, no e-mail address, no website.

"You're sure he's here to see me?" I asked again. "I've never heard of him or the Phoenix Trust."

"He's definitely here to see you. Even gave us your prisoner number to make sure he'd got the right guy." I got to my feet, figuring that talking to someone from the outside was much more preferable than vegetating in front of the television.

"Okay, lead on Mr McLoughlin."

The prison officer walked me to the visiting area, which was arranged like an examination room in a school, but with seats either side of each desk. He handed me a bright orange vest to put on as we walked through the door. Peeling magnolia paint covered the walls of the visiting area like most of the wing, and signs reminding everyone of the 'No Touching' rule were all over the walls. Not that many people took much notice of the rule, anyway. Another of the warder's punishments was a hard enforcement of this rule, along with strict searches. Everyone knew this dried up the inflow of life's little essentials on the inside, and it was one punishment that most of the prisoners dreaded. Personally, I wasn't bothered. I didn't do drugs and had no real need for anything from the outside world apart from the odd bit of cash to buy more cigarettes with. I was still off the smokes, but they were useful as currency on the inside.

"We had to put him in the visiting area as he's not on the approved lawyer list," Mr McLoughlin said, nodding toward a man sitting alone at a desk in the far corner of the room. I looked across at the man who was sitting calmly with his hands crossed on the desk in front of him.

A battered leather folio sat by the legs of the table. He seemed completely unfazed by being in a prison.

"I'll leave you to it," Mr McLoughlin said, walking off to join one of his colleagues on the other side of the room.

"Thanks," I called after him before crossing the room to meet my unexpected visitor. As I approached him, I examined him in more detail. He had to be in his late fifties, early sixties perhaps. Grey hair swept straight across his head, with a sharply defined widow's peak. He was wearing a suit. No surprise there. I'd never yet met a lawyer who didn't wear one, but as I got closer, I could see that it was a fine suit. Since Andy had bought me one to wear for my trial, I'd become quite the expert, and one of my idle daydreams was how many tailored suits I would buy when I got out. This Paul Dewar chap had a three-piece, double-breasted, finely dotted pinstripes over a navy-blue material. Very nice. He looked familiar, but I couldn't place him.

The lawyer looked up as I pulled the chair out from under the table on my side. He got to his feet, extending a hand.

"Mr Dawson, I presume?" he asked in a clipped South Coast accent. Not a local boy, then. I must have been mistaken about him being familiar as I didn't recognise his voice at all. I shook his hand, figuring that as he was a lawyer the prison officers wouldn't be too bothered about the rules.

"Yes, that's me," I replied. He had a firm handshake, and I had to resist the urge to stroke the material of his suit with my other hand. "You're Paul Dewar, I'm guessing?" He smiled at my reply, showing a row of perfect white teeth. They might have lived in a jar by his bed at night, I had no idea, but they gave him a reassuring smile. He was around my height, slightly less broad but still well built. As we sat down, I complimented him on his suit.

"Thank you," he replied. It was a retirement present to myself a few years ago. Holts of Saville Row." I didn't know who Holts were, but I'd heard of Saville Row so nodded to show my appreciation. "Except I never really retired properly, of course," he continued. If he had retired a couple of years ago, he had to be in his mid to late sixties, unless he had taken early retirement. I reassessed the man, impressed at the way he held himself. He looked like he could still pack a punch, that much was for sure.

We sat opposite each other for a few minutes in silence, him smiling at me and me looking back at him.

"So," I said, curiosity getting the better of me as I ended the little game we seemed to be playing. "What can I do for you?" He smiled again, the skin around his brown eyes wrinkling. "I'll be honest," I continued, putting his business card on the table between us. "I've never heard of you or the Phoenix Trust."

"No," he said, relaxing back in the chair and putting his hands flat on the table between us. I glanced down at what looked like a very expensive watch hiding under one of his cuffs. He splayed his hands on the table and I noticed a thick gold wedding band on his ring finger. I'd taken mine off to put in Jennifer's coffin the day we'd buried her and had regretted it ever since. "You don't know me, and very few people have heard of the Phoenix Trust." He steepled his fingers on the desk, his cuffs sliding back a couple of centimetres. Was that a Rolex? "They're rather, ah, what's the best term? Secretive? Yes, that'll do for the moment. They're rather secretive."

"So, what do they do? And what do they want with me?" I asked.

"We're getting ahead of ourselves, Gareth. May I call you Gareth?" he replied.

"Of course you can," I said, smiling at the formality of his request. "It's my name."

"Perhaps you could humour an old lawyer and talk me through where you are with your case? It'll all become clear, I promise." I looked at him, wondering where he was going with this. What the hell, I figured. It wasn't as if I'd got much else planned for the afternoon, and there was something quite endearing about the chap.

We spent the next thirty minutes going through my trial and the events leading up to it. Paul didn't take any notes. In fact, he hardly spoke at all except to ask the odd question when something wasn't clear to him. I opened up to him more than I had to anyone for a long time. I finished by telling him about the final stages of the trial, and about how my defence lawyer kind of fell apart and gave up at the end. Paul nodded as I said this.

"Yes, I thought so too," he said.

"You were there?" I asked, surprised. The penny dropped. That's where I knew him from. He'd been in the public gallery for the last couple of days of the trial. "You were there," I repeated, this time not as a question. "Why?"

"Call it professional curiosity, my old chap," he replied. "One thing I do like about Norwich is that there aren't many murder trials here. So when one came up," he paused for a second. "When your trial came up, I listened in to a bit of it."

"What did you think?" I asked him.

"About what? The trial, your defence lawyer, the verdict?"

"Well, all of it?"

"I didn't see the full trial, but I know the judge of old.

He's a good man. Very wise." Paul looked over my shoulder and beyond me. "Your defence? Not good, but public defenders often use cases such as yours to build their way to better things. Sad, but true." He looked at me directly, frowning. "And the verdict? Yes, in the eyes of the law it was the correct verdict. Assuming you did kill him."

His last statement threw me. What did he mean by that? I'd been convicted of murder. I was just about to ask him what he meant when he looked at his watch, nodded, and reached down for the briefcase. Assuming he was about to leave, I put a hand on his arm.

"Wait, please." I could see Mr McLoughlin frowning at me from his position on the other side of the room, so I removed my hand. "Don't go." Paul looked at me, balancing the briefcase on his lap and unbuckling it.

"Oh, I'm not going, my dear boy." He opened the case and reached in for a single sheet of paper. "But we need to change tack. Do you sail? Or rather, did you sail?"

"Er, no," I replied, confused by the sudden change in the topic.

"That's a shame. The Broads are lovely at this time of year what with the trees turning and everything." He put the piece of paper down on the table and returned his briefcase to its original position next to his leg. "Now, let's talk about the Phoenix Trust."

I sat back, relieved that he wasn't leaving. The truth was that I was enjoying talking to him. It wasn't just that he listened, but I didn't think he was judging me, either. Everyone else that I'd spoken to about my case in the last couple of months had judged me to one degree or another, but this rather odd man wasn't.

"The Phoenix Trust are, as I've said, rather reclusive. I'll be honest, until they approached me about your case I'd never heard of them," he said.

"Why did they approach you about my case? Who are they?" I leaned forward, intrigued.

"I can answer the first question, but I can't answer the second I'm afraid. One of the conditions of my being retained by them is that I don't try to find out who the people behind the Trust are, you see." He smiled, showing off his straight white teeth again. "I'm quite happy with that arrangement given how generous the terms of the agreement are." I frowned. I didn't understand.

"So why did they approach you about my case? You said you could answer that." Paul slid the paper round so I could read it as I asked this question. I scanned it as he spoke.

"They specialise in unusual cases, cases which are perhaps not as they seem. Such as yours." The paper was a lawyer engagement form. I'd signed one for Toby's firm to handle my appeal. Part of the form was a section releasing the lawyers handling the case. In the one I'd filled out before, this section was empty, but the piece of paper in front of me already had Toby's firm's details filled out.

"Sorry, Paul. I don't get this."

"It's a lawyer engagement form," he replied. He pointed at the section of the form I was looking at with Toby's firm's details. "This part releases your current lawyers." His finger moved to another section. "And this part transfers your case to my firm, such as it is. I am a one-man band at the moment, but I will bring additional resources to bear."

I frowned, re-reading the form in front of me.

"So, this form transfers my case to you?" I asked. His face lit up.

"Yes, precisely dear boy. That's exactly what it does. You sign that, and I am your new lawyer." I sat back, deflated, and pushed the piece of paper back at him. His face fell, and he looked at me, his disappointment obvious.

"Well it's a nice offer, Mr Dewar," I said, scraping my chair back a couple of inches. "But I'm going to have to refuse it. Thanks for coming to see me, and I'm sorry you've had a wasted journey." I got to my feet.

"Gareth, please, sit down," he pleaded. "Hear me out." I looked at him, trying to decide. This had to be some sort of scam. Taking on hopeless cases and fleecing people out of what little they had left. I was disappointed, not angry. I'd enjoyed talking to Paul, but I didn't have a penny to my name. I sat down, crossing my arms.

"Paul, I don't have any money. Not a brass button," I said. To my surprise, he laughed.

"Oh really, how delightful! Is that what you're worried about?" he asked. Now I was getting really confused. "You don't have to pay anything. Here, read this bit." He pointed at another block of text on the form that was in a much smaller font. I squinted as I tried to read it. The size and the language made it difficult to understand, but as I read it a couple of times, I realised that it said the Phoenix Trust would cover all expenses.

"There's a catch, right?" I asked Paul. "There has to be."

"No, no catch. The only stipulation is that you don't try to find out anything about the Phoenix Trust. The same agreement I've signed. They value their privacy, so to speak."

"But I still don't understand. Why my case?"

"They believe there are, now what was the word they used? Anomalies, that was it. Yes, they believe there are anomalies in your case that could be very useful in an appeal."

I stared at Paul. I was starting to get an idea of what

this was all about. The last time I'd spoken to Toby he was downbeat about the chances of even being able to mount an appeal, let alone have a chance of winning one. He'd even used the term 'bang to rights' at one point. If I hadn't liked the guy, I'd have slapped him for saying that.

"Gareth?" Paul said. I didn't reply, still trying to process the last hour or so. "Gareth?" I looked at him.

"They think you're innocent. Not only that, but they think we can prove it."

## 23

"David, it's Gareth," I said as soon as I heard the phone being answered. I wanted to keep the conversation short as I didn't have many minutes left on my phone card, and it wouldn't be topped up until next week. I pressed the earpiece hard against my ear to block out the ambient noise of the prison corridor.

"Hello, mate," David replied. His voice sounded gravelled as if he'd just woken up. It was almost three o'clock in the afternoon, so I guessed that this could be a possibility. "Everything okay? Me and Tommy are coming to see you this weekend."

"Oh, are you? Good stuff. Listen, David, could you do me a favour?"

"Of course I can, mate. You know that." His voice sounded brighter. "What can I do?"

"Have you got a pen and paper?" I could hear him shuffling around.

"Yep, I have," he replied a few seconds later.

"Could you have a look at something for me?" I didn't wait for him to reply. "There's a lawyer called Paul Dewar, lives in Norfolk somewhere I think but I don't know for sure. Can you look into his background for me?"

"Paul Dewar. Is that spelt D-E-W-A-R?" I looked at the card the lawyer gave me yesterday. The only thing that he had added to it was a mobile number on the reverse.

"Yep, that's right." I gave him the mobile number as well just in case it was useful. I paused, wondering for a couple of seconds whether to ask him to look into the Phoenix Trust as well, but I remembered Paul's warning and decided against it. Curious as I was, he'd been quite insistent. I listened as David repeated everything back to me.

"Nice one, David. You happy with that?" I asked him.

"No problem mate, leave it with me. I'll bring you what I get on Saturday. We're coming in the morning as Tommy's got us tickets for Carrow Road in the afternoon. Norwich against Sheffield United. Should be a good game."

"Cheers David, I'll speak to you then." I couldn't care less about Norwich City playing Sheffield United although there were many people on my wing who would care a lot. It was an unwritten rule that whenever Norwich was playing, the television in the recreation room was off and the radio was on. Withdrawal of radios when the football was on was perhaps the warder's most drastic punishment, and it hadn't happened in years apparently.

I spent the next couple of days itching to know what David had found out about Paul Dewar. I'd kept a copy of the re-engagement form that Paul had left with me and read it countless times. A couple of the older lags who knew their way around legal documents, or at least they said they did, had said they couldn't see anything wrong with it. Their reassurance didn't stop me being unsure about the whole thing, but the more I thought about it the more I realised that I didn't have anything to lose. Even so, it wouldn't hurt to check out Paul as much as I could, or at least as much as David could.

Saturday rolled around just like every other day in prison. Slowly. Very slowly. I was up early, keen to meet with David and Tommy even though getting up early wouldn't make them get here any sooner. Visiting time started at ten, and I knew they'd be there pretty much bang on time so they could get the visit out of the way and get back to Norwich for as much time in the pub as possible before the football started. When it got to ten o'clock, I was waiting by the entrance to the visiting room as the door was opened from the other side.

"Morning, Mr Dawson," Mr McLoughlin said as he opened the door. "You're keen this morning." He had a clipboard in his hand which he looked down at. "Your visitors are just in processing." I thanked him and followed him into the visitors' room, fumbling my way into the orange vest Mr McLoughlin had given me. A couple of other prisoners entered the room behind me, so I made my way to the far end of the room. Not far away from the table I'd sat at with Paul.

After a few minutes' wait, the door on the other side of the room opened and Tommy walked through, followed by David who was holding a bunch of papers in his hand. Tommy looked around the room and when he saw me, waved and made his way over. They both sat down, David offering a hand for a handshake which I had to decline as Mr McLoughlin was watching us. David's face fell as I shook my head at him, but it brightened back up when I pointed to the sign on the wall with its bright red, angry capital letters.

"Not allowed mate, sorry," I said.

"I know, I know," he replied. "Bloody forgot." David

leaned forward with an excited look on his face. I knew he'd found something and was desperate to find out what, but I didn't want the prison officers to think I was planning something. We made small talk for a few minutes, caught up on some local gossip. Tommy gave me an update on the business, which to my surprise seemed to be doing well without me. I'd had to sign the whole thing over to him as I figured not many people would use a company whose CEO was inside for murder. Tommy promised me he'd keep my share of the profits separate for when I got out. Whether he'd keep them separate for fifteen years, I doubted somehow. I figured the first time things went south my share would be the first pot that got dipped into.

Once I was sure that none of the guards were paying much attention, I turned to David.

"So, David," I said in a low voice. "What have you got, mate?" His face lit up with a broad smile as he put some papers on the table, spreading them out so I could read them. I leaned forward, my hands clasped behind my back. It was probably overkill. I doubted that the guards would rush over if I picked up a piece of paper, but better safe than sorry. The first couple of sheets I looked at were a CV for Paul Dewar. He was indeed a lawyer, with a law degree from Oxford. I went there once, and it all looked a bit posh, so that was good enough for me. Paul had an impressive stack of letters after his name, a whole bunch of alphabet soup I couldn't understand. They looked impressive, though. He'd worked in a bunch of firms in London, none of which I recognised, and had spent the last ten years of his career running his own firm called 'Broadland Legal' in Norwich before retiring two years ago. I'd heard of the firm but didn't know anything about it until I read the next sheet.

It summarised the business from start to finish, and it

looked as though when he'd retired the company had wound up. There were six partners, including Paul, and their names were listed. My eyes were drawn to a section marked 'Turnover' towards the bottom of the page. I sucked in a sharp breath.

"Six million pounds?" I said. "Is turnover the same as profit?"

"Kind of," David replied. "I looked it up," he continued, looking pleased with himself. "That's the amount of money they had coming in, but it doesn't include money going out." This confused me, so I asked David to explain. "For things like rent, electricity, stuff like that. But what's left over would get split between them, wouldn't it?" I did some rough sums in my head. The address of the office had been right in the middle of the city, so wouldn't have been cheap, and they must have had more staff than just the partners, but even so. Paul must have been pulling in close to a million pounds a year. No wonder he had a nice suit on. I figured it must have been a Rolex on his wrist after all.

"Wow," I said. "That's lottery money wages, that is." Both Tommy and David laughed.

"Bet you wish you'd studied more at school now, don't you?" Tommy chuckled. "Well you and me both, mate."

"Okay, ready for the next lot?" David said. I nodded, and he gathered up the pieces of paper before replacing them with different sheets. I leaned forward again and examined them.

"What have we got here then?" I asked.

"I've called it a 'Character Assessment'," David said, the pride obvious in his voice. Sure enough, the first piece of paper I looked at had those words in capital letters on the top of it. Underneath it was a list of websites. "They're the websites he visits the most. Nothing naughty there, all quite boring. It looks like he enjoys keeping fish and foot-ball. He's a Norwich fan as well. Had a season ticket there for years, but in the Jarrold Stand." Tommy laughed as David said this.

"Yeah, well," Tommy said. "I couldn't see him in the Snakepit, somehow. Slagging off the opposition in a posh voice." The Snakepit was a small corner of the Carrow Road Stadium which was particularly vocal, and not shy about language. David pointed at the next sheet of paper.

"They're his financials. He's got a cracking credit score, and the best part of half a million quid floating about in various accounts."

"You hacked into his bank record?" I asked, looking up at David.

"No, they're screen grabs from when he was doing his banking online," he replied. "He's got more than one offshore account, but I couldn't get any information on them. They're in the Canary Islands or something like that."

"Cayman Islands, mate." Tommy leaned into the conversation. "Not the Canary Islands, they're off the coast of Spain." The two of them bickered about whether the Canary Islands were closer to Spain or Portugal, but I tuned them out as I turned my attention to the next sheet of paper.

As I read a whole bunch of text with a load of medical sounding words, I started to get a sinking feeling about what I was reading.

"David, please tell me these aren't his medical records?"

"Er, well, yeah. Of course they are," he said. "He's in good nick for his age, though. Not about to drop dead if that's what you're worried about."

"I hope I'm half as fit at his age," Tommy added. "If I

get to his age, that is." David glanced at him, uncertain for a second, before breaking into laughter. I ignored him, looking at a list of medication that Paul was taking. I recognised a few of the names, but most of them might as well have been in Greek. It wasn't a long list of tablets, though.

"What's this one?" I asked David, pointing at the next sheet across. It had tiny writing on it, no chance of me being able to read it properly without a magnifying glass. David reached across and swivelled the paper round.

"That's his will, that one," he replied, stabbing his index finger at the paper. "But you're not in it, so you've lucked out there. Whatever's left is getting split among his nieces and nephews." I stared at him, incredulous. He prodded the last bit of paper. "That's a summary. It's all I've got." Apart from his medical and financial records, I thought as I looked at the last sheet. It was a printout of a spreadsheet, and not much more than a list of columns.

"What is this?" I asked.

"That's the title." He pointed at the first column. "That's the username or login." His finger moved across the columns before coming to rest on the last one. "And that's the password."

"For what?" I asked, scanning the list. David didn't reply, and I looked up at him. He stared back at me for a few seconds.

"Er," he replied. "For everything. Whatever he does on the internet, they're the logins and passwords for it. I've not gone as far as looking into his shopping history, but I can if you want me to?"

"Jesus, David," I said. "I asked you to have a look at him, not hack his entire life." David's face fell, and he looked like a disappointed spaniel. I caught the look on his face and felt bad. "But this, my friend." I pointed at the paperwork in front of us with my index finger. "This is absolute gold. You are a star." His expression returned to where it had been a few minutes before, and a smile split his face.

"I did a good job, did I?" he asked, grinning.

"Oh yes, you did," I replied, returning the smile.

"Cool. Great. Need a piss." He got to his feet without another word and wandered back toward the visitors' door. Tommy looked at me, also smiling.

"Man, he's something else," he said. "He was chuffed to bits with being asked to look into that lawyer, you know that?" I didn't know that but thought I knew why he was pleased. It would have felt, to David, as if he was doing something for Jennifer. Which he was, even if it was indirectly.

"I wasn't expecting that much information. How the hell did he get all of that?" I asked Tommy.

"Yeah, like he'd tell me that," he replied with a laugh. "Even if he told me, I wouldn't bloody understand it, anyway." I smiled. Tommy was right. The few times I had spoken to David about technological stuff he'd lost me in jargon within seconds. Tommy was telling me about a new client he was working on when David came back to the table.

"Those toilets are bleak, aren't they?" he said as he sat down.

"Have they run out of potpourri again?" I said. "I'll have a word with the maitre'd, get him to sort it out." David looked at me, confused until he realised I was joking.

"Yeah, they have. It ruins the ambience," he said, looking at us with an expectant face that both Tommy and I recognised. We both laughed, which was exactly what David was hoping for.

Tommy and David didn't stop for long. As I suspected, they were keen to get away for the football match. Or rather, to get away to the pub to prepare for the football match. Knowing Tommy, this would involve a large amount of lager and a burger of some description. I'd given the paperwork back to David to take away with him. Not the sort of thing I wanted the prison officers to find, really. I left the visitors' room after they had gone and went back to my cell for a while to think about what David had uncovered.

As I stood in line for the phone about half an hour later, I thought I had four or maybe five minutes left on my phone card. Plenty of time to speak to Paul Dewar and ask him a few pointed questions. He answered the phone even before the second ring had finished.

"Hello? Is that Gareth?" his voice was muffled, and he sounded almost out of breath. I wondered for a second what he'd been doing before realising that he could have no idea it was me on the phone. I was calling from a prison pay phone, which I knew for a fact would have come up as an 'unknown number'.

"How did you know it was me?" I asked, caught unawares.

"Well who else would it be?" he replied, a sharp edge to his voice. "You're the only person who's got this mobile number." I paused, trying to think on my feet and not doing particularly well at it. Paul continued. "I would imagine, seeing as your friends Tommy and David have just left, that you now know all about me?" I remained silent. How did he know they'd just left? Did he have a contact at the prison? It wouldn't take much for one of the guards to let him know when Tommy and David had gone. Probably about a tenner. "You can't kid a kidder, Gareth. I watched your young friend trawl his way around the areas of my private life I was prepared to let him have access to, and I resisted the temptation to knock on his electronic front door as it were." I felt a smile creep across my face. This man was no fool.

"So," Paul continued. "I imagine that now you know how much money I've got, you're phoning me up to ask me why I'm getting involved." I started to say something, but he cut me off. "Because I'm quite obviously not in it for the money. How am I doing so far?" I nodded, not realising that he wouldn't be able to see me. He was angry, no doubt about that. "I could put the phone down now and walk away. Leaving you where you are, for the next fifteen fucking years." I flinched at him swearing, not because I was shocked by the language, but because hearing him swearing surprised me. I could feel my fingers tightening on the handset of the phone. This phone call wasn't turning out at all how I'd expected it to. We both remained silent for maybe a full minute. I was racking my brains for something, aware that my time was limited when Paul broke the impasse. "Anything to say, young man?"

"Er," I stumbled over the word. "Er, sorry?" To my surprise, Paul started chuckling before it developed into a full-blown laughing fit that left him coughing. When he'd got his composure back again, he carried on.

"Good lad, good lad. Right then, I'll be there in twenty minutes."

## 24

"You're in the lawyer's room this time," Mr McLoughlin said as he opened the door for me. I'd been in there several times before with Toby for various depressing discussions. I wasn't sure how Paul had wangled getting in there when he wasn't my lawyer just yet.

"How come?" I asked.

"Warder said so," Mr McLoughlin replied. "I wouldn't argue." He smiled as I walked past him into the room. "They'll be here a few minutes." They? I was expecting Paul, but he'd not said anything about bringing anyone with him. I sat on the chair and tried to relax. This room was different to the main visiting area. The chairs were padded. There was no graffiti carved on the table, no cameras in the corner of the room, and no posters on the walls. The only thing that made it different to a normal room in a house was the reinforced glass in the doors, and the fact that the doors were about eight inches thick. I could see shadows moving behind the thickened window, and the door opened. Paul walked in, followed by a young woman. Behind them, I could see two of the larger guards doing what they did best, which was hang around looking big and ugly.

"Mr Dawson, how are you?" Paul smiled, extending his hand and shaking mine like we'd not seen each other for years. "Thank you so much for seeing us at such short notice." Yeah, right, I thought. I found a space in my diary to see you. He turned and gestured to the young woman who'd walked in with him. She had a battered leather briefcase clutched across her chest and looked, in a word, terrified. "This is Laura Flynn, my assistant." I shook her hand and watched her eyes dart around the room. As we sat down I had to resist the temptation to wipe my hand down the side of my trouser leg. I've heard the saying 'horses sweat, ladies glow' but the poor woman's palms were definitely sweating.

Paul sat down, put his briefcase on the table, and flipped open the lid. He pulled out some paperwork and set the briefcase beside him on the floor.

"Right," he said. "This is another copy of the same paperwork I gave you last time we met. The paperwork that signs your case, and the appeal, over to me." I looked down at the papers which he'd swivelled around for me to read. The top one had my details, and Paul's, already filled out with the date. The only thing left were three boxes for signatures. One for me, one for Paul, and one for a witness. That explained Laura's attendance, at least. Paul pulled a fancy looking pen out of his pocket and set it on top of the paper.

"Well then, Gareth," Paul said. He glanced at his colleague for a second. "Ignoring your friend Mr French's little indiscretion, do you have any questions for me before we sign this off?"

I had a million questions, but none that needed answering right at that moment. I picked up the pen. It was heavier than I was expecting it to be, jet black with a white blob on the end of the cap. When I unscrewed the cap, I realised it was a fountain pen instead of a normal biro. I'd not written with a nib since I was at school, but gave it a go, anyway. I pulled the top sheet of paper toward me and scribbled a rough approximation of my signature in the box next to my name. It would have to do. Paul took the pen from me and signed in his box, a flamboyant signature with plenty of loops and whorls despite his normal sounding name. He pushed the paper to Laura and handed her the pen. I looked at her as she stuck her tongue slightly out of her mouth when she signed, and I tried not to smirk. She looked at me when she'd finished signing, and I could tell from the way she frowned and her tongue disappeared that I'd failed.

"Could I have the lid back?" Paul asked. I realised that I was holding the cap of the pen in my hand and gave it back to him. "I would say keep the pen, but it was rather expensive, and I don't think you'd be allowed to hang onto it." He tucked it back out of sight inside his suit jacket and shuffled the paperwork together before returning it to his briefcase. "There'll be more paperwork to sign in due course, but it'll have to wait until Laura's drafted it." I glanced across at Laura as Paul mentioned her name. "Now," he continued. "We'll be here for a while, so why don't I see if I can rustle up a cup of tea for us all." Paul got to his feet and opened the door to the room. I was amazed it was open as I'd assumed that the prison officers always locked it. Obviously not. Paul disappeared through the door, leaving it open, and I could hear him talking to Mr McLoughlin.

I looked at Laura. She was the first woman I'd seen in months, so I guess you could say that this is what made her attractive, but it was more than that. She had fine brown hair, cut in a bob that extended down to her shoulders, and a simple business suit that was so dark it was almost black. The cream blouse underneath her jacket matched her pale face. I looked as her eyes darted from me to the open door, and back again. She didn't look any less terrified than she had when she'd walked in. If anything, she looked even more scared.

"Are you okay?" I asked, trying to sound normal, reassuring even. I guessed that this was probably her first time in prison. Or at least this far inside one. She stared back at me, her pale green eyes wide open.

"Oh God, I'm sorry. I'm so nervous," she blurted out. "I can't believe I'm sitting in a prison." Her voice fell away as she looked at me. "Er, with you I mean."

"With a convicted murderer, you mean?" To my surprise, she laughed at me, and as she smiled I saw dimples appear in her cheeks.

"Okay, yes. I'm sitting in a room, in a prison, with a convicted murderer and my boss has buggered off to get a cup of bloody tea." I laughed as well because when it was put like that it was actually quite funny. "Sorry," she said. "It's just all unexpected, that's all. He just said 'Laura, come with me'. Didn't tell me where we were going or anything. It wasn't until we turned into Knox Road I realised we were going to the prison." I bet someone in the local council was having a right chuckle when he came up with that name for the road that led to the prison.

"Have you worked for him for long?" I asked her.

"Two weeks," she replied. "I only graduated from Law School three weeks ago. Had a week off in the Lake District with my boyfriend and started with Mr Dewar straight away. He hired me on the recommendation of my tutor. They've known each other for years, apparently. Mr Dewar told him he had a big case coming up."

I thought about what she'd said for a few minutes. That meant that, unless Paul had another case on the go, he'd hired Laura before he'd even come to see me. He must have been sure I'd sign on the dotted line but then again, why wouldn't I?

"What, this case?" I asked her, trying to get it straight in my mind.

"Yes, your case," she replied. "That's all he's got on at the moment." We both turned to look at the door as Paul reappeared, followed by Mr McLoughlin who was carrying three cups of tea. As mine was put in front of me, the prison officer mumbled something.

"Don't get used to it, Mr Dawson," I heard him say in a gruff voice, but his half smile was a giveaway.

"Thank you," I said as he walked out of the room, and we waited until the door was firmly closed. I didn't hear it being locked though, which again surprised me.

"Gareth, I'm now representing you as your lawyer, and the lovely young Laura here will be helping me out." I took a sip of my tea, grimacing at the lack of sugar. "Happy so far?" Paul asked.

"Yep," I replied. "No sugar, but I'll live with it." They both smiled at me before Paul carried on.

"Right then. Let's get down to it. Now, we're protected by lawyer-client privilege, so you can say anything at all to us. Even if it's incriminating, do you understand?" I nodded as he reached back into his bag before pulling out a small digital tape recorder, a normal biro, and a small notebook. Paul put the recorder on the table in front of us and handed the notebook and pen to Laura. She flipped over the cover of the notebook and got ready to take notes as Paul pressed a button on the recorder to start it up.

"Did you kill Robert Wainwright?" he asked. I almost

choked on my tea at the question. Talk about getting right to the point.

"No, I didn't," I replied, wiping my mouth with the back of my hand.

"But you did clatter him with the baseball bat?"

"Yes, I did. I admitted that at the trial. I pled guilty to manslaughter, for God's sake."

"I know you did, my dear chap," Paul said. "But bear with me. So, you admit that you hit him with the baseball bat?"

"Yes, that's correct," I replied. Paul waited until Laura finished writing.

"How many times did you hit him?"

"Once."

"Put that into a sentence, would you?" Paul asked. I looked at him, uncertain.

"I hit Robert Wainwright — once — with a baseball bat." It sounded like I was playing Cluedo. Paul watched Laura write my reply down and then took the pen and notebook from her. He underlined part of her final sentence and turned the notebook around so I could read it. Laura's handwriting didn't really match her appearance. The letters were almost block capitals, more like a man's writing than a woman's. I read the final line.

"I hit Robert Wainwright <u>once</u> with a baseball bat." Paul pointed at the underlined word 'once' with the tip of the pen.

"That, dear boy, is your entire appeal in one word."

## 25

Another Saturday, another round of visitors. It was three weeks since Paul and Laura had visited, and I'd not heard anything from them since. I'd not seen Andy or Jacob for ages either, so when I found out Jennifer's family would be visiting it had lifted my spirits for the whole week.

I walked into the visitors' room, put my orange bib on, and made my way to the table where Jacob was sitting. There was no sign of Andy. As I approached, Jacob got to his feet, and we nodded at each other. He was looking well, dressed in a tight t-shirt that showed off tanned, muscular arms. My upper arms weren't in bad shape, but even I wouldn't show them off like that. If they looked like his though, I might well consider it. He was looking good.

"Hello, mate," I said. "How are you doing?" Jacob sat back down, a smile on his face.

"I'm fine, Gareth," he replied. "More to the point, how are you? You're looking thinner. Is that on purpose?" I smiled but didn't answer his question.

"Is your Dad not coming today?" I asked. "I thought I saw his name on the list."

"He's just in the toilet," Jacob replied. "We took longer to get here than I thought it would. I thought I would have to stop off in a lay-by and let him out for a pee at one point."

"How's he getting on?"

"Not great, Gareth," Jacob said. "I'm worried about him, to be honest. He's just got no, I don't know how to describe it, no life in him anymore." I didn't know what to say to that, so kept silent. "He's just moved house though, so I'm hoping that once he's settled in, he'll be happier."

"Where's he moved to?" I asked.

"Sheringham of all places," Jacob said with a laugh. I knew the town well, and it was in a lovely part of the country. One of the few happy memories of my childhood I had was going on holiday there. I'm not sure how old I would have been — probably only seven or eight — but I remember looking for crabs when the tide had gone out and getting my legs soaked. My mum had been furious and the smack she gave me hurt a lot more than the nips from the crabs I'd found.

"Very nice," I said. "Let me guess, sea view?" Jacob laughed harder as he replied.

"Oh yes. It's supposed to be a flat, but it's bigger than your old place and mine put together. Right on top of the hill, fantastic views out over the sea."

"That doesn't surprise me," I said. One of the best things about the North Norfolk coast was the sky. For some reason, there seemed to more of it than anywhere else in the country. I tried to imagine what it would be like to have a flat right on the coast. What it would be like to sit with a glass of beer watching the sea, not a care in the world. If I was going to buy a flat in Sheringham, I'd make sure it was

one with a sea view. "Does he know many people up that
way then? I thought most of his friends are in Norwich?"

"We'd better change the subject, mate," Jacob said,
nodding over my shoulder. "Dad's here." I got to my feet
and turned to greet Andy.

"It's great to see you, Andy," I said. Jacob was right.
Andy had changed. He looked drawn, almost gaunt. It
seemed that I wasn't the only one who had lost weight.
"Thanks for coming in, I really do appreciate it." Andy
shook his head as I said this.

"Gareth, please. I feel bad enough for not coming to
visit more often, and you saying that only makes me feel
worse." Andy had visited me more often than anyone else,
but he wouldn't know that.

"Dad's been moving house," Jacob said, looking at
Andy. "That's why he's been so busy."

"Oh right, I didn't know you were moving. Where have
you moved to?" I asked. Jacob obviously didn't want Andy
to know we'd already had this conversation, so I played
along.

"I've moved into a flat in Sheringham, close to the
seafront," Andy replied with a faint smile. "It's a nice little
place," Andy sighed. The way Jacob had described it made
it sound far from little. "To be honest, there was nothing
left in the old house for me, not anymore." I watched as
the smile faded from his face.

"Plus, it's on the ground floor," Jacob said, grinning.
"He was having trouble getting up the stairs." Andy
laughed and mimed hitting Jacob round the back of the
head.

"Yeah, course I was. Needed to be closer to the toilet
for that four o'clock in the morning pee. I can't start, and
then once I do, I can't stop." He laughed as he said this,
and for a few seconds the Andy I knew of old was back. It

was good to see him laugh, and I silently thanked Jacob for turning the conversation back round. I guessed he'd had a fair bit of practice at doing that.

The three of us sank into an easy conversation, talking about everything and nothing. It wasn't like the conversations I had with the other prisoners, or even the prison officers, as there was no nonsense. No hidden agendas, no ulterior motives. It was just three men with something in common that wasn't the fact we were in prison. It was that we'd all loved Jennifer. And we'd all lost her, but we were careful not to talk about that. After fifteen minutes or so, Jacob put an index finger in the air and reached into the pocket on the back of his jeans.

"I almost forgot," he said as he pulled a folded piece of paper out and lay it flat on the table, unfolded. Written across the top of it were the words 'INFORMATION WANTED' in large, black letters. Underneath this was a photograph of me. It looked like a still from the camera that had caught me coming out of the alleyway the night Robert died. Below my photograph was the text 'Did you see this man?' I scanned through the paragraph that followed, which was an appeal for anyone who might have seen me on the evening that Robert was killed. The text ended with 'Call Laura on' and a telephone number.

"Right, okay," I said slowly. I was surprised that Tommy or David hadn't told me about this, but then I'd not talked to either of them for a couple of weeks. "Is there a reward?"

"Don't know for certain," Jacob said. "But one of my mates heard it's ten grand." Ouch. Ten thousand pounds was a hefty reward. I wondered if that was ten grand for information leading to a successful appeal, or just for information. It had to be for the former, but even so, every nutter in Norwich would come out of the woodwork to claim that. "Can you get the Eastern Daily Press in here, Gareth?" Jacob asked.

"Er, yeah we can. We have to order it in though, and pay for it," I replied.

"There'll be a piece on the case this week, off the back of this poster. My other half works for the publishers," Jacob explained. "He's not sure when it'll come out, but it'll be this week at some point."

"Can we get it for you?" Andy asked. "Order it on your behalf? I'm guessing your hourly rate isn't brilliant."

"No, I wish that was how it worked," I laughed. "I've got a bit stashed away in my off-shore account, so should be able to stretch to getting the EDP for the week." I re-read the poster and jabbed at it with a finger. "Where did you get this from then?"

"There's one on almost every tree and lamp post in Thorpe St Andrew, mate," Jacob said. "And the pubs, the shops. There's even one in the fish and chip shop on Yarmouth Road."

"What's happening with your appeal and these new lawyers then, Gareth?" Andy asked, tearing me away from a brief daydream about battered sausage and chips from a chippy. It didn't have to be the one on Yarmouth Road, any chippy would have done. I paused before replying. There wasn't much to say.

"Not a lot, to be honest. At least, I didn't think there was, but then I'd not known about these posters." I'd told Andy about the appeal in a rushed phone call just after I'd signed the paperwork a few weeks ago. "I've not heard anything back from Paul Dewar at all." I saw Jacob frown. "He's the lawyer chap," I explained. "It's his firm that's now in charge of the appeal."

"What firm is it?" Andy asked.

"The Phoenix something or other," I replied. "Or

that's the name of the lot that are funding it." Jacob looked across at Andy, and I considered telling them what David had found out about Paul before deciding against it. "I didn't know there was a reward out, that's for certain."

We chatted for a while before visiting time ended. Andy told me more about his new flat, which sounded really nice. He promised to bring in some pictures for me to look at the next time he visited, which he said would be soon. When the bell rang to signal the end of visiting time, I was disappointed. I'd really enjoyed talking with them both. As they got to their feet, both Andy and Jacob said they would come and visit again, as soon as they could.

Once I'd handed in the high-visibility vest, I made my way back to my cell. As I sat on the edge of the bed, I unfolded the piece of paper with the appeal for information and spread it out on the table. I wasn't that concerned about it being contraband, as it was only a piece of paper, but even so hanging on to it was against the rules.

I was reading the text on the paper again when my cell door swung open and two of the biggest bastards I'd seen in years lumbered their way into my cell.

## 26

"Who the fuck are you?" I was on my feet in an instant, fists bunched, the piece of paper forgotten. I'd gone from being fairly relaxed to being prepared for a scrap in less than a second. Looking at the two gorillas in my cell, this would not be a scrap I would come out of on top. They were both very, very big lads, and that is no understatement. Well over six feet, the pair of them, broad shouldered, not gym big but just big. They could have been brothers, and as I looked at them a bit more closely, I realised that they probably were. I had no idea where Mac was, but given the size of these two, he wouldn't have been much help, anyway.

Neither of them replied to my question, so I repeated it. "I said, who the fuck are you?" They both just looked at me with impassive expressions, and a few seconds later the one nearest the door moved to let a third man walk into my cell. It was getting cosy.

"Mr Dawson?" the new arrival asked. He was nowhere near the size of the other two, but he carried himself with the air of a man who was used to being in charge. Aged late forties at a guess, his grey hair was cut almost to the skin in a crew cut. He didn't have the pallor of long term prisoners or any prison tattoos. I was sure that if I'd seen him and his two monkeys wandering around Whitemoor, I would have noticed them. I said nothing but just stared at him. "You are Mr Dawson?" he repeated his question, and I caught a clipped accent. Not an English one.

"Who wants to know?" I replied, trying to make myself look as menacing as I could. Given the circumstances, it was the only thing I could do. The man just laughed in reply, but I didn't think it was with any trace of humour.

"I do, Mr Dawson. You don't have to be so defensive." I tried to place his accent. Polish, maybe? "May I sit down?" My visitor gestured toward the only chair in the room and, when I nodded, sat down. The other two rearranged themselves on either side of him and he pointed at my bed. "Please, sit down. I only want to have a, how do you say it, a chat?"

I sat on the bed, feeling slightly less apprehensive but not by much. The fact that this gentleman had brought two bodyguards along for a 'chat' meant that either a lot of people wanted to kill him so he needed the protection, or he wanted to threaten someone. In this case, me. Neither option was very palatable.

"My name is Mr Demeter, but please, call me Gejza. This is Lasho," he said, pointing over his left shoulder, "and Yoska." He pointed at the other gorilla. I looked back and forth between the two of them. They stared back at me, expressionless. "And you are Mr Dawson, yes?"

"I think you know I am. Sorry, what was your name? Gejza?" I replied, grim-faced.

"Yes, that's correct. You almost pronounced it correctly, which is unusual," he said. "It's more of an 's' sound than a 'z'." He looked at me with his eyebrows raised, so I said

his name again. With more of an 's' sound. "Perfect,"
Gejza laughed. "Now, Mr Dawson, we need to have a chat
about a friend of yours."

"Who?" I replied.

"Robert Wainwright."

"He's hardly a friend of mine. You know why I'm in
here, I take it?"

"Yes, I do," Gejza said. "You murdered him." I
thought for a second about correcting him and pointing
out that although I'd been convicted of his murder, I didn't
kill him. We looked at each other for a few seconds before
he continued. "I used to work for a gentleman called Mr
Caran. Now I work for another gentleman who took over
Mr Caran's business interests after a disagreement back in
Romania. Your friend," he put his fingers in the air and
mimed air quotes around the word 'friend'. "Well, Mr
Wainwright owed my new employer quite a lot of money."

"What's that got to do with me?" I asked.

"Well, it's got everything to do with you. Where I come
from, where we come from, a debt doesn't die when a
person dies." He narrowed his eyes. "It gets transferred."

"Transferred? Where?" I said.

"To you."

"Well, that's bollocks."

"No, I'm sorry. Not in this case. The debt is outstand-
ing, and if you hadn't killed Mr Wainwright, then it would
have been re-paid. Therefore, it's now your responsibility,"
he replied. I still thought it was bollocks, and I told him so.

"Look, Gejza," I said, emphasising the 'z' just to annoy
him. "Robert Wainwright has nothing to do with me.
Whatever he owes you, or your employer, is none of my
business." Gejza looked up at one of his gorillas, either
Lasho or Yoska, I had no idea which one, and then back
at me.

"I'm afraid you're wrong, Mr Dawson," Gejza said, almost in a whisper. "That's not how it works where I come from." I considered telling him that in this country, at least, what worked where he came from didn't mean shit, but thought better of it.

"How much are you talking about?" I asked. When he told me, I let out a low whistle. That was a lot of money.

"Well I'm sorry to disappoint you, Gejza," I said. "But even if I was liable for that amount of money, which I'm not, there's no way I could pay it. I don't have any money." I sat back on my bed and regarded my visitor. "And my earning potential is a bit limited for a while. So, I think you'll have to forget about that debt. Write it off to experience perhaps?"

"I don't think so, Mr Dawson," Gejza said. I saw his gaze shift over my shoulder and rest on something on the wall behind me. The only thing on the wall was a photograph of Jennifer. "If you can't pay, then we will have to take payment another way." The threat hung between us for a few seconds, and I stared at the man sitting opposite me.

"That's a photo of my wife you're looking at," I said. He paused for a few seconds before replying.

"She's beautiful," he said, almost whispering. "It would be such a shame if anything happened to her while you were in here."

I looked at the man who was threatening my wife. My dead wife. He obviously didn't know she was dead, and I considered my next step. I could say nothing about what had happened to Jennifer, let him find out for himself. I could tell him, but I couldn't see how that would help in the slightest. What I really wanted to do was to launch myself off the bed and attack him. I knew it wouldn't last long and that his two gorillas would be on top of me in seconds, but if I got one good punch in it would be worth a kicking. As if he knew what I was considering, Gejza got to his feet and moved to stand between his bodyguards.

"Have a think about things, Mr Dawson," he said. "Work out what the best way ahead is for you." His eyes flicked back to the picture of Jennifer, and I pushed my hands against the bed, springing to my feet. The second I did that, Gejza took a step back and the two gorillas both stepped forward in a choreographed move that left me looking between their shoulders at the smaller man. "I'll be in touch," Gejza said as he turned to walk out of my cell. His bodyguards followed him and as he got to the door, he said something else which I didn't understand. It wasn't in English.

Out of the corner of my eye, I caught a flash of movement from the gorilla nearest me. By the time I'd realised what was going on, it was too late to do anything to avoid the fist coming towards my face.


There was a flash of white light, a brief split second of pain, then everything went black.

## 27

I was lying on the bed in my cell, reading a book, when the sound of the cell door opening made me jump. I looked at the door, wondering if my unexpected guests from the previous day had come back to see me, but it wasn't them. I'd spent most of yesterday afternoon in the prison infirmary with a tampon in each nostril, but apart from a splitting headache and faint bruising underneath each of my eyes, there was no permanent damage, according to the duty doctor at least. A succession of prison officers had interviewed me in the infirmary, but I'd not deviated from the 'walked into a door' story. None of them believed it, but, no-one pressed me too hard for the truth. I folded the corner of the page I was reading to mark my place and got to my feet just as Mr McLoughlin walked into my cell.

"Your legal team is here to see you, Mr Dawson," he said.

"Are they? I wasn't expecting them today."

"Well, they're here," Mr McLoughlin replied, looking irritated. "Are you coming or not?" He walked out of my cell and I followed him onto the walkway. We walked in silence to the door at the end of the block. I wanted to ask him if he was okay, but he didn't seem in the mood for idle chit-chat. Of all the prison officers, he was the one who I got on the best with. I guess our relationship was about as close to a friendship as it was possible for a convicted murderer and a prison officer to have. He seemed deep in thought as we walked through the corridors to the lawyer's room. Was he pissed off that I'd not told them who had attacked me in my cell? While we stood waiting for the door to be opened from the control room, I decided to break the silence.

"Are you okay, Mr McLoughlin?" I asked. His solemn expression changed to one of surprise, and I wondered if I'd made a mistake.

"I'm fine," he said sharply. His face then softened. "But thank you for asking." We stood in silence for a few seconds. "You're not though, are you?"

I sighed. This wasn't a conversation I wanted to have.

"I told your colleagues, Mr McLoughlin. I walked into a—" He cut me off with a sharp laugh.

"Of course you did. And I'm playing up front for Norwich City this weekend." He held up a hand at the prison officer who was about to open the door from the control room. "Look, I know you can't tell me what happened. Or at least, you can't be seen to tell me what happened. But at the end of the day, you were attacked on my wing when I wasn't on duty. And that pisses me off." He paused, looking at me with a hard stare. "But I will find out what happened." There was another uncomfortable silence before he nodded at the control room window. With a metallic thump, the door to the lawyer's room swung open and he pointed inside the room. I walked into the room, and the door swung shut behind me.

Paul and Laura both got to their feet as I entered the room.

"Gareth, my dear boy," Paul said. "How are things?" he asked as he shook my hand. "My God, whatever's happened to your face?"

"Nothing, nothing at all," I replied.

"That doesn't look like nothing, Gareth. Are you in trouble?" I could see him examining my swollen nose and black eyes.

"Not too bad," I replied. "I didn't know you were coming." Paul shot a dark look at Laura, who was staring at my ruined face with her mouth open.

"Yes, sorry," she mumbled. I felt bad as I hadn't wanted to get Laura in trouble. Maybe she had should have organised the visit, but hadn't?

"Laura, good to see you." I extended a hand to Laura, which she looked at for a few seconds before shaking it. I flashed her a quick smile, hoping that she would return it and I would get a glimpse of her dimples.

"Gareth," she replied in a muted voice. No smile for me today.

"I'm just glad my secretary arranged my meetings so that there was a free slot in my diary for you both," I said, attempting to lighten the atmosphere. I looked at Laura as I said this and saw a brief smile appear on her face. Not broad enough to show her dimples, but it was something.

We all sat down, and Laura pulled a notepad and manila folder from her briefcase. She was wearing the same business suit I'd seen her in before, but this time with a satin green blouse that threw me completely. I was taken back to a day with Jennifer in the large Marks & Spencer in the middle of Norwich. She was trying to find something to wear for a job interview and had found a green blouse just like the one Laura was wearing. It must've been the fifth or sixth blouse that Jennifer had tried on that day, and by that time I was happy to say anything she tried on looked amazing.

"Gareth?" Paul's voice snapped me out of my daydream. I realised that I'd been staring at Laura's blouse, and that she had pulled her jacket across her chest.

"Sorry," I said, looking at Laura's face and realising she was blushing. "I'm so sorry. Jennifer used to have a blouse just like yours, and I was just remembering the time she bought it." Laura tilted her head, not unlike the way Jennifer used to, and looked at me with a shy smile creeping across her face. I could just see the faintest outline of her dimples through it, but they didn't last for long. The minute Paul started talking again, her smile disappeared completely and Laura was straight back to being business-like.

"I'm going to speak to the guards about this. You've been attacked."

"Paul, please. Don't do anything," I pleaded with him. "It's nothing, honestly. Nothing I can't deal with." I looked between him and Laura. "Please don't." Paul stared at me for what seemed like ages before taking a deep breath in through his nostrils.

"Right, if you say so," he said. I could tell from the look on his face he wasn't happy at all, but for the time being at least, would let it go. I gave Laura a wan smile but got nothing in response. "So, Gareth," Paul said, getting back to business. "There are two reasons for us visiting today. I want to bring you up to date on the progress towards your appeal, and then Laura here will walk us through the lead up to the attack on Mr Wainwright." The preliminaries were over, and Paul was straight down to it. I leaned forward and crossed my arms on the table, mirroring Paul's body language.

"Sounds good," I said.

"Now then, it's been two weeks, or is it three, since we last spoke?" Paul said. It had been four weeks and two days, not that I was counting the days or anything like that. Paul leant back in his chair as he continued. "Now obviously we missed the first twenty eight day window for an appeal. Or at least, your previous legal team did. I know they looked into it, but decided against lodging one." I remembered Toby and I arguing about this at the time. He had said lodging an appeal without enough evidence could be prejudicial. I couldn't see how that could be the case. If I'd understood it correctly, if we'd lodged an appeal anyway the worst thing that could have happened would be that my sentence could have been extended by a few weeks. Believe me, when you're staring at a life sentence, a few weeks is nothing.

"Effectively, we need to launch an appeal from scratch," Paul continued. "And the only way we can do that is with new evidence or new witnesses." I nodded, the poster now making a lot more sense.

"Did you have any responses to the poster?" I directed the question at Laura, who looked up and to my surprise, laughed. She looked across at Paul, who was also smiling, before replying.

"Yes, you could say that," she said. She was about to say something else when Paul interrupted.

"I'd like to come back to that in a little while, if I may?" From the look on Laura's face, this wasn't a question. Her laughter hadn't lasted long, which was a shame.

"Now, where was I? Witnesses and evidence," Paul said, looking at the ceiling of the room. "We need either new witnesses — or new evidence — to take to the judiciary. They'll then decide if an appeal is what is called 'safe' before it gets sent to the Court of Appeal." From what I'd read, this was a court in London, not Norwich. "Now, you've heard about the posters obviously. I've also hired a superb investigator to help us out. Ex-policeman, in fact, which I think will be useful. Still well connected, although he left under, shall we say, a cloud." I saw Laura suppress a smile as Paul said this. I wondered what their investigator had done. "He's still bitter about it, which helps us," Paul concluded, which left me even more curious.

"As soon as we have new evidence, or new witnesses, or — even better — both, I'll lodge the appeal at Norwich with Judge Watling. He'll then sign it off. At least, that's the plan. I know James well, so have got a good idea of how to put it to him." It was no surprise to me that Paul knew the judge.

"What sort of timeframe are we looking at?" I asked them. They looked at each other briefly before Paul replied.

"Well, witnesses and evidence will take time to collect and prepare. But I'm very optimistic that we'll get there. It will just take a while to do it properly. I can't really put a timeframe on that." He shrugged his shoulders. "It could be weeks, but more likely it will be months." Although what Paul said made perfect sense, I couldn't help but be gutted, especially after what had happened yesterday. From the sympathetic look that Laura gave me, I knew my disappointment was obvious. She slid her hand across the table and wound it around mine. I almost jumped at her touch. She was the only woman I had touched since Jennifer had died. Even though it was only a brief touch of her hand, it still sent a shock wave through me. I looked down at her hand, her cool fingers touching the back of my hand. No rings, no nail polish.

"So, Gareth. Once we have the witnesses and evidence

prepared, and the judge has signed the appeal paperwork, it'll be quick from there," Laura said, giving my hand a quick squeeze before letting go of it. I resisted the temptation to grab it back and realised that I was probably reading far too much into what was an innocent touch. "Once the papers are lodged with the Court of Appeal, the waiting time should only be a week or so," Laura said, breaking my concentration which was probably just as well.

"Yes," Paul said, his voice so low it was almost a growl. "Nothing to do with justice, but everything to do with compensation." I frowned, not understanding his point.

"What do you mean?" I asked him.

"The compensation clock ticks from the day the appeal is launched. Quite reprehensible in my opinion, but what would I know?" Paul explained. I had not even thought about compensation. Thinking about it, I realised that I couldn't care less about it, anyway.

"So, that's where we are with the appeals process," Paul said. Although I didn't really know anything now that I hadn't known already, I was grateful to them both anyway. "So, moving on to the appeal itself, there's not much to tell you really. We might have found another witness, though." My eyebrows shot up in surprise.

"Really?" I said. I was sure that there were no other witnesses, apart from the dog walker and he was miles away from me. Mind you, I'd been sure there were no CCTV cameras either, and I'd got that very wrong. Paul turned to Laura.

"Why don't you tell Gareth about the response to the posters?" The smile returned to her face.

"Okay," she said. "There was, how can I put it, quite an enthusiastic response to them." Laura laughed. "I never realised Norwich had so many nutcases." I smiled at her, hoping she would continue. She flipped open her note-book. "Right, there were three people who say they saw you even though they weren't even in Norwich on the night in question. There was another witness who is convinced that you're her long lost son, and finally, the star witness and front runner for the reward." She looked at me, her eyes sparkling, but said nothing.

"What? Tell me?" I asked.

"Well, according to this witness, you were in fact dropped off at the recreation ground just prior to the murder." Her eyes sparkled even more. "In a spaceship."


A few seconds later, Mr McLoughlin's face appeared at the door to see what we were all laughing so hard about.

## 28

Almost a week later, I sat on the hard plastic chair in the lawyer's room while Mr McLoughlin plugged a telephone into the wall. I had been in this room I don't know how many times, and never noticed a socket on the wall for a landline. He lifted the telephone and pressed the plastic prongs on the top a couple of times as he held it to his ear.

"Okay," Mr McLoughlin said. "Good to go." I wasn't sure if he was talking to me or talking to himself, so I remained silent. He pulled a small piece of paper from his pocket and unfolded it. Moving so he was blocking my view of the telephone, I heard the keypad beep four times before he looked down at the paper. There must have been a PIN lock on the telephone. The next session of beeps would be the number I could see written on the piece of paper. He paused, the handset to his ear, before speaking a few seconds later.

"Hello? Is that Miss Flynn?" He paused. "HMP White-moor here. I've got Mr Gareth Dawson with me. Will I put him on?" Another pause before he nodded. He turned and handed me the handset. "You know the drill," he said fixing me with a hard stare. I wasn't sure what I'd done to warrant a look like that, but maybe he was just having a crap day at the office. "Just bang on the door when you're done," he reminded me as he walked away.

I waited until he had left the room, and I'd heard the lock being closed. The other times I'd been in here, the lock had stayed open. I guessed that was only when there were other people in the room.

"Hello, Laura?" I said. "It's Gareth."

"Hi, Gareth," I heard Laura reply. The line was terrible. It sounded as if Laura was in a wind tunnel. I missed the next few words she said as they were too broken up for me to understand, only catching a few partial words through the hiss.

"It's not a great line, Laura," I said, tightening my grip on the handset. This wasn't what I needed. I heard her say something but again couldn't make it out. Something about a pullover? "I can't hear you," I almost shouted down the line.

"I said, I'll pull over," she yelled back, the line suddenly clear. Wincing, I pulled the handset away from my ear. I'd heard that okay.

The next time Laura spoke, the line was much clearer. Almost as if she was in the next room.

"Sorry about that, Gareth," she said. "I'm in the car and had you on Bluetooth. It's a crap connection at the best of times, but I'm in the middle of nowhere at the moment."

"Where are you?" I asked her, fascinated because I had a link to the outside world even if it would only be for a few minutes.

"Er, I'm somewhere between Elveden and Thetford," she

said. I closed my eyes for a moment as I knew the area well. Thetford was a large forest maybe half an hour away from Norwich. It covered miles of land, some of it shut off but a lot of it open to the public. I'd always imagined that it would be a fantastic place to take kids for a holiday and remembered a conversation I'd had with Jennifer one evening to that effect.

"So, Gareth," Laura's voice snapped me out of my daydream. "Thank you for getting back to me."

"No problem," I replied. "I wasn't busy." Laura laughed, her voice tinkling down the telephone line. It brought a smile to my face.

"I've got some news," she said. "Good news."

When Mr McLoughlin had said earlier that my legal team needed to speak to me, my initial reaction was mixed expectations. The last few times I had spoken to them, there had been no real developments at all. Lots of activity, but nothing tangible at the end of it. Laura telling me it was good news brightened my day a lot. Maybe there had been another result from their investigator, or some new evidence, but after all this time I couldn't see how either option would be possible.

"So Gareth," Laura said. Not for the first time, I noticed the endearing habit she had of starting most of her sentences with the word 'so' followed by the name of the person she was speaking to. It was almost as if she used it as a punctuation mark or a way of gathering her thoughts together before she spoke. "Are you ready for this?" She was talking quickly, and I could hear the excitement in her voice. I could feel my hopes raising.

"Yes, what is it?" I said.

"Well, I'm just on my way to London from Norwich. I've been at the Crown Court all day." I waited for her to continue. "Your application for an appeal went to Judge

Watling this morning," Laura said. I hadn't even known it was going in front of him, so this was a real surprise.

"What did he say?"

"I don't know for sure what he said, I wasn't there. But I do know the judge and Paul were in the judge's chambers for ages," Laura said. "Paul said afterwards they'd been talking about an appeal 'out of time', but judging by the smell of whisky coming off him, I don't think they'd been discussing it for that long." I could hear from the tone of her voice that she was smiling, and the thought of Paul getting pissed with the judge who'd sentenced me to life in prison brought an ironic smile to my face. "Anyway, it doesn't matter," Laura rattled on. "Judge Watling signed the paperwork, the NG, that's all that matters."

"What's an NG?"

"Oh, yeah, sorry," she said. "It's the form that goes to the Court of Appeal. They'll look at it and then decide whether or not to grant an appeal. That's why I'm driving to London, to take it down there and deliver it. Paul said it's a formality, but he still wanted it there as soon as possible."

"What happens next, then?" I asked. Her enthusiasm was infectious. I felt, for the first time in weeks, as if I might have a chance.

"Er, a single judge panel is first," she replied. "One judge has a look at it and decides if it should go to a full panel of three of them. Weeds out all the crap, basically," she said, laughing again. "Then, if they say yes — which they will — they'll order a retrial."

"How long will that take, do you think?"

"Paul reckons it might take a while. Up to two months, maybe longer." My heart sank. That was not what I wanted to hear. "Don't get your hopes up, Gareth. I'm being honest with you, that's all," Laura continued. I tried to relax my grip on the handset and just sat there, listening to the rumble of cars and lorries I could hear in the background thundering up and down the main road between Norwich and London. I couldn't think of anything to say, anyway.

"Are you okay?" Laura asked a moment later. I didn't reply. "It's great news, Gareth. Paul's put together a superb case. It went to the prosecution team last week, and they sent it straight back uncontested. Just like Paul said they would." I sighed, trying to process it all in my head. I needed time to think about what Laura had said, and what it meant.

"When are you coming in to see me next?" I asked Laura.

"I think Paul will be in at the weekend. He's got paperwork for you to sign, and he'll bring you up to speed on the appeal."

"Are you coming?"

"Oh, I don't think so. Me and Seb are going to Brighton for the weekend."

"Seb?"

"Sebastian. My boyfriend."

"Your boyfriend's called Sebastian?" I was trying not to laugh. "I bet he'd be thrilled to know you were on the phone to a convicted murderer." An image popped into my head of a fop haired Hugh Grant look-a-like, with an accent to match.

"I won't tell him if you won't," Laura replied, the smile back in her voice. "You're right, he wouldn't be impressed at all. I mean, he knows I'm a lawyer and that I have to deal with prisoners, but even so."

"Is he a pouter?"

"What?"

"Is he a pouter? Does he pout at you when he's

annoyed?" Laura laughed at my question. It was almost, but not quite, a cackle. In another life, I'd have described it as a filthy laugh, but that didn't seem to fit given the circumstances. I'd not heard her laugh like that before, but it was a sound I would love to hear more of.

"That's enough, I need to go." She was still smiling though. I could tell from her voice. "We'll talk soon, okay?"

"Okay," I replied, realising that I didn't want the conversation to end.

"Bye, bye, bye," Laura said in quick succession. The next thing I knew I was listening to a dial tone. Smiling at the memory of Laura's laugh, I put the phone down, got to my feet and banged on the door.

"How did that go?" Mr McLoughlin asked as we walked back to my cell. If it had been any other prison officer, I would have kept silent. His hard stare had disappeared, and I wondered again what all that was about.

"Pretty damn good, to be honest," I replied. "That was one of my lawyers. She's taking my appeal paperwork to the Court of Appeal in London. The judge signed it off."

"Really?" Mr McLoughlin stopped and looked at me. "You serious?"

"Yeah," I replied. "Straight up." To my surprise, he smiled. I don't think I'd ever seen him smile before. It changed the shape of his face and made him look like a different man. A much nicer one, to be honest.

"That's great news, Gareth," he said. I wondered for a moment if he was taking the piss, but looking at him, I didn't think he was. "You'll probably get shipped out if it goes through. Back to Norwich, I'd imagine."

"Seriously?" I replied. "That'd be magic if that happened." Mr McLoughlin carried on walking down the corridor to the door that led back to the general population.

"That's what normally happens," he said. "You'll get ghosted back to the original area, even if it's a lower cat. You've got a good record, so I can't see the Guv'nor objecting." Mr McLoughlin opened the door at the end of the corridor and stood back to let me go through it before he locked it behind me. "Have a good afternoon," he called through the observation window in the green metal door.

I stood with my hands on the bannister of the walkway and looked down at the prison wing in front of me. There was a bustle about the place, which was normal during 'sosh', or social time. I watched as prisoners hustled each other, doing deals, sorting out arrangements. If, and it was a huge if, if I got out of here, I would never be coming back. Not to this prison, not to any prison.

All I needed to do was to get out first.

## 29

I was lying awake on my bed when the note got pushed under the door. I'm not sure what time it was, but it was late. More than likely it was early. I'd not been sleeping well at all for the last couple of weeks and had been tossing and turning for what felt like hours when I noticed a shadow pass across the observation window of my cell door. The prison officers looked in at random intervals anyway, presumably to make sure that no one had hung themselves after lights out, but this time the shadow stayed in front of the window for longer than normal. I heard a noise at the bottom of the door, and when I looked up, I could see a single sheet of paper had been pushed under it.

Swinging my legs off the bed, I got to my feet to retrieve the note. I didn't have to worry about disturbing Mac as he was back on the hospital wing. Coughing up blood again. I'd never once seen him cough up anything other than thick phlegm, but he was insistent. Besides, he'd said, the food was better on the hospital wing. Although we bickered like a husband and wife most of the time, I missed him.

I knew some of the prisoners preferred to be in solitary, even to the point of staging fights to get assessed as high risk and locked up, but I didn't think I'd manage that for long. I'd even heard a story about a lad who wet the bed all the time just to get his own cell, but I'd heard it from so many people I figured it was an urban legend. I picked the paper up off the floor and held it to the light coming in the observation window so I could read it.

"Oh for God's sake," I muttered as I read the text. It was an instruction to pack my things up and be ready to move at lights up tomorrow morning. That didn't give me a chance to speak to anyone before I left. They always shipped prisoners out before the doors to the cells opened. I wouldn't be able to say goodbye to the few mates I'd made in Whitemoor, and that included Mac. The instruction didn't say where I was being moved to, just that I was being moved. "What am I supposed to pack my stuff into, anyway?" I said under my breath, looking around the cell. In reality, my personal possessions would fit into a shoebox.

One of the main advantages of being 'ghosted' out of Whitemoor was that Gejza or whatever his name was would be miles away. I didn't doubt he could find out where I had gone, but it put at least one degree of separation between me, the Romanian, and his gorillas. I still hadn't worked out what I would do about that problem, but perhaps being moved away would buy me some time until I'd come up with something. Lying back down on the bed, I stuffed the paper under my pillow. I stared at the bottom of the bunk above me, knowing I wouldn't be able to get to sleep now. I closed my eyes anyway.

The next time I opened them it was morning, and my cell door had just been unlocked. I'd drifted off to sleep after all. With a start, I realised that I'd not packed any of my stuff. Wherever I was going, I didn't want to leave any of it behind. I pulled the picture of Jennifer off the wall of the cell, trying to rub the congealed homemade glue off the back. It was made out of coffee whitener mixed with a dab of water and was as strong as superglue, but it messed the photos up for good. It was my one remaining photograph of her. I looked at it and frowned. I'd have to get Andy to send me another one in and hope it got through the postal system intact.

"You sorted, then?" a voice shouted through the open door. It wasn't Mr McLoughlin, but one of the other prison officers. Mr Philips, I think his name was. "Come on, I haven't got all day." I moved about the cell, trying to get as much of my stuff together as I could.

"Have you got a box or anything?" I asked. "Please?" I heard a muttered swearword in response and a few seconds later a battered shoebox came sailing through the door. I dumped my few possessions into it and picked it up before leaving the cell without a second look.

Mr Philips was standing on the walkway outside my cell with a look of complete indifference on his face.

"Follow me," he said as he walked off down the walkway. I set off after him, listening to the jeers and catcalls that always accompanied anyone getting moved with almost no notice. I ignored most of them until I walked past one of the cells and heard my name being called out. I looked across and could just see one of my friends from the library, Jimmy something or other, armed robbery. He was looking through the observation window of his cell door.

"Good luck Gareth," he said. "Wherever you end up."

"Mate, can you tell Mac goodbye from me when he gets back?" I slowed my pace as much as I dared. "Tell him I'll be in touch, yeah?"

"Yeah, course mate," Jimmy replied. "No worries."

"Come on, Dawson," I heard Mr Philips shouting at

me. "You don't want to miss the happy bus." His words were followed by a chorus of laughs and jeers that echoed around the wing.

I followed Mr Philips through the wing and out of the locked doors that separated us from the outside world. As I stepped out into the courtyard, I shivered. It was freezing, a typical cold November morning. I looked up at the sky, enjoying for a moment a different view of it than from the exercise yard, but it was just as grey and dismal. I followed the prison officer towards the Serco Sweatbox, as the white prison vans were known. Ironic really, as the only time you ever sweated in them was in the middle of summer. The rest of the year they were bloody freezing. I took my place in the metal cage in the back of the van and sat on the hard metal seat as Mr Philips locked both my cage and the rear door of the van. There were eight compartments in the back of the van, each one separated by metal bars. An opening in the door of each one allowed you to put your hands through to have handcuffs put on or taken off. I leaned back against the bars, wincing at the cold of the metal I was sitting on, and waited.

It was an hour, maybe an hour and a half later when the door to the back of the van was reopened. I was sitting in the same position, arms wrapped around me to try to keep warm. I felt the van's suspension dip a little and saw Mr McLoughlin step into the back of the van.

"I heard you were being shipped out at Morning Prayers," he said. I had to think for a moment before I worked out he must be talking about their morning briefing session. Not many of the prison officers struck me as churchgoers. "So, I thought I'd stop by and say good-bye." That was a surprise. I got to my feet to speak to him.

"Thanks, Mr McLoughlin," I said. "I appreciate that." He shook his head.

"Now don't get soppy, Gareth," he smiled. "No tears, you hear?" I grinned back at him, and we stood there in silence for a few seconds. "Anyway, I would say it's been a pleasure, but I'm sure you wouldn't agree with me."

"I think the pleasure's been all Her Majesty's," I said, and we both laughed. The next thing Mr McLoughlin did really surprised me. He put his hand through the slot in the door and into my cell, palm extended. As I shook his hand, I realised that this was the first actual contact I'd had with any of the prison officers in Whitemoor.

"You don't know where I'm going, do you?" I asked him, deciding to take advantage of the situation. He smiled back at me, and again I reflected on how different he looked with a smile on his face.

"I'm not allowed to tell you where you're going," he replied. "I don't understand why, but rules are rules."

"That's fine, I get that," I said, feeling bad for putting him on the spot.

"I'm sure wherever it is, it's a fine city." My smile widened at his words. At every entrance to the city of Norwich was a sign proclaiming it as 'a fine city'. I was going home.

Mr McLoughlin let go of my hand and walked towards the back door.

"Thank you, Mr McLoughlin," I called after him. He stopped and said something that I didn't quite catch. "Sorry, I missed that?"


"My name's Richard," he said. "I said my name's Richard."

## 30

Compared to Whitemoor, HMP Norwich was like a Holiday Inn hotel. Not a great Holiday Inn hotel, but a hell of a lot better than the previous place. I didn't have a cell to myself, but at least the beds didn't have plastic mattresses or pillows. The bedding had a thin plastic covering, but it wasn't made of the stuff. The two beds in the cell were side by side, separated by a small desk area with a solid looking metal chair, and only one of them was made. A pile of linen at the foot of the unmade bed marked it as mine. The chair looked solid enough to be used as a weapon, but also solid enough not to be taken apart easily. The cell was lit by an opaque window high up in the wall. At least it was natural light and not just fluorescent tubes buzzing away on the ceiling.

I sat on the edge of the left-hand unmade bed, thinking about the last couple of hours and wondered who my new cellmate was. The journey down to Norwich had been uneventful. There weren't any other prisoners in the van, which was a bonus. I'd heard stories of the sweatboxes doing the rounds of loads of different prisons, dropping prisoners off, picking other prisoners up, with some of the occupants spending twelve hours or more in the vans until they got to their final destination. I'd had none of that.

When we'd eventually left, the drive took around an hour and a half at the most. The two guards up front were decent enough, but that might have been because they weren't prison officers but contracted security guards. They'd even bought me a Big Mac and fries when they'd stopped off to get lunch somewhere off the A11 on the way back to Norwich. I'd sat there in the back of the swaying van, enjoying the unexpected treat. Before I'd been sentenced, I hardly ever went to McDonald's, but I enjoyed the lukewarm burger and soggy fries more than I'd enjoyed a meal in years.

When we arrived at Norwich, it was back to the same routine I'd been through a couple of times before. Straight from the van to the processing area, where I sat with a couple of twitching junkies and some nut job who kept asking me what I was in for. He must have asked me nine or ten times before I told him, at which point he stared at me before sitting on the other side of the processing cell. When I heard my surname being called, I'd gone through into the processing room itself. I was photographed, asked if I did drugs, told the rules, stripped, searched, the whole works. It was the only environment I'd ever been in where another man told you to bend over and cough and you did so, knowing full well that he was staring up your arsehole.

A prison officer gave me a light blue t-shirt and scratchy tracksuit to wear and led me into the general population. As I followed him through the wing, I could feel lots of pairs of eyes on me. I looked around, careful not to meet anyone's gaze for more than a couple of seconds at the most. I was trying to tread the line between not being a wet, and not being seen as a hard man. Both ends of that spectrum would cause a scuffle of some description as the locals would try to put me in my place. The last thing I wanted was to get into any bother. I was confident enough that if somebody started, I could hold my own, but you never knew. All it would take is someone to have a shank and it could be game over before it had even begun. I was shown into my cell and told to wait for my personal officer. This would be interesting, I thought as I waited. I'd never had a personal officer at Whitemoor, or at least if I had I'd never met him. After about ten minutes, a prison officer walked into my cell. I took one look at him and figured out straight away he probably didn't see much in the way of trouble. He was huge, way bigger even than the gorillas back at Whitemoor. It's not often that I look at people with a sense of trepidation, but this time I did.

"Dawson, is it?" he asked in a deep voice that suited his build perfectly.

"Yes sir, that's me," I replied, standing and inclining my head down a touch. The classic 'please don't hit me' pose. He stood there, staring at me, as I looked at him from underneath my eyebrows. He had a good five to six inches on me height wise and was broader than me by about the same amount. Although it was November, the heating here was the same as it was at Whitemoor which meant it was freezing. He had a tight fitting short sleeve white shirt on that looked as if the buttons on the front of it would burst if he sneezed.

"Sit down, Dawson," he said, nodding at the bed behind me. I did as instructed, and he pulled the chair away from the desk and sat on it. He looked like an adult sitting on a child's chair, and I had to stop the corners of my mouth from creeping up into a smile. We sat opposite each other, him looking at me and me looking at him, again from under my eyebrows. I wondered if this was some sort of psychological trick to see what I would do, so I remained silent and waited. I figured that I had less to do with my day than he did, so I could wait him out. After what seemed like ages, he broke the impasse. "Look at me properly, please."

I raised my head and looked at him, meeting his stare full-on. He had a crewcut, number one all over from the looks of it, and dark brown eyes. I could just see the ends of a couple of colourful tattoos snaking down from beneath both shirt sleeves, some sort of weird inked designs winding their way around his enormous arms.

"I'm Mr Jackson," he said. "But you can call me sir." He smiled, but it was a forced smile that was nothing more than the movement of some muscles around his mouth. "I'm your personal officer while you're here at Norwich, which means you belong to me. So if you've got a problem, it's my problem." I looked at him, not sure what he meant.

"I won't cause any problems, Mr Jackson," I replied. "Sir," I added as an afterthought. He sat back in the chair, which complained with a loud creak as he did so.

"No, I don't think you will," he replied. "I've read your file from Whitemoor. Model prisoner by all accounts, bar one isolated incident the other week, which either means you've been a good boy or that you've just not been caught." I tried a self-deprecating smile and thought about telling him about the 'isolated incident', but gave up after a few seconds when I saw his eyebrows knit together in a frown.

"I've been well behaved, sir," I replied, feeling like I was back at school in front of the headmaster. Which was a fairly common occurrence back in those days. Tommy and

I used to joke that we'd got season tickets to his office, we were in there that often.

"I don't doubt you have been," Mr Jackson replied, leaning even further back on the chair. If it broke, I knew I wouldn't be able to not laugh. "But to be honest, it's not really you I'm worried about. In terms of causing a problem, that is. My concern is that the problems might come to you."

That was interesting. I'd been determined since I was sentenced that I would be the grey man in whatever prison I ended up in, the man that no one really noticed. I relied on my size to deter any chancers, but at the same time had been careful not to be the big man.

"Can I ask what you mean by that?" I asked, risking the question. The chair creaked again as he leaned forward and put his shovel-like hands on his knees. It could have been my imagination, but he looked as if he was relaxing a bit.

"This is a Cat B prison," he said. "And you're still a Cat A prisoner. Not only that, but you're on C3 wing."

"Okay," I replied with a frown, not understanding the significance.

"C3 wing is mostly sex offenders. There's a few Rule 45's on here, but don't worry. We keep them separate." Rule 45 prisoners were classed as 'vulnerable prisoners' because most people wanted to cut them to ribbons. That much I did know.

"Nonces? I'm in the same wing as the nonces?" I said.

"They're not nonces," Mr Jackson replied. "Well, not all of them are. But you don't need to worry about them." He paused, smiling grimly. "I don't think you're their type, to be honest. You look like you'd probably fight back pretty hard." Damn right I would.

"We're going off track," Mr Jackson said. "My point is

that you're a target because you're a Cat A prisoner, and there might be certain individuals in here who might want to make a name for themselves. Be the 'Top Boy' as it were." He was starting to sound like a football hooligan and, looking at the size of him, he'd probably have made quite a good one. I'd have stood behind him on the terraces, back in the old days. Definitely behind him though, not in front.

"Okay, I've got that," I said. "But what do I do?"

"Nothing. You do nothing." He pointed at me with a stubby index finger. "Keep your head down, and your hands in your pockets." His forehead creased, and any sense I'd had of him relaxing disappeared in an instant. "You won't be here for long. In a few weeks, you'll get sent back to Whitemoor where you belong." He leaned further forward and pressed his index finger into my solar plexus. I resisted the urge to grab his finger and see how far it would bend backwards until it snapped. That wouldn't end up well. "Until then, you answer to me. You call me sir. Not gov, not boss. Only sir. Understand?"

I spent the rest of the day in my cell, not really wanting to venture outside. One thing that disappointed me after the conversation I'd had with Mr Jackson was that I wasn't on my own in the cell. Another problem was that I was starving, having decided not to venture out for scoff. What he had said earlier had rattled me. It was in part the thought of queuing up for food next to someone who might be a paedophile, or having a conversation with someone that started with the usual question 'what are you in for' and ended with the word 'rape'. I didn't know how I'd handle that, so decided not to find out. Going hungry was a small price to pay, in my opinion.

About ten minutes before the end of social, a shadow appeared at the door of the cell and a man dressed in the standard grey tracksuit walked in. I got to my feet slowly to greet my new cellmate. He was fairly small, at least compared to me he was, and a fair bit older. Anywhere between late thirties and early forties, by my reckoning. He had the face of a heavy smoker, and I caught the smell of roll-ups coming off his faded grey tracksuit. I nodded at him, and he smiled in response, showing me his yellow teeth with gaps between them that were way too big for a toothpick.

"Hello mate," he said, extending a hand out for a handshake. "You must be my new roomie."

"Yep, I am. I'm Gareth," I said. When I shook his hand, he winced, so I relaxed my grip a touch. He looked young for arthritis, but that's what his fingers felt like.

"I'm Pete," he replied. "Pleased to meet you." He followed this up with the standard question. "What you in for?"

"Fifteen for murder. Got sentenced a couple of months ago." I watched as his smile faltered and he let go of my hand. "I'm here on appeal though. That's what I got done for, but I didn't do it. I know everyone says that, but in my case it's true. How about you?"

"Shouldn't you be in Cat A?" Pete ignored my question. I smiled, trying to put him at ease.

"I guess they didn't want to be bringing me here every day from Whitemoor. My trial's being heard here."

"Maybe so." He didn't look convinced. "You from here then?"

"Yeah, about two miles that way." I pointed out of the window. I didn't know which direction I was pointing, but it was good enough. "Thorpe St Andrew."

"Right," Pete said, turning away and sitting down on his bed. "So, you might be on the out soon then?" He used the standard term for anywhere that wasn't inside a prison.

"I doubt it. Even if I get through the appeal for murder, they've still got me for attempted murder or grievous bodily harm at a minimum." That's what Laura had told me, anyway.

"How come?" Pete asked.

I sat on my bed and outlined what had happened. I had nothing to lose by talking to the bloke, it wasn't as if he could grass me up for anything. He sat there and listened, nodding occasionally. When I got to the part about attacking Robert his eyes widened.

"Mate, that's not murder," Pete said. "That's justice that is, right there."

"Yeah, that's not how the system saw it." I went through the original trial and sentence in a couple of minutes, not wanting to go into any detail.

"Harsh mate," Pete said when I finished. "Very harsh. Some countries they'd give you a medal for that, so they would." The sad thing was he was probably right.

"So, what's it like here then?" I asked him. "I was on remand here, but got shifted to Whitemoor pretty much straight away."

"Could be worse," Pete said. "I've been here for a year, got four for burglary. There's the usual crowd of idiots. The youngsters who all want to be the boss, and lags like me who just want a quiet life. The screws aren't too bad in the main, though. That's the main thing." The way Pete spoke told me that this almost certainly wasn't his first time inside. One thing I knew he was lying about was the reason he was in this wing. Cons who'd been done for burglary didn't get put in with the vulnerable prisoners.

A while later I was lying on my bed listening to Pete snoring. He'd gone to sleep about two minutes after he'd closed his eyes, which irritated the hell out of me. I tried to ignore the droning and get to sleep, but as usual, I couldn't.

With my hands laced behind my head, I let my mind wander back in time to when life was different. Before Jennifer died. Before I was put away for murder. It didn't do me any good at all, it never did. I knew it was negative, but I didn't really have anything positive to think about.

Not anymore.

## 31

The lawyers' room in HMP Norwich was a lot nicer than the one in Whitemoor. It was much larger for a start, and it was freshly decorated. Instead of stained grey walls, it was painted in an off-white emulsion and I couldn't see any graffiti anywhere. Mr Jackson and I were sitting in comfortable armchairs, instead of hard backed plastic chairs, and the table between us didn't have a single cigarette scar. The room even had a window. You couldn't see anything out of the window because of the reinforced glass, but it let in natural light which was always a bonus. We were waiting for Laura and Paul to arrive, and Mr Jackson had not said a word since we sat down. He sat opposite me and stared at the wall. That was pretty much the extent of how our relationship had developed in the week I'd been back in Norwich.

Mr Jackson sighed and looked at his watch, making it obvious that he had much better things to do than babysit me. I ignored him. There wasn't anything I could do about that. After about ten minutes, the door to the lawyers' room opened and a prison officer who I'd not seen before showed Laura in. There was no sign of Paul.

"Hi, sorry I'm late," she said, out of breath. "I got caught up in traffic. There was an accident between a bus and a learner driver on Kett's Hill. They've closed the whole road, and it's an absolute nightmare." She was dressed a lot less formally than normal, wearing a pair of jeans and a dark grey sweatshirt with a North Face logo embroidered across the front. Laura had jammed her briefcase under her arm and not for the first time I wondered what was wrong with the handle.

Mr Jackson got to his feet, and Laura took a small step backwards. He towered over her.

"Right then," he said. "I'll leave you to it." He looked at Laura and pointed to one of the top corners of the room where there was a small camera with a red flashing light. "We'll leave that on, seeing as you're here on your own with him. There's no sound, but we'll be watching." He stared at me to make sure I got the message.

"Paul is on his way. He texted me a minute ago to say he was held up in the same jam." Laura looked at Mr Jackson. "Mr Dewar. He's my boss at the law firm." Mr Jackson nodded and turned to leave the room. As he walked through the doorway, he had to angle himself a touch to fit through it.

"He's a big lad," Laura said with a smile as the metal door banged behind Mr Jackson. I smiled back at her.

"He is, yes," I replied. "Fine if you like the strong, silent type." Laura laughed, covering her mouth and dimples with her hand as she did so. She sat down in the chair that Mr Jackson had been sitting in and put the brief-case on the floor next to her.

"So, Gareth," she said. "Are you happy to be back in Norwich?"

"I am, yes," I said. "There seems to be a problem with my visitors' list, though. I spoke to Andy last night." Laura frowned, and I realised that she didn't know who Andy was. "Jennifer's dad," I explained. Laura's frown disappeared, and she reached into her briefcase to pull out her notebook and a pen.

"What's his full name?" she asked.

"Andy Elliott," I said. "Can I give you the list of all my visitors?" Laura nodded in reply, and I gave her the other names. It was a short list. As well as Andy and Jacob, there was only Tommy and David on it. Laura dutifully scribbled down their names.

"I'll ask Paul to sort it out for you," she said. "He should be here in the next few minutes, anyway." I didn't tell her I'd already handed in the paperwork three times to Mr Jackson. I couldn't see the point.

"So, Laura," I said. If she noticed that I was copying her standard opening words, she didn't give it away.

"How have you been? How's Seb?" I asked her.

"Sorry, who?"

"Sebastien," I replied. "Your boyfriend?" I could have imagined it, but was sure I saw a look of irritation flick across her face.

"He's fine, we're fine," she said. Perhaps I was seeing what I wanted to see?

We chatted for a while, waiting for Paul to arrive. I told Laura about the journey from Whitemoor to Norwich and enjoyed watching her laughing as I told her about the Big Mac and fries. I liked it when she laughed. It wasn't just the dimples, it was the way that her whole face lit up. One thing that was in short supply both in Whitemoor and Norwich prisons was people laughing, let alone a woman laughing. She was the only female contact I'd had since I'd been arrested, so she could have been twenty stone and a right munter and I'd still have enjoyed watching her laugh.

The sound of the heavy metal door behind her opening made Laura jump. She put her hand to her chest as the door swung open and Paul came through it. I could just see Mr Jackson over Paul's shoulder. The prison officer was staring at me as he pulled the door closed behind Paul.

"My God," Laura laughed. "I nearly jumped out of my skin." I got to my feet to shake Paul's hand, and to my surprise, he pulled me into a bear hug.

"Gareth, my dear boy," he said, slapping me on the back. "Good to see you." Paul smelt of soap and cologne. He released me, stepping back and putting a hand on each of my shoulders. "You're looking well," he said. It was nice of him to say that, but I didn't think I was looking particularly well. Paul, by contrast, looked great. His face was tanned, despite the fact it was November.

"Have you been away?" I asked him.

"Only for a few days," he replied. "I'm just back from a short golfing trip to Spain." Very nice, I thought as we both sat down. I knew absolutely nothing about golf, and the idea of chasing a little white ball around a golf course didn't appeal to me in the slightest.

"I do hope you two youngsters haven't started without me," Paul said, looking from Laura to me and back again.

"No, we haven't," Laura replied. "We've just been catching up."

"Excellent," Paul said. "Have you got the file?" Laura reached into her briefcase and pulled out a thick brown file. Written in large capital letters on the top of the file were the words 'Crown versus Dawson'. Seeing those three simple words written that way brought home how important this all was. It also highlighted the fact that it was me versus a very large system. I looked at Paul and Laura for a few seconds. It wasn't just me. It was the three of us and the other two members of my team were quite something, even if it was in very different ways. Laura opened the file and took a couple of sheets of paper from it, handing them across to Paul.

"Thank you, Laura," Paul said as he straightened the pieces of paper on the edge of the table. "Right then," he said in a businesslike tone. "Let's get cracking." I shuffled forward on my chair, eager to hear what Paul had to say. "I thought we would start with the batting order if that's okay with you?" He looked at me, eyebrows raised.

"That's fine by me," I replied.

"So, prosecution goes first, as always. In this case, the first few days of the trial will be a re-hash of the original trial. The jurors will all have to be brought up to speed on the case, and that'll take a while." Paul paused, rubbing his hand across his widow's peak and smoothing back an errant strand of white hair. "You won't be directly involved in that part though, you'll only come in to play when the prosecution's done." Paul looked across at Laura, who flashed him a brief smile. "It will be very, very tedious. I warn you now. I've been through a few of these, and they are as dry as anything. The prosecutor's main challenge is usually keeping the jury awake."

"Will there be witnesses, stuff like that?" I asked.

"No, nothing. It's a read through of the trial," Paul replied. "The second week is where it will get much more interesting. I'll lay out my case and start with the first witness. That'll be you." I must have looked surprised at this news as Paul asked me whether I'd been expecting that.

"Not really," I said. I wasn't called as a witness in my

original trial, as Toby had thought there was no point. I explained this to Paul.

"Yes," Paul sighed. "I might have done it differently, but I can see his rationale."

"I'm not sure I do," Laura said. Paul glanced at her before replying.

"Well, Wainwright was found dead with head injuries. Gareth had admitted lying in wait and hitting him around the head with a baseball bat. Based on the apparent circumstances at the time, the only difference was between murder or manslaughter. We're back to the premeditation argument again." Paul looked at me with a sad expression. "And there was no doubt it was premeditated, was there Gareth?" I avoided Laura's eyes as I replied.

"Not when you put it like that, no," I said.

"And of course, whether or not you intended to kill him is irrelevant. You attacked him in a premeditated manner, intending to do him harm, and he died as a result. Saying 'Yes Your Honour, I did lie in wait and hit him with a baseball bat but didn't mean to kill him' isn't a defence against a murder charge. Hence the murder conviction." I looked at the floor, still avoiding looking at Laura. It was stupid really, she knew exactly what I'd done, but hearing Paul speak in such blunt terms in front of her made me ashamed.

"The question they would have asked themselves was what benefit they would get from putting Gareth on the stand. They obviously thought there was nothing Gareth could have said that would have helped their case. Have I got that right, Gareth?" Paul asked me.

"Yes, that's a fair summary, I guess," I said.

"But this trial is completely different," Paul said. "This time the question is whether Gareth is innocent of both

murder and manslaughter, and in order to prove to the
jury he is innocent, we need them to not only see him but
to listen to him. To believe him. To believe in him."
Listening to Paul talking that way made me wonder what
he would be like in a courtroom, talking to the jury. I had a
sneaking suspicion that he would be very good indeed.

"Okay, thanks, Paul," Laura said. I finally looked up at
her to see her looking at me with a wry smile on her face. I
attempted to smile back, but my heart wasn't really in it.
Paul continued.

"So, we put you up first. That's a chance to introduce
you to the jury, and to set—"

"Sorry, jury?" I interrupted him. "I didn't realise that
there would be a jury?"

Paul looked at Laura, and I realised that I'd probably
dropped her in it again with Paul.

"But it's a trial, Gareth," he said. "You can't have a
trial without a jury."

"I thought judges heard appeals?"

"Well they do, but this isn't an appeal anymore. It's a
retrial. Has Laura not gone through this with you before I
got here?" Laura opened her mouth to reply but I cut
her off.

"No, no, she did. But I wanted to wait for you to get
here. She started to tell me stuff about the trial, but I asked
her to wait until you got here. I just didn't realise it had
gone straight to a retrial, that's all. Sorry." Paul looked at
me, and it was impossible for me to tell whether or not he'd
fallen for it. Despite my time in prison, I was still a sucker
for a damsel in distress. To my relief, Paul seemed to
swallow the lie.

"Okay, Gareth," Paul said. "Now Laura here will go
through some things with you before the actual trial.
Things like body language, the way you speak. When you

look at the jury and when you don't look at them. She's quite the expert." He smiled at Laura before continuing. "In terms of what I'm going to ask you, we'll start off with your relationship with Jennifer. How you met, your life together, that sort of thing. It's important for the jury to see you in context." I knew that part would be difficult, but I would have to get through it. "Then, we'll move onto the night that Jennifer died. I'll try and make it as painless as possible, but it will be hard for you. We have to do it, though." Paul paused and looked over at Laura.

"The jury has to see you, Gareth, for who you really are," Laura continued, and I wondered if they were tag teaming me. "The only thing they know about you when you step into that courtroom is that you're a convicted murderer. That's the opinion we need to change so they see you as a victim." I nodded, staying silent. I understood where they wanted to go, but it would be very painful.

"So, what else?" I asked. Laura opened her mouth to reply, but Paul got there first.

"Next, we'll go into your state of mind after Jennifer died. What led you to decide to attack Robert Wainwright." He shuffled the papers in his hand, looking down at the text on them. "Finally, we'll go through the attack itself, almost in slow motion. That's the crucial part as it will build the scene for the following witnesses."

"Won't that have already been done by the prosecutor?"

"It will, yes," Paul replied. "But not from your perspective."

"The only goal that the prosecutor will have had was to prove that you attacked Robert," Laura chipped in as Paul nodded in agreement. "It's not about the result of the attack, but the fact you attacked him in the first place."

"Then when I'm done, it'll be the prosecutor's turn to

ask you any questions she wants to," Paul said. This was the first time I'd heard the prosecutor referred to as a woman.

"She?" I asked. "Is it the same one from my original trial?"

"Yes, it is," Laura replied with a sideways look at Paul. "It makes sense, seeing as she was the prosecutor back then." I understood what Laura was saying, but that didn't mean that I had to like it. The thought of coming up against that witch, especially on the witness stand, was not an appealing prospect.

"What sort of things is she likely to ask me?" I asked.

"Well, to be honest, I don't think there's a great deal she can ask." Paul glanced at Laura as he answered. "Correct me if I'm wrong Laura, but as long as we keep it to you, your experiences, and your feelings, there's not much left for them."

"As long as you're one hundred per cent honest, Gareth," Laura said. I looked at her, surprised. What did she mean by that?

"Yes, of course, there is that," Paul said. He looked at me with a frown. "But there aren't going to be any surprises, are there Gareth?" I wondered if now was a good time to tell them I used to be a burglar, but I decided against it. I'd never even been under suspicion back in those days, so there was no way that my previous career could come back and bite me.

"Until the day I was arrested for murder, I'd not had a single brush with the law," I said confidently. Laura was looking at me quizzically. "I promise you, there are no surprises."

"I would think this will take a morning or an afternoon to go through everything," Paul said. My heart sank at the thought of being on the witness stand for that long.

"Don't worry, Gareth," Laura said as I shuffled uncomfortably in the chair. "I'll work with you on everything."

"Thank you," I replied. I was going to need all the help I could get.

"So, after you, I'm going to put the policeman on the stand." He peered at the paper in front of him. "Griffiths, isn't it? Yes, that's the chap. I'll go through the crime scene with him, why he went straight to you, that sort of thing."

"It's pretty obvious why Malcolm came after me though, isn't it?" I said. This struck me as stating the obvious. "Wainwright had killed my wife, and I was on CCTV leaving the alleyway where he was found dead."

"Hmm, yes, well there's a little more that I can pull out of his testimony than that," Paul replied. "I can use him to describe the scene you see and set up some interesting bits and pieces for later on." Paul sat back in the armchair and waved at the camera in the corner of the room. "I wonder if they'll be able to sort us out with a cup of tea," he said to no-one in particular. We all sat for a few seconds before he waved at the camera again. "Perhaps they'll be along in a minute."

"I wouldn't bet on it," I muttered. Mr Jackson was probably sitting in his control room waving back at the screen he was watching us on.

Paul returned to his papers, turning the top sheet over and folding it back. He squinted at the text, and I wondered if he'd forgotten his glasses even though I couldn't remember him ever wearing any.

"Next up will be my investigator, Alfie Nesbitt. The ex-policeman I told you about. Very, very good he is. We will need to get his history past the prosecutor, though. This worries me, because if we can't use the evidence he's gathered, then we're in real trouble."

"What evidence?" I asked.

"Oh, all sorts," Paul replied, dismissing my question with a casual wave of his hand. "Laura, we need to work on this element more back at the office. I can't risk not being able to include what he's uncovered." Laura nodded, scribbling on her notepad. I thought this was supposed to be a collaborative effort between Paul, Laura, and me, but Paul seemed more than happy to keep me in the dark about a lot of things that I'd like to know about. I decided to try to talk to Laura about it if I got the chance to speak to her again on her own.

"I think at this point we'll probably be drawing stumps by Thursday afternoon," Paul said. "Assuming we start on a Monday morning, that is, and there's no reason why we shouldn't. Opening arguments until lunchtime on the Monday, you in the afternoon." He pointed his index finger in my general direction. "The policeman and Alfie on Tuesday, and then the first of the big hitters on Wednesday."

"Doctor Klein?" Laura asked.

"Indeed, the lovely Doctor Klein," Paul smiled as he said the name. I'd never heard it before. "She's my wound specialist and absolutely charming." I saw Laura smirk.

"She should be, she's costing us enough," she said. Paul made a shushing sound, wagging his finger at Laura.

"Now now, dear. Don't be like that." If anyone else had said that it would have sounded rude and patronising, but Paul managed to get away with it. "I think she'll be on for a day at least, if not more. It depends on how brave the prosecutor's feeling."

"Who is she?" I asked.

"She's a pathologist, retired now. Well, almost retired. Her area of expertise is blunt force trauma and injury patterns, with a particular interest in cranial trauma. She's superb, and you know what the best thing is about her?"

"No, what?" I replied.

"She looks like she's just walked off the set of Miss Marple."

## 32

"All rise."

The courtroom stirred into life at the barked order from the court usher. The quiet murmur of conversation died as people rose to their feet. At the front of the courtroom, the door behind the judge's desk opened and Judge Watling stepped through. He'd not changed much at all since my previous trial. I was half expecting him to look much older than he did, or to stumble in on a walking frame or something, but he looked pretty much the same. Mouldy looking wig with grey hair sticking out from underneath it, and the same flowing red robes. Judge Watling examined his empire over the top of his glasses for a few seconds before sitting on his ornate chair.

"Please, be seated," he said in a quiet voice. As the sound of the gathered audience sitting down echoed around the courtroom, he turned and gave me a very slight nod. Enough to acknowledge my presence, maybe even enough to recognise our previous dealings with each other.

I knew from the clock on the wall opposite me that I had been sitting in the accused enclosure for just over an hour before the judge had called the court to order. It was now just before ten o'clock on Monday morning, and I'd been brought in a few minutes before nine. For the last hour, I'd sat on the hard wooden bench, flanked by Mr Jackson and another prison officer who I didn't know. One thing I did know about him was that he was a heavy smoker and had disappeared three times in the past hour only to come back stinking of cigarettes. I wouldn't have minded so much but he didn't offer to take me with him, even though I'd given up, preferring to leave me in the care of Mr Jackson. I wasn't sure what the rules were for guarding prisoners in a courtroom with only one officer, but an escape from Mr Jackson seemed very unlikely anyway unless I got a very good head start. The only consolation for sitting on the uncomfortable bench was that if I found it uncomfortable, Mr Jackson must be even more uncomfortable given his size.

We'd left the prison first thing in the morning, and I'd spent the best part of an hour sitting in the holding area underneath the courtroom. It was a soulless place, just a row of individual cells with bars instead of proper doors. No natural light at all, just fluorescent tubes in the ceiling. Although the courtroom itself was new, the interior decorators hadn't spent much time down here. The cells were arranged around a central area with a table and chairs where the prison officers and court officials sat around reading newspapers and drinking tea. The whole room was tired and depressing. To be fair to the staff, it wasn't much of a staff rest area for them either.

A few minutes after I was brought up to the courtroom from the holding area, the public gallery opened. I watched as Andy and Jacob came through the door to take up seats at the front, and they both raised their hands in my direction as they sat down. I didn't return their waves as it didn't seem like the right thing to do, so flashed a wry smile in their direction instead. A few moments later, once the public gallery had filled up completely, I looked back to see if I recognised anyone else. At one end was an elderly couple, a woman and a man deep in conversation, and there were a few other people sitting on their own who I thought might be from the press. Paul had told me that the front cover of the Eastern Daily Press, Norwich's local newspaper, was carrying a story about my retrial. He said that at some point it would almost certainly be picked up by the nationals as well and as I looked at the seats, I played a game in my mind to match the occupants to the media sources.

At about ten minutes before ten, there was a small commotion at the back of the public gallery. I looked up to see Tommy, David, and Big Joe making a noisy entrance as they asked people to make some space for them. I couldn't hear them from where I was sitting, but I knew them well enough to know that they wouldn't be asking nicely. Especially Big Joe. He was just that kind of bloke.

Paul, Laura, and the prosecution lawyers had arrived not long after I had. Laura had gone straight to the defence table, where she busied herself arranging files, notepads, pens, and bottles of water for her and Paul. She was dressed in a business suit and was wearing the satin green blouse that I had seen her in before. The one that was so like Jennifer's. Laura looked up at me and smiled, and I noticed that she'd had her hair cut. Paul had gone straight to the prosecution table and had been engrossed in conversation with the prosecuting lawyer. It was indeed the same prosecutor from before, Miss Revell, who still looked as evil as she had done at my original trial. She was just as thin, just as nasty looking. She had two young men with her, lawyers perhaps or maybe paralegals? I didn't know who they were and didn't care, anyway. The two men both wore very serious expressions but looked as if they were just out of school. One of them was arranging the prosecution table just as Laura was doing on the defence table, while the other one was pecking away at a laptop. On another table between the two lawyers' tables and the back end of the courtroom sat a man and a woman, both with impressive sets of folders in front of them. I had no idea who they were either, but they looked like legal types if there is such a thing. Both well dressed, comfortable sitting where they were, mumbling to each other occasionally. At one point the woman looked across at me but looked away with no change in her expression at all.

Paul and the prosecutor finished their discussion before sitting at their respective tables where they waited for the judge to make his grand entrance. A few minutes before ten, as if there had been a silent alert, they both put their wigs on. Paul slid his hand back across his widow's peak before he put his hairpiece on. One of the benefits of not having much hair, I guessed. It took Miss Revell a bit longer to sort her hair out underneath hers, and I watched her struggle with it. One of her grey-suited colleagues looked up at her but thought better of offering to help. She eventually got things under control and looked toward the bench with glasses halfway down her pinched nose.

Judge Watling cleared his throat, silencing the murmurs of conversation that had started back up again as people had sat back down. He looked towards the court usher, who was standing by a door on the opposite side of the courtroom.

"Please bring in the jury," Judge Watling said. The usher opened the door and I watched as the jury filed through. This was my first opportunity to see them. Paul and Laura knew all about them as they'd been involved in the selection process, but I knew nothing about the group at all. I sat with my head forward, and my shoulders down, as instructed by Laura. She had said it was important that the first impression the jurors got of me was of a man in the wrong place. A man who should not be sitting on the accused's bench. If I'd been sitting there with my head held high and my chest thrust out, Laura had said this would give the wrong impression to the jury, and I had no reason to disbelieve her. The other thing she told me it would be useful to do is to give them names in my head, just made up ones. Something about altering my body language if my mind thought I knew them, making me look friendlier and less like the convicted murderer I actually was.

I glanced at the jurors every few seconds as they filed into their seats. Most of them looked unremarkable, just normal people, but there were one or two who stood out. The third juror in the line was a large black woman, dressed in a multicoloured dress that shouted 'look at me'. She was staring in my direction as she made her way to her seat, and I cast my eyes back down as soon as I realised she was looking directly at me. She had eyes that bulged just a bit, like someone with that thyroid thing I'd read about in a newspaper once. I didn't want to stereotype, but she wouldn't have looked out of place in a gospel choir, so I named her Ella after Ella Fitzgerald. One of Jennifer's favourite singers. Further down the line was a man who was about my age, and about my size. He would be Mark, which was my middle name, just because he reminded me of me. He was followed by an elderly gentleman who was walking with a stick. On their own, they could have been father and son. I looked back down at my lap, trying to come up with a name for the older chap. The best I could do was Albert, who was a character in a sitcom I used to watch when I was younger. I didn't know many elderly people who I could name him after, so Albert would have to do. I heard the door close and then looked up to see who had walked in last.

The last juror to take her seat, and the one who was sitting furthest away from the judge and therefore the fore-man, was a middle-aged woman of about fifty. She was well built but not fat, and she was dressed in a jacket and trouser suit not unlike the one that Laura was wearing. The thing I liked most about her was her face. Framed with curly brown hair that was streaked with grey, she looked very kind. Almost maternal. I wondered for a few seconds if she was still called a foreman, even though she was female. Was she a forewoman instead? Did it matter? She had a passing resemblance to my old English teacher, Mrs Rose, who for some reason had quite liked me even though I was shit at the subject. I never knew what Mrs Rose's first name was, as I only ever called her 'Miss', but Rose was a first name as well, so that would do me. Rose she was.

I sat back on the bench and tried to make myself comfortable as the judge went through his preliminary statements. He went through the house rules, what to do and what not to do, and he reminded the jury of their obligations. No watching television, no reading newspapers or going on the internet, no discussing the case with anyone else. Once he had finished, and the jury was sworn in, Judge Watling turned and looked at the prosecution bench.

"Miss Revell, as the prosecutor you have already won the toss. The floor is yours." I watched Miss Revell nod in the judge's direction and get to her feet.

"Your Honour, thank you," she said before turning towards the jury with a brief glance at Paul and Laura. I noticed that she didn't look at me, and I wondered if that was deliberate. "Ladies and gentlemen of the jury, thank you for attending today. My role within this court is relatively simple. Mr Dawson has already been tried for murder, by a jury of his peers just like you, and found guilty. He has been sentenced to life in prison." As she continued, I realised her angle appeared to be to convince the jury that this was a waste of their time. That justice had already been done. Her opening comments only lasted for perhaps ten minutes, and she finished with a final reminder to the jury I was already a guilty man. When she had finished, she sat back down and Judge Watling looked directly at me for a couple of seconds before he spoke.

"Mr Dewar, if you would be so kind?" the judge said, but Paul was already getting to his feet.

"Your Honour, my learned friend." Paul looked at the judge and the prosecutor in turn. He put his hands out to his sides, palms facing towards the jury as if he was welcoming them to his own personal courtroom. "We are all here today at the behest of the Criminal Court of Appeal for the retrial of the young man sitting behind me, Mr Gareth Dawson."

As he said my name, I sat up a little bit straighter on the bench as instructed by Laura and looked across at the jury. All twelve pairs of eyes were staring back at me. I felt the colour rise to my cheeks as I realised that it wasn't just the jury who was staring at me, but that it was everyone in the courtroom. If I felt this nervous when everyone was just looking at me, how much worse would it be when I was actually on the stand? I glanced up at the public gallery, looking for Andy. When I caught his eye, he grinned and gave me a discreet thumbs up.

"As you all know, Gareth Dawson was tried and convicted, in this very courtroom, for the murder of Mr

Robert Wainwright." Paul stepped away from his table and walked across to stand in front of the jury's bench.

"Ladies and gentlemen, if it pleases the court I would like to establish some facts." He paced slowly up and down in front of the jury as he continued speaking. "It is a fact that my client, Gareth Dawson, planned an attack on Mr Robert Wainwright in May of this year. It is a fact he struck Mr Wainwright with a baseball bat. It is a fact he attempted to mislead the police following the attack." Every time Paul said the word 'fact', he raised his voice and emphasised it with a gentle punch of his right hand into the palm of his left. It was a very effective mannerism, and one which I was sure was well practised. Paul stopped pacing halfway along the jury's bench. He looked across at me briefly before continuing. "And finally, it is a fact he was convicted of murder by twelve men and women just like you in this very courtroom. They found that Gareth Dawson had murdered Robert Wainwright, and they were certain of that fact beyond…" The final three words of his sentence were delivered with an exaggerated pause between them. "All. Reasonable. Doubt.

If I may, I would like to focus in on the last part of that sentence. All reasonable doubt." Again, the same pause between the words. "That is the standard of proof which must be upheld in order for this murder conviction to stand. Now, an appeal such as this is normally launched within twenty-eight days of the original conviction. In order for an appeal to be heard outside that twenty-eight-day window, there are certain criteria which must be fulfilled. One of those criteria is, and I quote from the legal text itself, new and compelling evidence."

Paul walked back to the defence table and picked up one of the files that Laura had placed there earlier. "Ladies and gentlemen," Paul said as he stood a few feet in front of the jury's bench. "I do not believe Gareth Dawson killed Robert Wainwright." He raised the manila file in his hand. "I do not believe Gareth Dawson could have killed Robert Wainwright, and the evidence which I will present to you over the next few days will leave you, ladies and gentlemen of the jury, with exactly the same belief. And if you do not believe Gareth Dawson killed Robert Wainwright, if you have any doubt whatsoever that it was not him but somebody else, then it is your duty to find him not guilty of murder and to quash his conviction."

I looked at the jury. He had them eating out of his hand. The third juror, Ella with the brightly coloured floral dress, was fascinated by the manila folder in Paul's hand. I had no idea what was in the folder. It could have been this morning's newspaper for all I knew, but Paul used it as a prop to great effect. He tapped the folder with his free hand, drawing the rest of the jury's attention to it. "Ladies and gentlemen, it is not even a case of beyond all reasonable doubt. It is a case of having no doubt at all that Gareth Dawson, the young man sitting over there, is innocent of murder." He paused in front of them for maybe ten seconds, almost as if he was expecting any of them to ask him a question or perhaps challenge him in some way. He walked back towards the defence table, pausing to nod at the judge as he passed him. "Thank you, Your Honour," he said. As he walked towards the table, Paul looked at me and gave me the briefest of winks.

The rest of his face remained deadpan as he took his seat.

## 33

The first week of the trial was, just as Paul had said it would be, a complete run through of the original trial. As Miss Revell talked them through it, all the jurors were given a large black folder with a number on the front, identical to the ones that the man and the woman sitting behind the lawyers had. Within the folders, it soon became obvious, was a complete transcript of the trial right down to copies of the original crime scene photographs. Before the prosecutor got into the meat of the case, she made a short speech about what the purpose of her presentation was. It was simple. The point of it was for me to be found guilty all over again.

I watched the jurors as they flicked through the folders. Mark, who was the closest juror to me in terms of age and size, glanced up at me a couple of times as he leafed through the pages but none of the others looked at me, concentrating instead on the contents of the folders.

"If you could turn to page three of your folders," Miss Revell said to them, "we'll start with the statements of those witnesses who were not called to the trial." Within

minutes, I was bored and this boredom increased tenfold
over the next few days. Not because I'd heard it all before,
and it wasn't that I wasn't interested in what was happening, it was just that Miss Revell was going through the
entire folder. Page by page, line by line, almost word by
word.

The court soon settled into a routine for those first few
days. Miss Revell would start the day with a recap of what
had been covered the day before, and then the jurors
would turn to whichever page they were starting on that
day. Then they were led through it like a school class being
walked through a Shakespeare play, with Miss Revell
playing the part of the teacher. Every so often she paused
the narrative to explain one of the finer points to the jurors
even though it wasn't clear whether or not they understood
it. Paul wasn't joking when he'd told me it would be
tedious. The only things that punctuated the days were the
breaks for lunch and the occasional coffee break when the
judge thought the jury was flagging. The public gallery, full
on the first day of the trial, got emptier and emptier until
by the end of the week there was no-one left. Even Andy
and Jacob had found better things to do. Every evening,
the judge dismissed the jury, and I was taken straight back
to the prison just as Paul had told me I would be. By the
time I'd had scoff at the prison, I was exhausted. They
were long days, just sitting in a courtroom watching other
people reading.

The worst day, or at least the worst day from my
perspective, was the Thursday. This was the day that the
prosecutor walked the jury through the attack on Robert.
As it had done at the first trial, it sounded pretty bad. How
I'd planned the whole thing right down to the last detail.
What made it worse was that it was all true. The pre-medi-
tation behind the attack on Robert was laid out to the jury

with no gloss whatsoever. There was no way it could be sugar-coated, and that wasn't the intention of the prosecutor anyway. Throughout the entire piece, I kept my head down even though I could feel the eyes of the jury on me. I looked up at Paul and Laura a couple of times, and Laura gave me a brief smile at one point, but that was the only positive thing about the whole day.

By Friday lunchtime, I'd had enough. The prosecutor had just finished describing the moment that the original jury had come back with their guilty verdict. It was about the most animated that she'd been for the entire week, and about the only time she showed any degree of showmanship. I guessed that for the rest of the week she hadn't felt the need to, but on Friday morning, she put on an affronted air as she told the new jurors how their predecessors had found me guilty. Not only had they found me guilty, she told the new jury, but the verdict was unanimous.

"The jury from the last trial, ladies and gentlemen," Miss Revell had said, "they came back with their verdict, their unanimous verdict, within two hours. That is how certain they were that this man," she waved a bony finger in my general direction without looking at me. "That this man was guilty of murder."

I spent the journey back to Norwich prison that evening deep in thought. The jury would be thinking about that last day for the entire weekend which must have been why Miss Revell had finished on what for me was a very negative note. I tried to shake myself out of it, but I couldn't help go over it in my head. By the time I got out of the van and back into the prison, I was in a foul mood. Mr Jackson led me back to my cell without us exchanging a single word. My cellmate, Pete, was nowhere to be seen although it didn't take me long to work that one out. To be honest, I was pleased that Pete wasn't about. With almost an hour of social time left, I hoped that I'd have some peace and quiet. Being on display all day, consciously thinking about every movement I made or expression I wore, was exhausting. As I sat down on my bed, I saw something on the pillow. It was a postcard, picture side down with no writing on the side I could see. I picked it up and flipped it over, and my heart dropped.

I'd never been to Romania, but the postcard I was holding had the text 'Grüße aus Rumänien' written across it in a gothic looking font. There were four pictures on the front, one in each quadrant of the postcard, and as I looked closer at it I could see that they were hand drawn scenes of landmarks I didn't recognise. Two of them were churches of some sort, and the other two were just random tourist areas. I flipped the card over, my heart thumping in my chest, but there was nothing written on the other side apart from the text which told me what the landmarks were. There didn't need to be anything written on the card for me to get the message, though. It was pretty clear. Grezja knew exactly where I was.

I jumped as Pete walked into the cell, and I almost dropped the card on the floor.

"Alright mate?" Pete said in his heavy smoker's drawl. "How did today go?" I looked at him, my eyes wide. He faltered when he saw my expression. "Er, you okay?"

"What's this?" I took a step towards him, waving the card in his face. "Some sort of sodding joke? Who got you to put this on my pillow?" Pete took a step back toward the cell door as his gaze flicked from my face to the card and back again.

"I don't know nothing about it, mate," he said. "It was on your bed when I got back from scoff earlier. I left it there for you. Never even touched it, honest." I doubted that, but it didn't matter. I looked at Pete and saw real fear in his eyes. Realising that I was scaring him, I put my hand out, palm down.

"It's alright mate, sorry," I said, shaking my head. "It just put the frighteners on me, that's all."

"But it's only a postcard," Pete replied, relaxing. "That's all it is, a postcard. There's not even anything written on it, it's just a bunch of old buildings." I sat down on the bed and took a deep breath. How did he know it was pictures of buildings if he'd not touched it? I told myself that it didn't matter, so what if he had picked it up and looked at it? It changed nothing.

"It's a long story mate," I sighed.

Pete sat down on his bed, and we faced each other. I held my head in my hands and thought for a few minutes. What did I have to lose by talking to him? When I finally realised that the answer to that question was absolutely nothing, I told him the full story of the visitors to my cell back at Whitemoor. The money that Robert owed and the transfer of the debt over to me. The full story took maybe ten minutes, and Pete remained silent throughout.

"What do you think?" I said when the full story was done. Pete looked at me, frowning and playing with a piece of skin on one of his nails. He took a few moments to reply.

"I think it's bollocks," he finally replied, his watery blue eyes staring at me. "It makes no sense. You don't owe them anything. Just because you killed the bloke that did, that doesn't make sense."

My eyebrows went up before I had a chance to consider my reaction.

"I mean, just because they think you killed him," Pete continued quickly. "I'm not saying you did, I know you didn't because you said so. But I mean, not being funny like, you got done for killing him. That's what they'll think, isn't it?"

"It's okay, I get you," I sighed. "It doesn't seem to matter to them, whether I'm innocent or guilty that is." Pete nodded as I said the word innocent, but stopped nodding when I got to the guilty word.

"Can't you talk to them?" Pete nodded his head toward the door.

"Who? The screws?" I replied.

"Yeah," he said. "Why not?"

"What can they do?" I thought about Mr Jackson. He might be a big lad, but I didn't think even his size could help me with my problem.


If this gang could just walk into my cell unchallenged in a Category A prison like Whitemoor, finding me here would be a piece of cake.

# 34

"I swear by Almighty God, to tell the truth, the whole truth, and nothing but the truth." I spoke as clearly as I could before I handed the battered Bible back to the court usher. He was standing next to the witness stand with his hand outstretched like a homeless person begging for money. As I put the Bible in his hand, I wondered how many people had said those same words and of those people, how many of them had actually meant them. I hadn't been in a church for years, so the words themselves didn't mean that much. The sentiment behind them was something else, though. As I sat back down, I looked around the courtroom. It was Monday morning, and I'd had a crap weekend, wondering if I'd get another visit to my cell. Pete was a nice enough lad, but he didn't strike me as a fighter.

Laura pushed her chair back so she was sitting away from the defence table. I shook my head from side to side, trying to concentrate. The next few minutes, few hours perhaps, would be vital and I couldn't afford to get this bit wrong. Paul got to his feet, taking his time and shuffling

pieces of paper into some sort of order. I looked again at
Laura. She had her left hand on her leg, hidden from
everyone except me and the prison officers, except they
were paying no attention at all. She extended three fingers
across her upper thigh. Juror number three. That was Ella,
who today was wearing the same dress she had on the first
day of the trial. Loud as anything, bright red and covered
in ugly blue flowers. Perhaps she had a dress for each day,
and just rotated them?

Laura changed her hand into a fist and then put her
fingers and thumb across her leg followed by her index and
middle finger. Juror number seven, Albert, the old guy with
the stick. I watched as she repeated the movements to give
me juror number six, who was a tiny woman I'd nick-
named Minnie as she reminded me of a mouse. She was a
small tousled haired woman, maybe mid-thirties, who
looked as if she would cry if anyone spoke to her. She was
sitting next to Albert, skinny arms folded across a non-exis-
tent chest, and I watched as Albert leaned over and whispered something in her ear. These three jurors were the
ones I should play to during the first part of Paul's questioning. These were the ones that Laura thought would be
most affected by this stage, so they were the jurors I should
concentrate on. I sat in the witness box, running a finger
around my shirt collar, which was tighter than it had been
earlier. I could feel a trickle of perspiration making its way
down my back, and every time I moved I could smell my
own sweat.

"Mr Dawson, Gareth," Paul said in a sombre voice.
"What I would like to explore this morning is your relationship with Jennifer, your wife." Across the courtroom,
the prosecutor got to her feet.

"I must object, Your Honour. How is this relevant?"
she said.

"Really? Your honour?" Paul said. "I've only just—"

"Yes, thank you, Mr Dewar," Judge Watling said, cutting Paul off. "Miss Revell? Please proceed?"

"Your honour," the prosecutor replied. "I fail to see how Mr Dawson's relationship with his wife has any bearing on his innocence or guilt in this matter."

"Mr Dewar?" Judge Watling looked at Paul, who was looking affronted.

"Your honour, my client's relationship with his wife defines him, it is at the core of his nature. To even attempt to re-try this case without considering this relationship will do him a grave injustice indeed."

"I agree," the judge said after thinking for a few seconds. "Please do continue." Miss Revell sat back in her chair, expressionless. I couldn't tell whether she was annoyed at losing the opening skirmish or not.

"Thank you, Your Honour. Now please, Gareth, could you tell us about the night you met your wife, Jennifer?" Paul said.

I glanced up to look at Andy and Jacob in the public gallery before I told the jurors my story. Starting with the night that Jennifer and I had met, I told them all about the first time I met Robert Wainwright. As I spoke, my gaze flitted between Ella, Albert, and Minnie, as instructed by Laura. I turned to face the jury, and I told them all about the first time that Jennifer and I met. How she and Robert came into the pub I was drinking in and how they then ended up in an argument outside.

"Gareth, if I may ask. Why did you intervene in their discussion? It had nothing to do with you, surely?" Paul asked, as I knew he would. We'd been through his outline script, so I knew the direction he was heading in.

"I'm not sure, I've asked myself that so many times you wouldn't believe it." I continued, shifting my attention to

Minnie. "She looked like she needed my help, and I didn't want her to get hurt."

"Was there any suggestion that Mr Wainwright would hurt Jennifer?" Paul asked.

"I didn't know, but I wasn't going to take the chance."

"Did you assault Mr Wainwright that first evening you met Jennifer?" I remembered my hand around Robert's neck. Out of the corner of my eye, I saw Laura's hand move on her leg. Glancing down, I saw four fingers extended across her thigh.

"We had words," I lied, not thinking I'd burn in Hell for that small one. "I may have got in his face, but I didn't hit him, or hurt him." My attention shifted to juror number four, Mark. The closest one to me in terms of age and size. He was fiddling with a wedding ring on his left hand as I caught his eye. "I wanted him to leave Jennifer alone, that was all. That's what most men would have wanted to do, I guess." I looked back across at Minnie, who was sitting with a thin hand clutched to an equally thin chest, her jaw slightly open. Laura was good, there was no denying that. Minnie looked just like a woman who needed a big strong lump like me to protect her.

"Gareth?" Paul said.

"Sorry," I replied, breaking my gaze away from Minnie. I was drained already. Talking about Jennifer, back in the early days, had taken more out of me than I'd thought it would.

"Your Honour," Paul said, looking up at Judge Watling. "May I suggest a recess for lunch? I'm intending on going through what I suspect may be a particularly hard part of my client's testimony next, so perhaps starting after lunch may be better." I saw the prosecutor roll her eyes in response, but Judge Watling didn't appear to agree with her.

"Yes, I agree. Court adjourned until half past one." The courtroom audience started to get to their feet as Judge Watling made his way through the door behind him.

I was a lot more comfortable in the witness box after lunch. Maybe it was not having the fear of the unknown anymore, maybe it was just having a full stomach even if was full of lukewarm lasagne and soggy garlic bread with only a hint of garlic. Either way, it didn't matter. I knew the next bit would be hard, but at the same time, it would be crucial. This was my chance to get under the jury's skin. To make them see me not as a convicted murderer, but as a wronged man.

There was a delay getting started after lunch, and I took the time to examine in more detail the two individuals sitting at a desk toward the back of the courtroom. When Paul and Laura had visited me at the weekend, I'd probed them to find out who they were. The most that Paul could tell me was that they were 'court officials of some sort'. Laura had added that she'd seen a similar thing at an appeal trial she'd attended as a law student. At that trial, there'd been a man sitting in a similar position who was there to record everything for the court. I'd asked Laura why, if that was the case, there was a court reporter? Surely that was what they were for? Laura had been non-committal, shrugging her shoulders in response. Paul had been keen to get on with the main discussion, so the conversation was soon forgotten.

I looked at the two court officials, or whoever they were, while we waited for the court to resume. They were similar in terms of age, both in their mid-thirties at a guess. Obviously at home in a courtroom, dressed for the occasion, and not bothered by the files they had with them. I'd been keeping half an eye on them since the appeal began and had noticed that they didn't speak to anyone at all. Not even the usher. The only people they spoke to were each other. I didn't think they were just there to record the appeal, but at the same time, I had no idea who they were.

"Gareth, please tell us in your own words about the night Jennifer died," Paul said a few minutes later when Judge Watling had restarted the trial. Paul cut right to the heart of the topic with no preamble as he often did. I took a deep breath, blew the air out of my cheeks, and looked at Rose, the twelfth juror and the foreman, before replying. This wasn't at Laura's bidding, and I wasn't sure why I'd singled out Rose other than perhaps I thought she might be sympathetic.

"We'd had a bit of an argument, to be honest," I said. "Jennifer was going out with some friends, and either she'd not told me or I'd forgotten. I'd been planning on cooking something for us both, maybe spending the evening on the sofa watching a boxset or something, but instead, she went out for a few drinks with a friend." I paused and reached out to pick up the glass of water on the witness stand in front of me. My hand was shaking, but it wasn't on purpose. "She'd asked me if she looked okay before she left, and all I could say was 'yeah, you look fine' or something like that." I paused again, looking down at my feet. "Next thing I know, I was on my way to the hospital to see her before she went into the operating theatre. But when I got to the hospital, she was already unconscious. I kissed her, promised her everything would be okay. But I didn't say goodbye. I didn't know I would never see her again."

I stopped there, not for dramatic effect, but because I couldn't go on. The only image in my head was of Jennifer at that moment when I'd promised her something I couldn't deliver and had no right to promise her anything. I stared at my feet, unable to look up, unable to talk. Tears streamed down my face. Fuck me this was hard, I'd not been expecting this.

"Your Honour," I heard Paul say. "Could we take a short recess?" The next thing I knew Laura was at my side, her hand on my elbow.

"Gareth," I heard her whisper. "That was a fantastic performance. You did really well." I looked at her, wiping at my eyes with the back of my hand. For a second, I hated her. That was no performance.

That was me, laid bare in front of everyone.

## 35

I sat on the witness stand after the break, trying to stay composed while Paul rearranged his papers yet again. I looked across at the jury while I waited for him to restart. Ella was still dabbing at her eyes with a handkerchief, and Minnie looked just as upset. The young man I'd named Mark was staring at me, and as I caught his eye, he shook his head from side to side. I looked away from him and at Laura, who had four fingers extended on her thigh. The man I'd just been looking at, Mark, would be the focus for the next stage of Paul's questioning.

"Gareth, are you ready for me to continue?" Paul asked.

"Yes," I replied. The word came out almost as a croak. I cleared my throat and repeated myself. "Yes."

"Thank you," Paul said. "What I want to explore now is your state of mind following Jennifer's death. Could you tell us about that, in your own words?" Paul and I had argued about this last week. He was convinced that it was vital to the appeal, but it was easy for him to say. It wasn't him up here on the witness stand.

"I was in bits," I said. "Just torn to pieces. Jennifer was the best thing that had ever happened to me. I used to wake up next to her in the morning and wonder why she was in bed next to me. Not just in bed with me, but married to me." I paused, considering what to say next. With a glance at Mark, I continued. "In my experience, things like Jennifer didn't happen to people like me." Over the course of the next hour, Paul led me through those dark days just after Jennifer had died. We left nothing out. I told the jury about my drinking, and about how low I had sunk. Paul was careful to keep the questions specific in terms of how I felt, what I thought, and the effect on me of what had happened. Eventually, we reached the point of Robert's trial, and Paul wove in additional information for the jury.

He explained the legal loophole that Robert's legal team had used to ensure that the only thing that Robert was charged with was drink driving. At this point, Paul turned to the jury and addressed them directly.

"Ladies and gentlemen, it is vital at this stage you try to put yourself in Gareth's shoes. He has lost his wife, his soulmate, and regardless of the vagaries of the law, the man who took Jennifer from him was on charge." He turned back to address me. "Now I know this is in the transcript, but when the verdict was read out Gareth, can you recall your reaction?"

I looked at my hands, trying to look ashamed.

"Yes," I said. "I shouted at Robert."

"Do you remember what you shouted?" Paul asked. I remembered what I'd said word for word, but wasn't going to repeat it in the courtroom. Paul would do that for me.

"I shouted that I would kill him," I said. Paul shuffled through his paperwork until he found the piece of paper he was looking for. He looked down and then back up at me.

"For the record, and I apologise for the language I am about to use, you said 'You're dead, Wainwright. You're fucking dead. I'll fucking kill you myself'. Is that correct?" I nodded my head, still keeping my eyes downcast and away from the jury. "Gareth, please answer the question for the court transcript," Paul said.

"Yes, that's correct," I replied in a small voice. When we'd discussed this part of the questioning before the trial, Paul and Laura had explained how the prosecutor might try to use those words against me at some point. Paul wanted to get them in front of the jury, but in a way in which they would be sympathetic. It was better that they were brought out now.

"Why did you shout those words, Gareth?" Paul asked. The prosecutor shuffled in her chair, and I looked across at her to see if she was going to object. When she remained silent, I continued.

"I shouted those words because I had just watched the man who murdered my wife get away with it."

"Please, Your Honour." The prosecutor rose to her feet. "Robert Wainwright was not convicted of murder. The only convicted murderer—"

"Miss Revell," the judge warned.

"—in this courtroom is the man on the witness stand," she concluded, almost shouting over the judge as she did so.

"Miss Revell, that's quite enough." Judge Watling had what Jennifer would have described as 'a right face on'. He frowned at the prosecutor as she sat back down. "I will sustain your objection, but with a warning. The jury is to disregard the witness's last statement, and that of Miss Revell as well." Paul had said that something along those lines would happen. The prosecutor could object until she was blue in the face, but I'd still said what Paul wanted me to say. The jury might have been told to disregard it, but they couldn't un-hear it.

Paul continued through my story, and every low point in my life at that time was highlighted in painful detail. The gradual slide toward rock-bottom was laid out for the entire court. The only part of it that I'd not told anyone about was the night I'd thrown up on the carpet watching our wedding video. That was just between me and Jennifer, and I wasn't going to tell a soul about it. My half-hearted attempts to get help for my drinking were described, and Paul deftly brought me to the next key stage of my testimony. The decision to attack Robert Wainwright.

"Now at this point in time, Gareth, you had already started making steps towards your own recovery. Am I correct?" Paul asked, sounding like a psychiatrist. I'd never seen a shrink in real life, but I imagined that this is what they would sound like.

"Yes, that's correct. I'd cut back on my drinking and had started running again to try to give me a different focus."

"But yet you decided to attack Robert Wainwright. What prompted this decision?

"I had gone out for a run one evening, and I saw Robert driving his car. The same car that he had used to kill Jennifer." I looked across at the prosecutor who was stirring into life. "Sorry, the car that was in the accident." She looked at me through half open eyes as if she was daring me to continue. "I knew he was still banned, but he was driving anyway." I took a deep breath, remembering that evening. "Seeing him just driving around like nothing had happened just tipped me over the edge." I locked eyes with juror number four. "So, I decided to do something about it."

Over the course of the next hour, I described how I had planned to attack Robert even though the prosecutor had been through all this already. Everything from finding out where he lived, establishing his pattern of life, to buying the baseball bat at a car boot sale so it couldn't be traced. Paul walked me through the plans I'd put into place to avoid getting caught, and I hoped that if there was a God up there, He wasn't listening. It wasn't the truth, the whole truth, and nothing but the truth, but an amended version of it. I knew I had to protect Tommy, David and Big Joe, so I told the jury that I'd threatened them all. With Paul's help, I tried to paint a picture of me as a desperate man, so desperate he would even threaten his closest friends to get the revenge he so badly wanted. The few times I looked up at the jury, they were all listening, so I thought I'd got away with it. I didn't dare look up at the public gallery in case I caught Big Joe's eye if he was sitting up there. I knew he wasn't happy about having to 'confess' to being threatened by someone like me, but there wasn't anything I could do about that.

Paul got to where I'd laid in wait for Robert for the first time.

"What was your intention at this point?" Paul asked.

"I wanted to hurt him."

"To kill him?"

"No, that was never my plan. I just wanted to hurt him, to make him suffer for what he'd done," I said. "I never wanted to kill him. Only to pay him back."

"So, Robert Wainwright left The Griffin public house, and you followed him along Yarmouth Road?"

"Yes, I did. I was just plucking up the courage to go after him when someone else beat me to it." Paul slowed things right down and we went through what happened in the wasteland in excruciating detail. I told the jury about Robert getting to his feet and walking off after being beaten up by the two strangers.

"So you don't know who the two men who attacked Robert were?" Paul asked.

"No, I don't think I'd ever seen them before. I didn't get a good look at them, anyway. It was dark, and I didn't want them to see me, so I couldn't get too close."

"Would you recognise them again if you saw them?"

"No," I replied. "I don't think I would."

Paul paused for a moment, scribbling something on his notes. I knew that this was a deliberate ploy to let the unexplained attack on Robert sink into the jurors' minds, so I waited for him to continue. Paul lingered until he saw the judge shuffle on his chair.

"Your Honour, I now intend to go through the attack on Mr Wainwright in some detail." He stopped for a few seconds and looked up at the public gallery. I followed Paul's gaze and saw the elderly couple I'd seen earlier getting to their feet and making their way towards the door to the gallery. I wondered who the couple were as we waited for them to leave the court. Paul had obviously arranged this with them in advance, and my best guess was that they were Robert's parents. Seeing as I was just about to describe how I'd attacked Robert, it made sense for them to leave. I remembered the look on Andy's face when he had listened to Jennifer's post-mortem reports during Robert's trial and how that had affected him. No matter how much I hated Robert, if they were his parents, I couldn't blame them one bit for not wanting to hear the next part of my testimony.

Once the door had closed behind the couple and they were out of the courtroom, Paul returned to his questions.

"Gareth, please describe what happened next?"

"I saw Robert leave the pub and make a telephone call. I figured he was phoning for a taxi. He then went down the alleyway to the side of The Griffin pub, so I crossed the road and followed him down the alleyway."

"On the CCTV footage of you crossing the road, you can be seen pulling the baseball bat out of your pocket at this point," Paul said. I paused, unsure whether that was a question. "Which hand did you use to pull out the bat?"

"My right hand."

"Why?"

"I'm right handed."

"Thank you. So, you pulled the bat out with your right hand and followed Robert Wainwright into the alleyway." I nodded in reply. "What was he doing in the alleyway?" Paul asked.

"He was having a…" I stopped and paused. "He was urinating. I had the baseball bat in my hand, so I waited for him to finish and turn around."

"You waited for him to finish urinating?" Paul said.

"Yes. I couldn't hit him while he was, er, urinating. That didn't seem right and besides, I wanted to look him in the eye." I glanced at juror number four, who was leaning forward and listening. "When he turned around, I hit him on the side of the head with the baseball bat."

Paul paused, letting my comment echo around the courtroom for a few seconds.

"What happened then?" he asked me.

"He dropped like a stone."

"How many times did you hit him?"

"Once."

"Once? You only hit him once?"

"Yes," I said firmly. "I only hit him once."

"What happened next?"

"Well, I looked at Robert lying on the floor. To tell the truth, I was horrified. Absolutely horrified by what I had done." I took a deep breath before continuing. "I dropped the bat and knelt down by his side."

"Can you describe any injuries you could see?" Paul asked me.

"I couldn't really see any injuries as such. He had a few drops of blood coming from his nose, and a red mark on the side of his face where I'd smacked him, but there was nothing else."

"A nosebleed and a red mark? Those were the only injuries you could see, is that right?" Paul asked.

"Yes, that's correct," I replied.

"What did you do next?"

"I rolled him onto his side, so he wouldn't swallow his tongue or choke." I looked down at Laura, but she was busy scribbling something on a pad. I wanted her to look up at me, to acknowledge that even though I'd hit Robert with the baseball bat, it wasn't as bad as it had been made out. "He'd dropped his phone when I hit him, but it was still working, so I figured he could call for someone when he woke up."

"How did you know his phone was still working?"

"I could see the photo on the home screen. There was a crack in the glass, but it wasn't shattered," I said. "There was a photograph of him and Jennifer on the screen. From back when they were together."

"And then?" Paul asked after stopping for a few seconds to let that sink in with the jury. I knew he was going to use the phone later on, somehow, so went with it.

"I got up and left, back down the alleyway and toward the road."

"Ladies and gentlemen," Paul turned to the jury, "there is CCTV evidence that clearly shows my client entering the alleyway after Mr Wainwright and leaving again a short time later. The defence does not contest this evidence as it is obviously my client and is consistent with his version of events." Paul turned back to me. "What time was it when you attacked Mr Wainwright?"

"I'm not sure," I replied. "Ten o'clock maybe? Sometime around then, anyway."

"Your Honour, may I introduce Exhibit A, which is a map of the immediate area." Judge Watling nodded his head in response. Laura got to her feet holding a large rolled-up sheet of paper that had been resting against the defence table. She walked to the middle of the courtroom and was met by the usher who was carrying an easel. Laura unrolled the paper and pinned it to the easel before stepping back and adjusting it so that the jury and the rest of the court could see the map. The only person who couldn't see it was Judge Watling. Paul and Laura exchanged places and Paul put a large round red sticker on the map.

"This marker, ladies and gentlemen, is The Griffin pub where the attack took place. Could you describe the route you took from the pub, Gareth?"

As I described the route I had taken, Paul ran his index finger along the roads on the map to show the jury where I had gone.

"I stopped in the park just off Laundry Lane for a few minutes to get my head together." Paul pointed at a green patch on the map to show the jury where the park was.

"How long did you stay in the park?" Paul asked. I shrugged my shoulders.

"I'm not sure, maybe ten minutes or so. I went straight from there to The Heartsease, along St William's way." Paul turned back to the map and placed another red sticker on it.

"This sticker marks the location of The Heartsease pub, ladies and gentlemen. There is CCTV footage which shows my client arriving at the pub at 10:26 pm." He reached through his robes into an inside pocket and pulled out a thick black marker pen, using it to write 10:26 onto the red sticker over The Heartsease pub.

"Ladies and gentlemen of the jury, I am approaching the end of my examination of my client. It will shortly be the turn of the prosecutor to cross examine him, but I would ask you to consider this. My client has been one hundred per cent honest with this court today. That honesty has been brutally difficult for him. He has hidden nothing from you whatsoever." Paul returns to the judge. "I have no further questions for this witness, Your Honour," Paul said with a nod of his head.

The prosecutor got to her feet, slowly. She remained behind her table, and put both hands onto the surface of it, leaning on them with her palms flat on the table.

"Mr Dawson, first may I say how sorry I am for the death of your wife." I wasn't expecting her to say that, and as I looked at Paul and Laura, I didn't think they were either. "That must have been a particularly hard time for you." She paused for a few seconds before looking up at the jury. "Ladies and gentlemen, you'll be pleased to hear my cross examination won't take long." She took her hands off the table and stood up straight. "Mr Dawson, let me see if I understand this correctly. You decided to attack Robert Wainwright, and then planned this attack over a period of some weeks. You purchased a weapon that you thought could not be traced, you stalked Mr Wainwright to maximise your chances of successfully attacking him undetected. You put into place an elaborate series of measures that were designed to mislead the police. And finally, you followed Mr Wainwright into a deserted alley and struck him around the head with a baseball bat, rendering him unconscious." She looked at me, her eyebrows arched.

"Yes, that's correct," I said in a quiet voice, looking at my lap. There was nothing else for me to say.

"And then you hit him again, and again, until he was dead." My head shot up, and I stared at her.

"No," I said forcefully. "No, that's not true. I only hit him once." I could feel my voice getting louder and saw Laura looking at me. I met her gaze, and she gave me a warning look. I swallowed and tried to recover my composure. The prosecutor said nothing else, but just stared at me for what felt like ages.

"I have no further questions for this witness, Your Honour," she said.

## 36

"The defence calls Detective Superintendent Malcolm Griffiths," Paul said in a monotone voice.

I watched as Malcolm made his way to the witness stand, taking a copy of the Bible from the usher as he entered the small wooden enclosure. The policeman was wearing a smart fitted dark grey suit with a maroon shirt and a slightly darker coloured silk tie. He looked sure of himself, and I wondered how many times he'd given evidence in court. He'd been a copper for a while, so it must have been hundreds of times. Not for the first time, I thought it would have been useful to get some coaching from him before the trial if he wasn't on the other side.

Malcolm handed the Bible back to the usher and sat down in the witness stand. Age wise, he looked exactly the same as he had the last time I'd seen him. He'd been promoted to Superintendent since then, which is some-thing I hadn't known until Paul had used his full title just a few seconds ago, and he had a nicer suit on than he was wearing last time around. Other than that, he looked no different apart from perhaps a few extra pounds around the middle.

Paul led him through the preliminary questions, establishing who he was, how many serious crimes he'd investigated as a policeman, and what his role was in my particular case. I'd thought Paul would go over everything with Malcolm in the same way he had done with me, but that wasn't his plan at all.

"Detective Superintendent Griffiths, please could you tell the court how you came to regard my client, Gareth Dawson, as your prime suspect in the murder of Robert Wainwright." Paul was straight to the point, no messing about.

Malcolm looked surprised, and I figured that he'd been expecting to go through the case chronologically. He shifted in his chair before replying.

"Er, well," he said. "I knew Mr Dawson from prior to the events of the night in question. I was the Senior Investigating Officer following the accident in which his wife died." Malcolm was talking in the stiff, formal way I remembered from the last trial. He was every inch a policeman. "As soon as I found out who the victim was, Mr Dawson became a person of interest straight away given his previous relationship with Mr Wainwright." I don't know if I'd have called it a relationship.

"So, you went to see him?" Paul asked. "Popped round for a chat?"

"Yes, we went to interview Mr Dawson to ascertain his whereabouts during the evening in question," Malcolm replied.

"Did you have any other suspects at this stage? Any other persons of interest, as you put it?"

"Not at that stage, no. But we were actively pursuing

several leads. Door to door interviews, appeals for witnesses, that type of activity."

"Then why were there four of you?" Paul asked.

"I'm sorry, when?"

"When you went round to interview him. Why were there four of you?"

"Well, er, that's standard procedure." Malcolm was looking uncomfortable.

"Really? So when the police interview someone informally, it's standard procedure to send round four policemen, and hide one of them at the back of the property."

"Not every time." Paul paused, obviously thinking carefully about what to say next. "It depends on the risk assessment. In Mr Dawson's case, we considered that he could be a flight risk, so we took precautions against that situation developing."

"A flight risk?" Paul repeated. "But why would you think that? This is a man with no criminal record, no history with the police at all. Whatever would make you think he was a flight risk?" Malcolm paused for a second before replying.

"Experience, more than anything else," he said, looking uncomfortable.

"Did you have any other suspects at all? How many other people of interest did you interview?" Paul stared at Malcolm, unblinking. It was quite a few seconds before Malcolm replied.

"None," he said eventually.

"But you looked into Mr Wainwright's friends, acquaintances, that sort of thing?"

"We did the standard background checks into him, yes. But it was only a couple of hours later when we retrieved CCTV footage from a house just up the road from the alleyway. The footage clearly showed Mr Dawson heading in that direction with a baseball bat and leaving again a few minutes later. Mr Dawson then became a suspect, as opposed to a person of interest."

"Ah yes," Paul said as if he'd forgotten something. "The CCTV footage. I take it you watched the full tape."

"Yes, we did," Malcolm said confidently.

"And there was no one else on it?"

"No, there wasn't."

"Could you see the entrance to the alleyway on the tape?" Paul asked.

"No, the camera angle didn't extend to that area."

"So although you saw Mr Dawson heading to and then leaving the immediate vicinity of the alley, you couldn't actually see him enter or leave the alley itself?"

"That's correct," Paul said, frowning for a few seconds before sitting back in his chair. I knew exactly where Paul was going, and as I watched Malcolm's face I knew from how his expression changed that he'd worked it out as well.

"So if you couldn't see Mr Dawson enter the alleyway, you also couldn't see if anyone else entered it. If they approached from the opposite direction then the camera wouldn't pick them up, would it?"

"That's correct," Malcolm said. Paul looked at him expectantly, but Malcolm said nothing else.

"Were you able to get the time of the attack from the footage?" Paul asked after a pause long enough to let the idea of another attacker hang in the air. Malcolm explained that the time hadn't been set on the CCTV camera, but they'd been able to use the footage to calculate how long I'd been in the alleyway. Just under sixty seconds. "So how did you time the attack?"

"Mr Wainwright called for a taxi at 9:57 pm. The ambulance service received a 999 telephone call at 10:45 pm when the barman from the pub found the victim.

According to Mr Wainwright's phone records, his phone dropped from the network at 10:22 pm, so we assume that this was the actual time of the attack itself," Malcolm explained.

"Sorry, dropped from the network? What do you mean by that?" Paul asked.

"The phone was smashed, we assume during the attack. This was at 10:22 pm. These timings are from the carrier, so we know that time is accurate regardless of the time on the phone itself. That's when the signal from the phone stopped." Paul turned to the map and placed a sticker over The Griffin pub. Before he continued, he wrote 10.22 pm on the sticker, adding a question mark after it.

"Ladies and gentlemen, could I refer you to photograph number seventeen in your folders?" Paul asked the jury. They all shuffled through their folders with Paul watching until he thought they had all got to the right photograph. "As the picture shows, Mr Wainwright's phone is completely smashed. Broken to the point of destruction, I would suggest. Certainly more than just a cracked screen, which is what Mr Dawson reports." Paul paused, looking at Malcolm. "Those timings don't work though, do they? My client followed Mr Wainwright into the alleyway straight after the phone call was made to the taxi firm, so that would have been just after ten in the evening. He can be seen on the footage just after the victim finished his call, and leaving around 60 seconds later."

"Your Honour," the prosecutor called out. I'd almost forgotten she was there, she'd been so quiet. "Surely my learned friend is calling for his witness to speculate here?"

"Your Honour, this witness is a policeman with over twenty years service. This is hardly speculation." Judge Watling looked at them both before replying.

"Yes, but even so I do think that Miss Revell has got

this one right," he said. "Please rephrase or retract the question, Mr Dewar." Paul made a show of looking exasperated but again, he'd got his point across.

"I'll retract the question, Your Honour. I apologise." Paul looked down at his notes before continuing. "Detective Superintendent, in your experience, is it possible that while Mr Dawson did attack Robert Wainwright at or about ten o'clock, the victim was then subsequently attacked by an unknown party later on? And it was during this second attack that the phone was smashed, dropping it from the network?"

"It's possible," Malcolm replied. "But it's also possible that Mr Dawson came back to the alleyway from the opposite direction, when he wouldn't have been seen by the camera. We only have his word for the exact sequencing of events."

"But there's also CCTV footage from The Heartsease pub that shows Mr Dawson arriving there at 10:16 pm. If the attack that killed Mr Wainwright was at 10:22 pm, then it doesn't work." I glanced up at the jury to see several of them frowning. Paul crossed over to the map and wrote 10:16 pm on the sticker covering The Heartsease pub.

"You're right, but we discounted the accuracy of the CCTV timing at the Heartsease," Malcolm said. Paul turned back to Malcolm, eyebrows raised.

"Why?" Paul asked, frowning. My stomach lurched as Malcolm leaned forward and shot a dark look in my direction.

"Well, you know who installed the cameras at the pub?" He looked back at Paul.

"Please enlighten us," Paul said. Malcolm glanced back at me for a second, and I saw a slight frown cross his face.

"Mr Dawson did," he said. Both Paul and Laura looked at me. "Given the other measures he'd taken to avoid detection, we didn't believe the time on that camera was accurate." Oops. I'd not adjusted the time on the camera at The Heartsease, but hadn't mentioned to Paul and Laura that I'd installed it. I felt the colour rising in my cheeks.

Paul recovered from the surprise first, and continued talking after adding a question mark after the time marked on the sticker. As he asked Malcolm his next question, something about whether or not he'd been able to verify that the time on the cameras was incorrect or if it was only an assumption, Laura continued to stare at me, her face as dark as thunder. I looked down, ashamed.

"So were you able to verify that the camera had been tampered with?" Paul asked.

"No," Malcolm replied. "We sent the device to a firm we have a contract with for forensic analysis. They looked at it, and couldn't tell either way."

"What was the firm called?" Malcolm checked his notes before replying to Paul's question.

"Digital Solutions Incorporated," he said.

"But if they had confirmed that the time was accurate, would that be admissible evidence to the court?"

"Yes, it would. That's part of the contract, that they provide evidence that complies with the Criminal Procedure and Investigations Act 1996."

"Which then means it can be used in court, is that correct?" Paul looked over at the jury as he said this.

"That's correct, yes," Malcolm said.

"Okay, Detective Superintendent Griffiths, let me ask you a question. If it had been possible to demonstrate that the time on the CCTV camera was accurate, and Mr Dawson was in that location at that time, would this have changed your investigation?"

"It would, to an extent," Malcolm replied, looking

thoughtful. "But he's admitted hitting Mr Wainwright, so I don't understand how it would be possible."

"Thank you," Paul replied. "Do you know a gentleman called Florin Caren?" Malcolm frowned at the abrupt change in direction, as did most of the jury.

"Er, yes. I know of him," he said.

"Could you tell the jury about him, please?" Paul asked. "Just a précis will be fine." Malcolm shifted in his chair, and the creases on his forehead deepened.

"I wasn't expecting to be asked about him, but he was a Romanian criminal who SOCA put away earlier this year," he said. Paul was about to ask him a question when he continued. "Serious Organised Crime Agency, sorry." Paul nodded in response.

"And what was your involvement with the case?"

"It was quite minor as far as I remember. The individual in question was based in London, but had close links to Norwich so SOCA asked us for input. It was just in an advisory role as we know the area."

"Do you remember what Mr Caren was convicted of?" Paul asked as Miss Revell rose to her feet.

"Your Honour, how is this relevant?" she said. The Judge looked at Paul for a reply.

"It will become clear in due course, Your Honour," Paul replied.

"I shall hold you to that, Mr Dewar. Please continue." Miss Revell sat back down at the judge's words, turning to one of her colleagues and whispering something in his ear.

"Detective Superintendent, please carry on. Do you remember what this Mr Caren was convicted of?" Paul repeated his question.

"It was a long line of convictions if I remember correctly. Some quite serious ones. He was not a nice man,"

"And the most serious conviction?"

"I'm not one hundred per cent sure."

"In which case, allow me to refresh your memory. Mr Caren was arrested in April this year, and subsequently convicted of murder and conspiracy to murder. He is currently incarcerated in Belmarsh Prison." There was silence in the courtroom for a few seconds, probably as everyone tried to work out how this was connected to my case. "Thank you, Detective Superintendent. No more questions," Paul said, turning away from Malcolm.

I zoned out as the Prosecutor got to her feet and started asking Malcolm questions. They were all about how I'd 'confessed' to everything once I found out Robert was dead, and I tired of them quickly. Looking at the jury they looked as bored as I was. I saw one of them looking at me, the older chap Albert, with a curious expression on his face. I wondered what he was thinking. There'd not been much so far in the trial that was particularly explosive, but I knew Paul was laying the groundwork out carefully. I just wasn't sure what he was building up to. When we'd been preparing for the trial during the last few weeks, I'd tried very hard to find out what avenues he was going to explore. He'd refused to share his strategy and when I tried to press Laura, she clammed up immediately. I was going to find out at the same time as the jury.

I nodded at Albert as he was still looking at me, and to my surprise, he nodded back.

## 37

The next witness that Paul called to the stand was Alfie Nesbitt, his investigator. He was quite a small man, at least he was for a policeman. Or an ex-policeman, anyway. He stood maybe five feet five and was built like a runner. Thin and wiry. He took the oath with an air of boredom and sat in the witness stand as if he did this sort of thing every day.

"Mr Nesbitt," Paul said, "I would like if I may to introduce you to the jury. Ladies and gentlemen," Paul turned to the jury, "this is Mr Alfred Nesbitt, known as Alfie. He's an investigator who I hired for this case. I have brought him to the stand to enable me to introduce some new evidence that was not considered at the previous trial. Mr Nesbitt, Alfie, could you tell the jury what you did for a living before you became a private investigator?"

"I was a police officer, serving for eleven years in Suffolk Constabulary. I was a cybercrime specialist."

"But you are no longer a police officer now?"

"That's correct. I resigned from the force two years ago."

"Could you share with the jury the details of your resignation?" Paul asked. Alfie turned to face the jury square on, tilting his head upward.

"Yes. I resigned due to allegations about my behaviour. These allegations were never proven, and no formal action was taken against me, but I felt that my position within the police had become untenable."

"I see," Paul said. "So regardless of whatever these allegations were, no charges were ever brought against you?"

"They weren't criminal allegations," Alfie said. Paul shot a swift glance at Miss Revell, who was leaning forward on her desk.

"No criminal allegations, no formal action taken, is that correct?" Paul asked.

"Your Honour," Miss Revell stood. "If I may, could I question the impartiality of this witness?" The judge looked at Paul for a response.

"Your Honour, my learned friend is quite within her rights to question his impartiality, and this is precisely why I have raised the witness' former occupation. However, Mr Nesbitt is here to present tangible evidence he has uncovered in his role as my investigator," Paul said. It was obvious that he had been expecting the challenge. "He is not here to offer an opinion, nor to speculate. His character cannot be queried by this court, surely?"

The judge took a few seconds to consider what Miss Revell and Paul had said.

"Very well," he replied over the top of his glasses. "But Mr Dewar, I will be swift to intervene if your witness steps outside those parameters."

"Thank you, Your Honour," Paul said. As Miss Revell sat back down in her seat and whispered to one of her colleagues, I noticed Laura let out a deep breath. The

burning question I had, and I was sure everyone else in the
room had, was exactly what the allegations against Alfie
Nesbitt were. It didn't look like we would find out, though.
"Your Honour, I would like to introduce a new exhibit.
This is footage from a dashboard camera, or dash-cam,
that my investigator has uncovered." Judge Watling
nodded, and the usher wheeled a large flat screen television
to the centre of the courtroom. "Alfie, could you tell us
how you uncovered this footage?" Paul asked.

Alfie cleared his throat before replying. When he spoke,
he was softly spoken which was a marked difference to
when he had taken the oath.

"I canvassed the taxi firms operating in the area, asking
them to review their taskings for the evening in question. I
was trying to find any cabbies, sorry, taxi drivers, who may
have been in the area at the time of the attack." Alfie
spoke in a similar way to Malcolm, but not as stilted. I
wondered if this was something they taught at police
school. How to talk in court, or something like that.

"I see," Paul said. "And you found some, I take it?"
Alfie obviously had, or there would be no need for the big
television. I got the impression that Paul was just trying to
keep the momentum going and avoid everyone waiting in
silence for the usher to plug the damn thing in.

"Yes, I did," Alfie replied. "I found a taxi firm based in
Norwich, ABC Taxis, which had sent a vehicle for a pickup
in Dussindale. They put me in touch with the driver, and I
was able to confirm with him that he had a dash-cam
fitted. I was also able to obtain the device itself from the
driver." Paul looked across at the usher, who was still struggling with the television. If it wasn't for the two prison officers either side of me, I'd have gone to give him a hand
with it.

"So, what did you do with this device?" Paul asked.

"I sent it to a company called Digital Solutions Incorporated, based in Cambridge, for analysis."

"Why did you send it to that particular company?" It was obvious that Paul and Alfie were following a well-rehearsed script, but that didn't make it any less interesting.

"They're Home Office approved analysts of digital media and devices." Alfie glanced across at the public gallery where Malcolm was still sitting. I'd not noticed him come back into the gallery after he'd finished giving evidence. The look the two of them exchanged was fierce. Not much love lost there, then. I wondered again what Alfie had done to get himself thrown out of the police, and whether or not Malcolm had been involved. "They're the same company that Norfolk Police outsource all their digital analysis to."

"Yes, thank you, Alfie. A previous witness has covered that part already," Paul replied.

The court usher prodded at a remote control, and the screen flashed into life. He crossed the court and handed the remote control to Paul.

"Your Honour, I would like to introduce this footage to the court." The judge nodded in response. "Alfie, before we view the footage, could you just read out the introductory paragraph of the report from Digital Solutions Incorporated?" Alfie unfolded a sheet of paper he had pulled out from a pocket.

"Following detailed forensic analysis of the device, Digital Solutions Incorporated are able to state with certainty that the device settings have not been altered in any way since installation. These settings include the date and time, which have been confirmed to be correct at the time of the examination and unaltered since the device installation. The device has been found to be in full working order, including the Global Positioning Satellite functions which maintain the date and time stamp." Alfie's voice suited the dry jargon perfectly.

"So the date and time on the device are correct, and haven't been altered?" Paul summarised.

"That's correct."

"And this is confirmed by a Home Office approved analyst?" Paul said, hammering the point home for the jury. I leaned forward in my chair, eager to see the footage itself.

"Yes," Alfie replied.

"Thank you," Paul said. "Could the jury see the footage, please?"

The usher pointed the remote control toward the television and pressed a button. The DVD player underneath the television whirred into life, and the view through a windscreen flickered onto the screen. In the bottom right-hand corner of the screen, there was some small white text showing a date and time. On the television, the car was driving slowly, and I recognised the area it was driving through as Thorpe St Andrew. It even went past the primary school that I had gone to as a child. It stopped at a red light at the top of one of the main roads leading through the town, Thunder Lane, and a pedestrian could be seen crossing the road in front of the car. It was a very familiar looking pedestrian. Me.

Paul stabbed at the remote control just as I looked at the car, freezing my face on the screen. The quality was very good indeed, much better than the grainy images from the camera that caught me at The Griffin pub. There was no doubt who it was.

"Alfie, for the benefit of the jury, could you confirm the location of the vehicle and read out the date and the time on the screen please?" Paul crossed to the map, another red sticker in his hand.

"The location is the traffic lights between Thunder Lane and St William's Way, as you can see from the road signs. This is supported by the GPS chip in the dash-cam." Paul located the junction on the map and placed the sticker on it. It almost overlapped the sticker that was placed over The Heartsease pub, they were that close together. Paul took the lid off his marker pen.

"What is the time on the footage please?"

"10:20 pm," Alfie said.

Paul wrote 10:20 pm on the sticker and took a step back.

"Alfie, what is the distance between this junction and The Heartsease pub?" Paul asked.

"It's just under half a mile. I measured it using GPS when I walked the route."

"How long did that take you?"

'Five minutes," Alfie replied. Paul tapped the sticker over the Heartsease pub and looked thoughtfully at it, no doubt hoping that the jury was doing the same thing.

"And the distance between the junction and the location of Mr Wainwright's body?" Paul asked.

"That's one point three miles. It took me twenty three minutes at normal walking speed,' Alfie replied. "That was the direct route, not through the park," he added. Paul tapped again at the map, this time highlighting the sticker over The Griffin pub with '10:22 pm' written on it before turning to the jury. He said nothing, but just looked at them with his eyebrows raised, inviting them to make the conclusion themselves. There was no way I could have made it from The Griffin to the spot where the dash-cam had caught me in two minutes. Even Usain Bolt wouldn't have been able to do it that quickly.

The screen showing my frozen face stayed turned on as Paul returned to the defence table. Laura handed him another set of notes. Paul looked up at me briefly before he turned back around. He had his back to the jury, and I caught the faintest of smiles on his face before it disappeared as he turned back around.

"Now, Alfie, you also did some more work for me looking more closely at Mr Wainwright," Paul said. "Could you tell the court about that?"

"Yes," Alfie replied. He looked up toward the public gallery. I followed his gaze and saw that the old couple had returned and were sitting in their original location. "With the permission of Mr Wainwright's parents, I was able to access his laptop."

"Really?" Paul said with a note of what sounded like surprise. "They were happy to hand it over to you?"

"When I explained what we were looking at, yes." In the public gallery, the old man nodded at me. "Mr Wainwright's father was quite surprised that the police hadn't already asked for it," Alfie continued.

"Your Honour," I heard Miss Revell call out. "This is hearsay, surely."

"Yes, you're quite right," Judge Watling replied. "Mr Nesbitt, you should know better as an ex-policeman." Alfie managed to look suitably apologetic for a few seconds, but it didn't last for long.

"So, you had the laptop analysed?" Paul continued after the judge had finished telling the jury to disregard the statement. It was as if the objection hadn't even registered with Paul.

"Yes, using the same firm as before. Digital Solutions Incorporated."

"Which is the firm that the police would have used, had they analysed the laptop?" Paul asked.

"That's correct, yes."

Paul paused for a few seconds, looking at his notes. I

watched him as he stood there, and wondered what was coming next.

"Could you give us some information about what you found on the laptop, please Alfie?" he asked a couple of seconds later.

"There were three main elements. His social profiles, his e-mail, and his banking records," Alfie replied.

"Let me just check, you were able to access all this information through his laptop?" Paul said, no doubt trying to head off an objection from the prosecutor about whether or not they would be allowed in court. Just as Alfie was about to reply to Paul, the prosecutor got to her feet.

"Your Honour, may we approach the bench?" she asked. Judge Watling looked down at her, across at Paul, and back to her again. He raised his eyebrows for a few seconds before replying.

"Yes, please do," the judge said. Paul and Miss Revell both walked from behind their respective tables toward where the Judge was sitting. For a few minutes, there was a hushed conversation between the three of them. It was impossible to hear anything that was said, and their body language gave nothing away although it was difficult to get any cues as they were facing away from me. There was a quiet hubbub of conversation in the courtroom as the discussion went on, until Judge Watling lifted his head up to address the jurors.

"Ladies and gentlemen, I'm afraid that I am going to recess the court at this point for further discussions between myself and the counsels." Judge Watling looked up at the large clock on the wall of the courtroom. "It's now just after eleven o'clock, so we'll break here for lunch and reconvene at one o'clock this afternoon."

The usher stepped forward and half the people in the court were already on their feet by the time he had told us to 'all rise', no doubt keen to make the most of the extra time for lunch. The only people who didn't move were the two court officials sitting at the table behind the lawyers. Paul and Miss Revell walked behind the judge as they disappeared through the door behind the judge's bench. As I stood watching them, I tried to imagine what his chambers were like. Mahogany walls, comfortable armchairs, and an endless supply of cigars and brandy perhaps? Or was it magnolia walls and plastic tables and chairs like the rest of the courtroom? The chances of me finding out soon were slim, that much I knew.

Mr Jackson and his nameless colleague led me back down to the holding area underneath the courtroom and locked me into one of the cells. I sat on the plastic mattress, loosened my tie and undid the top button on my shirt. The cell doors and walls were just bars, so although I was locked in, I could see out through the chipped painted metal. I was the only occupant in there. The second prison officer disappeared back through the door, no doubt off for a smoke, and Mr Jackson sat on one of the chairs in the communal area between the cells. A battered copy of a newspaper sat on the table in front of him.

"What do you think then, Mr Jackson?" I tried engaging him in conversation. It was worth a try.

"About what? Norwich's chances against West Ham at the weekend?" he replied in a gruff voice. That was probably the closest I'd heard him ever come to humour. "I think City'll get stuffed," he said. I desperately racked my brains to try to remember something about the current team, but came up short.

"They're not bad at the back, but they've not got much up front," I tried, remembering a conversation I'd overhead back at the prison. Mr Jackson looked at me, a curious expression on his face. He made a sound that was somewhere between a grunt and a moan and opened the paper in front of him. I guessed that the conversation was over.

About ten minutes later, the other prison guard returned closely followed by Laura who was carrying a Sainsbury's carrier bag. She walked over to the cell and pushed the bag through the bars. I opened it to see a prawn sandwich, a packet of cheese and onion crisps, and a can of coke. I'd not had a prawn sandwich since before I'd been locked up, and it was quite possibly my favourite sandwich in the world.

"Oh my God," I said. "Who told you?" I looked up at her to see a broad smile on her face.

"Your mate Tommy mentioned that you had a bit of a thing for prawn sarnies, so I thought I'd treat you," she said, still grinning. I looked across at Mr Jackson, afraid for a second that he would come across and confiscate the bag. He didn't seem bothered in the slightest, so I tore open the sandwich and took a huge bite out of it. I closed my eyes and savoured the taste. When I opened them again, Laura was sitting on one of the plastic chairs just the other side of the bars. I'd been so focused on the taste of the soft bread and prawn mayonnaise that I'd not even heard her fetch a chair.

"So, what's going on?" I mumbled through another bite of the sandwich.

"Don't talk with your mouth full," she replied with a smile. "I'm not sure, to be honest. I think it's probably about whether what's on Wainwright's laptop is admissible or not."

"Why would it not be?" I asked.

"Er, because he's dead," Laura said, the smile fading. "All sorts of consent issues there. I wouldn't worry though, Paul's all over it."

"How important is what's on the thing?" I said, my appetite starting to fade. Laura looked at me, her face now deadpan. She blew her breath out through her cheeks.

"Well, I wouldn't quite say 'no laptop, no case', but probably not far off it, to be honest. It's pretty crucial."

I put the remains of the sandwich back in the plastic bag, my appetite now completely gone. This made little sense. Surely they all had to agree what could and couldn't be talked about in the court before the trial? Laura and I sat in silence for a few minutes before she looked at her watch.

"I need to get going, Gareth," she said. "I'm meeting Seb for lunch around the corner." I tried to hide my disappointment as I thanked her for the sandwich, but from the look on her face as she said goodbye, I didn't think I'd done a very good job of it. When she'd left the cell block, I slipped my shoes off and lay down on the thin plastic mattress, lacing my arms behind my head and staring at the ceiling.

I seemed to spend most of my life in this position, just thinking.

## 38

"Ladies and gentlemen, I trust that you all had an enjoyable lunch," Judge Watling said from his raised position at the front of the courtroom. I thought about my half-eaten sandwich that was in the bin of the cell block downstairs. I'd eaten the crisps and drunk the can of coke, but had not been able to finish the sandwich. "I apologise for the delay over lunch, but the counsels and I had a couple of the finer points of law to discuss. For the record, I have ruled that the evidence contained within Mr Wainwright's laptop should be allowed into evidence." I exhaled, not even aware that I'd been holding my breath. Laura turned around to look at me, and I tried to keep my face neutral but might have let a small smile slip through. I just caught the judge saying something about the Criminal Justice Act from the year two thousand and something or other. I couldn't care less what the legal point was, I was just relieved that it was going to be allowed. As Paul stood to face the front of the courtroom, I had to remind myself that I had no idea what the evidence actually was, but I trusted his judgement. I didn't have any other options.

"Mr Nesbitt," Paul said to Alfie who was back in his original position on the witness stand. "Let's start with social profiles, shall we?"

"Yes, certainly," Alfie replied. "Until almost a year ago, Mr Wainwright was an active social media user. He had accounts on Twitter, Facebook and also Instagram, and was active on all of them. These accounts have all been verified with the relevant service providers as existing and used until that point." Alfie stopped there and looked at Paul. This looked like it was a well-rehearsed play for the jury, but I guessed it didn't matter whether it was or not.

"Until around a year ago, you say. What happened then?" Paul asked.

"They were all deleted. I was able to retrieve most of the content from various internet archives that catalogue social media profiles, and there was nothing particularly contentious within them." Alfie looked down at his notes for a second. "But they were all deleted within a few days of each other, at about the same time he moved house."

"And was there anything unusual about his activity when he moved house?" It was obvious, at least to me, that Paul was leading Alfie carefully through a series of events to build a picture for the jury.

"Yes, there was," Alfie replied. "He became ex-directory at that point, and he also failed to re-register on the electoral role at his new address." Paul paused to let that sink in for the jury.

"Almost as if he was trying to hide from something or someone?" Paul suggested. I looked across at Miss Revell, expecting her to object. I was getting the hang of things. As I watched, one of the two young men with her leaned across and whispered something in her ear.

"Your Honour," Miss Revell said, half rising to her feet. "Counsel is leading the witness to speculate."

"Thank you, Miss Revell, you are quite correct," Judge Watling replied, giving Miss Revell a look somewhere between confusion and concern.

"I apologise, Your Honour," Paul replied, also looking at his counterpart. I couldn't read his face, and not for the first time I promised myself never to play poker with the man if I ever got the opportunity.

"So to summarise, in May of this year, Mr Wainwright deleted all of his social media accounts and moved house. At the same time, he became unlisted in public telephone directories, and also didn't register himself on the electoral roll?"

"That's correct," Alfie replied. Paul's previous comment about Robert hiding wasn't needed. It was obvious that was what he was trying to do. "So, I looked at his e-mail account to see if there was any further information there."

"Was this information password protected?" Paul asked, looking at the Judge.

"No, the password was saved onto the computer so wasn't required by the firm that did the analysis," Alfie replied. The judge nodded his head, and I figured that this must have been part of the discussions in the back room. Maybe something about the information being easily available and not hacked? I looked up at the public gallery and saw David sitting up there. When I caught his eye, he gave me a theatrical wink that I hoped no one else in the courtroom noticed. Saved onto the computer my arse.

"I examined his e-mail account, including his deleted items. He didn't empty his deleted items very often if at all," Alfie said. I didn't dare look up at David. "There was a series of increasingly threatening e-mails from an account with the e-mail address 'f.caran@posta.ro' regarding repayment of an unspecified sum of money throughout March and April. The last e-mail from this individual was on April 21st. Then there was a further e-mail from another Romanian service provider on April 25th. It's not clear who this came from as the e-mail address is a random collection of letters and digits."

"Your Honour, may I introduce these e-mails as exhibits? These are copies of the relevant e-mails to Robert Wainwright." The judge nodded as Paul handed him a copy of what must have been the e-mail. Laura then handed copies to the usher who walked across to Miss Revell, handed her a copy and continued to the jurors' bench after giving copies to the two court officials sitting behind the prosecution desk. As the jurors passed the papers down their line, Paul continued. "Could you read this e-mail out please, Alfie?" Alfie cleared his throat before replying.

"This e-mail is from 'XDY654R@home.ro', and is dated April 25$^{th}$ at 10:45 am. The text of the e-mail reads 'Last warning. Pay now.' The e-mail isn't signed."

"Were there any more e-mails from this e-mail address?" Paul asked.

"No, nothing," Alfie replied.

"Ladies and gentlemen, may I remind you that April 24$^{th}$ is the night that Robert Wainwright was attacked by the unknown assailants, as reported by the defendant." He then turned back to Alfie.

"Mr Nesbitt, could you let us know what you found out about Mr Wainwright's finances when you had his computer examined?" Paul said.

"Yes. Digital Solutions Incorporated was able to retrieve all his bank statements from his online account. Again, his passwords and access codes were all saved onto his computer." I didn't look up at David.

"So, what did they show in terms of financial activity?"

"Well, the bulk of his transactions were pretty routine," Alfie replied. "Direct debits, cash withdrawals, that sort of thing. Nothing out of the ordinary from January at all."

"How about prior to January?" Paul asked. "In terms of, as you put it, anything out of the ordinary?"

"Yes. Prior to January, there were a series of regular payments to six different online gambling companies. We could only go back three years, but they increased in amount over time. In January, the total payment to all six companies was just over £10,000." Several sets of eyebrows in the courtroom, including my own, shot up.

"In one month?" Paul asked, doing a good impression of incredulity.

"That's correct," Alfie replied. "But at the same time, there were also a series of payments into the account." Alfie stressed the word 'into'.

"Were you able to trace where this money was coming from?"

"No. They were cash payments into the account, usually in the first week of the month. Untraceable. Like the outgoing payments, they slowly increased over about two years. This was separate from his wages which were paid by bank transfer at the end of the month," Alfie explained.

"Did the incoming cash payments and outgoing payments to the gambling companies match?" Paul asked.

"No, not quite. Some months there was more coming in than coming out, but most of the time it was the other way round. He was haemorrhaging money. There was also a regular series of unusual outgoing bank transfers, usually just after he got paid for his regular job."

"And what made them unusual?"

"It was where they were going to," Alfie replied. "That's what made them unusual. There's no way of tracing the actual account holder, but the IBAN was from an overseas account." A frown creased Paul's forehead and as if he realised what the gesture meant, Alfie carried on. "An IBAN is an International Bank Account Number. The first two letters show which country the account is in."

"So where were these payments going to?" Paul asked.

"The IBAN started with the letters 'RO'. That's the identifier for Romania,' Alfie replied.

"Mr Wainwright was making regular payments to an account in Romania?"

"Yes," Alfie said. "Until March. That's when the payments to the Romanian account stopped."

Paul paused, making notes on a pad.

"Mr Nesbitt, let me make sure I understand this," he said, looking across for an instant at Miss Revell before returning his gaze to the investigator. "Mr Wainwright was paying cash into his bank account regularly, separate to his wages. He was spending a lot of money each month on internet gambling, and making regular payments to an unknown account in Romania which stopped in March." Paul stopped at that point, looking toward the jury. It looked as if he was contemplating carrying on, but he didn't say anything further.

"No more questions, Your Honour," Paul said, turning to face the judge for a second before returning to his seat. As he sat down, Laura put her hand on his arm and squeezed it, coaxing a brief smile from him.

"Miss Revell?" Judge Watling said. I looked over at the prosecutor's bench. She was deep in conversation with one of the suited men, and I didn't think she'd heard the judge call her name. "Miss Revell?" the judge said again, louder than the time before. He looked pissed off which I thought was a good thing.

"Sorry, Your Honour," Miss Revell replied, rearranging

the wig on her head where it had slipped forward. "Er, yes, I do have some questions."

Alfie crossed his hands in his lap as Miss Revell got to her feet.

"Mr Nesbitt, you have specified that all of the data you obtained from this laptop was easily available? Not password protected in any way?"

"Yes, that's correct," he replied. Miss Revell turned to Judge Watling.

"Your Honour, as we discussed in chambers, I have serious concerns about the integrity of this laptop's data. You offered me the opportunity to explore this in open court." The judge nodded and she turned back to Alfie. "Mr Nesbitt, you are quite au-fait with computers, are you not? Given your history working within the computer crime unit of Suffolk Police?"

"Yes, I am."

"And one of the tasks that you undertook within that unit was the forensic analysis of computers, which included password retrieval?" Alfie started to reply when Paul cut him off.

"Your Honour, please. My witness appears to be about to be accused of a crime by my learned colleague," he said. Miss Revell shot an immediate response back at Paul.

"I am not, I simply suggest that the laptop could have been compromised."

"Miss Revell, you are skating on rather thin ice with your suggestion," Judge Watling warned her. "There is a fine line between suggesting a compromise, and linking the witness to this compromise." Miss Revell looked at the judge, and I wondered if she was taking one for the team to put the suggestion into the jurors' heads.

"Judge Watling?" I heard a voice and realised that it

was Alfie. The judge looked at him, as surprised as I was to hear him interrupt the argument.

"Yes, Mr Nesbitt?"

"Perhaps I could point out I never had possession of the laptop. It was collected directly from Mr and Mrs Wainwright's address by courier and taken to Digital Solutions Incorporated. It was never in my possession at all," Alfie said. "Nor the defence team. It was sent directly from Mr and Mrs Wainwright's house to the analysts by courier."

"I have an audit trail to support that, Your Honour," Paul chipped in, and I had to concentrate on keeping a straight face and not look at David. Who could possibly be a better courier to collect a laptop than him? Miss Revell looked crestfallen at this news, looking back to her colleagues on the bench who both gave her blank stares in return.

"Oh," she said as Paul sat back down in his chair. That hadn't gone well for her at all. She rallied and went on to ask Alfie more questions about not being able to trace the origin of the cash payments made to Robert or the recipient of the payments, but the questions soon petered out.


I looked across at the jury and could tell from the look on their faces that this innings had definitely gone to Paul and Alfie.

## 39

It took me a second or two to realise that I'd been stabbed. Well, stabbed may be a bit dramatic. Slashed with a homemade knife is a more accurate way of describing it. I was queuing up for supper back at the prison, chatting with Pete about the day's events and the investigator, Alfie Nesbitt. We were discussing what he might have been accused of when he was a copper. Pete was sure Alfie had been on the nick, perhaps using computers to syphon off money somehow, when someone brushed past me in the queue, knocking me toward the food counter. I was just about to say something to the prisoner who'd barged into me when I felt a white-hot pain across my buttock. I put my hand on my backside and it came away covered in blood. My blood.

As soon as other prisoners saw the blood on my hand, a commotion started up that soon got the attention of the prison officers. Several of the prisoners shouted and jostled about, and I heard someone shout "knife" at the top of his voice. I wasn't sure whether they were just doing it to create confusion to allow whoever had sliced me to get away, whether it was a genuine concern for my welfare, or both. It didn't matter anyway. The prisoner with the knife was long gone.

"Move, move," Mr Jackson shouted as he cleaved a path toward me through the prisoners, closely followed by another two officers. His bulk cut through the small crowd with ease. Once he reached me, he looked at me with an impassive expression before reaching out and grabbing my shoulder with a huge hand. He spun me around and looked down at my tracksuit trousers which were getting heavier with the blood pouring out of the cut. I'd still not seen the extent of the damage, but started to feel light headed. I'd never been good with the sight of blood, and when it was mine it was ten times worse. "Right, let's get you to the infirmary," he said, pushing me away from the food counter. "You're not going to faint on me, are you?"

"No, I'm good," I replied, even though I wasn't.

Other than asking me if I'd seen who the prisoner with the knife was, Mr Jackson didn't say another word as he led me to the infirmary, a room the other side of two very serious doors. I knew there was a small ward attached to it from what Pete had told me, but I'd never been here as a customer. A male nurse came out to meet us as Mr Jackson pointed toward the single examination couch in the room. I shuffled onto it, face down.

"What've we got, then?" the nurse said. He was dressed in the same pyjamas I'd seen at the hospital when Jennifer died, but his were blue instead of green.

"Knife wound to the buttock. Looks deep," I heard Mr Jackson say. "His name's Dawson."

"Mr Dawson?" the nurse said. I turned to look at him. "My name's Damien, I'm the nurse practitioner here. I'm just going to have a look at this wound, okay?" I wasn't sure what the difference between a regular nurse and a nurse practitioner was, but he looked like an okay bloke, so I let that one go.

"Yeah, that's fine," I replied. The nurse pulled some bright purple gloves from a box attached to the wall and snapped them on before pulling the back of my tracksuit trousers down.

"Hmm," I heard him say. "That's going to smart a bit."

"You're telling me," I replied as he prodded at my buttock.

"It's not too bad though. Only went as deep as fatty tissue from the looks of it, bleeding's pretty much stopped already. Do you know what the weapon was?" I wasn't sure if he was asking me or Mr Jackson, so I kept quiet. The nurse kept prodding at my arse cheek. "Looks like it was probably a razor blade to me, it's quite surgical." I figured if anyone would know about weapons inside a prison, it would be a nurse practitioner who worked in one. The nurse mumbled something I didn't quite catch, and I heard Mr Jackson reply with a curt 'yep'.

When I heard the door clang shut, I raised my head and realised that the nurse had left the room. Mr Jackson was sitting on a plastic chair, looking at me.

"He's gone to get some stuff to patch you up," he said. "So what's going on, then? Who've you pissed off?" I didn't reply at first, but thought I'd better say something to the man.

"I didn't see who it was," I replied. "One minute I was standing there talking to Pete, the next I've got blood pissing down my leg." He fixed me with a hard stare, no doubt used to having conversations like these. "I don't know who I've pissed off." That last statement at least was the truth. I had no idea who had slashed me, but thought I probably knew who had put him up to it.

The nurse came back in a couple of minutes later,

breaking the uncomfortable silence that had developed between me and Mr Jackson. He had a handful of very clinical looking stuff in his hands, including what was quite obviously a syringe and needle.

I groaned and put my head on my forearms.

## 40

"The defence calls Doctor Anthea Klein."

The court settled down as the small woman in the witness box took the Bible in her hand. As she recited the oath in a much louder voice than I had been expecting, I could see what Paul had said about her being straight from the set of Miss Marple. Dr Klein, Paul's favourite witness if he was to be believed, was only about five foot tall if that. She was thin, dressed in a grey tweed jacket and matching skirt, and had curly grey hair that would have looked fine with a blue rinse. As she sat down, I half expected her to pull out a ball of wool and a couple of knitting needles, although I'd had enough of needles for one week.

"Dr Klein, before we begin, I would just like to introduce you to the jury if I may?" Paul said. Would you mind telling them a bit about yourself please?"

"Certainly," Dr Klein replied, smiling warmly at the jury. I looked across at them, and pretty much all twelve of them returned her smile. "I'm now retired and only undertake consultative work, but I first qualified as a Medical

Doctor back in the late nineteen seventies, and then as a pathologist in the early nineteen eighties." She described her career in some detail, listing courses, degrees, fellow-ships, all sorts of stuff I didn't really understand. I was concentrating more on the fact she'd qualified as a doctor before I was even born. She carried on detailing her career and explaining all the qualifications and awards that she'd got along the way. Dr Klein got my attention back when she started talking about the time she'd spent in the United States, as a specialist examiner in New England. "I developed a keen interest in a specific type of trauma. Blunt force cranial trauma." I was beginning to understand why Paul was so keen on Dr Klein in this particular case. "I authored a book titled 'The Pathophysiology of Low Velocity Cranial Trauma," she said in a light voice, as if she was about tell a joke. "It's now in its tenth edition, but is used by most pathologists in the United States and the United Kingdom as a definitive resource in the investiga-tion of blunt force trauma to the head."

Paul looked across to the prosecution table as Dr Klein offered this, as if he was expecting Miss Revell to object. When she didn't respond, Paul turned to the judge.

"Your Honour, I would like to introduce this witness as an expert witness in the analysis of blunt force trauma to the head." Judge Watling looked across at Miss Revell when Paul asked this. She half got to her feet before replying.

"No objection, Your Honour," the prosecutor said. "She seems eminently qualified in the field." I looked back at Dr Klein who put her hands together as if she was praying and smiled at the jury. To my surprise, most of them were smiling back at her, even Albert who didn't seem to pay attention at the best of times.

"Your Honour, I would also like to take this opportunity to remind the jury that the forensic accounts from the original trial have been entered into evidence with no challenges from the prosecution." I saw Miss Revell grimace, and then nod her head.

"Very well," Judge Watling said.

"Dr Klein," Paul continued. "I asked you to review both the murder scene itself and also the post-mortem results. Could we go through your analysis of the murder scene first, please?"

"Of course," Dr Klein replied. "I do hope that you've all had breakfast, though," she continued, looking at the jury. I looked up at the public gallery, concerned for a moment that Robert's parents were still there, but they'd not returned this morning. The usher was manoeuvring the television back into place as Dr Klein introduced the material she was going to talk about.

"Now obviously I wasn't involved at all at the time of the incident, so my analysis of the scene is based on the reports. I commenced with a thorough examination of the murder scene reports, provided by the police." She looked at the public gallery and catching Malcolm's eye, smiled at him and I realised that they must know each other. Dr Klein wasn't in the courtroom when Malcolm was giving evidence, and I wondered how their paths had crossed. "I must say they did a thoroughly good job of documenting the scene. It made the analysis so much easier for me." I looked up at Malcolm. Was he blushing?

The usher brought the screen to life and Laura walked over to the television carrying a laptop. She plugged some cables in and the television flashed a couple of times before showing a mirror image of the laptop screen. Laura opened up a presentation, and on her way back to the defence table she handed Dr Klein a small remote control.

"Thank you, my dear," Dr Klein said to Laura before

turning back to the jury. "Ladies and gentlemen, I'm afraid that some of the photographs in this presentation are rather gruesome. I do hope that everyone's okay with that?" I wondered what would happen if one of the jurors put their hand up and said they weren't, but none of them did. Dr Klein pointed the remote control at the laptop, and the screen changed to a photograph. I recognised it straight away as the alleyway behind The Griffin pub, and Robert's body lying at an angle in the middle of the photograph would identify the location for everyone else.

"This is a photograph showing the entire scene, illuminated by police spotlights. As you can see, there is the body of the victim, identified as Mr Robert Wainwright, in the centre of the frame. Can I ask you to pay attention to the position of his body in the photograph?" Dr Klein pressed the remote control again, and the picture changed to a zoomed in image of Robert. He was lying on his side, pretty much exactly as I'd left him, facing towards the back wall of the alleyway. The only difference between how he looked in the photograph on the screen and how he'd looked when I'd left him was that in the photograph, his head was completely smashed in. On the screen, a large depression in his skull was obvious, as were the flecks of white tissue splattered around. Were those bits of bone? Or was it brain tissue? I felt slightly nauseous, and as I looked at the jury several of them looked how I felt. I saw juror number three, Ella, dab at her forehead with a tissue as she looked at the screen.

"Now the piece I want to focus in on is the position of the body, and the injuries that the victim has sustained. I will go into more detail on the injuries later, so for the time being this is just an overview," Dr Klein said. "As you can see, the victim is lying on his side with his face toward a wall. He is approximately eight inches away from the wall.

The scene was examined carefully by the forensic science team who confirmed the body had not been moved. The post-mortem also confirmed this, as there was grit embedded in the other side of the victim's face." Dr Klein paused, looking at the jury as if she was assessing whether or not they understood her. "When the fatal blows took place, the victim was in exactly the position you see him in now."

Dr Klein looked at the bench just behind Laura as a man who I'd not noticed before got to his feet and walked into the middle of the courtroom. There was another man sitting on the same bench and from how they were both dressed, I figured that they were together. They both wore grey suits, white shirts and black ties, and for a moment they reminded me of the two men who'd attacked Robert before I got to him, although they looked nothing like the attackers that night. "This is my colleague, Daniel," Dr Klein said. "Daniel, if you would, could you assume the position that the body in the photograph is in, please? If you would use the judge's bench as the wall, that would be great."

Daniel looked at the screen, and lay on the floor of the courtroom, manoeuvring his body into an approximation of Robert's. He lined himself up so he was the same distance away from the judge's bench as the wall was in the photograph. Dr Klein looked back at the screen, pressing the remote control. On the screen, a red line appeared superimposed across Robert's head. It intersected with the depression in the side of his skull, and pointed away from the wall and into the main part of the alleyway.

"This line represents the angle of the blows on the victim. It has been calculated from the injury patterns and the blood spatter on the wall behind the victim using a standard set of forensic algorithms." She pressed the button again, and an image of a baseball bat replaced the red line. "As you can see, this was the angle that the bat was being held at when the blows were struck.

"This is my other colleague, Jeremy," Dr Klein said as the other grey suited man got to his feet. He was holding a baseball bat in his hand, and I saw the surprise on the faces of some of the jury as they saw it. He stepped forward and walked towards his colleague on the floor. "Jeremy, please could you kneel down with the baseball bat in your right hand." Jeremy did as he was instructed. "Now raise and lower the bat as if you were hitting Daniel. But please, don't actually hit him." There were a few nervous laughs from the jury bench and as I looked across at them, I could see that Dr Klein had their complete attention. As if he was hitting his colleague in slow motion, Jeremy raised the bat over his shoulder and brought it down until it was lying across the other man's face. "Could you do it again please?" Dr Klein asked. He did as instructed and the bat ended up in the same position. Dr Klein pressed the button again and another line appeared on the screen, but this time it was at an opposite angle to the first one. The two lines made a large X over Robert's face.

"The second line is the angle that Jeremy is showing us now. As you can see, it's quite different to the actual angle of the bat as it struck the victim." Most of the jurors were leaning forward and staring at the screen. Several of them were looking at the screen, down at Daniel on the floor, and then back at the screen again. "Jeremy, is it possible for you to adjust your position so you are striking Daniel at the actual angle the victim was struck?" Jeremy pantomimed moving around Daniel with the bat, trying to match up the angles, but the judge's bench stopped him getting anywhere close.

"Now, could you swap the bat to your left hand please,

and repeat the same motion?" Dr Klein asked. When Jeremy changed the bat to his left hand, the angle matched the line on the screen perfectly.

"Ladies and gentlemen," Dr Klein said. "This rather simple demonstration proves only one thing." Paul looked at her, his eyebrows raised in a question. Dr Klein said nothing for a few seconds, building the dramatic tension in the courtroom by a notch.

"And what is that Dr Klein?" Paul asked.

"The blows which killed the victim were delivered by someone holding the baseball bat in their left hand. Of that, there is no doubt."

The silence in the courtroom was deafening. I could see several of the jurors exchanging glances as they connected Paul's earlier question in my testimony about which hand I had used to pull the bat out of my jacket. Paul looked up at the clock. It was almost ten o'clock.

"Your Honour," Paul said, and I knew what he was about to say. "The next part of my case is a change in direction. May I suggest we break for lunch at this point?"

I was led back to the holding cells by Mr Jackson, and true to form, his colleague buggered off for a smoke. As I sat in the cell waiting for a cup of tea, I shifted on the bed to take the pressure off the stitches in my backside. I'd ended up with fourteen, the nurse had told me, and would have them in for the next week. I hoped that they wouldn't hurt as much coming out as they had done going in. Budget cuts in the prison system seemed to apply to anaesthetic as well as everything else.

The door to the main holding area flew open, and Paul walked through accompanied by Laura. I looked at her, hoping to see a Sainsbury's carrier bag with a prawn sandwich, but she was empty handed. Something lukewarm out of a microwave it would be then.

"Good, good, good. That's a wicket taken right there, my boy," Paul said as he walked toward my cell, grabbing a couple of plastic chairs as he did so. "What do you think of the lovely Dr Klein, Gareth?"

"She's good, isn't she," I replied.

"Oh yes, very good indeed," Paul said. "And she's only just getting started."

Mr Jackson walked over and handed me a cup of builders' tea. He knew I took two sugars, so there wouldn't be any in there.

"Now that looks like a most excellent cup of tea, young man," Paul said, examining the polystyrene cup. "I don't suppose we could get one as well, could we?" Mr Jackson looked at Paul with his trademark hard stare, and I was sure the answer would be no when I saw his face soften. Glancing over at Laura, I could see she was beaming at the prison officer. Dimples and all. Mr Jackson shuffled back and flicked the kettle back on. Paul and Laura sat on their chairs, both leaning in toward me. As I did the same, I caught my stitches on my trousers and winced. "Are you okay?" Paul asked.

"Yeah, I got stabbed last night."

"What?" Laura's loud exclamation caused Mr Jackson to look across at us. She repeated the word, quieter but just as insistent. "What?"

"Well, more slashed than stabbed. With a razor, the nurse thought." I explained. "But I got stitched up at the hospital wing, so it wasn't too bad." Laura put her hand to her chest.

"My God," she said. "That's awful. Where?"

"In the queue for supper."

"No, where did you get stabbed?"

I paused before replying. "Across the backside," I said.

Paul started smiling, and then laughing. Laura shot him a fierce look.

"Paul, what's bloody funny about that?" she barked. Paul's laughter died away, and he managed to look apologetic. "What's going on, Gareth?" She stared at me with her arms wrapped around her chest, unblinking.

"Nothing, it's just life inside."

"I don't believe you."

"Well, what can I say?"

"First you get battered and end up with black eyes and a broken nose." I remained silent. Technically, my nose hadn't been broken, but Laura didn't look in the mood to argue. "Then, you end up being stabbed. What's going to happen next?"

Laura was right to ask that. It was a question I'd asked myself several times. What was going to happen next?

## 41

"Ladies and gentlemen," Paul said to the jury. His voice was bright, enthusiastic. "I do hope that you all had a good lunch. Now, no doubt you'll be pleased to hear I am approaching the final part of my defence." Most of the members of the jury smiled as he said this. "I would like to call Dr Klein back to the witness stand." The now familiar figure of Dr Klein made her way to the witness stand. I looked up at the public gallery as she settled herself into her seat, and I could see Andy and Jacob sitting next to each other, Tommy and David to their left, but I couldn't see Big Joe or Robert's parents. I scanned across the faces of the other people in the public gallery, wondering who they were, when I saw a familiar face. Mr McLoughlin, the prison guard. As I caught his eye, he half raised a hand. Laura had instructed me several times not to engage with anyone in the public gallery, but I risked a nod to acknowledge his greeting, anyway.

"Now, Dr Klein, you are still under oath, so we won't need to swear you in again," Paul said for the benefit of the jury.

"Thank you," Dr Klein replied, her trademark smile still present. Just as when she had first sat down in the courtroom, I expected her to pull out some knitting needles.

"I want to talk this afternoon about the mechanics of Mr Wainwright's injuries," Paul said. "Now I know that you weren't present at the post-mortem, but can you confirm that you are up to speed on this issue?"

"Absolutely. The pathologist's notes and slides were extremely well done. I was able to get all the information that I needed from them."

"Could you describe Mr Wainwright's injuries, in general terms?" Dr Klein checked her notes before replying to Paul's question.

"Yes, of course. According to the post-mortem report, there were two areas of injury to Mr Wainwright. The most obvious of these areas was obviously to Mr Wainwright's head, but the pathologist also noted some old bruising to his ribcage."

"Old bruising?" Paul asked. "How old exactly?"

"Yes, now it's always difficult to be too accurate with the time of partially healed bruises, but as a rough estimate the pathologist suggested two to three weeks."

"Which would mean that those injuries were inflicted at some point in the weeks before he was killed?"

"Yes, that would be correct. But it's not possible to be more specific than that." Robert's old injuries had been brought up in the original trial, but Miss Revell had argued that it was impossible to ascertain how Robert had sustained them. I looked across at her, wondering if she would raise the same objection again, but she remained silent.

"Did Mr Wainwright have any other injuries at all,

other than the bruising to his chest and the head injuries that we are going to explore in a moment?"

"No, he didn't," Dr Klein replied.

"Did he have any defensive injuries to his hands?"

"No, it was just the bruising to his chest and the head injuries."

"Thank you, Dr Klein," Paul said. "But before we get to those particular parts of the jigsaw puzzle, could I ask you first to tell the jury a little bit about what happens when somebody is hit around the head with a blunt object? Such as a baseball bat?"

Dr Klein turned to face the jury, smoothing out a wrinkle on her tweed skirt with the palms of her hands.

"Ladies and gentlemen, I will try my best to explain this in straightforward language. You see, the head can be thought of in the same way as an egg. If you consider an egg, it has a hard outer layer or shell. The head has a skull. Inside the egg is the important part, the yolk. Or the brain. Finally, surrounding the yolk is a protective fluid, or egg white, which is very similar to the liquid the brain floats in. It's called cerebrospinal fluid." Dr Klein paused and looked at each of the jurors in turn. I figured that she was making sure they were all keeping up. From where I was sitting it looked as if they were. "Now imagine that you tap the side of an egg. Quite hard, but not hard enough to break the shell. The yolk is protected by the egg white, and while it may wobble around inside the shell, there is enough fluid to protect it from too much damage. If you hit the side of a human head with a blunt object such as a baseball bat, it has exactly the same effect." I saw several of the jurors nodding at Dr Klein's explanation. "The brain is protected to an extent by the cerebral spinal fluid it floats in, as the yolk is by the egg white.

The effects of this wobbling, for want of a better word,

will vary according to several factors. The force of the blow is probably the most important factor, but others are the direction of the impact and where the impact hits. For example, a blow to the side of the head can cause various internal injuries without the skull itself being broken." Dr Klein paused, again surveying the jurors. Although a few of them were frowning, they all seemed to be following along. I half expected one of them to put their hand up at some point as if they didn't understand, like children with a teacher.

"Because the brain is mostly fluid, any force travels through and around the brain tissue, often in small swirling currents or eddies. When the skull remains intact, this force is reflected within the cranium as it has nowhere else to go. This bounces around inside the skull which can set in motion a sequence of events inside the brain tissue. Perhaps the most dramatic of these events is immediate unconsciousness."

"So, it is quite possible to hit somebody with a baseball bat, without breaking the skull, and for them to be rendered unconscious immediately?" Paul asked.

"Yes, indeed," Dr Klein replied. I thought back to the night I attacked Robert. That was exactly what had happened. He had gone down like a sack of potatoes when I'd hit him.

"If an individual is struck as described, and is lying unconscious, what then is happening inside their brain?" Paul asked.

"Well, a lot of that depends on the factors I have previously mentioned, I would expect that there might be a degree of bleeding within the brain. This might be quite obvious bleeding, such as a subdural haematoma or a bleed in between the layers of tissue which surround the brain. Or it could be microscopic in nature."

Miss Revell got to her feet as Dr Klein finished speaking.

"Your Honour," the prosecutor said, "the witness is quite clearly speculating."

"Your Honour," Paul barked. "I fail to see how an expert witness in blunt cranial trauma who is describing the pathological and physiological responses from a blow to the head can be said to be speculating."

"I agree. Thank you, Miss Revell," Judge Watling said. Miss Revell sat back down in her chair, looking defeated. One of her colleagues put a hand on her shoulder and leaned forward to say something in her ear. Whatever he said, Miss Revell didn't agree with it and her face turned even sourer.

"Dr Klein, thank you. Would you now explain to the jury what happens when blows which are hard enough to break the skull are delivered?" Paul asked.

"Yes, certainly. The egg analogy is another useful one in this case. If you imagine hitting an egg hard enough to break the shell, the egg white then stops protecting the yoke, or the brain. Once the protective layer of the skull is breached, the brain can be disrupted much in the same way that an egg yolk can break, spilling its contents. If the area of disruption includes an area of the brain which is crucial to life itself, then this can have fatal results."

On the jury bench, Ella was holding a tissue to her mouth, and Minnie had gone a deathly pale colour. As I watched, the juror next to her leaned across to comfort her. I wondered if I should say something to Laura, or get her attention somehow. The poor woman on the jury bench didn't look well at all.

"The hypothalamus is one such area," Dr Klein continued, oblivious to the plight of Gloria and Minnie, which surprised me. "It controls the heart rate and respiratory rate. If the damage to this area is severe enough, then the heart stops beating and respiration ceases. Life itself ceases." As Dr Klein spoke these words, there was a genuine look of sadness on her face. I glanced back across the jury to see many of them frowning, one or two wearing the same expression as Dr Klein's. Ella let out a loud sob, and the juror next to her put her arm around her shoulder.

"Your Honour," Paul said in a soft voice. "Perhaps now would be a good time to take a break?"

## 42

W hen we all re-entered the courtroom about half an hour later, both Gloria and Minnie were looking a bit better, but still pretty ropey. A few of the other jurors glanced in my direction as they filed back into their seats, but it was impossible for me to read their expressions. One of them, Mark, who I'd pitched to in my testimony, looked almost sympathetic. Dr Klein took her seat and looked at Paul, her eyebrows raised.

"Now Dr Klein, as you know, there were some anomalies in the timelines of the night in question," Paul said. "My client has put forward one version of these timelines, while my learned colleagues and the police have put forward another. I'm keen to see what the forensic evidence says." Paul paused, and looked at the jury before returning to Dr Klein. "Could you tell us what you found when you reviewed the results of the post-mortem?" During the break, the television and laptop had been put back into position. Dr Klein raised the remote control in the direction of the screen, but paused before pressing the button.

"Ladies and gentlemen, some of these images are, I'm afraid, rather graphic," Dr Klein said in a quiet voice. "I apologise in advance for having to show them, but I can't explain things to you properly unless I do." Some of the jurors nodded as she looked at them, and I saw Ella close her eyes for a brief second before opening them again and taking a deep breath. She looked directly at me, her eyes wide and unblinking. I held her gaze for a second before looking down as Laura had told me to do if any of the jurors stared at me. 'Try to look penitent and repentant,' Laura had said before having to explain what those words meant.

Dr Klein pressed the button on the remote control, and there was an audible gasp from the jury bench. On the screen, in glorious high definition Technicolour, was a close-up image of Robert's head, much closer than the earlier images which had shown the whole scene. The damage that had been inflicted on his skull was plain to see. Jagged fragments of white bone could be seen poking through bloodstained tissue and hair. Off-white flecks of what could only be brain matter were spattered around the wounds. Whoever had done this hadn't been messing about at all. I was quite aware that the jury might well still think it had been me, so I looked from the screen straight back down to my lap.

"As you can see here, the skull is severely damaged and the brain itself is disrupted," Dr Klein said in a matter of fact voice, as if she was describing a damaged plant in her greenhouse. She pressed the button again and the gruesome image was replaced by an x-ray image of what must be Robert's head. "This is an x-ray image that shows the bony damage underneath all the soft tissue." As if the previous image hadn't been dramatic enough, she pressed another button on the remote control and a small red dot from a laser pointer built into the remote danced on the screen. She steadied her hand and located the red dot onto an area at the base of Robert's skull, using it to draw a rough circle around a shard of bone.

"This area just here is the hypothalamus, the area I was talking about just before our little break. It controls the body's most basic functions necessary for life, such as heartbeat and respiration." She paused and looked at the jury before continuing. "As you can see, there is a sharp piece of bone which has gone straight through it. In the post-mortem report, the pathologist highlights this fragment as having completely transected the hypothalamic area."

"So in other words, that piece of bone killed Mr Wainwright?" Paul asked. I guessed he was trying to make things simple for the jury.

"Well, some of the other injuries are very severe, but yes. That would be a fair statement."

"And when that piece of bone, what was the phrase you used, transected the hypothalamus?" Dr Klein nodded in response to Paul's question. "That would stop Mr Wainwright's heartbeat?"

"Yes. That's correct."

"So up to that point, the point at which that particular blow was struck, Mr Wainwright's heart was still beating? Do I understand that correctly?" Paul asked. Even though I knew that this was a well choreographed exchange, that made it no less riveting. As I looked over at the jury, I could tell they were as fascinated as I was.

"Probably," Dr Klein replied.

"Probably?"

"Yes, probably. It's impossible to say for certain. He could have received a blow before the one that caused the hypothalamus to be transected which was in itself fatal."

"But if there had been a blow prior to this one which was not fatal, would it be possible to identify that?"

"Yes, I believe it would."

There was a palpable tension in the courtroom as Dr Klein gave the answer to this question, and I knew instinctively that the next few minutes of her testimony were crucial.

"Could you explain that in a little more detail please, Dr Klein?" Paul said in a low voice. Dr Klein didn't reply at first, but just pressed a button on the remote control. The picture on the screen changed back to the close-up of Robert's shattered skull.

"When I read the original trial transcript to prepare for this case, there was an obvious discrepancy between the defendant's version of events, and the version of events that the prosecution presented." Dr Klein glanced across at Miss Revell, who didn't respond. "So I re-examined the evidence with this discrepancy in mind. I wanted to look for evidence of a time lag between the original assault and the fatal blows, to see if it was possible to confirm or deny either version of events from a forensic perspective."

Dr Klein pressed the button on the remote control again. The screen changed to a close-up of some pieces of tattered flesh.

"This is a highlight of the wounds on the victim's head." The red laser dot reappeared, circling a darkened area of tissue. "This area is interesting. There is evidence of some clotting here underneath the skin. A bruise if you will." She focused the red dot on the darker area. "But the clotted area has then been overlaid with another, far more traumatic, injury. The fact that there is clotting underneath suggests a delay between the blow that caused the clotting, and subsequent wounds." I risked a glance at the jury. There were one or two nodding heads, which I took as a good sign. "Clotting takes between five and ten minutes to appear, you see," Dr Klein said.

"So, is that conclusive evidence of a delay between the two injuries?" Paul asked.

"No, it's not conclusive. It's highly indicative, but not conclusive." Dr Klein's face changed into a wan smile. "Sorry, there are just too many variables involved in soft tissue injuries such as this one," she said, looking at the jury. "But there is evidence which I believe is conclusive."

You could have cut the atmosphere in the courtroom with a knife as Dr Klein said this. I couldn't help but lean forward in anticipation, and as I did so I noticed a few of the jury members doing the same thing. Dr Klein pressed the button again, and the image changed. The change on the screen was accompanied by a few gasps in the courtroom.

"This is a photograph of a slice of the brain taken following the post-mortem of Mr Robert Wainwright," she said. I was glad I'd had something to eat. Dr Klein waved the red dot around a fuzzy looking area on the picture. It almost looked as if something had gone wrong with the camera taking the picture. "This area is the most damaged area of the brain. What you can see here is disruption to the brain tissue itself. However, that's not the area I'm most interested in. I'm just going to show you a different version of the same image to make it easier to explain."

The screen changed to show a black and white image, similar to an x-ray or CT scan. Regardless of whether or not it was easier to explain, it was a lot easier to look at now it wasn't in glorious Technicolour. Dr Klein repositioned the red dot over a small white circular area on the opposite side of the brain to where the damage was. "This area here is quite normal, and you can see another similar area on the other side. It's known as white matter and is a part of the brain that passes messages from one part of the brain to another. The darker areas are grey matter and are where all the important bits are. The neural cell bodies, axon terminals, and dendrites, as well as all the nerve synapses, are in these grey parts. Now the interesting thing is—"

"Dr Klein," Paul interrupted. "Those white and grey areas are normal, you say?" I got the impression that he was throttling her back a touch and reminding her to keep things simple for the jury.

"Well, they look normal in these pictures," she replied, taking a sip of water from a glass in front of her. "But they're not."

"In what way are they not normal?"

"Well, perhaps I should rewind slightly before explaining this next part?" Dr Klein smiled at the jury. "I don't want to lose anyone." Several of the jurors returned her smile.

"Please do, Dr Klein."

"Now, if you remember what I was saying earlier about the brain being bounced about inside the skull. When a blow is struck that doesn't fracture the skull?" Dr Klein said, looking at the jury. Several of them nodded in response and I realised that I had done exactly the same thing. "The force that is reflected through the inside of the skull affects different areas in different ways, depending on the density of the brain tissue." She used the laser pointer to draw a circle around the white area on the screen. "These two areas, the white matter and the grey matter, have different densities. They move slightly differently in response to this force and as they do so, there can be small tears in the tissue at the junction of the two types." Dr

Klein was speaking much slower than she had been, and I figured that my suspicion about Paul's interruption was correct.

Dr Klein took another sip of water before continuing. "I wanted to have a closer look, so I examined this area under a microscope." She pressed the remote control again, and the screen changed to a mottled grey colour with some red streaks. Frowns appeared on the faces of a few of the jury members as they craned forward to look at the screen. Dr Klein said nothing, but just sat in her chair looking at the screen.

"Dr Klein, could you explain what we are looking at?" Paul said a few seconds later. Dr Klein jumped back into life.

"Yes, these red streaks here," she said, pointing at the screen with the laser pointer. "They are haemorrhages within the brain tissue. Tiny areas of bleeding between the grey and the white matter, where the tissue has torn."

"I see," Paul replied. I was glad he did because I didn't. "And what is the significance of these haemorrhages?"

"Well, one area of significance is that they are only seen in closed head trauma. If the skull is ruptured, then they won't occur as the force that's required to cause them has been dissipated. But that's not the most important thing," Dr Klein said. Paul paused, letting the obvious question hang in the air.

"What is the most important thing, Dr Klein?"

"In order for these haemorrhages to form, two things are required. One of them is time. They don't form immediately." Another pause from Paul, and another obvious question left to simmer for a second.

"And the other?" Paul asked.

"A heartbeat," Dr Klein replied. "They need time, and

a beating heart. If there is neither, then they won't form. They can't form."

"So how long does the heart need to be beating for after the initial injury for these haemorrhages to form?"

"At least ten minutes, if not longer."

## 43

The next morning dawned with blue skies, but it was freezing cold. As I was being led from the door of the prison to the van, the wind tore through me. Even though it was still only November, it felt cold enough to snow but the blue sky said otherwise. I sat on the metal seat in the van, wincing as I did so as the temperature irritated the stitches in my buttock. At least it was only a short journey to the courtroom.

The difference in the temperature between the van and the interior of the court cells when we arrived was enough to make me break out into a sweat. The court heating must have been running at full pelt, and it was much warmer than it had been earlier in the week. Once the holding cell locked behind me, the first thing I did was take off my suit jacket. I was looking around for something to hang it on when I heard a voice behind me.

"Do you want me to hang that up for you?" I turned to see a young man with an earnest expression looking through the bars at me. He was thin, about my height, and dressed in the white shirt and black trousers that so many people who worked in the system seemed to wear. There was an embroidered patch on his shirt with a company logo, some squiggle in red and white that I couldn't quite make out. Another couple of men in the same uniform were milling about behind him on the other side of the room. "There's nothing to hang it up on in the cell, you see." His accent gave him away as being local to Norfolk, and it was too broad for him to be from Norwich itself. "People would only try to hang themselves off of it if we put a hook in there." He laughed at his own joke, even though it wasn't very funny. I handed my jacket through the bars of the cell.

"Thank you," I said as he took the jacket from me. To my surprise, he walked over to a cupboard and pulled out a proper hangar, sliding the jacket onto it and smoothing the fabric as he put the jacket back into the cupboard. I'd been half expecting him to throw it over the back of a chair.

"Do you want a cup of tea or coffee?" the young man called over.

A few minutes later, I was sipping a cup of tea from a polystyrene cup. It was the nicest cup of tea I'd had since before I'd been arrested. The young man — I wasn't sure quite what to call him — had asked me about milk and sugar, the whole works. He'd even checked that it was the right colour before passing me the cup. That was, I thought, the reason it tasted so good. There was a bit of effort that had gone into it. It wasn't just a cup of brown muck that had been handed over. I sat in the cell for maybe ten minutes before Mr Jackson came into the room. He stood next to the man who'd made the tea chatting for a few seconds before they both walked over to my cell. Mr Jackson made the other man look even thinner. I knew it wasn't a fair comparison, but I couldn't help it.

"You're on, Mr Dawson," Mr Jackson said as the man in the white shirt unlocked the door to the cell. I walked through, handing him the empty polystyrene cup. I figured that me walking over and putting it in the bin wouldn't go down too well with Mr Jackson.

"Thank you very much for the tea," I said. The young man smiled in return.

"Oh, no problem," he replied. "I'll just grab your jacket for you." As he headed across the room to the cupboard, I looked at Mr Jackson. He stared back at me, with his normal sullen expression.

"Did you have a good evening?" I asked him on the off chance he might speak to me for once. To my surprise, he replied a moment later.

"Yeah, was okay I guess." That was it, though. It was progress of sorts. I shrugged my way into the suit jacket and followed Mr Jackson up the stairs and into the courtroom.

In the courtroom, the only people that were there when we arrived were Paul and Laura. When they saw me come in and take my seat, they both walked over to speak to me. Paul was dressed in his standard black robes over a dark grey suit, and Laura had her usual business suit on. Her blouse today was cream, not the green one I liked the most, and she had tied her hair up into a French plait. At least, I think that's what it was called.

"Gareth, my dear boy," Paul went first. "How are you? I must apologise for not visiting you last night." He nodded toward Laura. "I'm afraid that we've both been rather busy." I looked across at Laura and a bizarre image of the two of them together, as in properly together, somewhere in a seedy Norwich hotel room came into my head. Despite the unwanted image, I smiled. "I'm confident, you know," Paul continued. "Really confident." Laura smiled at me, and I immediately felt bad for the previous thoughts I had about her. I had been in prison for a while, though.

"I'm sorry too," she said. Laura dropped her voice as Paul turned away and walked back toward the table, his black robes billowing out behind him. "How are you doing?" she asked in a half whisper. "Is everything okay?" I didn't reply, but smiled to let her know everything was fine. I got to see her dimples for a few seconds, which was a result.

I sat down, forcing Mr Jackson to shuffle over on his seat to make room for me. There was a space on the other side of my chair where the other prison guard had nipped outside, no doubt trying to get his nicotine levels as high as possible before the court sat. I didn't blame him. Mr Jackson sniffed loudly.

"I think she likes you," he said. I turned to look at him, but he remained sitting in the same position staring forward with his enormous arms folded across his chest. "Shame you're in nick really," he continued. That was the most sociable thing he'd said since the first day I'd arrived at Norwich. I looked at him, trying to work out if he was joking, taking the piss, or just making a statement. As I was wondering what to say in response, or whether to say anything at all, Miss Revell breezed into the courtroom. She was followed by her two stooges, both dressed in the same type of suit. One of them was carrying a laptop, the other one a box file of some description. When he saw her, Paul walked over to their table and within seconds they were deep in conversation. I couldn't help but wonder what they were talking about when I noticed one of Miss Revell's stooges saunter over to Laura and say something to her. She glanced up at him and laughed. Even from this distance, I could see her dimples. I looked at Mr Jackson and thought for a second I saw a smile on his face, but I couldn't be sure. Bastard.

The public gallery was filling up, so I concentrated on the people who were filing in so I could get my attention away from Laura. A lot of the people I didn't recognise, but I saw Andy and Jacob make their way in, as well as Robert's parents. There was a small group of four men who took their seats in the second row. They were all dressed in pretty much the same way in scruffy jackets and jeans, all with notebooks clutched in their hands. They had to be from the press, but from which press I couldn't tell. I wouldn't recognise a reporter from the Evening Daily Press at the best of times. It was obvious from how they were talking to each other that they knew each other. The gallery filled up pretty quickly, and the twenty or so seats were filled within a few minutes. I looked at the clock on the wall of the courtroom and saw that it was almost ten minutes before nine o'clock. As the minute hand ticked onto the number ten, both Paul and Miss Revell reached for their wigs and adjusted them on their heads. Paul was fussed over by Laura, while one of Miss Revell's suited assistants helped her. A hush descended over the courtroom as the minute hand of the clock made its way round the clock face until it reached five minutes to ten.

The door behind the judge's desk opened halfway, and the familiar face of the court usher peeked out of the opening. He glanced around before turning back to say something to someone still in the room, presumably the judge. There was a pause before the door opened fully and the usher stepped through. He stood to one side of the door and drew himself up to his full height, preparing for his moment in the spotlight. I looked through the door behind him, eager to get a glance into the judge's inner chambers or whatever they were called. I couldn't see much, but there was a man in a suit in there who looked very familiar. I looked back into the courtroom at the desk where the man and woman who didn't really fit in had been sitting. Court employees, Laura had called them. Their desk was empty, and I was ninety nine per cent certain that one of them was sitting in the judge's private room. They might both be in there, but I couldn't see that far into the room.

The usher took a deep breath.

"All rise," he said in what he presumably thought was a commanding voice. It wasn't, but who was I to criticise? We all got to our feet as Judge Watling walked through the door, swinging it closed behind him and cutting off any view I had of his inner chamber. He sat on his throne and took a second or two to assess his little empire.

"Please, be seated," he said after a pause. There was a rustling noise in the court as everyone sat down and made themselves as comfortable as they could.


It was showtime.

## 44

J udge Watling welcomed the jury back, sounding
reasonably sincere when he said he trusted that they'd
all had a good evening. He said a few words about not
discussing the case outside the courtroom, or reading about
it in the newspapers or on the internet. The judge said this
every morning, and not for the first time I wondered how
this was policed. For all anyone knew, just before their door
opened the jurors had all been sitting there on their phones
reading up on whatever the Eastern Daily Press was
pushing out today. I knew for a fact that my trial had made
the front page of the newspaper as I'd seen a copy downstairs in the holding area. The headline had been something bizarre which made no sense, but I recognised a
picture of Jennifer and me on the front page, so knew there
was a story on the trial in there somewhere. I'd been
tempted to ask one of the officers working in the holding
area if I could read it, but thought better of it. Whatever
the article said, I'd figured, no good would come of me
reading it.

"So without further ado, ladies and gentlemen, I would

like to ask the counsels for their closing statements. Mr Dewar," the judge said, looking at Paul over the top of his reading glasses. "As the defence, you have the privilege of batting first." As if Paul didn't know that. As Paul got to his feet and rearranged his robes while he turned to face the jury, I looked up at Judge Watling who gave me his trademark cursory nod.

"Your Honour, ladies and gentlemen of the jury, thank you," Paul said in a quiet voice. Several of the jurors leaned forward slightly as if they couldn't hear him very well. I looked at Ella. She was wearing a louder dress than she normally wore, this one covered in bright red and green flowers. The only way it could be any less loud was if you were colour blind. She caught my eye and I glanced down, breaking eye contact.

"I stood in front of you at the beginning of last week and made some introductory comments which I would like to refer back to now if I may," Paul continued, speaking in a louder voice now he had the jury's attention. I glanced at them, and saw all twelve pairs of eyes were fixed on Paul. He spent the next fifteen or twenty minutes describing what I had done, how I'd planned for and carried out an assault on Robert Wainwright. I let my head hang in front of me, trying to look penitent. "But, ladies and gentlemen, once Gareth Dawson had struck the man who had killed his wife, what did he do?" Paul paused, and I looked up at him. For a second, I thought he was asking me the question. Paul was standing still, looking at me with a puzzled expression on his face. I flicked my eyes across to Laura, who was staring at me with wide eyes and raised eyebrows. I got the message and looked back at my lap. "What did he do next?" Paul repeated himself, and I could tell that he'd turned back to face the jury.

"My learned colleague, Miss Revell, would have you

believe Gareth Dawson then struck Robert Wainwright again, and again." I could hear Paul's hands hitting the table, punctuating his words, and I flinched at the sound. "Struck him so hard that he killed him, murdered him. And that is the alleged crime for which my client, Gareth Dawson, was found guilty here in this very courtroom and sentenced to life in prison.

One of the things I spoke to you about last Monday morning was the concept of 'beyond all reasonable doubt'. In order for the conviction to stand, you must be one hundred per cent certain that Gareth Dawson carried out those fatal blows. He has admitted striking Robert Wainwright once, hard enough to knock him to the floor and render him temporarily unconscious." I risked a quick glance up at the jury and could see that several of them were looking at me. "But he denies striking him again. He says that he threw the bat to the floor and fled, disgusted with himself, after rolling him onto his side so he wouldn't swallow his tongue."

Paul reminded the jury of the evidence that showed me leaving the scene. The CCTV footage with no time or date stamp. He then went through the other CCTV footage that was taken from the taxi driver's dash-cam and the camera in The Heartsease.

"The police didn't bother to try to find the dash-cam footage, so certain they were that they already had their man, and they discounted the footage in the pub stating that the camera's time could have been altered when Gareth Dawson installed the camera. But they were not able to offer any proof either way that the camera's time had been changed. Their analysts couldn't say. So, it's just as likely that this time was accurate as it is that it was inaccurate."

He turned to the map on the easel, pointing at the red

stickers with the times written on them. "These timelines don't work, ladies and gentlemen." Paul jabbed at the sticker over The Heartsease with his finger. "If he was here at 10:26 pm, and then here…" Another jab at the map, this time over the sticker at the junction of Thunder Lane and St William's Way. "If he was here at 10:20 pm, then he couldn't have killed Robert Wainwright at 10:22 pm, which is the time that the police have ascertained was the time of the fatal blows from the victim's broken phone." He left his index finger over the sticker covering the location of The Griffin pub and paused for a few seconds, taking a sip of water from a glass on the table. I watched from under my eyelids as Laura filled the glass back up as soon as Paul had put it down. "A phone which Gareth Dawson reports as being intact, and not smashed, when he left the scene. He even checked the victim's phone as he left to make sure he could call for help when he came round." Paul paused again, looking at each of the jurors in turn.

"Now, what about the medical evidence?" he said, picking up a few sheets of paper from the table and studying them for a few seconds. "This, ladies and gentlemen," Paul said as he waved the papers in the air. "This is crucial in terms of reasonable doubt. Dr Klein, a well respected academic in the field of trauma, has demonstrated that Robert Wainwright was struck and sustained a head injury. Then, perhaps longer than ten minutes later, he sustained further serious injuries which killed him. These injuries were inflicted — probably by a left-handed person — at 10:22 pm when according to the evidence my client would have been somewhere between the road junction and a pub over a mile away. The prosecution has offered no evidence to the contrary."

Paul was really getting into his stride by now, and he

had let a hint of indignation creep into his voice. I forgot all about not looking up and studied him, fascinated. He was staring at the jury, and although I couldn't see his expression I could see his head going from side to side as he looked up and down the row. "So if Gareth Dawson didn't kill Robert Wainwright, the obvious question is who did?" Several of the jurors looked across at me, but I couldn't read their faces. "I don't know," Paul said, exhaling as he did so. Several of the jurors frowned as he carried on. "There are no other suspects in the case. What there is is plenty of evidence to suggest, and I emphasise the word suggest, that Robert Wainwright was in trouble with some quite serious people. He was heavily in debt to a criminal organisation and he was being threatened by them." Paul picked the papers back up from the table where he'd put them when he was taking a drink. "The medical evidence shows that Robert Wainwright was the victim of a sustained beating some days before he was killed, which my client himself witnessed. It's not unreasonable to suggest that perhaps this beating is related to Mr Wainwright's murder. As a suggestion, it cannot be disproved." Paul paused again before bringing his hand back down on the table with a thump. This time, I wasn't the only one who flinched at the noise. "So, why did the police not investigate this angle?"

I looked up at the public gallery to see if Malcolm was up there. It was fairly obvious where Paul would go next, at least it was to me, and I didn't think Malcolm would come out of it particularly well. I could see Andy and Jacob sitting at one end of the public gallery, and Tommy and David were huddled together at the other end, but I couldn't see Malcolm anywhere. Why would he attend though, I asked myself as Paul's indignation rose a notch.

"Why did the police not investigate this angle?" he

repeated his question before turning back to point in my direction. "Why should they? They had already found their prime suspect. A man who, by his own admission, had planned for and carried out an attack on the man who he considered had murdered his wife." I waited for an objection from Miss Revell, but she stayed silent. I looked down, feeling not just the jury's but every set of eyes in the courtroom focus on me. "Why would the police look for anyone else when they had what amounted to a confession already? Why would the police look for anyone else when all the facts pointed toward my client?" I looked at Laura who stared back at me with a pained expression. Paul's voice dropped, and the next words were spoken with an air of resignation, not indignation.

"Except the police didn't have all the facts. They only had one or two of them. But their absolute focus on my client as the sole suspect meant that they didn't look for any more. They only looked for information that incriminated my client for the murder of Robert Wainwright, and then they adjusted that information into so-called facts at the exclusion of a full investigation." Paul drew himself up to his full height, and I sensed that he was reaching his conclusion. The indignation was starting to creep back into his voice. "Ladies and gentlemen, my client could not have murdered Robert Wainwright. Yes, he struck him. But did he kill him? No. He couldn't have. Because at the exact moment that Robert Wainwright died, at the exact moment those killing blows were delivered, my client was well on his way to a pub over a mile away."

Paul stopped speaking, picking up the glass that Laura had refilled and taking a sip. His hand was rock steady, not a hint of nerves at all.

"Ladies and gentlemen, let me put to you an alternate theory. One which I believe has just as much, if not more, credibility as a chronology of events. I put to you that Gareth Dawson's version of events is a true one, as every shred of evidence which my team has uncovered points to. Evidence which the police did not even begin to look for, as they were so focused on my client as the guilty party. Was Robert Wainwright being followed by the thugs who had beaten him up the previous week? Perhaps they saw my client leaving the alleyway and entered it after he had left. We will never know as the camera that captured my client crossing the road didn't cover the entrance to the alleyway." Paul paused, taking a deep breath which I unconsciously mirrored. "Perhaps, as Gareth Dawson was approaching The Heartsease to meet his friends, these unknown assailants were in the alleyway with Robert Wainwright as he lay there slowly bleeding into his brain? Perhaps they were delivering the fatal blows that overlaid the damage that my client had done?" Paul paused again, taking his time. The silence in the courtroom was almost palpable.

"I don't think there's any 'perhaps' about it, ladies and gentlemen. I can't produce a suspect, or suspects, in this case. But I don't need to. The evidence speaks for itself. If you have any doubt whatsoever that Gareth Dawson didn't kill Robert Wainwright, then it is your civic duty to overturn this wrongful conviction." Paul remained on his feet for a few seconds, looking at the jury, before he sat back down in his chair and reached for the glass of water. Laura put her hand on his shoulder and leaned toward him, whispering something in his ear. Paul nodded in response, and turned back to look at me. As he did so, I saw a thin sheen of sweat on his forehead reflected in the harsh fluorescent light of the courtroom.

Miss Revell got to her feet and clasped her hands in

front of her as though she was about to say grace before a meal.

"Your Honour," she said in a voice so quiet I had to strain to hear her. "May I approach the bench?" Judge Watling's eyebrows shot up in surprise and he looked at her over the top of his half-moon glasses.

"Of course," he replied, taking his glasses off and folding them as she made her way over to him. I watched as she leaned forward and talked to the judge. Keeping her hands clasped in front of her, she looked as if she was pleading with him, almost begging. The judge frowned, then his frown became deeper, and then he just nodded. The only words I could make out were his final words to her, which could be lipread from where I was sitting. He said 'thank you' to Miss Revell before she turned and walked back toward her table with a brief sideways glance at Paul. I looked at Paul, but couldn't see his expression. The only thing I saw was Laura looking at him and shrugging her shoulders when she caught his eye.

Judge Watling cleared his throat to silence the conversations that had burst into life as Miss Revell was walking back to her table.

"Ladies and gentlemen, I'm afraid that I must adjourn the court for a period of time." He looked up at the large clock on the wall which read just before ten o'clock. "We will reconvene at eleven o'clock sharp."

With that, he got to his feet and disappeared into his inner chambers before the usher had a chance to open the door for him.

## 45

Mr Jackson led me back down to the cells underneath the courtroom as his colleague peeled off to the smoking area. I had thought at one point that we were just going to sit in the courtroom for an hour, but after a heated whispered argument about smoking, Mr Jackson had appeared to give in. I was deposited in the cell and Mr Jackson sat at the table and opened up a newspaper. I declined the offer of a cup of tea from the cell assistant or whatever he was called. My stomach was churning, and I wasn't sure I could keep a cup of tea down.

The door to the cell area opened and Laura rushed in, heading straight across to my cell. She looked flustered and had her lips pressed together into a thin line.

"What's going on?" I asked her. "Why has it stopped?" I couldn't remember what the proper word for stopping court proceedings was, and to be honest I didn't care. Laura waited as the cell assistant brought over a chair for her to sit on, declining his offer of a cup of tea as she sat down. With a disappointed look, he made his way back to the table and sat down opposite Mr Jackson who just ignored him. At least it wasn't just me, then.

"I don't know," Laura said. "I haven't got a clue." Her words were spoken like a machine gun. "I tried to speak to Paul about it, but he disappeared to call someone." She was speaking so quickly that I had to concentrate to understand her.

"Have you seen this before?" I asked.

"No," she shot back. "I mean, yes, I've seen adjournments before." That was the word I'd been looking for. "But never at this stage of the trial." Laura took a few deep breaths, puffing the air out of her cheeks. "Sorry," she said. "I'm a bit wound up."

I had to stop myself laughing at her words. She was wound up? How did she think I felt? I had to fight the urge to try to reassure her, reach through the bars and take her hand to tell her that everything would be okay. Although I didn't laugh, I couldn't help but smile. She looked at me, and returned the smile complete with dimples.

"Sorry," she repeated herself. "That was a stupid thing to say." This time I did laugh.

We passed the time making small talk about everything but the trial. I was grateful for that, at least. Laura kept checking her phone, explaining that she was waiting for something from Paul. I didn't think that she'd be able to get a phone signal in an underground room, but after a few minutes, the phone buzzed when she was halfway through telling me a story about going shopping at the weekend. She looked at the screen, her face lit up by the blue light, and frowned.

"Paul's gone back to the office," she said. "He's not said why. Just that he's had to nip back to check something." She paused for a moment before slipping the phone back into her jacket pocket and carrying on with the story. I laughed dutifully at the punchline of what turned out to be a not very funny story, but I was still grateful to her for taking my mind off what was going on upstairs in the judge's chambers.

After a few minutes, we ran out of small talk. It wasn't that I didn't want to talk to her, but despite her best efforts to take my mind off it, I kept thinking about what was happening. I didn't really have any recent funny stories either, and the stitches in my buttock were itching like mad.

"So, what do you think's going on?" I asked her. She shrugged her shoulders in the same way as she had done earlier at Paul.

"I honestly don't know. The last time I saw a court adjourned like that was for the judge to check on a point of law, but it was raised in open court, not a sidebar."

"How do you mean?" I asked.

"There was a legal point I saw raised in a case I went to while I was still in law school. It started out as an objection, then it became a sidebar, then it became an adjournment. Legal arguments don't normally happen in front of the courtroom, especially if it means that someone ends up looking stupid," Laura explained. "The judge in that case wasn't sure, so she adjourned the court to check the law books."

"But what point of law could they be checking?"

"I don't know. It might not be that. It could be something else entirely." Laura sighed, looking as frustrated as I felt.

The next thirty minutes or so dragged by. Laura had excused herself. It was a few seconds after her mobile had buzzed on the table, so I figured Paul had texted her. I jumped as the phone on the wall rang, breaking the silence. Mr Jackson answered it, grunted a couple of times, and lumbered over to my cell. We made our way back up the steps leading to the courtroom. I sat back in my appointed spot and tried to make myself comfortable as he did the same thing next to me.

While we waited for the jury to come back in, I looked up at the public gallery. Andy gave me a broad smile and a thumbs up as I caught his eye. Jacob was sitting next to him, his eyes downcast. It looked as if he was scribbling something in a notebook, but I couldn't see exactly what he was doing. Tommy and David were sitting in the back row, deep in discussion about something and not paying any attention at all to their surroundings, and Robert's parents were still nowhere to be seen. I was just wondering where they were when the door behind the gallery opened and Robert's father shuffled through, taking the last available seat.

"Ladies and gentlemen, I must apologise for the unexpected adjournment," the judge said, looking up and down the line of the jury. "There has been a most unexpected development in the case, one which I have not experienced before in over thirty years of sitting in courtrooms. I had to refresh my memory of what to do in such cases." The silence in the courtroom was absolute. You could have not only heard a pin drop, but it would have been deafening. "The prosecution has stated that there is no evidence upon which a reasonable jury could uphold the conviction, given the additional evidence presented by the defence counsel." Judge Watling looked over his glasses directly at me. There was a pause of perhaps ten seconds, the longest time he had ever concentrated on me. His eyebrows went up as he refocused his attention on the jury. "What this means ladies and gentlemen, is that you are no longer required to reach a verdict in this case. I am taking that responsibility away from you and directing a verdict." His gaze returned to me. I sat up straighter in my chair.

"Gareth Dawson, on the charge of murder which you have been convicted of, I hereby declare that conviction null and void and overturn both the conviction and sentence. Furthermore," he paused as a collective gasp echoed around the courtroom, followed by hushed conversations. I closed my mouth, realising that I had opened it as the judge had spoken, and looked at Laura. She stared back at me, not open mouthed, but with a broad grin on her face. I expected the judge to bang his fist on the table to silence the courtroom or something like that, but he just waited for the hubbub to die down. I think most people in the room realised he had more to say, and quietened down to hear it. "Furthermore," he continued, "on the advice of the Crown Prosecution Service who have been in attendance during these proceedings, they do not consider that there is a case to answer for in relation to the original offence for which you pled guilty, namely that of manslaughter." It took me a few seconds to work out exactly what he was saying. No case to answer for manslaughter? My heart thumped as I realised what that meant.

"Given the time you have already served for what was, in effect, a wrongful conviction, they also do not think that pressing charges for a lesser offence such as assault would be in the public interest. You are as of this moment a free and innocent man." There was a loud gasp in the courtroom, and as the noise in the courtroom increased I realised that it was from me. What the fuck? The judge rose his voice as several people in the public gallery pushed their way to the door. "Ladies, gentlemen, silence please." He spent the next ten minutes talking to the jury, reminding them of what they could or couldn't do after the trial, and thanking them for their service. I wasn't listening to what he was saying, I was just numb. I didn't know what to do, where to look. I didn't want to look up at the public gallery out of respect for Robert's father, but at the same time, I wanted to jump to my feet and pump my fists in the air. Point at Andy and Jacob, wave at Tommy and David. Maybe even give anyone from the press who was still there a two fingered salute. I did none of those, I just sat there with my hands in my lap, trying to process what had just happened.

I didn't even look up at Paul and Laura.

## 46

When Mr Jackson led me back down to the cell room underneath the court, my instinct took me straight toward the cell I'd been put in so many times before. As I walked toward the door, I heard a noise I'd never heard before behind me. I turned to see Mr Jackson laughing.

"Where are you going fella?" he said. "You don't belong in there any more sunshine." He pulled out a chair from under the main table in the room, the one I'd seen him reading his newspaper at so many times over the last week. "Have a seat, Gareth. All we're waiting for is some paperwork, and then you'll be on the out."

I didn't reply, but just sat on the chair he had offered me. It didn't feel right, and I looked over my shoulder toward the cell. As I did so, Mr Jackson bustled around by the kettle.

"White with two, isn't it?" he asked me, throwing two teabags into mugs and flicking the switch to the kettle on. Mugs, not polystyrene cups. As it heated the water, he turned to face me and crossed his massive arms over his chest. "Well, I didn't see that coming, did you?" he asked. I shook my head in reply, not sure what to say. "I mean, blimey, you've just gone from being a convicted murderer to a free man in the space of about an hour." Mr Jackson continued talking, and I tried my best to tune him out. It was weird the way he'd gone from being sullen and uncommunicative to my new best friend, but I guessed it was just the way he related to prisoners versus people who weren't prisoners. Maybe I had misjudged him after all?

The door to the cell room flew open and Laura came through it, almost running. I got to my feet and turned to face her and to my surprise, she threw her arms around me and hugged me. I stood there for a second before I remembered what to do, and put my arms around her to return the gesture. Her hair was lying against my cheek, and I could smell the shampoo she used. I had no idea what sort of shampoo it was, but it smelt amazing. The feel of her body against mine felt amazing. I let go of her, embarrassed but not really knowing why. She released her grip on my shoulders and took a step back. I looked at her and saw that her face was flushed with excitement.

"My God, can you believe that?" she said, almost squealing. There were two red patches on her cheeks, just where her dimples appeared when she smiled. "Can you believe that?"

"That's just what I was saying," Mr Jackson added. "Look at him though, I don't think it's sunk in." They both looked at me, and Laura smiled before starting to laugh. Her dimples punctuated the red patches on her cheeks perfectly.

"No, I don't think it has," she said.

Mr Jackson, whose first name I found out was Craig, finished making the tea just as a man in a suit who I'd never seen before came in with a bunch of paperwork for me to sign. Laura explained what the various bits and pieces were, but I couldn't care less. All I wanted to do was get them signed and get out of the place. As he left, clutching the freshly signed forms in his hand, he walked past Paul who was just coming into the room.

"Gareth, my dear boy," Paul said as he reached me, pulling me into a bear hug. I wasn't that bothered about smelling the shampoo that he used, though. "What an amazing result," he whispered in my ear. Once we had completed the back slaps of two men hugging, we extricated ourselves and sat down.

"What's next, Paul?" I asked him.

"Well, once the paperwork has been countersigned by the judge then you're a free man. I've been talking to Jennifer's father, Andy is it?" I nodded. "He's waiting to collect you and take you back to his place while everything else is sorted out." I suddenly realised that I had nowhere to go. The flat that Jennifer and I had rented now had new tenants in it, and as what had just happened had been so unexpected, I'd not even thought about it. Paul must have realised what I was thinking. "I've just spoken to Andy outside. There's bloody press all over the place, though," Paul said. "Did you want to speak to them?"

"Er, no thanks," I replied. "I'd rather not."

"Good lad, that's what I like to hear. Although I suspect that you could be quite the celebrity for a while if you wanted your fifteen minutes of fame."

"No, not my style. I'm not interested in the slightest."

"Okay, no problem. Andy's son has a car parked at the rear of the courtroom. Most of the hacks know about the rear entrance, but they're pretty good about not bothering people if they leave from there, so I'm told," Paul said. "So as soon as we get the nod from the judge, you're good to go." I looked at Laura, who had a broad smile on her face. She looked as pleased as I was.

A few minutes later, I flinched as a phone in the corner of the room rang. Mr Jackson walked across to answer it in the absence of any of the court staff. I guessed that now I was innocent they didn't need to be here anymore. I heard Mr Jackson, now Craig, say a few words to the person on the other end of the line before he put the handset back down. He turned to me with a grin.

"That's it, sunshine. You're all good," he said, his smile broadening. I got to my feet and he walked toward me. For a horrible moment, I thought he was going to give me a hug like Paul had done, but he just held out a hand. "We'll sort out your personal belongings down the line, yeah?" he said as he gripped my hand like a vice. I thought for a second about what those belongings actually were.

"You can keep them if you want, or burn them," I replied. "But would you say goodbye to Pete for me?"

"Course I will," he said. "You take care of yourself, you hear? Don't take this the wrong way, but I never want to see you again."

I laughed and followed Paul up the stairs leading back toward the courtroom. Instead of entering the courtroom, he pushed open a door with a sign saying 'Court Employees Only' in bold red letters. I must have walked past the door a hundred times and never noticed it. Laura was behind me as I followed Paul down a well-lit corridor toward a fire door at the back of the courtroom. He paused at the door and turned to me.

"Gareth, we'll meet again soon to tidy everything away. But well done chap, that's a real result." We shook hands. I didn't want to say anything as the lump in my throat was threatening to overwhelm me. I looked at Laura, wanting to give her another hug, but I knew if I did I would lose it completely. We all exchanged handshakes again, and I blinked to keep the tears at bay. Laura didn't bother, and I could see them gathering in the corner of her eyes.

With a flourish, Paul pushed the fire door open, and I stepped out into the sunshine.

## 47

I kept my head down as Andy accelerated the car hard out of the courtroom's rear car park. As Paul had said, the small crowd of journalists in front of the courtroom didn't take too much notice of us. I saw one of them raise a camera and take a picture of Andy's car, but other than that they paid us no attention at all.

Jacob was in the back seat of the car, at his own insistence. I'd tried to get him to sit in the front, but he wasn't having it at all.

"Where to then, Paul?" Andy asked me as he made his way through the traffic. "I think a drink is called for, don't you?" I thought for a few moments before replying.

"How about The Buck?" I said. Andy glanced across at me before returning his eyes to the road in front of him.

"Are you sure?" he asked. The Buck was the pub that Jennifer had been drinking at on the night she'd died. For some reason, I'd not been in there at all in the period in between her death and my imprisonment. I'd been past it many times, but never crossed the threshold.

"Yeah, please. I mean, if that's okay with both of you?"

I realised too late that going there might be just as difficult for them as it could be for me.

"Fine by me," Jacob leaned across the back of my seat and clapped me on the shoulder. "But the first round's on you." Both he and Andy laughed as I patted my pockets, pretending to look for a wallet they both knew wasn't there.

We spent the rest of the short journey in silence. I looked out of the window as the streets of Norwich flashed past. People, lots of people going about their business, whatever that business was. It all looked so normal but at the same time, so alien. I almost asked Andy to stop at one point just so I could walk up and down the street for a moment or two, because I could. Andy and Jacob seemed to sense my mood and both remained silent, allowing me some space to think. I had a lot to think about.

Twenty minutes later, Andy eased his car into a space just down the road from The Buck. I climbed out of the car and stood on the pavement, looking around and breathing deeply as Jacob climbed out of the back seat. The three of us set off down the pavement toward the pub, and I noticed a bunch of fresh flowers tied to a tree. It was pretty much at the spot where Jennifer had died. Jacob and I stopped to look at them while Andy carried on walking.

"Dad left them here this morning," I heard Jacob whisper in my ear. "Every time he comes into Norwich he brings some fresh ones." I looked up at Andy as he paused outside the pub. He didn't look back at me, but at the river on the other side of the road. I looked at Jacob, lost for words. He shrugged his shoulders at me. "Come on mate, let's get a pint inside you. It's been a while."

As we waited for the barmaid in the pub, I looked around the interior and wondered where Jennifer had been sitting the night she died. It was bizarre, I can't think of

Blind Justice

another way of describing it. I closed my eyes for a few
seconds, imagining hearing her laughter echoing around
the inside of the pub. This was a far cry from The Heartsease. It was a decent place for a start. The building must
have been hundreds of years old, and I thought for a
moment about how many generations of drinkers had
spent their hard-earned money inside. How many
convicted murderers had decided to have their first pint as
free men in here? Maybe I was the first one?

Andy, Jacob and I sat at a small round table near a bay
window that looked out over the road outside, and across
the river to a row of boats moored on the opposite side. I
looked at the pint in front of me, the condensation on the
outside of the glass, and the tiny bubbles spiralling their
way up the amber liquid. I picked up the glass and took a
small sip, wanting to down it in one but not trusting my
stomach.

"Cheers, gents," I said in a quiet voice. They both took
their glasses and clinked them off mine even though they
were both drinking Diet Coke.

"Cheers." It was a strangely muted celebration. When
the second pint came my way, Jacob proposed a proper
toast.

"What shall we drink to?" Andy asked me. I thought
for a moment.

"I think we should drink to justice." I picked up my
glass, enjoying the cold sensation on my fingers. "To blind
justice." They both raised their glasses and repeated my
words.

"To blind justice."

I sat in the back of the car for the drive from Norwich
to Sheringham, much to Jacob's disappointment. The only
way I could persuade him was to say I wanted to sleep on
the way back. The two pints I'd had in the pub had

knocked me for six, or at least that's what I'd told him. I
spent the journey with my eyes closed, pretending to sleep
while thinking about the future. I had no idea what I would
do. I couldn't go back to my flat, not with the tenants, and
I didn't think that throwing them out of what was now
their home was the right thing to do. There was also the
issue of the Romanians to deal with. In my mind, being
found not guilty of Robert's murder would get me off the
hook with them. That would only work if they followed the
same logic I was trying to follow though, and there was no
guarantee of that. They could decide that as I was last
man standing as it were, the debt would stay with me. I'd
have to cross that bridge if I came to it, though. For the
immediate future, I didn't have many places I could stay.
Andy had offered me a bed for as long as I needed it, and I
was sure that Tommy would put me up if necessary. Even
Jacob had offered me his spare room, but when he'd said
that in the pub earlier on I got the impression he wasn't
that keen. I didn't know his other half, and while the idea
of staying with two gay men didn't bother me in the slightest, something about Jacob's tone made me think twice
about accepting the offer.

It took about an hour to get to Sheringham, and Jacob
and I said goodbye in the car park in front of the small
block of flats that Andy now lived in. We promised each
other we'd catch up soon, grab a few beers and chew the
fat properly. He hugged me before he left, and I was
reminded how well built he was.

Andy's flat was in a two storey block with a sign outside
advertising the fact there were a couple of flats available
for the semi-retired. Not quite sheltered housing, but not
far off it. I followed Andy through the communal hallway,
wondering why he'd decided to move here, to this flat. He
was hardly ready for retirement from the look of him.

Andy opened the door and led me into the thin hallway of his flat, past an old-fashioned coat stand.

"So why did you choose here, Andy?" I asked as I followed him through to the kitchen. He turned with a smile.

"I've always loved Sheringham. We used to come here for family holidays years ago." His smile faltered just a touch. "When Jennifer was young, you know?" I didn't know that, but I kept my silence. The flat was bigger than it looked from the outside, and Andy had covered the walls with photographs. As I looked at the photos in the hallway, I realised that they were of a much younger Andy. There were photographs of him, his wife, and Jennifer and Jacob as babies. One of them was taken on the seafront of Sheringham, which had changed little over the last twenty or so years. Further back toward the front door were even earlier photographs, Andy in cricket whites wielding a bat. I took a step back to look at the earlier photographs, interested in what he looked like when he was my age. There was one of his cricket team, all smiling, with a young man front and centre holding a trophy on his lap. I scanned the faces in the black and white picture, looking for Andy. I found him in the back row with one of his colleague's arms draped across his shoulders. Both men had broad grins on their faces, and eyes full of promise.

"That was the championships, when my school won the ESCA One Day Cup," I heard Andy say over my shoulder. I turned, frowning at him. "Sorry, English Schools' Cricket Association," he continued. "I think they're still going, even now. 1971 that picture was taken, though. A long time ago." The next picture along was a close-up of a young Andy, cricket bat angled backwards as he waited for a ball to be bowled. A real action shot. There was something off about the picture, but I couldn't quite put my finger on what it was. "Do you want a cup of tea?" Andy interrupted my thoughts.

"Yeah, that'd be great. Thank you," I replied, following Andy into the kitchen. As he rummaged through the cupboards, I looked around the small but functional space.

"Have you got a dog, Andy?" I asked him, pointing at a bowl of water on a mat by the back door of the kitchen.

"Yeah, I've had her for a while now," he replied, putting two mugs on the granite worktop. "I got her from a rescue centre not long after Jen died. Bit of company, you know?" The next words Andy said cut me like a knife. "I think you'd stopped coming round by then."

I looked at him, wondering for a second if he was having a dig or just making a statement. He didn't look at me, but carried on making the tea. I decided that he was just making conversation, or at least that's what I hoped.

"Where is the dog anyway?" I asked, looking around. I couldn't see or hear one anywhere, and there couldn't be that many places for one to hide.

"Jacob's other half has been looking after her while we've been at court the last few days. She's getting on, and I didn't want to leave the poor old girl on her own all day." Andy's face softened and the sad expression I remembered so well returned. I realised that he was going to have to face yet another bereavement at some point soon.

"I really appreciate you putting me up, Andy," I said when we were both sitting at the small table in his kitchen. He shook his head in reply.

"Not at all, you stay as long as you need to." He looked relaxed, comfortable, quite at ease with the whole situation. "And I mean that. I don't want you thinking you have got nowhere to stay, or that you're not welcome." He reached across the table and gripped my hand, looking at me intently. "I'm so pleased you're out, Gareth. A bloody travesty, that's what it was."

I'd figured that I'd stay with Andy for perhaps a day or two. A week at the very most. Just until I got myself together. Looking at him now, he seemed quite happy for me to be here. I sipped the tea, relishing the fact that it was made with decent teabags and not the cheap rubbish that was the only thing you could get in prison.

"Thank you," I said, almost in a whisper. "That means a lot." Andy didn't reply, but stared at his tea. We sat in silence for a few moments, each of us lost in our own thoughts. I tried to think about the future, what I would do now that I was out of prison. I'd have to find somewhere to live for a start, somewhere of my own. I wasn't sure how long I could stay with Andy for, despite his offer. A week was probably about the longest that I'd be comfortable with. As if he was reading my thoughts, Andy spoke.

"So what are your plans then, Gareth?"

"I really don't know, to be honest," I replied. "Sitting here having a cup of tea with you is a bit of a surprise, that's for sure."

"I bet it is," Andy laughed. "Bit of a turn-up for the books, eh?" That was the understatement of the century.

"I think maybe a holiday," I said. "Somewhere hot, with a beach. Just for a few days." The more I thought about having a holiday, the more sense it made. After being cooped up for so long with so many other people, sitting on a deserted beach somewhere appealed a lot. I'd be fine on my own, I'd even prefer it.

Andy and I spent the rest of the evening sitting in his lounge, watching nonsense on television. He'd suggested the pub, but I'd declined. I was happy just chilling out and, if anything, had found going to The Buck overwhelming. Andy popped out at one point to the corner shop and came back with a couple of bottles of wine, but after one glass I'd had enough. The two pints from earlier had pretty much finished me anyway, and the last thing I wanted to wake up to on my first proper day of freedom was a hangover. At around ten o'clock, I decided that I'd go to bed, and I let Andy faff around me for a bit. He showed me the bathroom, gave me a towel and a spare toothbrush, and showed me into what he called the guest room. It was only just bigger than my old prison cell, with a single bed and a small set of drawers. As far as I was concerned though, it was paradise.

I lay in bed for a while, enjoying the luxurious feeling of both the soft mattress and what must have been the cleanest duvet I'd been under in months. I could hear Andy moving around the flat, and after around half an hour I heard him close the door to his bedroom. For the next hour, I tossed and turned in the narrow bed. Although I was exhausted, both physically and mentally, sleep evaded me. I gave it another twenty minutes, and then decided to get up and find a book to read. If the flat had been bigger I would have put the television back on and moved to the sofa, but I didn't want to disturb Andy. I swung my legs out of bed and made my way as quietly as I could to the lounge.

On top of the bookcase in the lounge was a photograph I'd noticed earlier. It was of Jennifer and me on our wedding day, and was another one of David's unposed snaps. I had my back to the camera, and Jennifer was looking over her shoulder at the camera. She had a broad smile on her face that was so genuine it hurt. I could feel a lump forming in my throat, and sat on the sofa with the photograph in both hands. As I touched Jennifer's face with the tip of my thumb, I let the tears flow. There were no sobs, no clenched fist pressed against my mouth, no gripping pain in my chest. Only tears.

I put Jennifer's picture back on the top of the bookcase once I'd decided that I'd cried enough for that evening, and picked a book out from Andy's small selection without looking at it. I didn't really care if I'd read it or not. I just wanted something to take my mind off not being able to sleep. On the way back to the guest room, I diverted to the kitchen to see if there was any wine left. Maybe a large glass would help me get to sleep, I reasoned with myself as I filled the largest one I could find to the brim. Putting the glass and the book back in my room, I padded to the bath-room for a pee. On my way past the photographs of Andy on the wall, I looked again at the one of him about to smack a ball for six. There was definitely something odd about it.

I was mid-pee when I realised what was off about the picture. I finished my business and washed my hands before returning to the hallway, turning on the light as I did so. Leaning forward to examine the photograph, I could see that I was right. It was the wrong way round. I looked at the scoreboard behind Andy's shoulder and realised that it wasn't the photograph that was the wrong way round, it was Andy. His right shoulder was toward the camera when it should have been his left if he held the bat the way I would hold it. The only reason he would face the way that he was would be if he was left handed. I looked at his hands, gripping the cricket bat so hard that even in the photograph I could see his knuckles had whitened.

My mind went back to the night I'd attacked Robert, and I looked over at the coat stand. I picked up a hat that was hanging on one of the arms and looked at it in profile. Beneath it was a dog's lead, hanging from the same hook. My heart rate increased a notch as I realised that I recognised the shape of the hat. When had Andy got the dog? Just after Jennifer had died, he'd told me. Dogs had to be walked. I knew that as I'd seen the silhouette of a dog walker that night. A dog walker wearing a hat just like the one in my hand. I looked back at Andy's hands wrapped around the cricket bat and imagined them wrapped around another type of bat.

I moved back across to the photograph of the team and looked at the man with his arm draped over Andy's shoulder. Although there were no names on the photograph, I didn't need them to recognise the man. The widow's peak was less distinct in the photograph than it was now, but there was no doubt in my mind I knew him. Paul Dewar.

Behind me, I heard a soft click as Andy's bedroom door opened. I turned to see Andy peering around the door. His hair was awry, and his eyes were half closed against the light.

"Are you okay, Gareth?" he asked, glancing at the hat in my hand. "I heard the toilet then saw the light come on under my door."

"Sorry, Andy," I replied, not sure what to say. "I didn't mean to disturb you." I put the hat back on the stand. We stood in silence for a few seconds, and I waited to see if Andy would say anything else. When I realised that he wasn't, I carried on. "I see that you've known Paul Dewar for a while," I said, my finger pointing at the team photograph. A slow smile appeared on Andy's face as he smoothed his hair over his head.

"I have, yes," he replied. "We go back a way, Paul and I."

"You kept that quiet."

"Not really, no reason for you to know," Andy said.

"Shall we have a drink? A proper one? I think a chat is needed, don't you?"

Andy and I sat in the lounge, a bottle of whisky on the table in front of us. When I drank whisky, I always went for quantity over quality, but tonight I had both. Andy had poured out two very generous measures into tumblers, adding a splash of water to each from a small jug he'd brought through from the kitchen. It was all done in silence as I contemplated what to say to him. With a glance at Jennifer's smiling face on top of the bookcase, I decided how to approach things.

"So, you've known Paul since school?" I asked.

"Yes, we're old friends," he replied, curling his fingers around the glass in his hand.

"Did you ask him to look into my case?"

"I may have mentioned it to him," Andy said, almost in a whisper. "I do know he likes a challenge."

"But I don't understand why you'd do that, Andy. Unless you knew I was innocent, that is."

"But you always said you were, Gareth. Right from the start. Is that not enough for me, to take you at your word?"

"But what if it's not enough?" I replied. "What if you knew for certain I was innocent? Because you knew who the real killer was?"

He put his glass down on the table, and I took a large sip of whisky from mine. As the liquid burned its way down my throat, Andy looked at me with his eyebrows raised.

"And how would I know that, Gareth?" He was smiling, his eyes no longer wrinkled with sleep.

"What's your dog's name?" I asked. His smile faltered for a second before returning.

"She's called Phoenix," he replied. "I didn't name her.

That was the name she already had when I got her from the rescue centre, but it seemed apt in any case."

"Were you walking her the night Robert died?" I asked. There it was, out in the open. The killer question, as it were.

We sat in silence, both knowing the reply to the question would change both our lives. The knowledge that we would share of who had really killed Robert Wainwright, who had really avenged Jennifer's death.

"When I saw you convicted, Gareth," Andy said after a few minutes. "I knew I couldn't let that go. I couldn't see the man who loved my daughter being convicted for a crime I'd committed." He looked at me, his eyes serious and unwavering. "What sort of a man would that make me? If Paul hadn't managed to get the conviction overturned, my next step would have been to take your place."

Jennifer stared at us both from the top of the bookcase. Two men who'd loved her, one who'd wanted to kill for her, and one who actually had.

"Your toast in the pub, to blind justice," Andy said, picking up his glass from the table. "It was very apt. But justice isn't always blind. Sometimes she just needs a bit of a hand to see the light."

"Maybe another toast is called for?" I replied. "What would you suggest?"

Andy raised his glass in the air and looked over at Jennifer's picture, tilting his glass in her direction.

"How about we toast that young lady over there?" He got to his feet, and I followed him. We both raised our glasses toward the photograph on the bookcase and spoke in unison.

"To Jennifer."

# A NOTE FROM THE AUTHOR

I hope you enjoyed reading *Blind Justice* as much as I enjoyed writing it. If you did enjoy it, perhaps you would consider leaving a review on your book site(s) of choice?

Thanks for coming this far with me! I'd love to stay in touch with you, so please do visit nathanburrows.com where you can sign up for occasional updates. Or just drop me a line—I'll always reply.

In the meantime, happy reading!

*Nathan Burrows*

nathan@nathanburrows.com

# ALSO BY NATHAN BURROWS

# THE GARETH DAWSON SERIES

## Finding Milly - Gareth Dawson Series Book 2

Jimmy Tucker is dying. There's only one person he wants to tell. His daughter—Milly. But when he gets home from the hospital, she's vanished without a trace.

The inoperable brain aneurysm deep within Jimmy's head could burst at any time—a cough, a sneeze, or a blow to the head could kill him instantly. With the police not interested in Milly's disappearance, Jimmy takes things into his own hands and begins to look for his only daughter. But it doesn't take him long to realise that his daughter is not the woman he thinks she is.

As he gradually discovers Milly's shocking private life, Jimmy enlists the help of Gareth Dawson, an ex-crook with a big heart. But Gareth can only help Jimmy up to a point.

As the pressure mounts, can Jimmy uncover the truth about Milly's disappearance before it's too late—for either of them?

Finding Milly is available on Amazon

## Single Handed - Gareth Dawson Series Book 3

When a dismembered hand is discovered in a lobster pot off the North Norfolk coast, it's one less missing person for the police to look for. Until something much darker emerges…a blackmail note.

Gareth Dawson, a reformed criminal whose gruff exterior hides a kind heart, is trying to deal with the aftermath of his brother-in-law's death. But if the extortionist reveals the shameful secret that Gareth's brother-in-law has been hiding, the truth will destroy both his memory and the lives of those mourning him. As well as those who aren't.

With his sister refusing to go to the police, Gareth realises that he will have to deal with the situation—alone and single handed. But who is telling the truth? And who is lying?

Can Gareth identify the blackmailer and uncover the truth about his step-father? Or are some family secrets best left hidden…?

Single Handed is available on Amazon

The first three books in the series are also available as an eBox Set and is available in Kindle Unlimited.

View the Gareth Dawson Series (Books 1-3) eBox Set on Amazon

# THE PAUL ADAMS SERIES

## Man Down - Paul Adams Book 1

You don't have to be killed in action to be a casualty of war.

Medics Paul Adams and Lizzie Jarman are one of the most welcome sights to injured soldiers in the war-torn poppy fields of Afghanistan. With red crosses on their arms and medical equipment strapped to their backs, they thunder into battle in a Chinook helicopter – straight into areas everyone else is desperate to get away from.

In the middle of the fiercest fighting British troops have seen since the Falklands War, the medics are the last defence from death on the ground in some corner of a foreign field. But in Afghanistan, where a hostile is only obvious when they raise a weapon, there's no such thing as a non-combatant. And not all enemies are on the other side.

Despite the heroic efforts of the medics on the ground and in the air, someone in the field hospital is determined to finish what the Taliban has started. Wounded soldiers – who should be living – are dying. Their deadliest enemy is much closer to home than they realise.

As the death toll and the temperature rise, can the medics finish their tour of duty, or will it finish them?

Man Down is available on Amazon

~

## Incoming Fire - Paul Adams Book 2

Even when you're flying a desk, Afghanistan is a dangerous place.

Medic Paul Adams thought he'd seen the last of Afghanistan after his last tour almost killed him and his colleague, Lizzie Jarman. They'd been there, done that, and got the medal. But he can't turn down a temporary promotion. Just as he arrives in Kandahar air base, rockets start raining down, dealing death and destruction in equal measure.

Unknown to Adams, Lizzie isn't where he thought she was. Now much more than just a colleague, he thought she was safe and sound back at home. Sent out to replace a fallen medic, Lizzie's on patrol outside the wire where the risk of horrendous injury or death is far higher, utterly random, and ever present.

The insurgents outside the air base aren't the only threat to Adams and Lizzie. There's another enemy, far closer, who is much more threatening - and they're both firmly in the centre of his sights.

It's no longer simply a question of survival. But when none of their enemies are wearing a uniform, how can Lizzie and Adams recognise them before it's too late?

Incoming Fire is available on Amazon

~

Both books in the Paul Adams series are also available through Kindle Unlimited. The third in the series will be released in mid 2021.

Made in the USA
Las Vegas, NV
03 August 2021

27497731R00222